W9-BIT-314

CALICO

CALICO

Lee Goldberg

**SEVERN
HOUSE**

First world edition published in Great Britain and the USA in 2023
by Severn House, an imprint of Canongate Books Ltd,
14 High Street, Edinburgh EH1 1TE.

severnhouse.com

British Library Cataloguing-in-Publication Data
A CIP catalogue record for this title is available from the British Library.

ISBN-13: 978-1-4483-1013-5 (cased)
ISBN-13: 978-1-4483-1014-2 (e-book)

All Severn House titles are printed on acid-free paper.

Typeset by Palimpsest Book Production Ltd.,
Falkirk, Stirlingshire, Scotland.
Printed and bound in Great Britain by
TJ Books, Padstow, Cornwall.

Praise for *Calico*

"A genre-bending, gripping read"
Harlan Coben, #1 *New York Times* bestselling author

"A mind-bending thriller unlike anything I have read before.
I couldn't turn the pages fast enough"
Linwood Barclay, *New York Times* and *Sunday Times*
bestselling author

"A superb twin-track thriller featuring constant intrigue and a
huge secret – could be Lee Goldberg's best ever"
Lee Child, #1 *New York Times* bestselling author

"A tour de force of a novel. The authenticity is
overwhelming, the writing is taut, and the mystery is
thoroughly engrossing"
James Robert Daniels, author of *The Comanche Kid*, a Spur
Award finalist for Best Western Novel

"Lee Goldberg delivers with the unapologetically savvy Beth
McDade, a detective unafraid of following the dead bodies and
the mystery surrounding them. *Calico* couples history with good
old fashioned detective work"
Yasmin Angoe, award-winning author of the Nena
Knight series

"One of the most compelling novels I've read in a long time.
Great characters, a vivid historical setting, and intriguing plot
twists had me staying up late to finish it. Goldberg always
delivers the goods, and *Calico* is something special"
James Reasoner, Spur Award finalist and author of more than
350 westerns

"A two-fisted western mystery with a compelling heroine in Beth McDade. If you like the *Yellowstone* series and its spinoffs, you'll love *Calico*!"
Peter Brandvold, multiple Spur Award finalist and Western Fictioneers Lifetime Achievement Award honoree

"*Calico* is stunningly original – a magical mixture of a murder mystery and an old-fashioned Western, set in the California desert. It's also a heartwarming, epic story of one family that spans the centuries. Read it today – you won't soon forget it!"
Matt Witten, author of *Killer Story*

Praise for the Eve Ronin mysteries

"Fast-paced, riveting"
Library Journal Starred Review of *Movieland*

"Typically classy police procedural from Lee Goldberg – giving Michael Connelly a run for his money"
Ian Rankin on *Movieland*

"Assured prose matches the tight plot"
Publishers Weekly on *Movieland*

"Lively descriptive prose enhances the tight plot . . . *Columbo* fans will have fun"
Publishers Weekly on *Gated Prey*

"A riveting, intense story. Readers of Karin Slaughter or Michael Connelly will want to try this"
Library Journal Starred Review of *Bone Canyon*

"Goldberg knows how to keep the pages turning"
Publishers Weekly on *Bone Canyon*

"Lee Goldberg puts the *pro* in *police procedural*"
Meg Gardiner, international bestselling author, on
Bone Canyon

"A heroine for the ages."
Michael Connelly *on Lost Hills*

"A cop novel so good it makes much of the old guard read like
they're going through the motions until they can retire."
Booklist on *Lost Hills*

"A gripping premise, a great twist, and all the smart, snappy ease
of an expert at work."
Tana French on *Lost Hills*

"Goldberg is every bit the equal of Michael Connelly. Superb
reading entertainment."
The Providence Journal on *Gated Prey*

About the author

Lee Goldberg is a two-time Edgar Award and two-time Shamus Award nominee and the #1 *New York Times* bestselling author of more than thirty novels, including *Lost Hills*, the Ian Ludlow trilogy, fifteen Monk mysteries, and five internationally bestselling Fox & O'Hare books co-written with Janet Evanovich. He has also written and/or produced many TV shows, including *Diagnosis Murder*, *SeaQuest*, and *Monk*, and is the co-creator of the hit Hallmark movie series *Mystery 101*.

As an international television consultant, he has advised networks and studios in Canada, France, Germany, Spain, China, Sweden, and the Netherlands on the creation, writing, and production of episodic television series. He is also co-founder of the publishing company Brash Books.

www.leegoldberg.com

To Valerie & Madison – my past, present and future.

ONE

Saturday, February 2, 2019

The walls in Beth McDade's dark bedroom were bare. Her bed was simply a mattress and box spring. Her nightstands, on either side of her bed, were a steel gun safe and a cardboard moving box topped with mismatched desk lamps.

Beth was shirtless and straddling Chet Rogoff on her bed, her hands working to unbuckle his jeans. She was eager to get to that sweet moment when the flirty banter, the alcohol, and the right touch would combine to free her from her anxieties and her boredom.

That's when her cell phone vibrated on the gun safe.

She let go of his belt buckle. 'I've got to get that.'

'Now? Really?' Chet said, breathing heavily.

'I'm on call.'

Her shift as a homicide detective at the San Bernardino County Sheriff's Barstow station ended at 5 p.m. but she was on call 24/7 for the next two weeks, even on her so-called days off. That's because the station only had 2½ detectives, two full-timers and one deputy, who rotated in from patrol to take up the slack.

She reached for the phone and checked the screen. It was 2:20 a.m. The caller ID displayed: WATCH COMMANDER.

'McDade,' she answered, gently grinding against Chet, keeping some hope alive for them both.

'Sorry to wake you,' Sergeant Ripley said, with a tone that indicated he knew she wasn't asleep. It wasn't a big secret that she was at Pour Decisions on Main Street until eleven. The majority of the bar's patrons were Sheriff's deputies, Barstow cops, or other first responders. The rest were military types from Fort Irwin or the Marine Corps Logistics Base eager to get off the base and wash the sand out of their throats.

'No problem, Rip,' Beth said. 'Who needs to dream when you're living it in Barstow? What's up?'

'I am,' Chet whispered. She put her free hand over his mouth to shut him up but she kept moving her hips.

Ripley said, 'Twenty minutes ago, a guy was hit and killed by a motor home outside of Peggy Sue's.'

She knew the place. It was cheesy roadside diner out in Yermo, a bleak smattering of gas stations and fast-food joints off Interstate 15 in the Mojave Desert, thirteen miles east of Barstow. The diner was surrounded by dinosaur statues to draw the attention of motorists or, more likely, their bored and car-sick kids.

'Who responded to the scene?' Beth asked. They only had twenty-five officers in total, including the command staff, to cover the 9,200 square miles under their jurisdiction, though most of it was uninhabited desert.

'A deputy is out there, a kid named Willits, and CHP is handling traffic.'

Meaning Willits was sitting on his ass, she thought. No cars were on the desolate street at 2:20 a.m. and only a trickle during daylight. A tortoise could cross the road at noon without much danger of getting hit before he reached the other side.

'Is the coroner there yet?'

'He's on the way,' Ripley said.

'So am I.' She ended the call, stopped moving, and looked down at Chet. 'I got a body in Yermo.'

She began to climb off of Chet but he grabbed her firmly by the hips to keep her in place.

'You got a body right here,' he said.

'Very funny.'

'The guy is DRT.' Cop talk for Dead Right There. Chet was a California Highway Patrol officer. 'He's not going to get any deader if you finish what you started. Besides, why arrive before the coroner does? You'll just be sitting on your ass. Wouldn't you rather kill the time here?'

'Good point.' She dropped her phone on the bed and got back to work on his buckle. They rushed themselves and climaxed together in less than five minutes.

There was no time for post-coital anything. Beth jumped off of Chet, took a quick rinse in the shower, gargled some mouthwash, ran a brush through her brown hair, and got dressed in the same blouse, blazer, jeans, and shoulder holster she'd worn the previous day.

Beth squatted in front of the gun safe, took out her Glock, holstered it, and then searched for her phone.

Chet held her phone out to her from the bed, where he was still lying, naked and disheveled. He was thirty-two, a couple of years younger than her, and in perfect shape, though she'd noticed some gray hairs on his chest. He was easygoing and good-humored, two qualities that were hard to find in men living or working in Barstow. It wasn't a place that attracted the best and the brightest, which she knew didn't say much about her, either.

'We drank a lot tonight,' he said.

She'd got off work at five. The drinking started at six, and she'd had her last beer and a chaser around ten. She figured she'd be fine now, as long as she didn't have to shoot anyone.

'How's my breath?' Beth blew in his face.

'Redolent of Listerine.'

'Redolent? Wow.'

'I'm not just hot, I'm educated.'

'You went to Barstow Community College.'

'That counts.'

She gave him a quick kiss and stood up.

'Stay as long as you want. There's breakfast in the freezer.' And lunch and dinner. The only appliance in her kitchen that got a workout was her microwave. 'Just lock up when you leave.'

'You don't want me to keep the bed warm for you?'

'I won't be back before my shift starts.' Her shift started at 7 a.m. It was a good thing she kept a spare blouse and slacks in her locker. Going two shifts in the same clothes didn't send a great message to the command staff.

'This was good,' he said. 'Let's do it again sometime.'

'We'll see.' She smiled at him and dashed out.

There was a saying about Barstow that Beth heard when she'd arrived from LA three years ago.

The interstate here only goes in one direction: away. Nobody wants to be in Barstow and those who do, you don't want to know.

She thought of that, and how true it was, every time she got on the freeway.

Barstow was built on the banks of the Mojave River in the 1800s as a railroad hub for the booming silver and borax mining operations in the desert. In the mid-1900s, the city's Main Street was a stretch of the legendary Route 66 and was lined with eye-catching motels, hotels, and restaurants that were always packed with travelers. But when the new, much bigger, much faster, eight-lane interstate was built on the outskirts in 1957, Main Street took a bullet in the head and Barstow began its long, rotting decline. Beth felt that living there was like visiting a vast hospice. Or being a patient in one.

The interstate was an asphalt dividing line between the Barstow city center to the north and College Heights suburbs to the south, up in the rocky hills, close to the Community College. Beth lived in a rented tract home in the Heights, just like every other deputy who didn't commute from Victorville or Apple Valley. It was the only place to live in Barstow without having a meth lab or a gang member as a neighbor, though some wealthier, original gangsters, the ones who shopped at the Ralph Lauren at the Barstow Outlet Stores, and who had kids in school and speedboats in their driveways, liked it up there, too.

She drove her unmarked Ford Explorer, a police interceptor model outfitted for off-road driving, at seventy-five miles per hour, eastbound on the interstate, without lights or sirens. There were only a few vehicles on the road at that hour.

The interstate spilled down onto the Mojave Desert valley, the Calico mountain range to the north, and the Marine Corps Logistics Base to the south. Beyond that, a wide expanse of parched earth, occasionally dotted with homes, inhabited by military families, alfalfa farmers, retirees, turkey ranchers, off-the-grid survivalists, and, in Beth's mind, way too many in-bred families of meth-tweakers. The three gas stations, one dreary hotel, and four fast-food joints in Yermo were the last real outpost of commerce until Baker, fifty miles east.

Peggy Sue's was located south of the interstate, across from the MCLB, with open desert on either side. Their nearest neighbor was a Jack-in-the-Box a hundred yards west, by the on and off ramps to the interstate.

A sheriff's patrol car, its lightbar flashing, blocked off the deeply cracked asphalt street. Beyond the cruiser, a huge, bus-sized motor home was parked on the shoulder. A San Bernardino County coroner's wagon was parked in front of Peggy Sue's.

Beth parked beside the coroner's wagon and approached the young deputy, who was measuring skid marks on the road behind the motor home and taking photos. Willits looked like a kid dressed up in an oversized deputy costume. Further up the road, a coroner dressed from head to toe in white Tyvek, his back to Beth, was crouched over a body, taking photos. The air felt like a hot towel on her face.

'What's the story?' she asked.

'The driver of the motor home was heading eastbound on the interstate, got off for a cup of coffee, but he got distracted by the lightning storm and then a big blast from the Marine base.'

She hadn't heard any thunder or anything about a lightning storm. 'A lightning strike?'

Willits shrugged. 'I don't know. But there was smoke and a lot of activity over there. It's quieted down now.'

Beth glanced at the logistics base. Beyond the cyclone fence were rows and rows of vehicles and equipment, ready to be sent out to a battle somewhere or for use in the desert war games staged at Fort Irwin, on the other side of the Calico Mountains. She thought it was ironic that the Marines kept their toys in the desert, about as far from the ocean as it was possible to be.

Willits was still talking. 'Anyway, when the blast happened, the driver glanced over there for a second, and when he turned his eyes back to the road, a guy ran right in front of his motor home.'

'Ran from where?'

The deputy gestured to Peggy Sue's, the dinosaurs, the freeway beyond. 'The Peggy Sue's parking lot. He was screaming.'

'After he was hit?'

'Before. He wasn't making any sound after.'

'Any idea what he might have been running from?'

'Nope. There was nobody there, at least according to the driver and his wife.' Willits gestured to an elderly couple standing beside their RV. 'They're on their way to Las Vegas.'

Of course they are, she thought. Anywhere but here.

The elderly couple were both shaped like pears and looked

distraught. The man wore suspenders and sneakers with Velcro tabs instead of laces. The woman wore a loudly floral, pull-over house dress. Beth would eat her gun before wearing one of those.

'Did you give them a breathalyzer?'

He nodded. 'They're clean.'

'How long did it take you to get out here after they called 911?'

'Only a few minutes. I was getting coffee at Eddie's.'

It was a truck stop several miles further east with a sixty-five-foot-tall cherry-topped ice-cream sundae for a sign and twenty-six gas pumps. It was fortunate that the deputy happened to be so close by. On a good day, there were two patrol cars out per shift. With so few deputies, and such a vast patrol area, it often took an hour for a deputy to respond to a call.

Beth went over to the body, smelling it before she got a look at it. She smelled shit and blood, but mostly body odor, weeks of sweat in his clothes.

She came up behind the coroner and aimed her flashlight at the body. Her first impression, based on the B.O. and his ratty, dirt-caked clothes, was that he was a transient. He was bearded, long-haired, and deeply tanned. There was blood everywhere. His torso was flattened, but with the exception of some exposed broken bones, everything else in his body remained contained inside of his clothing. His head was mostly intact, except for an indentation on one side.

The coroner stood up and Beth recognized her as Amanda Selby. Even in darkness, lit only by their flashlights, Amanda looked tired and generally disheveled but, Beth thought, who wouldn't at this hour?

'I'm not used to seeing you on graveyard,' Beth said.

'I'm working some extra shifts. We need the money and I'm not sleeping much lately, anyway.'

Beth pointed her flashlight beam at the body. 'Cause of death?'

'Motor home.'

'Can you be more specific?'

'He was hit mid-chest, smacked his head against the windshield, cracking his skull open, then dropped under the vehicle, which rolled over him, crushing his torso, causing massive internal injuries. Hard to say exactly which severe trauma actually killed him. There are so many to choose from. Excuse me.'

Amanda pushed past her and vomited into the desert scrub in the empty lot beside Peggy Sue's.

Beth stepped up beside her. 'I thought you'd be used to this by now, given your line of work.'

Amanda spit out the bad taste in her mouth. 'It's morning sickness. My third child is due in September.'

'Congratulations.'

'I wouldn't say that. We wanted to stop at two. But I learned the hard way that the only birth-control methods you can trust are celibacy, a vasectomy, or getting your tubes tied. One of us is going under the knife after this baby drops or we're never having sex again. We may not anyway with three kids and only one of us earning a decent living.' Amanda seemed suddenly self-conscious and glanced at Beth. 'Sorry for venting, but I spend my days with corpses. Not a lot of opportunity for conversation.'

'No problem,' Beth said. 'The dead man looks like a homeless person.'

'Smells like one, too.' Amanda led her back to the body.

'Did you get his ID?'

'I was just about to check his pockets when you came over.'

'How many homeless can there be in the desert?' Beth aimed her phone at his face, called up the photo app, zoomed in tight to hide the injury, and snapped a photo. She looked up to see Willits ambling over. 'You know this guy? Maybe seen him around?'

Willits looked down at the dead man as Amanda carefully went through his pockets with her gloved hands.

'Nope,' he said.

'No ID,' Amanda said. 'But this is odd.'

She held out her gloved hand and shone her flashlight on her open palm, revealing some old coins.

'Antique coins?' Beth said.

'I'm not a numismatist – say that three times fast – but people find all kinds of interesting stuff out here. Old utensils, dishes, belt buckles, bones,' Amanda said, putting the coins into a transparent evidence baggie that she pulled from one of her pockets. 'Back in the 1880s, this was the railhead for the Calico silver-mining camp. The desert floor was full of tents and crudely built huts.'

Beth was familiar with the Calico Ghost Town, a tourist trap up in the mountains, three miles north of the interstate, built by the

Knotts Berry Farm guy. It was a re-creation of the original town built atop its ruins and populated by 'performers' and shopkeepers wandering around in period costumes.

'Anything else in his pockets?'

'Just this.' Amanda pulled a vintage tin of Eve Chewing Tobacco from his pocket. The text on the tin was in an old-time font. The art depicted a naked woman with a leaf strategically positioned over her crotch standing under an apple tree. The slogan read *Chewing Paradise.*

Amanda opened the tin. There was a glob of black tar inside. 'Imagine putting that in your mouth.'

'No wallet or anything?'

'Not unless he has it up his ass.' Amanda closed the tin, put it into an evidence baggie, and stood up.

'Be sure to look.'

'No orifice goes unexplored in my business.' Amanda walked to the empty lot and, with her back to Beth and Willits, dry-heaved over the dirt.

Beth turned to Willits. 'Is that motor home still roadworthy?'

'I think so. Just a dented grille and a cracked windshield.'

Beth glanced at the couple, who looked back at her, worried. But she didn't think there was any need to talk to them. They could have fled instead of calling 911 and probably never would have been caught. But instead, they stuck around. They wanted to do the right thing, and so did she.

'Then you can send them on their way.'

'Is it OK if I head out, too?' Willits said. 'I've taken my measurements and photos. There's nothing else for me to do here right now. It's a tragedy, not a crime.'

Beth knew the deputy only came to that conclusion because he was inexperienced, so she decided to make this a teaching opportunity. She pointed at the dead body. 'What was he screaming about?'

'He was probably drunk, on drugs, or nuts. What difference does it make?'

'What if he was running from someone?'

He nodded toward the couple. 'They said there was nobody out here.'

'But they were distracted. It's a big desert and it's dark. That's not even counting the lightning storm, the explosion, and running over a guy.'

'I see your point. Sorry about that.'

'No worries,' she said, both surprised and impressed by his apology. 'It's late. We're all tired.'

'What can I do to help?'

'Take a picture of him, cropped so it isn't too gory, and see if anybody around here recognizes his face. Off-roaders, people who work at the gas stations.'

'I got it.'

She glanced at the restaurant and the dinosaurs. Peggy Sue's opened at seven, still four hours away. 'And I'd appreciate it if you'd pull the security camera footage when the restaurant opens up and drop it off at my desk with your report when your shift ends.'

'Will do.'

'Thanks.' This kid might just make it out of Barstow with that attitude, she thought.

Beth turned to her car and spotted someone strolling over from base. She knew who it was from his unmistakable lope. It was Bill Knox, the security chief for the Marine Corps Logistics Base. Fifties, buzz-cut, chest like armor-plating, hands like bricks. She walked over to meet him in the road.

'What brings you over, Bill?'

'You. When I saw the coroner's wagon pull up, I thought there was a chance you might be here. What happened?'

'Motor home vs man. Motor home won.'

'Why didn't the driver see him? It's an open road.'

'He was distracted by the lightning storm,' Beth said. 'And the explosion on your base.'

Bill gave her a strange look and glanced up at the clear sky. 'There was a lightning storm?'

'Isn't that what caused the blast and got you out of bed so early?'

He put on his poker face. 'It was just a dumpster fire. No big deal. An idiot tossed a cigarette inside, ignited some soiled rags.'

He must not play much poker, she thought. He was lying. Badly. She wondered why. Now she wanted a look at his security camera footage, too, not that anything on the base was any of her business.

'Why did you want to see me?'

'We should get together again some time,' he said with a smile. 'It's been too long.'

Three months ago, they had dinner at Oggie's Sports Brewhouse at the Outlets and then got a room at the Hampton Inn. That qualified as a night on the town in Barstow. She hadn't heard from him since. She glanced at his wedding ring. His wife lived in the Bay Area, but he was stationed out here in the desert. Sex with him was like combat training and just as bruising, but in a good way.

'How are things at home?'

'The same,' he said. 'Does it matter?'

Not really. Not to her. There wasn't much else to do in this hell-hole when she wasn't on the job. The alternative was being alone with her thoughts, her past, and her mistakes. His marriage was his problem, not hers.

'You have my number. You don't have to wait for someone to get killed outside of your gate to see me.'

She turned her back on him and walked into the desert, looking for any clues that might tell her where the dead guy came from.

TWO

B eth didn't find anything in the desert around the diner and spent the next few hours at the Kampgrounds of America site north of the freeway and at the Calico campgrounds in a canyon below the ghost town. She visited every tent and RV, waking people up and showing them the dead man's photo. She hoped to either find someone who'd seen him or to stumble upon his abandoned tent or RV. But she had no luck.

Dawn was breaking across the Mojave Desert valley as she drove south on Ghost Town Road, across a dry lake bed, toward the interstate, where the first rays of the sun glistened off the shiny silver trailers of passing big rigs.

Her phone rang. It was Ripley, the watch commander, calling again.

'We've got a burglary in progress at 43700 Tahiti Road, Lake Betty.'

Beth floored the gas, put on her flashers and siren, and sped onto the freeway on-ramp, heading east. The address was about fifteen miles away. It would take her at least twenty minutes to get there.

Lake Betty was one of a two dozen private, shallow, spring-fed, man-made lakes in the valley. Several of the lakes were long and narrow, built specifically for tournament water-skiing. A few were bleak fishing holes at long-abandoned resorts. And the rest were failed 'lake-front' tract-home developments. When they broke ground on Lake Betty in 1974, it was supposed to be the first of three lakes, surrounded by three hundred homes and a Tahitian-style country club. It ended up being one lake with eleven homes and the rusted-out ruins of a train caboose.

'Why are you calling me?' she asked Ripley.

'You're the nearest unit. The closest patrol car is handling a domestic dispute in Lenwood and is thirty minutes out. CHP is sending backup, but they are ten to fifteen behind you.'

'I meant, why are you calling me on the phone and not through the dispatcher?' She had her radio unit on at a low hum, subconsciously listening for anything major.

'This could be the same crew Hatcher has been chasing down,' Ripley said, referring to Glen Hatcher, the other, full-time detective, 'and he thinks they may be monitoring our radio calls. And I've got the homeowner on the phone. He's watching it go down on his live video feed. I'll patch him through. His name is Morty Grenlick.'

'Where is he?' Beth asked, knowing that the odds were he was hundreds of miles away. Most of the lake homeowners were out-of-towners who only came out on weekends and holidays.

'La Jolla.' There was a click and a hiss of static on the line, then Ripley continued. 'Mr Grenlick, you're on with Detective Beth McDade, who is on her way to your residence. I'll sign off now.'

Beth turned off her siren so she could hear Grenlick and because sound carried a long way in the open desert. No sense announcing her arrival ten minutes before she got there.

'How many others are rolling?' Grenlick's voice was gruff and tempered with frustration.

She said, 'Just me. Tell me what you're seeing.'

'You've got to get more people out there.'

'There are no more people, Mr Grenlick. Tell me what you are seeing.' Beth peeled off onto the Mineola Road exit, and made a screeching right on to the southbound two-lane road through the middle of sandy nothing.

'Three men with balaclavas over their faces. They've backed an SUV with a toy hauler up to my garage like it's their own fucking place.'

At the moment, it basically was their place. Her SUV hit the railroad tracks and, for just a moment, was airborne before it hit the asphalt with loud thud. The impact jacked up her adrenaline. It felt good.

'Are they armed?'

'What the fuck for? The house is empty. But they are in for a fucking surprise. My neighbor Duke has a sawed-off that'll cut those assholes in half. He's probably out there now.'

Her lights were pointless, so she switched them off. There wasn't a single car on the road for miles. She was still ten minutes away from the lake.

'Do you have his number? Tell him to stay inside. Tell him not to get involved.'

'Jesus Fuck, they're loading my Sea-Doo into their trailer,' Grenlick said, then he raised his voice, as if speaking to someone else in the room. 'Hey, fuckwad, I can see you. Get your fucking hands off my shit.'

Beth felt a cramp of anxiety. 'Are you talking to them? Can they hear you?'

'Hell yes, when I want them to,' Grenlick said, then raised his voice again, presumably into the mike on his computer. 'This is the voice of fucking God. The cops are on the way, asshole. You're going down.'

Great, she thought, why not tell them exactly when I'm arriving?

'Don't do that, Mr Grenlick.'

'The sonofabitch is flipping me off and grabbing his nuts.'

'You're not helping the situation,' Beth said.

'Fuck me! Another one of 'em is driving away with my Razer. There goes $18K, into the desert. Where the fuck are you, lady?'

'Almost there,' she said, making a hard right onto an unmarked dirt road, but she knew it was over. There was no chance of catching them now.

'They're getting away,' Grenlick yelled, and she heard the whap of his fist on the desk. 'You need to get a chopper up there.'

'We don't have a chopper.'

At least not for this, tracking stolen ATVs across a wide-open desert. Maybe for a serial killer, or a kidnapping, or a Transformer from outer space marching across the valley, firing rockets from its head. The helicopter was based in San Bernardino, a hundred miles south, on the other side of a mountain range. In a pinch, they could call on the CHP or even the military for air support. This wasn't a pinch.

'Now the sonofabitch is taking out his dick and pissing on my couch,' Grenlick said, then yelled into his computer: 'I will cut that baby dick off and use it for bass bait, you white-trash piece of shit.'

Beth kept the gas pedal floored. 'How do you know the suspect is white?'

'I saw his dick,' he said, 'which I wish I could unsee.'

Lake Betty was about five miles away. The grove of trees around the lake was impossible to miss in the vast flatlands.

'They're getting in their truck. They're leaving. They are getting away. Where the fuck is Duke?'

'I need you to call your neighbor and tell him to stand down.'

'Stand down from what? If Duke was out there, you'd be hearing gunshots. What good is a fucking alarm and enough cameras to film the fucking Super Bowl if anybody can just walk in, take your stuff, and piss on your couch?'

She was closing in on the lake. 'Can you tell which way they are going?'

'Away from my fucking house, where do you think?'

'Which way? Straight out into the desert or on the road?'

'How the fuck do I know? My cameras are watching my property, not the entire fucking desert.'

She knew they weren't coming in her direction. They would likely stay away from main roads and freeway, go through the desert and alfalfa fields. They would be long gone before she got there.

She arrived at the twenty-five-acre melanoma-shaped lake. The one-story cinder-block-and-stucco houses around the shore were spaced widely apart and shaded by trees. There were a few low cyclone fences, strictly to keep pets and kids from wandering away. People who came here wanted wide open spaces. The backyards all had docks, some with speedboats, most with paddle boats, rowboats, or battery-powered cocktail-party cruisers.

Grenlick's house was easy to spot. It was between an open lot and another, almost identical home. The four-car garage door was open, a Jeep Cherokee inside, and an alarm was shrilling from a speaker mounted under the eaves. She pulled up in the far side of the garage, careful not to roll where another vehicle might have been. If nobody had been here for a while, the breezes across the valley would have blown most of the surface smooth.

'Is there anyone still in the house or on the property?'

'They're fucking gone,' he said, morose. 'Thanks for nothing.'

'What about your neighbor?'

'Fucking gutless, that's what.'

Beth hung up on him, grabbed her radio mike, and called the dispatcher. 'This is 8D2, show me at 43700 Tahiti Road, responding to the 4-5-9. It's all clear.'

'10-4, 8D2,' the dispatcher said.

She got out, noting the tire-tread marks in the dirt in front of the garage. They had a distinctive pattern. At least she could get some good casts of tire treads. She faced the camera she saw mounted over the garage.

'Can you please turn off the alarm?'

The alarm went off. He'd heard her over his camera mike. She waved her thanks to Grenlick, then glanced over at the neighbor's house.

Why didn't he come out?

She wandered over to Duke's house. A few cardboard Amazon packages were yellowing on the cracked concrete stoop and she got a bad feeling.

As Beth got closer to the house, she heard the TV on inside. She walked around back to the lake side of the house. The drapes were slightly parted across a sliding glass door. She leaned close to the glass and saw the decomposing body of a man in a recliner, watching Hallmark Movies and Mysteries, a TV tray in front of him.

It wasn't the first time she'd had this experience. There were lots of retirees living in isolation in the desert. They could go weeks without seeing or talking to anyone. And it could be even longer before anyone, particularly out-of-town relatives, got worried enough to call the Sheriff's department to ask for a welfare check.

She tugged on the sliding door. It was unlocked, and even opening it a crack let out a blast of the putrid stench.

Breathing through her mouth, she went in and did a cursory check of the small two-bedroom house to make sure there weren't any other residents or animals inside, dead or alive. He'd died alone, led into the afterlife by the *Garage Sale Mysteries*.

She went back to her car, reached inside for the mike, and radioed the dispatcher.

'This is 8D2, responding to the 4-5-9 at 43700 Tahiti Road. The resident expressed concern about his neighbor at 43702 Tahiti Road. I did a wellness check and have a confirmed 1144.' That was the radio code for a dead body.

'10-4. We'll contact the coroner.'

'Copy that.' She replaced the mike and saw a CHP cruiser arriving. It was a welcome and common sight. The first responders looked out for each other out here.

Beth stepped into the road to stop him before he could run over any tread marks and walked up to his driver's side door. His window was already rolled down. It was a patrol woman named Rita Lopez.

'I appreciate the backup, Rita, but the show is over.'

'Figured as much.'

'Did you happen to see an SUV with a toy hauler go by?'

'Nope. Wish it was that easy.'

'Thanks again. I owe you.'

'Don't be silly.' Rita smiled, made a U-turn, and drove off.

Beth walked up to Grenlick's house and waved at the security camera over the garage.

'Mr Grenlick? Can you please send me a link to the security camera videos?' she said, then gave him her email address.

'Where's fucking Duke?' His voice boomed out over the desert from the camera's speaker. It was startling and disembodied. It really did sound like the voice of God.

'Duke is dead. He has been for a few days now.'

'Just my luck.'

Mr Warmth, Beth thought. She went back to her car, popped the trunk, and opened up the large gym bag that contained her forensics kit. Out here, CSI was only called for homicides, shootings, and other major, violent crimes. Otherwise, the detectives were on their own when it came to gathering evidence.

She took out a one-pound bag of Shake-N-Cast, which contained a unique plaster powder inside and an 'easy-break' capsule of water pre-measured to create just the right amount of slurry to capture the impression of a single shoe- or footprint. It came with a separate plastic cookie cutter-esque thing that unfolded to create a frame around footprints or tire treads in the dirt.

She unfolded the frame, placed it around the tire tread. Then she crushed the bag in her hands, breaking the capsule of water inside, shook and gently kneaded the contents, tore off the perforated top, and poured the contents over the impression.

That done, she went back to her car, took out her phone, and checked her email. Grenlick had sent her a link to the video. She pulled up the footage and watched the burglary go down, pretty much as he'd described the play-by-play, right up to one guy pissing on the couch and flipping off the camera.

She paused the image. The finger he was holding up to the camera was slightly crooked. He was wearing gloves and booties. The man was very careful and was clearly an avid viewer of TV cop shows. But he shouldn't have peed on the furniture.

Beth went back to the trunk, took out a collection vial, evidence baggie, sealed Q-tip, and a sealed plastic scalpel, and went into Grenlick's house through the door in the garage. His home had the same floorplan as Duke's, but had been remodeled with higher-end materials. The furniture was also more contemporary.

She crouched by the urine, tore open the Q-tip, and rubbed it over the sample, then stuck it into the vial.

'I wouldn't want your job,' Grenlick's voice boomed through the house, startling her. She glared at the camera. She forgot that he was watching, then she realized it might actually be helpful.

'This is the glamorous part,' she said, breaking the stem of the Q-tip and sealing the cotton end inside the vial, which she put into the evidence bag. 'Can you please send me this video to document the collection of the evidence?'

'Sure. Hey, sorry if I was an asshole earlier. It's hard to see $60K worth of your stuff go out the door and not be able to do a thing about it.'

'I understand, sir. No problem.'

She asked him to watch her while she walked through the house and tell her what he saw missing. As he did, she made a list for her report. All of that killed another forty-five minutes, just in time for the coroner's arrival. It wasn't Amanda this time, but a guy named Griswell, who'd been bald since he was twenty and, Beth suspected, a virgin since his birth forty years ago. He came with an assistant, presumably to help him lug the body away.

Griswell mumbled an irritable hello and went inside Duke's house with his assistant. A moment later, a sheriff's patrol car pulled up. It was Willits. He joined Beth.

'My shift's ending.' He handed her a thumb drive. 'Here's the video footage from Peggy Sue's DVR. I'll leave my report on your desk.'

'Thanks.' She really would have appreciated it if he'd brought her a cheeseburger and fries from the diner, too. It was only a little after 9 a.m. but she hadn't eaten since 6 p.m. and was starving. It may have been her imagination, but the thumb drive smelled like pizza. 'Did you take a look at the footage?'

'Yeah. It's weird. He comes running across Peggy Sue's parking lot, eastbound from the direction of Ghost Town Road, waving his arms around like he's on fire. He nearly shits himself when he sees the dinosaurs, starts really wailing, running and looking over his shoulder, when WHAM, he's hit by the motor home. I didn't see anybody chasing him.'

'Did you show his photo to anybody?'

'I went by all the gas stations and fast-food joints along Yermo Road. Nobody recognized him.'

'I appreciate the legwork.'

'It's something interesting to do besides drive around,' he said, glancing out at the lake. 'It can be pretty dull out here.'

'Sometimes dull is nice.'

'Then you found the right place to work.'

'I didn't have a lot of choices,' she said, but she suspected he already knew that. Why else would she be here?

The deputy got back into his patrol car and drove off. Her shift had only just begun and she was already exhausted. She sighed and went back to Grenlick's front yard to pull up the plaster cast of the tire tread.

The excitement never ends, she thought.

THREE

The Barstow Sheriff's station was on the north end of Mountain View Drive, adjacent to the San Bernardino County Courthouse, and across the street from the California Highway Patrol station and Barstow City Hall. With the exception of all the large radio towers, and the numerous California State and US flags flying around it, the low-slung, boxy buildings could easily be mistaken for drab strip malls that couldn't even entice a Subway or 7-Eleven to rent space.

Beth spent most of the day at her desk, filling out the paperwork on her two death cases, one accidental and one natural. It was the busiest day she'd had in weeks. The detective office was a small room with three desks separated by chest-high cubicle partitions. It was a tight fit when all three detectives were working, but today she had it to herself.

It was after 4:30 when she finally had a chance to look at the security video from Peggy Sue's. She plugged the thumb drive into her computer. The video was divided into six quadrants, each one showing a different angle of Peggy Sue's exterior.

There was thirty seconds of stillness, of nothing moving, and then the small portion of the sky she could see was alive with lightning, crackling loudly like electricity, but without any thunder, and flashing outward, more like shooting particles than zigzagging bolts. An instant later, there was a loud blast, deep and full, almost volcanic, illuminating the parking lot in a yellowish-orange flash from the southwest, the heart of the Marine base.

That was no dumpster fire.

As the flash dissipated, the dirty man ran out of the darkness, from the direction of Ghost Town Road, across the back of the parking lot. He seemed terrified, looking repeatedly over his shoulder, as if he was being chased. He turned, saw the raptor statue atop an outbuilding, and staggered back, screaming.

He ran towards Yermo Street. Beth shifted her gaze to a different camera angle, showing the front of the diner, and saw him dash into the street, looking over his shoulder, just as he crossed into the path of the motor home. It slammed right into him, taking him down, and then rolled right over him.

Beth played it back again, this time watching the other cameras to see if anyone came out of the desert darkness, but nobody did. If the dirty man was being chased, whoever his pursuer was didn't appear.

Her guess was that he was on drugs. Why else would he be terrified by a ridiculous dinosaur statue on a diner?

But there was no question he was killed by accident, at least as far as the motor-home driver was concerned. The old couple did everything right.

Beth finished her reports and looked at the clock on the wall, which always made her feel as if she were in a high-school class-room rather than a police station. It was 5:15, past the end of her shift. She was too wired up to go home. But even if she wasn't, she still was in no hurry to go there. She never was. So she headed to the bar.

Pour Decisions was on the corner of 1st Street and Main, a few blocks north of the Civic Center, in a cinderblock building surrounded by vacant lots for blocks and facing a row of boarded-up storefronts. Further up 1st Street was the city's old iron truss bridge, which stretched over the railroad tracks and down to the Harvey House Railroad Depot, the nicest building in Barstow. Beth wished the bar was in the depot, a beautiful Moorish mishmash of tiled domes, long colonnades, and brick that evoked a sense of elegance, wealth, and class that was missing entirely from in the city.

Pour Decisions had the ambience of a Chevron gas station mini-mart that had cleared out the shelves of chips, candy, and jerky to make room for two pool tables, a jukebox, wooden tables, plastic chairs, and a granite-topped bar.

For reasons Beth didn't understand, Pour Decisions was adopted decades ago by law enforcement, first responders, and just about anybody else with a uniform or badge as their clubhouse. The tweakers, gang members, whores, and drunks in Barstow knew better than to step inside, even though it was across the street from the dreary Route 66 era motels on Main Street where they all did business or indulged their vices.

The bar was already packed when Beth walked in, some of the regulars acknowledging her with a wave or a smile.

She sidled up to the bar, took a handful of salted nuts from the plastic bowl, and overheard the conversation between two off-duty Barstow cops a few stools to her left. One cop had a beer gut that he was attentively nurturing tonight with a pitcher for himself, the other had a scar on his cheek, supposedly courtesy of a hooker who came at him with a broken bottle.

'We get there at the ass-crack of dawn,' Beer Gut said, 'and the old guy is just livid, standing there on his porch in his tighty-whities, saying someone broke into his house and left a truck engine in his living room.'

'Why would someone do that?' Scar Cheek asked.

'Nobody would or could,' Beer Gut said. 'He obviously built it there himself for some crazy reason and forgot he'd done it.'

'How do you forget something like that?'

'How do you forget who your wife and kids are? It's Alzheimer's. That ever happens to me, put me down like a rabid dog. You'll be doing me a favor.'

Sally the bartender set a beer and a shot down in front of Beth without being asked. She was a big middle-aged woman, with a beehive hairdo that actually looked right on her, wearing a tank top with the words POUR DECISIONS across her massive grand-motherly bosom. It wasn't just an advertisement for the place. It also seemed to Beth like she was making a statement about the trouble those breasts had gotten her into. Or perhaps it was a warning. Or all of the above.

'You read my mind,' Beth said.

'You look exhausted, just like everybody else in here.'

'Don't we always?' Beth took the shot.

'It's worse today. That lightning storm last night was like a full moon on steroids. It was a wild couple of shifts for every first responder in town. You want a cheeseburger with extra meat and extra cheese?'

'Sure.' Beth set the shot glass down. 'A side of heart disease to go with a main course of liver failure is just what I need.'

'Good thing you're sitting two stools away from an ER doctor and an EMT.'

Sally went back into the kitchen to get the cook started on her burger. Beth turned to her right to see a man, still in his Barstow Community Hospital surgical scrubs, talking to a young red-headed EMT she'd seen respond to a few shootings in the desert. Everybody called the EMT Caruso, after that pompous actor on *CSI: Miami* whose idea of acting was whipping off his sunglasses to punctuate every line.

The doctor said, 'They wouldn't tell us anything about the fires at Fort Irwin or MCLB, but they medevac'd six guys to us with second- and third-degree burns at the same time you were bringing us victims from the pile-up on the I-15. It was chaos. What caused that accident?'

Beth's ears perked up.

It must have been a hell of a dumpster fire. But why would there be a fire at *both* bases at the same time? It seemed like an unlikely coincidence to her.

Caruso said, 'A boulder. How the hell does a one-ton boulder end up on a freeway in the middle of the desert? It's not like a tumbleweed.'

A guy walked by, wearing a T-shirt with the California Highway Patrol logo, their badge within the C of CHP, the letters written in an ugly gold font that went out of style with disco music. 'Maybe it fell off the back of a boulder truck?'

Caruso turned to the CHP guy. 'What's a boulder truck?'

'Like a turnip truck but with boulders, for decorative landscaping in Vegas,' the CHP guy said. 'You'd be surprised the stuff we see being transported.'

It really was a shit-show last night, she thought. All things considered, she'd had it easy. She did wonder, though, what was going on at those two military bases and if it had anything to do with Bill's unusual interest in that dead transient.

She ate her burger, washed it down with another beer, and went home where, to her surprise, she discovered the bed made, and the kitchen and bathroom cleaned. She'd never had a one-night stand who threw in a free house-cleaning.

On her kitchen table, she spotted a bowl, a spoon, and a box of Captain Crunch set out on the table for her. A dialogue bubble had been drawn next to the Captain's mouth and it contained a phone number.

She smiled. Maybe it wouldn't be a one-night stand after all.

* * *

Beth slept from 7 p.m. until 6 a.m. on Sunday, which barely left
her enough time to shower and eat a bowl of Captain Crunch before
rushing into the station for her next shift. She walked into the
detective office and found Glen Hatcher at his desk, watching
the lake house burglary video, right at the moment where the guy
urinated on the couch. Glen liked to wear cardigan sweaters in
the office, saving his suit jackets for court or work in the field.
He looked like Mr Rogers with a Glock.

'The homeowner really pissed him off,' Hatcher said, laughing
at his own joke.

'At least now you know one of the perps you're looking for is
white.'

'How do I know that?'

Beth pointed to the screen. 'His dick.'

Hatcher squinted at the screen. 'Trust a woman to spot that. No
offense intended.'

'God forbid you should be caught zooming in on a guy's junk,
even in an official capacity.'

'Especially in an official capacity.'

'You think this is the same crew you've been chasing?'

'Same M.O. Same ski masks,' Hatcher said. 'They always seem
to know when we're stretched thin and nobody is around to respond
if they trip an alarm.'

'Which is most of the time with only four people on patrol on
any given shift,' she said, taking a seat at her desk. 'I took a plaster
cast of the tire tracks and a sample of piss for the DNA.'

'You're kidding me.'

She pulled the plaster cast out from under her desk, set it on his
lap, then opened her desk drawer and took out the evidence baggie
containing the vial, which she placed on his desktop. 'They might
come in handy.'

'The tire track, maybe, but since when do we run DNA on a
burglary?'

'When you don't have anything else to go on except a white
dick.'

'Oh, that old adage.'

The phone rang on Beth's desk. She snatched it up and answered
with her name. It was Amanda Selby, the coroner.

'I've completed my autopsy on the man hit by the motor home.'

'Do you have an ID for me?' Beth asked.

'There were no hits on his fingerprints and no dental matches. But I'm not surprised.'

'Why is that?'

'Come over and I'll tell you.'

That meant Beth would have to go to the Barstow Hospital, which had been abandoned a few years earlier in favor of the new Barstow Community Hospital that was built across the street. The old one-story 1958 structure was temporarily being used as a satellite county morgue while the one in Needles was being remodeled. The old hospital had the benefit of being only a block away from the Sheriff's station, but she hated the place. The long, dark, empty halls seemed to reek of pain, despair, and death.

'Tell me now,' Beth said.

'I'd rather show you, along with a few other odd things.'

'This isn't like that dead guy you showed me who had an extra testicle.'

Hatcher leaned out of his cubicle and looked at her. She waved him off.

Amanda said, 'I don't think there will ever be another guy like that. What you saw was a medical rarity. This is different.'

'So not some strange deformity.'

'This is more of a mystery.'

'One for me to solve,' Beth said, 'or for medical science?'

'Maybe both.'

Beth had to walk down a lot of dark, empty halls before getting to the morgue. The deserted hospital struck her as the perfect setting for a slasher movie. Every time she visited the place, she was glad that she was packing her Glock.

But Amanda, despite often being alone with the dead in this abandoned, echoey building, didn't seem to Beth to be the least bit uncomfortable. Now they stood on either side of an autopsy table, the mangled corpse laid out naked between them, his chest cavity surgically split wide open.

'He's a Caucasian male, roughly thirty years old, cause of death was massive internal trauma,' Amanda said.

'No surprise there.'

'But before we get to the body, I want you to see his clothes.'

Amanda led Beth over to the adjacent autopsy table, where his clothes were piled in large transparent evidence bags.

Amanda picked up a bag containing the dead man's pair of ragged jeans, which were caked with red dirt, and soiled with his blood, urine, and excrement. It still stunk, even in the bag.

'Not only were his clothes filthy, but they were infested with lice.'

Yucky, Beth thought, but not unusual for a homeless person. 'I'm glad you searched his pockets and not me.'

'His clothes, hair, and skin were also covered with this red iron-oxide dust. So I checked his lungs. He had thickened alveoli and scarring indicating that he's been inhaling heavy metals for years.'

'Meaning he's been living in a cave or maybe working one of the abandoned mines in the Calico Mountains. Or both.'

'You're probably right, mercury is used to separate silver from rocks but I'm getting ahead of myself. Let's stay with his clothes.' Amanda held up the bag of jeans, turning it around to display it from all sides. 'There are no labels or tags of any kind. There are also no zippers, plastics, or polyblend fabrics. It's all natural material. The buttons on his shirt are made of wood. And look at these rivets on his pants.'

Beth did. 'I have those on my jeans.'

'Yes, but your rivets are machine-made, smooth and uniform. These are not. They are irregular, hand-hewn, and hand-applied, the way it was done a hundred years ago,' Amanda said. Beth looked closer and could see that now. 'This is vintage stuff. A hand-made pair of jeans made like this today would cost hundreds of dollars.'

'Unless he's wearing his great-grandfather's jeans,' Beth said. 'I'm told they last forever.'

Which was possible. Beth knew there are quite a few families in the Mojave, living on the same property for generations, but not passing down great wealth. It's why they didn't leave. And why she suspected they in-bred, too. It would explain some of the dumb-ass crimes they committed.

'Then he must also be wearing his great-grandfather's boots.' Amanda set down the jeans and picked up the bag containing the boots. 'These have leather soles attached to canvas bodies. You only find leather soles now on dress shoes. The shoelaces also have metal tips. Nobody makes work boots like this today. But they did when those pants were made, back in the 1880s. I checked on Google.'

'So maybe this guy was living off the grid, wearing old clothes, trying to be some kind of mountain man, living off the earth,' Beth said. 'What does his body tell you?'

Amanda went back to the body at the autopsy table and lifted up the man's left hand. 'We'll start with his fingernails. They are yellowed and ridged. That suggests poor liver function due to lead or mercury poisoning.'

Beth leaned down, studied his fingers, and saw the yellowing and ridges Amanda was talking about. 'More evidence for the theory that he's been mining.'

'There are minute bug-bite scars, some quite old, all over his body.' Amanda pointed to some of the scars on his dirt-caked arms and legs. 'I'd say he's been infested with lice for years. And he has plantar lesions on the bottom of his feet.' Beth followed Amanda to the end of the table and looked at his feet. The soles covered the ugliest blisters she'd ever seen. They were pustules that appeared were ready to burst.

Repulsed, Beth instinctively took a step back. 'Is that from walking with lousy shoes?'

'It's from fucking. It's syphilis and it's gone untreated for some time. It looks like this guy avoided all modern medicine.'

'Not to mention soap and water.'

'And toothpaste,' Amanda said, 'which brings us to something really strange.'

'Stranger than the idea of anybody sleeping with him, even for money?'

Amanda went to the head of the table and used her gloved hands to force open his mouth. He didn't have many teeth, and the ones he had were crooked and yellow. 'He's had a lot of teeth pulled, and a few that remain have cavities that were filled with an amalgam comprised of copper and an unacceptably toxic amount of mercury, at least by today's standards.'

Beth peered into his mouth and saw the fillings, but they didn't look much different than her own. 'When was it standard?'

'Not since the late 1800s.'

'Who does that kind of dental work now?'

'Nobody,' Amanda said.

'Not even an unlicensed dentist?'

'It wouldn't make any sense. It's easier and cheaper to use existing, pre-packaged amalgam. But the fillings were the least of the problems in his mouth. His gums show early signs of oral cancer, most likely from sucking tobacco, which he may have been doing for medicinal purposes, unaware he was only making his dental issues worse.'

'I'm beginning to understand why this guy was running around screaming.'

Amanda walked back over to the other autopsy table, sorted through the bags, and came back with one containing the tin of tobacco.

'I had this analyzed. Modern tobacco is loaded with additives and chemicals. Not this. It's old-school. Just tobacco, sugar, and plant flavorings.'

'Homemade and put in an antique tin?'

'That's got to be it because I checked the brand online. It's from the 1880s, just like his pants and the coins in his pockets.'

'You should be a detective,' Beth said.

Amanda put the bag back with the others. 'I am. I just do my detecting with corpses and Google.'

'Don't we all,' Beth said. 'He probably found the tobacco tin and coins rooting around in the desert and the caves.'

'If so, I'd expect them to be rusted or oxidized after a hundred-plus years in the dirt. But these are in mint condition.'

'He must have cleaned them.'

'Then it's the only thing he's ever cleaned.'

She had a point, Beth thought. 'Maybe it's because he intended to sell them and wanted them to sparkle. Or perhaps he bought this stuff at the Calico Ghost Town.'

'You're probably right, but you have to admit this case is weird,' Amanda said. 'It's like he walked out of the 1800s and into the path of a motor home.'

'Is that going to be the conclusion in your report?'

'Of course not. I'm pregnant-crazy, not crazy-crazy.'

Beth looked down at the dead man. 'If this guy was living in the mountains like an old-time prospector, people out in the Mojave must have known him. He was too weird not to have stood out, even among the Yermites. But we've been showing the photo around to people out there and so far nobody has recognized him, or at least is willing to admit it.'

'It's a big desert.'

'Yeah, but he still needed to get food and water from somebody,' Beth said. 'And he certainly didn't get the clap on his own.'

She knew of a whorehouse, a collection of trailers in Newberry Springs. She'd check it out. Or ask patrol to do it.

'He sure went to a lot of effort to live the way people did over a century ago,' Amanda said.

'And to die the way they did, too.'

'He certainly would have, if the motor home hadn't hit him first,' Amanda said. 'The driver did him a favor.'

FOUR

Beth printed out photos of the mystery man and gave them to the watch commander to distribute to the deputies so they could ask around about him. In the meantime, she decided to drive out to the Calico Ghost Town, which was once a private tourist trap, but was now a San Bernardino County Regional Park, giving it the sheen of historical significance. If the mystery man fancied himself a miner, she figured the park rangers might have seen him in the mountains around the hundreds of abandoned silver mines and caves.

She drove out to Yermo, then north across the dry lake bed up to the graded, but sloping ridge at the base of the jagged mountains, where Calico was squeezed in between the steep edges of two deep canyons. There was a guard shack and a gate where the road forked between the graveyard and the town. The graveyard was a mix of real tombstones and fake ones, which made no sense to her.

Beth pulled up to the shack and rolled down her window. The ranger was Jan Houty, a wilderness nut about her age, born and raised in Barstow, who she'd met a few times at Pour Decisions.

'What brings you up here, Beth?' Jan asked. 'Finally broke down and decided to take a ride on the choo-choo train?'

'I'm working a case that I hope you can help me with. Have you ever seen this guy around?' Beth held up her iPhone with her close-up picture of the mystery man's face.

'No, why?'

'We think he may have been working and living in the abandoned mines up here.'

'That'd be suicide.'

Beth knew that wasn't hyperbole. Most of the mine shafts were horizontal, rather than vertical, but many had collapsed into the tunnels below. There were also some open pits, and every few months a Sheriff's department rescue team was called to recover the body of some idiot hiker who thought the caves would be fun to explore, despite all the warning signs erected everywhere, and got himself killed.

'That isn't an issue for him now. He was run over last night,' Beth said. 'Do you sell vintage clothes and boots in the park?'

'Just some souvenir stuff. You know, T-shirts, cowboy hats, leather vests, belt buckles, even some Sheriff's badges if you're in the market for a new one.'

'I'll keep that in mind if I ever lose mine. Can I airdrop you this photo to show to other rangers? Maybe one of them might have run into him in the mountains.'

Jan picked up her iPhone. 'OK, but I'm not sure they will pay much attention to this. They're really distracted right now, as you can imagine.'

Beth sent the photo and heard the swoosh. 'Distracted by what?'

She heard the ding of the photo landing on Jan's phone. 'You didn't hear what happened at Big Bear last night?'

'A lot happened last night. It was crazy.'

'A male grizzly bear attacked a campsite and slashed a woman's arm half-off. A park ranger emptied his Glock into the bear and it still ran after him for fifty yards before it went down.'

'Sounds like quite a bear,' Beth said.

'It was an eight-foot-tall, two-thousand-pound grizzly bear,' Jan said. 'In Big Bear.'

Beth was confused. 'Is that unusual? I mean, isn't that why they call it Big Bear?'

'Yeah, it is,' Jan said. 'But the only bears up there now are black bears.'

'What's the difference?'

'A California grizzly is bigger and brown and *extinct*.' Jan pointed to the California State flag that was mounted on the shack. It depicted a bear loping on all fours across a patch of green over the words *California Republic*, towards a five-pointed star in the upper left corner. 'It's the one right there. The flag is the only place anybody has seen one since 1924. Finding a living one now is a miracle. The ranger who killed it hasn't stopped crying. It's such a tragedy.'

Beth was sure the woman who nearly lost her arm didn't feel that way. But, out of respect for Jan's feelings, she said: 'Maybe the bear had a mate. Or even cubs.'

'That's the hope and the distraction. They've shipped the bear up to UC Berkeley for a thorough necropsy and genetic analysis. It'll probably be stuffed and put in a museum. But now every ranger in the county wants to be the one who finds the next grizzly.'

I hope he's well armed, Beth thought.

She thanked Jan for her help and drove up into the ghost town, parked in the near-empty lot, and wandered up the single street, which was flanked on both sides by typical Western false-front facades for establishments like 'Stoby's General Store & Post Office', 'Lil's Saloon', and 'Judge Orville's Courthouse and Jail'. At a shack that once housed the Calico Print, park visitors could dress up in vintage clothes and have their pictures taken and printed on the front page of the newspaper, suitable for framing.

She knew the place was built on the ruins of the actual mining town, but it all felt about as authentic as capped teeth.

Beth went into the gift shop, leather shop, candy store, photo shop, woodwork shop, candle shop, rock store, the Lane House museum, and the restaurants, and visited the Maggie Mine, the Mystery Shack Tour, and the Calico–Odessa railroad, and showed all the shopkeepers, tour guides, concessioners, cooks, wait staff, and 'cast members', who were all dressed in 'Old West' costumes, the dead man's photo.

Nobody recognized him.

She got into her Explorer and headed back down toward the valley floor, where she could see a CHP patrol car two miles away, snaking up Ghost Town Road from the interstate.

Beth slowed as she approached the CHP cruiser and they stopped in the middle of the empty road, driver's side to driver's side. The officer was Chet.

'Hey there, stranger,' he said.

'I'm sorry. I'm not ghosting you. Honest to God. I've been working that case pretty much since the minute I left.'

Coptis interuptus.

'That was a first. I've never had a woman leave me behind in bed before.'

'Never?'

'At least not in her own home.'

'I guess that isn't exactly how a one-night stand is supposed to go.'

'Is that what it was?' he asked, but with a smile, to show there was no edge to it.

She smiled back, to share the same message. 'I don't know. It depends. Did I hurt your feelings?'

'Of course not. You have a job to do. I get that.'

It was one of the benefits of only dating men who were first responders, too. They understood the job. 'I'm glad you do. Have you ever seen this guy before?'

She held up her phone to him.

'Nope,' Chet said. 'Is that the vic?'

'We've got no ID on him and I think he lived around here. Probably in the mountains. You mind showing his picture around? See if any other officers or locals have seen him?'

'Sure.'

She airdropped it over to him. 'Now you have an excuse to text me.'

His phone dinged, indicating the photo had arrived. 'Do I need one?'

Her phone rang. She glanced at the screen. Shit. 'It's my watch commander.'

'At least this time we aren't in bed.' Chet laughed and drove off.

Beth put the call on speaker and continued down the road toward the interstate. The watch commander today was Jim Sanderson, a big guy who volunteered as a wrestling coach at the local high school.

'What's up, Jim?'

'There's an LAPD detective out here working a case who wants to talk with you. He's waiting for you at Peggy Sue's.'

Beth felt a twinge of anxiety in her gut. She couldn't imagine why any LAPD detective would want to talk to her or why she'd want to talk to any of them after what had happened. 'What's his name?'

'Trent Hardy.'

Beth nearly threw her phone out the window.

The outside of Peggy Sue's looked like a giant jukebox surrounded by dinosaurs. The interior was equally bizarre, a 50s-style diner stuffed with memorabilia and souvenir items celebrating Route 66, old movies, Betty Boop, Lucille Ball, Marilyn Monroe, Elvis Presley, and dinosaurs.

She found Trent at an outside table in the 'Diner-Saur' park, eating a hamburger at a concrete table by the tree-shaded duck pond and a ridge-backed stegosaurus statue. Seeing him sparked both anger and desire, but mostly anger.

He was in his late twenties, with blond hair, laugh-lines on his cheeks, and a natural, heart-warming smile that made his blue eyes sparkle, an unusual trait for a police officer. Even killers wanted to give him a hug. Today he was dressed in a jacket and tie, an outfit she'd only seen him wear once before, at her LAPD Board of Rights hearing, which immediately brought back bad memories. He seemed pleased to see her, flashing her that amazing, knee-weakening smile, until he saw the look on her face. But that only dimmed his smile by a couple watts. It still sent a charge through her, to her dismay.

'What the hell are you doing here?' she said as she marched up to the table.

He carefully set down his burger. She noticed a thin manila file folder next to his plate. 'Having lunch. I'm starving. Can I get you something?'

'Don't be cute. Answer my question.' She stood facing him, hands on her hips. They hadn't spoken or seen each other face to face since the hearing, which ended with the department taking her badge.

'I'm working a missing person case. A guy from West LA. His last known location was a gas station in Yermo, so I came out to investigate.'

'You could have called and I would've run it down for you.'

'I wanted to see how you are.'

'Now you have. Welcome to hell,' she said. 'Satisfied?'

'Come on, Beth. You know I never thought you did anything wrong. I feel terrible about what they did to you.'

'Really?' Beth sat down across from him and lowered her voice, though the nearest people were a couple of weary parents with two screaming little kids. 'The last time I saw you, you were a uniformed patrolman. But now you're a detective. How did that happen?'

'Beth—'

She didn't let him answer, caught up in her anger now, wanting to ride with it, let it steamroll over any attraction she felt.

'Let me guess. Your lawyer argued that you were the victim, that you were sexually assaulted by a superior officer, and if the city didn't want to be sued, and risk paying out millions in a settlement, they'd give you a gold shield and shut the fuck up. Is that about right?'

'They were going to fire me, too, even though I didn't violate any rules.'

'But I did,' she said.

'I didn't say that. They did.'

And they were right, she did, if you went by the book.

But the hypocrisy was that detectives were dating other cops all the time. Her only mistake, she believed, was doing it with a junior officer. They were two consenting adults, but the brass treated her like a teacher who'd slept with one of her underage students. So did the media. At same time she was being persecuted and prosecuted, she knew that there was a deputy chief having an affair with a female captain, but nobody said anything about *that*. And Beth never brought it up in her defense. She wouldn't tear down the LAPD to save herself. Her late father devoted his life to that badge. She wouldn't tarnish it.

Trent studied her face. 'What we had was great, Beth. It was totally consensual. I told them that. Again and again. But what was I supposed to do? Let them fire me when I did nothing wrong? What good would that have done? All I've ever wanted to do was be a cop. So my lawyer did what he had to do to make that happen.'

'Congratulations,' she said. 'You turned the scandal into a win for you.'

'Not really. Everyone resents me. They think I slept my way into a promotion.'

'Well, as it turned out, you did.' She stole one of his French fries and ate it. He took a slurp of his soft drink. They both seemed to feel better after getting that ugliness out into the Diner-Saur park and gave it a minute to dissipate.

'How did you end up with the San Bernardino Sheriff's Department?'

Beth took another fry. 'I wanted to stay in California and this was the only department that would hire me. They had an opening in Baker that nobody wanted.'

He passed her the catsup bottle. 'Baker? But that's just a highway rest-stop with a giant thermometer.'

Beth squirted some catsup in a corner of his plate, dipped some fries into it, and continued eating as she talked.

'It's where everybody stops before going into Death Valley, the Mojave Desert, or on to Las Vegas. So there's a deputy posted out there at all times,' she said. 'It's a one-man job, five days on, five days off. You live behind the station in a decked-out double-wide and you're basically your own boss, like the town marshal.'

'I didn't think anybody actually lived out there.' Trent picked up his burger and continued eating.

'It's a tiny immigrant community. They work hard and mind their own business. There are some domestic disputes, of course, but mostly the trouble comes from the half-a-million people who stop there every year to gas up or get Alien Jerky on their way to or from Vegas. Mostly I dealt with drunk drivers, shoplifters, some car break-ins, and an occasional hold-up.'

'It sounds miserable and remote.'

Like being exiled to a hot Siberia, she thought. But she didn't have a lot of choices if she wanted to be a cop in California.

'It's exactly what I needed. For a while, anyway.'

Or it was what Beth thought she'd deserved. She was punishing herself, no doubt about it. To some degree, she knew she still was. But at least she was out of the spotlight, and quietly getting back on her feet.

'I bet you couldn't wait for those five days off,' Trent said.

'It was the five days off that were killing me.'

'I don't understand.'

'In Baker, you know everybody, and everybody knows you, you're always in the public eye. You have no personal life and no time to think, which was a benefit,' Beth said. 'But when I came back to my place in Barstow, the closest city, I had nothing to do.'

All she did was drink and masturbate. But sex was her drug of choice and she ached for it after a few days. She hadn't discovered Pour Decisions yet, so her vibrator got a workout.

'You could have spent time with friends,' Trent said.

'I didn't have any,' Beth said. 'The only people who understand us, our way of life, have the same life.'

'Other cops.'

'Oh no, I'm not making that mistake again. I won't get involved with anybody with a Sheriff's badge. They are officially off-limits, but other first responders are fine. EMTs, firemen, CHP, park rangers, local police. But I didn't meet many in Baker.' At least not any that she wanted to take to bed. 'Those five days off always felt like five years, so the instant there was an opening in homicide here, I took it.'

And her jurisdiction expanded, putting her into contact with more first responders. She also found her way to Pour Decisions. As a result, her pool of potential lovers greatly expanded and her vibrator went into the moving box by her bed.

Trent dabbed his mouth with a napkin. 'Still, it must be boring compared to LA.'

'It's a lot of wide-open space, it takes forever to get anywhere, so everything moves slower,' she said. 'But people still find reasons to rob and kill, so at least I have plenty of work to do.' Which reminded her of why he was sitting there. 'You came here to do a job, so let's do it. Who disappeared?'

'His name is Owen Slader. Thirty-five years old. Lives out in Silver Lake.' He slid the file folder across the table to her.

She opened the folder. There were several pages of information and two photos inside. She looked at the pictures. One was taken on an alley stoop, at the rear of a restaurant, a corner of the kitchen visible in the open doorway. Slader was in his early twenties, lanky and loose, wearing a chef's sauce-stained tunic and jeans, his hair a bit too long, his eyes bloodshot, taking a drink from a bottle of beer. She got the impression from his posture, or perhaps something in the expression on his face, that he was a hard-partying guy, but she couldn't say why. Perhaps because she'd seen the same look in her own reflection once. The photo also looked posed and staged, like it was taken for publicity purposes to show him in his element. It just seemed lit too well.

'That's an older photo of him,' Trent said, then tapped the other one. 'That's him today.'

In this photo, Slader looked older, and less cocky. Clean-shaven, hair nicely cut, wearing a Tommy Bahama shirt, khaki shorts, and sandals. He was sitting on a bench at a food truck, digging into a bowl of noodles with a pair of chopsticks. He'd gone up-scale with age. The drink on the table was a Coke. The picture appeared to be a candid shot, but at the same time, it also seemed professionally lit to her. He'd grown up.

'What's he do for a living?' Beth asked.

'He's a wannabe Anthony Bourdain, only not as talented, a former gourmet chef who is now a writer and a social-media influencer with his own popular YouTube channel.'

The photo on the bench must have been a publicity still taken while he was shooting one of his videos, Beth thought. That explained why it looked candid and slick at the same time.

'Slader was driving back to LA from Las Vegas on Friday night,' Trent continued. 'He was supposed to pick up his twelve-year-old daughter at his ex-girlfriend's place on Saturday morning and take her for the weekend, but he never showed. His ex said it wasn't like him, not anymore.'

'Anymore?' she asked, browsing the pages in the folder, which listed his basic personal details like his place of birth, his home address, his phone numbers, his bank accounts, and his credit card accounts.

'He used to party hard, but now everything is about his daughter.' Beth was pleased with herself for reading his pictures accurately. 'The ex, her name is Sabine Denier, claims he'd never miss a weekend, certainly not without calling and offering a good excuse. We checked his credit cards. The last activity was at EddieWorld in Yermo. We checked with his cellular provider, and the last ping from his phone came from there, too. So did the last ping from his car.'

She looked up from the photo. 'His car?'

'It's a 2018 Mercedes GLC, a mid-sized SUV. It has an app that allows you to see everywhere the car has been or where it is now. So can law enforcement if they serve a warrant on the car manufacturer.'

That was a trick she didn't know and it embarrassed her that Trent did.

'Why would the pings stop?' she asked.

'Only two reasons, besides a network failure, which there wasn't,' Trent said. 'And that would be if the car wasn't running, due to the vehicle being turned off or involved in an accident, or if the unit that sends the signal was intentionally disabled or jammed, which is something sophisticated thieves will do.'

'What time was his last ping?'

'Around 2 a.m. Why?'

Owen Slader went missing on the same day, at the same time, and in the same area that the mystery man ran out of nowhere and got hit by the motor home.

Beth looked again at Owen Slader's photo and tried to imagine him with a beard, long hair, and wearing filthy, old clothes. 'I don't suppose he had lice, bad teeth, and syphilis?'

'Of course not,' Trent said. 'Why would you ask that?'

'Taking a long shot,' Beth said and stood up. 'Let's go to EddieWorld. I'll drive.'

FIVE

EddieWorld was a gas station, fast-food place, and tourist trap, all rolled into one, right off the interstate's Yermo exit and across from Liberty Park, a vacant weedy lot dotted with various sculptures, including a huge bust of Crazy Horse, erected by a dissident Chinese artist to oppose human rights abuses in China. Beth didn't get what Crazy Horse had to do with Communist Party oppression, but it was bizarre enough to fit with EddieWorld's sixty-five-foot-tall LED-illuminated ice-cream-sundae cup as a backdrop.

Over two dozen gas pumps and two dozen electric vehicle charging stations took up most of the EddieWorld property. The main building was set back from the pumps and resembled some kind of Spanish mission, minus the religious iconography.

Beth parked in front of the building and the two detectives went inside. The place was a huge candy store, souvenir shop, and mini-mart in the center of a food court. Beth approached one of the cashiers, flashed her badge, and asked to see the manager, who came out from some back office to meet them. Beth explained to him that they were looking for a missing person and were interested in seeing any security camera footage recorded shortly before and after 2 a.m. on Saturday.

The manager led them to a windowless security office, sat them down in front of a bank of monitors, cued up the footage, showed them how to work the DVR playback, and even offered them a complimentary EddieWorld thumb drive to download any footage they needed, then he left them alone.

'Wow,' Trent said. 'I wish people in Los Angeles were as cooperative.'

'They know how much they need us out here,' she said. 'It's the Wild West.'

She started the playback.

They saw Slader drive up in his black Mercedes GLC to one of the pumps at about 1:25 a.m., fill up his tank, and then walk into the store. There were only a few other cars at the pumps, but no one approached him.

He walked inside, spent some time browsing the aisles, before selecting several bags of beef jerky and going to a self-serve soft drink dispenser, where he got himself a large drink. There were three or four other patrons in the building, but he didn't have any interactions with them.

'It doesn't look like he's under any duress,' Trent said.

No, she thought, it didn't.

Slader went to the cashier, chatted with her while she rang up his order, then he walked back to his car. Nobody followed him out.

He got into his car and drove off. She noted the time code. It was only five minutes before the mystery man got hit by the motor home at the next exit on the interstate.

Beth watched to see if any cars tailed Slader out of EddieWorld, but none did. She stopped the footage and copied it to the thumb drive.

Trent shook his head. 'There were no altercations, nothing out of the ordinary. He was fine when he drove off.'

'You were hoping for a road-rage incident or some other confrontation?'

'That would have been nice,' Trent said.

'Not for Slader.'

She pocketed the thumb drive. They left the room, thanked the manager for his help, and asked him not to erase the day's footage until he heard from them. He agreed. The two detectives got back in Beth's Explorer and she headed back to Peggy Sue's.

Trent looked out at the passing desert. 'Could he have had an accident, maybe lost control and driven off the freeway?'

'Sure, it happens all the time. People fall asleep at the wheel, veer off the road. But this is a wide-open desert. Look around, Trent. Do you see his car? Somebody would have spotted it by now.'

'Maybe he was forced off the road and car-jacked.'

'I suppose it's possible,' Beth said. 'But then he could be anywhere.'

'Or his car could be anywhere and his body could be somewhere in that desert, out in the open or in a shallow grave.'

It wasn't uncommon for gang members to come out to the desert to execute someone, or bury a body, but they rarely seemed to bury them deep enough, or far enough away from road or dirt-biking paths, to avoid discovery. But she'd never heard of a car-jacking and murder happening out here.

'There's no evidence to indicate that's what happened,' she said.

'There's no evidence to indicate that it didn't.' Trent knocked a knuckle on the window. 'This is where he disappeared, but I don't know what to do next.'

'Don't worry about it,' Beth said. 'It's not your problem now, it's mine.'

He turned to her. 'He's from LA. It's my case.'

'And he disappeared here,' Beth said, just as Peggy Sue's dinosaurs showed up on the other side of the road. She took the exit. 'My jurisdiction. My case.'

'We can work it together.'

'No, we can't.' She drove under the overpass toward the MCLB and the Jack-in-the-Box on the corner. 'We can't do anything together ever again.'

'Why not? We aren't wearing the same badge anymore.'

She turned left on Yermo Road.

'I'm trying to rebuild my career, dumbshit. Do you think it helps having the officer I was fired for fucking show up at my work place? What the hell were you thinking? That we'd pick up where we left off?'

Yes, he did; she could see it on his face.

'No, of course not. Jesus,' Trent said. 'I care about you, Beth. That didn't stop because you got fired.'

'It should have.' She pulled into the Peggy Sue's parking lot and braked hard beside his unmarked LAPD-issue Dodge Charger to express her anger. 'Don't come back, Trent. If I find anything on Slader, I'll notify you.'

He smiled that damn smile and said: 'It was good seeing you.'

She hated that she still felt the pull to him. 'I'm so relieved that you got some closure. It was keeping me up nights.'

His smile abruptly disappeared. He got out and slammed the door behind him.

Beth made a sharp U-turn and drove off as fast as she could.

The next three days moved very slowly. It was often like that in Barstow, a rush of activity, followed by nothing but delayed paperwork and sheer boredom.

There were no new leads on the mystery man or Owen Slader, though she spent a lot of time driving around the Mojave Valley, including the collection of trailers in Newberry Springs where the prostitutes plied their trade, showing people photos of the two men. There was also no sign of Slader's Mercedes, though she had all the deputies looking for it.

At the end of her shift on Wednesday, she wandered into Pour Decisions. There were two guys playing pool and the radio was on, tuned to Alan Vernon's talk show. Vernon was a crazy conspiracy theorist, broadcasting his own show from a trailer in middle of the Mojave, out near Fort Irwin. He was a local celebrity, though a reclusive one.

Beth took a seat at the bar, dragged over a nearly empty bowl of nuts, and listened to Vernon while Sally filled up a beer mug for her.

'The truth isn't hiding, it's right out in the open. The government admits that Goldstone Space Communications Complex at Fort Irwin exists to communicate with our space craft and search the cosmos for alien signals. They admit it because the array and its purpose can't be hidden—'

Sally set the beer down in front of her. 'The burger will be right up.'

'You can skip the burger, but keep the nuts and drinks coming.'

'But they aren't searching the cosmos for alien signals. They are responding to them.'

Sally refilled Beth's bowl from a big canister of mixed nuts under the bar.

'Bad day?'

'Usual day.'

'That array exists so the shadow government in DC can remain in constant communication with their alien overlords and continue their plans for the ultimate invasion.'

Beth had heard that conspiracy theory, and variations on the theme, many times before. It was one reason why the jerky store in Baker was called Alien Jerky, and why the owner wanted to build an alien-themed flying-saucer-shaped hotel behind his store. There were lots of people who were convinced extraterrestrials were behind the strange lights in the skies above the vast military base. She figured it was just the Air Force testing top-secret military aircraft.

She gestured to the radio. 'Why do you listen to that lunatic?'

'It's how I keep up with my ex-husband.'

'He listens to this crap?'

'That's him,' Sally said.

The woman never ceased to surprise Beth. She'd been coming in for six months and kept learning new things.

They both looked at the radio now as Vernon went on.

'Half the soldiers out there are human . . . but the other half are aliens in human form . . . wearing our military uniforms. We've known that for years.'

'I'm sorry,' Beth said.

'Don't be. Alan's insane, I know that, but if he's on the radio, and pitching his alien conspiracies, then it means he's at home, taking care of himself, and not getting into trouble.'

'But that lightning storm is evidence that their plans are moving into the next phase . . . and big things are happening . . . good for the aliens, bad for mankind.'

'He really believes all that crazy stuff?' Beth asked.

'Sometimes there's some truth buried in the shit he says. Otherwise the government wouldn't keep trying to shut him up,' Sally said. 'I admire his tenacity, he truly thinks he's saving the world, but it's impossible to live with him.'

'You still care.'

'I'm a big softy.' Sally went over and turned off the radio.

'Don't mind me,' Beth said. 'You can keep it on if you want. This is your place. I'm just a guest.'

'I've heard enough and it's about time for the Marines to start drifting in. I don't want to piss off the aliens. I'm not insured for laser-beam damage.'

Sally went to serve another customer. Beth drank some beer, and idly turned to watch the guys playing pool. One guy, with a Tom Selleck mustache, was running the table. He kept casually putting balls in the pockets, to the mounting, visible frustration of the other player, a stocky guy with a cleft chin that looked like a tiny ass.

The Mustache said, 'I make this shot, you owe me hundred bucks.'

'You aren't that good,' Ass Chin said.

Beth didn't know much about pool, but it looked like the shot would require Mustache to use the cue ball to knock another ball just right, so it would ricochet off the side and knock another ball into a corner pocket.

Chet slid on to the barstool next to Beth and gave her arm a squeeze. 'Is this stool taken?'

'I'm saving it for Chris Hemsworth, but you can keep it warm until he gets here.'

'Have you had anything to eat yet?'

Beth held up the bowl of nuts. 'I'm eating now.'

The Mustache made his shot, and grinned at Ass Chin. 'Want to go double or nothing?'

Ass Chin flipped him off. With a crooked finger. 'I'm not a sucker.'

Beth nearly choked on a cashew and started coughing. Chet patted her back.

'Are you OK?'

'Fine.' Beth washed down the cashew with the last of her beer. 'You know that guy?'

Chet glanced at the Mustache. 'Yeah, that's Cliff Decker, a firefighter in town, and an aspiring pool hustler.'

'I meant the sucker,' she said, gesturing to Ass Chin.

'Dave Salem. A Barstow PD patrolman. Why?'

A cop, she thought. That was how he knew where Sheriff's deputies always were. He monitored the police band because he was on it.

'I'm not too bad at pool myself. He looks like an easy mark next time I'm low on cash.' She'd never played pool in her life.

'Want to share a pizza?' Chet asked.

'You know they're frozen and microwaved here, right?'

Chet nodded. 'That's home cooking for you. You should love it.'

'Sure, I'm in,' she said.

'Great, I'll order us one. But you have to promise to leave room for dessert.'

'What did you have in mind?'

'The box of Eskimo Pies in your freezer.'

'The whole box?'

'Depends if we work up a sweat.'

Beth smiled. 'You're pretty sure of yourself.'

He smiled back. 'I'm just a man who believes in finishing what he starts.'

This was the kind of easy banter that got them into bed the first time.

'I like a man with strong beliefs.' She got up. 'I'll be right back. I've got to make a call.'

Beth went outside and scanned the cars parked on the street. There were four pickups, all Ford F-250 SuperDutys. She went to each one and found what she was looking for on the third truck – tire treads that matched the cast she took at the lake house.

Damn.

She took a picture of the treads and the license plate and then was faced with a dilemma.

Should she arrest the guy or not?

She only had a beer, and with some food, so there was no way she'd test as intoxicated if things got ugly.

And they could easily get ugly.

It was also Hatcher's case. How would he feel about her snatching the arrest out from under him?

If she arrested a cop, she'd certainly be making enemies with the Barstow Police, which would be bad enough. But this was Hatcher's case. He'd be pissed off and she didn't need enemies at the Sheriff's department, too, especially given her problems in LA.

All she could see were the ways making an arrest right now could go very wrong for her.

But there also wasn't any pressing need to act now. Ass Chin

Dave Salem wasn't going anywhere. He'd still be in Barstow tomorrow. The arrest could wait.

So she went back inside, ordered another beer and shared a pizza with Chet. She saved room for dessert.

Two hours later, Beth and Chet were sitting naked on her bed, their backs against the wall, each of them enjoying a post-coital Eskimo Pie. It was a refreshing treat after the sweat they'd worked up.

Chet looked across the room at the blank wall. 'You ever think about putting up some artwork?'

'Like what?'

'I don't know. Something you like, someplace you love.'

'I've never bought any artwork,' she said.

'Ever? Not even posters of singers or movie stars or cartoon characters when you were a kid?'

'Sure, but my parents bought the posters and I'd deface them within a week or so, which would really piss off my mom.'

'Why?'

'I got bored looking at them,' Beth said. 'I still feel the same way. I don't want to look at the same faces, or vase of flowers, or misty seascape every day.'

'How about a photo that means something to you? You must have taken a few in your life.'

'Crime scenes, mostly,' she said, a piece of chocolate coating breaking off and landing on her breast. 'I don't want that on my walls.'

Before she could wipe it off, Chet leaned down and licked it off her skin. 'Most people, you visit their homes, and it's like taking a walk through their lives.' He sat up again and looked around her room. 'Then again, I guess this is, too. That nightstand is a real focal point.'

He gestured to her gun safe with his popsicle stick, which had chocolate on it.

'It belonged to my dad.'

'Really? He liked guns?'

She licked the chocolate off his stick. 'He was a cop. Almost twenty years on the LAPD.'

'He retired early?'

'Got killed early.'

'I'm sorry,' Chet said.

Beth licked the remaining ice cream off her own stick. 'He walked into a liquor store for a pack of gum and didn't know there was a robbery in progress. He was shot in the head before he knew what happened.'

'How old were you?'

'Old enough to enter the police academy.'

'How about your mom?'

Beth tossed her stick across the room. 'She'd left us years before that. I came home from school one day and everything was gone except his clothes, their bed, his gun safe, and the stuff in my room.'

'That's cold,' he said.

She took his stick from him and tossed it across the room, too. 'What's your story?'

'Happy childhood in Redlands. Joined the military to serve my country. Went to Afghanistan. Came back whole and joined the CHP.'

'You traded one desert for another.'

'Different uniform but more comfortable vehicles and no snipers or IEDs to worry about.'

'You like the job?' she asked.

'It's restful after Afghanistan, but still gives me what I need.'

'What's that?'

'To serve. To drive fast. To carry a gun. To go after bad guys,' he said. 'What about you? Why do you do it?'

'It's all I know how to do,' she said. 'It's the family business.'

'Why here?'

She gave him a look. 'That wasn't my choice. But I'm sure you and everybody with a badge out here knows that.'

'I know why you aren't in LA, but not why you picked Barstow.'

'I didn't have many options.'

Chet shook his head. 'There are forty-nine other states. You could have found somewhere else. But I think the desert suits you. I mean, look around.' He swept his arm in front of him, indicating the whole room. 'It's a perfect fit.'

'Are you saying my home is bleak, dry, and desolate?'

'Except for the cactus,' he said.

'I don't have a cactus.'

'I was talking about you.' He rolled on top of her.

'Aren't you worried about getting jabbed by my thorns?'

'Maybe I'm a cactus, too.'

She smiled. 'I'm feeling at least one prick already.'

SIX

Detective Glen Hatcher was at his desk, in his Mr Rogers cardigan, when Beth arrived at the station on Thursday morning.

'I have a lead for you in those home burglaries,' she said.

He turned in his desk chair to look at her. 'You've been investigating my case on your own?'

'All I did was go out for a drink.' Beth went on to explain about Dave Salem, the ass-chin cop with the crooked right middle finger. She finished by showing Hatcher her photos of Salem's tires.

'It's thin,' Hatcher said.

'It's his finger. His tire. His piss.'

'He's a cop.'

'Which is how he always knew where we'd be,' she said. 'Or, rather, where we *wouldn't* be.'

'If we arrest a cop and next time a lone deputy needs police backup on an armed robbery on the outskirts of Barstow, nobody is gonna show.'

'That's a chance we have to take, because if we don't do anything, then we're essentially covering up his crime for him,' Beth said. 'That makes us accomplices.'

'If you're so gung-ho about this,' Hatcher said, 'why didn't you arrest him last night?'

'It's your case, Glen. I didn't want to show you up and take all your glory.'

'You mean you didn't want all this shit on you.'

'I'm a team player.'

That's when Jim Sanderson, the shift watch commander, stuck his head in the room, and held out a piece of paper. 'We got a call

from patrol. A construction crew out in Newberry Springs has dug
up some bones. They're human.'

Beth snatched the paper from his fingers. 'I'm on it. Glen is busy.
He's working a big break on his burglary case.'

She rushed out before Hatcher could object.

Newberry Springs was east of Yermo, but just another swath of desert,
roughly bordered by Interstate 15 to the north and Interstate 40 thirty
miles to the south. The particular patch of sand Beth was heading
for was only a few miles below I-15, barely across the invisible border
with Yermo. The lot was filled with a couple of bulldozers and
water trucks, a Morlock Construction trailer, a water tank, several
pickup trucks, and a big drill operated by Herbert George Well
Drilling, presumably to tap the springs the area was famous for. There
was also a coroner's wagon and a sheriff's patrol car on scene.

Beth parked beside the patrol car and approached the deputy, an
old-timer named Charlie Morrow with a gut so big, he made good
money at Christmas playing Santa at the Outlets.

'What have we got, Charlie?'

'They're grading for a new lake development and hit a wooden
box. It appeared to be a casket with an old skeleton inside.' Morrow
gestured to an open pit staked out with crime-scene tape. 'I took
some photos and sent them over to the coroner for examination. In
the meantime, the developer's got an archeologist on the payroll
who came by and says it's definitely a casket from the 1800s, based
on the nails and the construction.'

So far, it was all standard operating procedure. A deputy would
sit on the bones until a coroner came to collect them all. But
homicide was only called if the coroner determined the bones were
recent and there were signs of violence.

'So why call me?'

Morrow led her around behind the construction trailer, where
she saw Amanda hunched down in the sagebrush, vomiting. 'You'll
have to ask her.'

Beth went over to Amanda, crouched beside her, and placed a
comforting hand on her back. 'Morning sickness again?'

Amanda shook her head. 'This time I think it's the burrito I had
for breakfast from that food truck in Daggett.'

'It's a pickup with a camper lid parked at an off-ramp.'

'A food truck, like I said.'

'It's a random guy making tacos with mystery meat that he's grilling on a Hibachi on his tailgate. You know better than that.'

'I had an intense craving that overruled my better judgment.' Amanda stood and led Beth over to the staked-out hole. 'Morlock's staff archeologist says it's an old burial and there's a complete adult male skeleton in the casket. I'm not a forensic anthropologist, but judging by the oxidation, the bones appear to be very old, probably over a hundred years. There's also no obvious signs of violent death or homicide.'

They got to the edge of the hole. Beth saw bones in a rotting wooden casket. The bones were still in some swaths of clothing. 'Then why did you want me here?'

Amanda crouched beside the body and pointed to something shiny in the skeleton's right elbow. 'He has a titanium radial head in his elbow and two dental implants.'

Now Beth crouched beside her. 'So these aren't old bones.'

'The bones are,' Amanda said. 'But the implants aren't.'

'That doesn't make any sense.'

'That's why I called a detective.'

Beth took a closer look at the bones. The clothes appeared to be the remnants of a white-collared shirt and jeans. The belt buckle was the Louis Vuitton logo. Even if it was a natural death, burying the body out here was suspicious. 'I don't suppose you found a wallet in there?'

'Nope, but I can get an ID off the serial numbers on the elbow and dental implants. It'll take a few hours.'

'I'll get CSU out here to process the coffin and the hole.'

The crime scene investigators would be dispatched from San Bernardino, an hour or so away, if they weren't at some other far-flung crime scene. And that's if CSU prioritized old bones in the desert. It could be a full day if they didn't.

Beth excused herself from Amanda and went to the Morlock construction trailer, where she found the manager, a heavy-set, sunbaked guy in his fifties named Carson Edlow, wearing a hard hat, though she couldn't imagine what might fall on his head out here.

'How long are we going to be held up?' Edlow asked.

'I'm not sure yet, but at least the rest of the day. What was this lot before?'

'At one time, there was a ranch here, but it's been vacant for a century.' She knew it wasn't unusual for people back then to bury their kin in their backyard. She'd come across old bones many times before. 'Some ground-breaking this turned out to be.'

'So this was the first day of construction? The land hasn't been disturbed at all when you got here?' She was wondering if it was a fresh grave, given the modern implants in the skeleton.

'Not unless you count parking the trailer and sticking a couple of stakes in the ground,' Edlow said. 'We were just starting preliminary grading, and testing where to sink the wells, when we hit that grave.'

'Who owns this property?'

'Desert Lake Ventures, a real-estate development firm out of LA. We're the local, general contractors for them. As a company, we've got over a century of experience building in the Mojave Valley.'

'What are you building here?'

He pointed to some blueprints on his fake wood-paneled wall. 'A lush private lake surrounded by estate homes for watersports and off-road enthusiasts.'

She thought about Grenlick's lakefront home. 'It's been tried here before.'

'Yeah, I know about those others, and most of 'em have become white-trash watering holes, but this time it's gonna be different. Those places were built thirty, forty years ago, were under-funded, and went for a different demographic. Tract homes and trailers around a fish pond in the desert,' Edlow said. 'The people behind Desert Lake Ventures have deep pockets and have done this kind of thing before in Arizona and Nevada. They know how to make it work and attract a higher class of people, the kind with private jets and homes in Park City, New York, Malibu, and Palm Beach.'

'If I had that kind of money,' Beth said, 'I'd buy a place where there are great restaurants, great shopping, and a real lake.'

'Las Vegas looked like this once,' Edlow said. 'All it took was one man with a vision who built a resort.'

'A mobster.' Bugsy Siegel. She'd seen his story in a Warren Beatty movie.

'Desert Lake Ventures is legit. No Mob involved.'

'That's a relief,' Beth said.

She went back outside, put in a call to CSU, then took a few photos of the grave and the property, just to be doing something useful. Amanda couldn't take the bones away until CSU gave the OK, so she was stuck there waiting, too. But she spent most of her time talking on her phone.

To the surprise of both women, a lone forensic investigator arrived a little over an hour later, which was blazingly fast, all things considered. His name was Russell Parmalee. He was in his late twenties and kept his head shaved bald, and frequently ran an electric razor over his face, to make sure he never left his own hair behind at a crime scene. Beth thought it was strange. She thought everything about him was.

Parmalee huddled with Amanda for a while at the grave, they talked a bit, then he let her collect the bones in a body bag.

Amanda carried the body bag over to Beth, who was watching Parmalee work.

'I'm gonna head out,' Amanda said. 'By the way, the tox results came back on Motor Home Man. He had outrageously high levels of mercury and lead in his body.'

Motor Home Man. Beth liked that name. It was more descriptive than Mystery Man or Dirty Man. 'Aren't those results what you expected?'

'He also had cholera. We found the bacteria in his intestines. Who gets cholera in America anymore?'

'The man was cursed,' Beth said.

Amanda looked over her shoulder at Parmalee, then moved closer to Beth's open window, crouching down and lowering her voice to a conspiratorial whisper. 'I think you should know that I'm unofficially running some more tests on Motor Home Man.'

'Why unofficially?'

'Because the tests are scientifically unjustified, factually unnecessary, and ridiculously expensive and will only satisfy my twisted curiosity, so I'm having them done myself.'

That worried Beth. She knew how tight money was for Amanda. 'You're paying out of your own pocket?'

'Hell no. I could barely afford that burrito I threw up. I sent a tooth and a small bone from Motor Home Man to a physicist at UC Irvine who owes me a favor. Actually, he still pines for me. We dated before I was married.' Amanda grimaced. 'I probably shouldn't have told you that.'

'Why not?'

'Because what I did was probably unethical, potentially illegal, and would certainly compromise the chain of evidence if this were a homicide investigation, so thank God it's not, but if I get in trouble for this, which isn't likely, since this is a low, low-profile case, it's better for you if you can deny knowing anything about it. How good of a liar are you?'

'I hope we don't have to find out. I've already had enough scandal for one lifetime,' Beth said and saw the unconvincingly disinterested expression on Amanda's face. 'Well, now we know how good a liar you are.'

'I haven't lied.'

'Your face just did. You tried to pretend like you don't know about my past.'

Amanda dropped her disinterested facade. 'Is it all true?'

'Yep.'

'Any regrets?'

Beth had a lot of time to think about it and her feeling was that she was unfairly singled out. Nobody was hurt, at least not until the brass meddled in their relationship. 'Only that I got caught.'

Amanda smiled and stood up straight again. 'The tests probably won't lead to anything. I'll call you later with my preliminary report and the ID on this guy.' She shook the bag of bones for emphasis.

'Thanks,' Beth said.

Amanda left. Beth waited a few minutes, then got out of her car to see what Parmalee was up to.

He saw her coming and rose from the graveside to meet her. 'You need an archeologist, not a crime-scene technician.'

'How do you know that already?' she asked.

'I've seen a bunch of graves like this out here. This was a thriving mining community and people died young and were pretty much buried where they dropped. These nails are more than a hundred years old.'

'The implants in the skeleton aren't.'

'Yeah, Amanda mentioned that. But until she gets the bones in the lab, she can't be sure. All I can figure is that it's a recent burial in an old casket.'

'You ever heard of anybody doing that?'

'No,' he said. 'But what other explanation is there?'

'I don't know what we're dealing with here or if a crime has been committed. So I'm treating it like a homicide until I do. Make a note of everything you find, especially anything that doesn't fit in with an old burial.'

'Sure,' Parmalee said, 'my pleasure.'

It obviously wasn't. But she didn't care. There were too many mysteries in her life now and she didn't like it. She liked answers.

SEVEN

Beth grabbed a burger at Jack-in-the-Box, ate it in her car, then went back to the station, and ran into Hatcher as he was emerging from their office.

'Perfect timing,' Hatcher said. 'I've got Officer Dave Salem here to give us some advice on the home burglaries we're investigating.'

'You're kidding. He just walked in?'

Hatcher grinned. 'I called him. I said I needed an expert on the off-road-vehicle scene in the desert, and heard he was really into it, being that he was born and raised out here. He's off duty today but said he'd come right over.'

'He wants to hear what we have.'

'He's a cocky bastard. I have him in the conference room to put him at ease. I'm just getting him a Coke from the vending machine.'

Now Beth grinned. She knew exactly why Hatcher was being so hospitable. 'What convinced you he's your man?'

'The tire treads, the crooked finger, and he was off duty each time there was a burglary. I also cruised by a patch of sand he owns in Daggett. It's a warehouse big enough to hold a lot of toys. How does he afford that on a Barstow PD officer's salary?'

A good question. 'Bring him his Coke, chat him up a bit, and I'll come in and drop the hammer, if that's what you'd like me to do.'

'That's exactly what I want,' he said. 'I'd appreciate the assist.'

'He's a cop,' she said. 'Are you sure you want to do this?'

'He's a criminal,' he said. 'We can't treat him different because he wears a badge or we might as well be his accomplices.'

She agreed, of course, and was glad that he did, too, despite the blow-back he'd get for it as the lead detective on the case.

Beth went back outside, got a collection vial from her trunk, ran a Q-tip over her own car seat to get the tip dirty, stuck it in the vial, and sealed it. She stuck the vial in her pocket, went back to her office, picked up the cast of the tire tread, and carried it into the conference room.

Hatcher and Ass Chin Dave Salem were sitting across the table from one another, some files spread out between them with pictures of various stolen ATVs. She set the cast down on the table and took a seat beside Hatcher, who was in full soft-talking, Mr Rogers mode. She half-expected Hatcher to start singing 'Won't You Be My Neighbor?'.

'Thank you for coming in, Officer Salem,' Beth said, offering him her hand. 'We really appreciate your help.'

'We're all on the same team.' Salem gave her a handshake. 'You look familiar.'

'Detective Beth McDade. You've probably seen me at Pour Decisions.'

He snapped his fingers and pointed at her. 'Yeah, that's it. You're one of the regulars.'

Hatcher said, 'As I was saying, Dave, we thought you might look at the evidence we have and see if any of the pieces connect for you, because frankly we're stuck and you're a born-and-raised local. We're both outsiders, city-folk, and always will be.'

'Be glad to help.'

'Let's start with the most recent burglary,' Hatcher said, and glanced at Beth to pick up from there.

She explained they got a call of a burglary in progress at a Lake Betty home in Newberry Springs from an out-of-town owner who was watching it all in La Jolla on his security camera feeds.

'The homeowner was shit-talking the perps, so one of them flipped off the security camera.' Beth took out her phone and showed Salem a still of himself, face covered with a balaclava, giving the camera the finger. 'Anything about him seem familiar?'

'Nope.' Salem took a swig of his Coke.

Hatcher said, 'We're having a real hard time IDing these guys. We can't see their faces or even any skin.'

'Well, some skin,' Beth said. 'He whipped out his itty bitty dick and pissed all over the place.'

She saw a flash of anger pass across Salem's face, pinching his ass-crack chin.

He wanted to defend his dick. Instead he said, 'These aren't shit-head tweakers looking for a quick score. You're dealing with pros. They won't leave a trace.'

Beth pointed to the cast on the table. 'We have a cast of tire prints from the last scene.'

Salem waved her off and named the brand of tire.

Hatcher cocked an eyebrow. 'How do you know that?'

'Those are probably the most common off-road tires you can get for an SUV. Just about everybody out here has those, including me. Hell, some of your department vehicles use them, too.' Salem crinkled the empty can and tossed it in the trash across the room with a satisfying *thunk*. He was pleased with himself.

'You're right, Dave, those tires are common,' Beth said, 'but the tread wear is as individual and unique as a fingerprint.'

'That ain't much. Sounds like you two really have hit a dead end.'

'We have this.' Beth held out her phone again and showed him the video of her collecting the urine off the couch with a Q-tip and putting it into a vial.

Salem looked up at her. 'You collected his piss?'

'That's right.' She took the vial out of her pocket and set it on the table.

Salem shot a grin at Hatcher. 'And here I thought that being a detective was glamorous. Seeing that, I'll stick to patrol, thanks.'

'We like to be thorough,' Hatcher said.

'That's not only disgusting but pointless.' Salem leaned back in his chair. 'The fact is, neither the city nor the county is gonna pay to run DNA on a burglary. Besides, even if they did, that piss only helps you if his DNA is in the system. And if it's not, what are you gonna do? Test the DNA of everybody you question?'

'I don't think that's going to be necessary,' Beth said and looked at Hatcher, who took out a pair of latex gloves from a sweater pocket. 'Do you?'

'Nope. This should do it.'

Hatcher got up, gloved his hands as he walked across the room, and then removed the Coke can from the trash. He tugged an evidence baggie out from another pocket and dropped the can into it.

It's a beautiful day in the neighborhood.

Salem sat up straight and looked quickly between Hatcher and Beth.

She smiled at Salem. 'We've got you, Dave. The DNA on that can is going to match what we pull from your piss.'

Salem stared at it for a moment. 'Even if that were true, which it isn't, you can't use that can. You don't have a warrant.'

Hatcher sealed the evidence bag and peeled off his gloves. 'We don't need one, Dave. You came in here voluntarily to discuss the burglaries, you were given the Coke freely, you tossed the can in the trash, giving up possession, and I recovered it. It's all on the security camera.' He pointed to a camera in an upper corner of the room. 'But, speaking of warrants, Dave, we've got one to search your warehouse in Daggett. Imagine what we will find.'

Salem swallowed hard, his throat going dry. A tell.

Beth added, 'And that's not even counting the plaster cast that's going to match your tires and the video of that crooked finger of yours.'

Hatcher sat down again. 'All that's left is reading you your rights, slapping on the cuffs, and taking you to your cell. Unless, of course, you'd like to help us round up your crew, then you can avoid a cell . . . at least for a day or two, assuming you can make a deal with the DA.'

Salem got some color in his cheeks, flushing from anger and embarrassment. Beth had seen it many times.

'You two aren't exactly Joe Friday or you wouldn't be here in this shithole.' Salem gave Hatcher a hard look. 'You were getting kickbacks in Chicago . . .' he shifted his gaze to Beth '. . . and you were making junior officers fuck you in LA. You two are no better than me. So cut the bullshit and tell me how we can work this out, cop to cop. You want a cut, is that it?'

Hatcher leaned forward on the table. As a physical act, it wasn't much. But his entire facial expression changed, from kindly Mr Rogers into a disgusted Dirty Harry.

'I wasn't on the take, Dave, but I knew everybody else in my precinct was and I said nothing about it. I didn't go to prison, but I still got flushed down the toilet with them. That's not happening again, and certainly not for a white-trash, arrogant, tiny-dick clown like you. So, do you want a deal or do I take you to a cell? It makes no difference to me. You're going to prison either way.'

She didn't know about Hatcher's past. She'd never thought to check. So it was true what she'd heard years ago about the Barstow Sheriff's department. It really was the land of misfit toys. Nobody else would have her or Hatcher now.

Hatcher leaned back in his seat. Salem glowered at them both for a long, hard minute, then seemed to deflate like a punctured floatie. 'Call the DA.'

'Stand up,' Hatcher said. 'Put your hands behind your back.'

Salem stood and did as he was told. Hatcher walked around the table and cuffed him while Beth read him his rights.

'Sit down,' Hatcher told Salem. 'We'll be right back.'

Beth gathered the cast and the vial and the two detectives walked out. Once they were back in their office, out of earshot of Salem, she turned to Hatcher.

'Did you really get a warrant for his place?'

He shook his head. 'That's my next call, then the DA. But I don't want to search the warehouse yet, it'll tip off his crew.'

She nodded in agreement, setting the cast on her desk and tossing the prop vial in the trash. 'Makes sense.'

'I owe you one,' he said.

'It was pure luck.'

'Seeing him flip off the pool player in the bar, yeah, that was luck, but not the rest. That was top-notch policing. Thanks for that.'

'You may not thank me once his friends at the Barstow PD hear about what we've done.'

'The Captain has our back on this. He OKed it, he'll take the flak.'

She doubted that, but she didn't want to kill his enthusiasm. Politics in Barstow were probably as brutal as LA, maybe worse because it was a small town. The generals always sacrificed the soldiers to save themselves.

Hatcher added, 'I almost lost it when you made the comment about his tiny dick.'

'So did he,' she said.

'I saw that on his face. That's when I was sure we had him.'

Beth gestured to the Coke can in the evidence bag. 'You think the DA will have that tested for DNA?'

'Hell no. Or the piss. It's just enough for Dave to know that we could if we wanted to.'

They basked for a moment in the shared glow of their success. Beth's cell phone rang, killing the moment. She answered it. The caller was Amanda.

'I was able to use the serial numbers from the implants as well as dental records to get a positive ID on the bones we discovered this morning in Newberry Springs,' Amanda said.

Her lucky streak was holding. If his teeth were in the system, that meant he'd been reported as a missing person. Half her job was done already. She got out a pen and pad to jot down his name.

'How long has he been missing?'

'About a week, which doesn't make sense, since his bones appear to be over a hundred years old.'

'What's his name?'

'Owen Slader,' Amanda said. 'You're not going to believe what day he went missing.'

Beth was already shaking. She sat down. 'Saturday, February 2nd at 2 a.m.'

'Two a.m.?' Amanda's voice quivered. 'Really? How do you know that?'

'It was the time of the last GPS ping from his car and his phone.'

'That's some coincidence,' Amanda said.

Beth McDade didn't believe in coincidences.

EIGHT

Saturday, February 2, 2019

Owen Slader was in a hurry, speeding west at ninety miles per hour on Interstate 15 across the barren Mojave Desert to Los Angeles.

He'd waited until the last second to leave the blackjack table at the Wynn because he'd had an amazing run of luck, turning a $10 bet he'd made as an afterthought on his way to his room into three grand over a couple hours of play. It felt like he was just getting started.

But by then it was nearly midnight on Friday, and it was his weekend with Nicky, with his twelve-year-old daughter. If he didn't show at 10 a.m. on Saturday, or if he arrived late looking like the Walking Dead, well, that would prove everything his ex-girlfriend Sabine had said when they were fighting over custody, wouldn't it? That he was a hard-partying, self-absorbed, irresponsible, undependable, womanizing asshole, which he absolutely, unapologetically was back then. He was a changed man now.

And to prove it, he'd walked away from the hot cards, the hot dealer, and all that hotness in general, to give himself enough time to make the four-hour drive home and even get a few hours of sleep before presenting himself at Sabine's door.

How long could his streak have lasted? Could he have jacked it up to ten grand? Twenty? He'd never know. He'd had to fight himself on a spiritual, cellular, and molecular level, in an epic battle worthy of a Marvel movie, just to get in his car and drive out of the parking structure.

But he was proud of himself for doing it. It was so selfless, so mature. So responsible.

And so stupid. How could he walk away from the best lucky streak he'd ever had?

As he left the lights of Vegas behind, and sped into the dry, open desert, he kept telling himself that he was still leaving the city as a big winner. He had a fat wad of cash in his pocket and the hours of great footage he'd shot on his iPhone for his hugely popular YouTube show of quirky, off the Strip eating – the retired grandma with her kosher food truck, the bakery making gourmet pastries out of sugary breakfast cereals, and the all-nude strip club serving amazing Texas barbecue. Those places, and his commentary on them, were gold . . . his ticket to becoming the next Anthony Bourdain.

And he'd score big points today with Nicky, taking her to brunch downtown in Smorgasburg LA, the open-air food market of stalls and trucks in what was once a grimy, industrial factory district. She loved it and so did he. What was more important than that?

He'd made peace with himself about the time he hit Baker, home of the world's largest thermometer, gateway to the Mojave. But now, two hours into his drive on the desolate highway, his adrenaline high was gone and he was crashing, afraid he might fall asleep at the wheel, if his 2018 Mercedes GLC didn't run out of gas first. He'd just noticed the tank was on empty and a red light was flashing.

But luck was still on his side, because at that moment he was rolling into Yermo, a rest stop in the wasteland, the bleak midway point between Las Vegas and LA, and saw EddieWorld's huge ice-cream sundae topped with a ten-foot-tall glowing cherry.

He took the exit, drove up to one of EddieWorld's twenty-six pumps, got out, and stretched. It was chilly, and he wasn't dressed for it in his Tommy Bahama aloha shirt, jeans, and Nikes, but the cold helped wake him up. While he filled the tank, he glanced at the three other cars at the pump, then gazed into the desert, where statues of a Tiananmen Square dissident in chains and Chief Crazy Horse's head were displayed amidst the sagebrush.

They made no sense being there, but he thought the fact that they were was a true reflection of the psychotic mental state of anybody who'd live out here, a godforsaken place people only passed through to shit, pee, or fill their gas tanks and stomachs.

He topped off his tank, locked the car, and walked over to the main building. There was a sign stenciled on the glass door: Executive Chef Miguel's Kitchen. Owen's idea of living hell would be ending up as an executive chef at a gas station in the Mojave Desert and he certainly wouldn't advertise his shame.

He knew about shame. He'd spent years as a chef in LA, getting fired from one kitchen after another (for his attitude, not his food) before his down-and-dirty blog, podcast, and YouTube channel on the city's dining scene took off (for his attitude, not his food) and brought in enough advertising dollars that he could make a living criticizing other people's dishes instead of making his own.

He went inside EddieWorld. There were only three customers in the huge space that was filled with aisles of candy, nuts, dried fruit, and stuffed animals in the middle of a fast-food court. The restaurants, all closed at this hour, offered 'Fresh Gourmet food' like hot dogs, fruit cups, hamburgers, hummus, 'handcrafted' sushi, 'artisan' pizza, and the most expensive beef jerky he'd ever seen at $70 a pound.

Out of culinary curiosity, and because he had lots of Steve Wynn's cash in his pocket, he grabbed quarter-pound bags of lemon pepper, Sweet & Spicy, BBQ, and Tropical Sweet & Spicy Mango jerky to sample with Nicky. That'd be fun, a father/daughter bonding thing. He could even film it, humanizing himself for his audience. He helped himself to a Big Gulp Coke at the soft-drink dispenser, then went up the cashier, a bored, bone-thin young woman with painful-looking piercings in her lip, eyebrows, and in the bridge of her nose, and dropped the jerky on the counter. She rang him up.

'That'll be $115.67,' the cashier said.

He took out his roll of cash and peeled off two crisp hundred-dollar bills with a theatrical flourish. She wasn't impressed.

'I've never been to a gas station with an executive chef or a sushi bar before,' Owen said.

'Our fish is two hours fresher than Las Vegas.' She said it by rote, like it was something she'd memorized for situations like this.

'What does that mean?'

'The same seafood that's served at the finest restaurants on the Strip is delivered on a truck from LA that stops here first.'

'Yes, but how many Michelin stars do you have?'

'We don't sell tires here.'

She'd missed his point, but he'd amused himself, and that's what mattered. He smiled, picked up his jerky and drink, and went back to his car, taking a long sip of Coke on his stroll. Feeling refreshed, he got into his car, dumped the jerky on the passenger seat, and sped back onto the westbound interstate.

Owen wondered if he could devote an entire episode of his show to gas station dining. He vaguely remembered hearing that a Chevron station in West Adams served kick-ass tacos. It was something to think about, which is what he was doing when there was an explosion.

Startled by the sound, he swerved and saw a fireball rise in the desert, somewhere behind Peggy Sue's, dramatically illuminating the unmoving dinosaurs, making them appear truly menacing.

Almost immediately, the air crackled with bolts of lightning, but unlike any that Owen had ever seen before. They weren't jagged streaks of light. These bolts looked more like tears in the cloudy sky, as if something was clawing through the curtain of darkness.

A big rip opened right in front of Owen's car, only a few yards away, and it was astonishing. It was wide enough that he could see through it, to the same horizon. But the night sky within it, unlike everywhere else, was cloudless and the freeway ahead was gone. He was so fascinated and confused by what he saw that, before he knew it, he drove right into the center of whatever it was.

It felt like hitting a wall, the force of the impact slamming him back into his seat, even though his airbags didn't go off and there was nothing in front of him but open desert. And then, out of nowhere, a bearded, filthy man, wide-eyed with terror and holding a corn cob, appeared in his headlight beams.

Owen swerved hard to avoid hitting him, bouncing the car over rocky, rutted terrain, smashing through brush, into what should have been the median between the east- and westbound lanes of the interstate. But where was the steel divider? He slammed on his brakes, the car stopped, and he felt an overwhelming urge to vomit. He opened the door, leaned out into the dirt, and threw up, deep and repeatedly, until he was dry-heaving, drool and bile dripping from his mouth.

Light-headed, he grabbed some napkins from the map pocket on the door, wiped his mouth, spit out more bile, and then, using the door for support, stood up and looked back the way he'd come.

The strange lightning was gone. It was a bright, clear, moonlit night, and much hotter outside than it was a few minutes ago at EddieWorld.

Owen reached inside the car, grabbed his iPhone from a cup holder, and looked at the screen. It was 1:48 a.m. There was no signal, of course. A donkey brayed nearby, somewhere in the night.

He began to shake and wondered if he was about to faint. He sat back down in the front seat . . . and took a sip of Coke, which made him feel better and washed the bad taste out of his mouth, but it didn't make things any clearer in his mind.

Staring straight ahead, his headlights illuminated a tiny crudely built lopsided stone hut, and the remains of a campfire, the embers still glowing in the middle of a ring of small rocks. Someone lived here.

Was it that guy he'd almost hit?

Or did he hit him?

Oh, God, no, he thought. Tell me I didn't kill a man.

Owen turned on the flashlight app on his phone, got out of the car, and followed the flattened brush and his tire tracks for about ten or twenty yards. The tracks abruptly stopped, as if his car had come from nowhere. There was no sign of the bearded man with the corn cob.

He also didn't see the interstate, the gas stations, the dinosaurs, or the giant ice-cream sundae.

They were all gone. Without a trace.

And yet, the landscape itself was unchanged and familiar to him. It was the same dry, ancient lake bed he'd driven across dozens of times on his way back and forth between Los Angeles and Las Vegas.

He saw the flickering lights of what appeared to be campfires along the desert floor and heard an incessant, almost rhythmic pounding from the rugged Calico Mountains to the north. He turned his head toward the sound and he could see dozens of lights in and around Calico, which sat on a steep, narrow ridge that sloped down from the mountains a few miles away. But he knew that Calico was a ghost town, a cheesy tourist attraction. It shouldn't be open at this hour. It made no sense.

He turned back to his car and walked past it to the dying campfire. Beside the embers was an antique Dutch oven – a big pot with three legs and some congealed grease inside – and a tin coffee pot, a tin cup, a tin plate, and a tin spoon.

He continued to the stone hut. It was small, something an elf might live in, made of stacked stones with a doorway framed out of pieces of rough planks of wood, a ratty blanket for a curtain. The roof was covered with tent cloth, pulled taut, and covered with branches and leaves.

'Hello? Anyone here?'

He aimed his iPhone light at the blanket, cautiously parted it, and peered inside the hut. Torn burlap sacks covered the ground like rugs. A canteen, a pair of jeans, a shirt, and a filthy wide-brimmed hat, covered with red dust, hung from pegs wedged between the rocks. Against one wall there was a dirty, sweat-stained bed roll atop two bales of hay. On the opposite side of the hut was a wooden barrel, some burlap sacks, and a pile of corn cobs.

This was definitely the bearded man's shelter.

Owen walked out, heard the donkey bray again, and followed the sound. A few yards behind the hut was a large pile of rocks and dirt and, beyond that, the opening of a cave, where he saw a donkey tied to a wooden cart filled with more rocks. He approached the cave, the opening about the size of a single-car garage, and peered inside. The first few yards were wide, and seemed natural, unsupported by any wooden braces, and then narrowed in the back, where the digging looked fresh and a shovel and pick were propped against the side. There were ruts in the dirt from the wheels of the cart and a saddle of some kind beside them.

Was the bearded man a prospector? A miner? It didn't matter. Owen had wasted enough time here as it was.

He turned and walked to his car. He needed to get to Los Angeles. To his daughter. He couldn't be late.

Owen climbed into the driver's seat, slammed the door, and made a wide U-turn back to . . .

What?

Where?

There was no roadway to follow.

Interstate 15 was gone.

Everything was.

How the fuck could that be?

A horrifying thought dawned on him. Maybe he'd fallen asleep at the wheel . . . and crashed. Maybe he was dreaming. Maybe he was in a coma in an ICU somewhere. But none of his dreams had ever been this vivid or detailed. Did comatose people dream? He didn't think so.

Maybe he was dead, and this was Purgatory, but that was too terrifying to even consider. Besides, he felt too corporeal to be dead, to be some kind of spirit. Did spirits puke? Unlikely.

That left only one other explanation, something that only happened in movies and books: time travel. He'd driven through a tear in time into the past. Was that possible? Of course not.

There had to be rational explanation for all this, but he couldn't think of any.

Whatever the answer was, he knew one thing with absolute certainty: he shouldn't have left the damn blackjack table.

NINE

The next few hours passed very slowly. The only way Owen was able to control the panic percolating inside him, to avoid just curling up into a ball and crying, was to look into the camera of his iPhone and tell his story, like he was filming another segment of his show. It gave him the distance and perspective he needed, and the comforting, if totally false, sense that he wasn't alone. He had an audience.

As the sun began to rise over the Mojave, revealing the tents dotting the dry lake bed, the railroad tracks stretching east and west, and the constant pounding from what appeared to be mills of some kind nestled in the craggy Calicos, he got out of the car and took a long piss into the sage.

And as he was peeing, his limp dick in his hand, he decided he wasn't in a coma, pissing into a catheter. A dream wouldn't be this drawn out and death, be it Heaven, or Hell, or something in between, wouldn't be this mundane. He definitely wouldn't have any need to piss.

So he was in the past. That was the only conclusion that explained everything.

He assumed the time travel had something to do with the explosion and the strange lightning, not that it mattered. He had no idea how to get back to his time, or if the lightning would ever happen again, or if anybody would come back to rescue him.

I'm so fucked.

Owen stuffed himself back in his pants, zipped up, and started to cry, not for himself, but because he'd never see Nicky again. She'd believe he'd abandoned her, that he'd never loved her, and that he was the selfish prick Sabine had always said he was.

He felt the panic come roaring back and whipped out his iPhone like it was an EpiPen that he could jam in his leg to stop a devastating allergic reaction. Instead, he held it up to his face, touched the record button, and accomplished the same thing.

'I am so cosmically, titanically, biblically fucked. I'm stuck in the past. Can you believe it? I can't, but here I am. What am I going to do? All I know about time travel is from TV shows and movies, which is all bullshit, because nobody has ever done it before. Until now. Hurray for me.'

He looked around and took a deep breath.

'I remember a story where a guy goes back to prehistoric times to hunt dinosaurs, steps on a butterfly, and destroys mankind. God, I hope that's bullshit.' He lifted up each foot and checked under his shoes. He hadn't stepped on anything. 'Mankind is safe for now.'

And future me, he thought. And future Nicky. That's what he had to protect.

Oddly, that thought calmed him. It gave him a purpose, something to invest in besides terror and hopelessness. He felt the panic subside. He glanced back at his Mercedes.

'But the sun is about to come up, and I'm in the open desert, so soon people will be able to see my 2018 Mercedes. That's got to be worse than stepping on a butterfly . . . it's certainly a violation of the prime directive. Looks like I've got some work to do.'

He pocketed his phone, got in his car and drove it into the cave. It was a tight fit, the jagged outcroppings scratching the length of his car. The leasing company wasn't going to like that.

As he got out, he remembered he had an earthquake kit in the spare tire compartment. The kit contained some bottled water, first-aid supplies, batteries, light sticks, a rain poncho, lifeboat rations, duct tape, emergency blanket, a solar-powered flashlight/radio, and lots of other stuff. But most important, it had a pocket-sized solar battery charger for electronics. He'd need that to keep his phone going, rather than the car battery. It would be important to conserve the gasoline so he could keep the car battery charged for as long as possible . . . so he could use the heater or A/C in a pinch . . . or, if absolutely necessary, he could drive away from here, if only to hide the vehicle somewhere else. He climbed out of the car and saw the donkey staring at him.

'From now on, you're Mr Ed, but if you start talking back to me, then I'll know I am insane.'

He gave the beast a moment to reply and was greatly relieved when he didn't.

The cave was in a butte that was an island in a sea of dirt off the shore of much larger, craggy mountain to the south and was obscured from view by boulders and big clumps of brush. It faced the open desert, the dry lake bed at the base of the Calico Mountains a few miles north.

Owen looked down at the hut. The bearded man hadn't returned and maybe never would. It was Owen's place now, so he went down to take a look at the man's belongings.

The wooden barrel, about waist high, was full of water and he noticed a dipper hanging on a peg near it. The burlap sacks contained flour, potatoes, ground coffee, and some pieces of hard, stale bread. There was a wooden box with a wet cloth over it. And suspended over that was a tin cup that dangled by a string from the ceiling and dripped water on the cloth. Under the cloth, Owen found a slab of bacon that was surprisingly cool to the touch. He figured the contraption was some kind of desert refrigerator. Who knew there was such a thing? He saw a piece of paper pinned under a rock. It was a handwritten form indicating the miner-mining claim to the property was deeded to Louis Grant by order of Justice of the Peace Josiah Orville.

His gaze drifted to the bag of corn cobs. What was he saving them for? Maybe they were for the donkey.

He began moving the supplies to the cave, except for barrel of water, which was too heavy, and the bedding, which he had no intention of touching. He'd sleep in his car. But the donkey might like the hay.

Owen swept away the rocks holding the tenting to the top of the hut, dragged the canvas over to the cave, and draped it over the back of his car.

By now, the sun was up and it was already scorching. Owen offered the donkey a corn cob, but the animal wasn't interested. So he brought over a bale of hay, which the donkey liked much better.

Owen realized he was hungry, too, so he ate some of the jerky he'd bought at EddieWorld and washed it down with some Arrowhead water from his earthquake kit. That's when he realized that he'd soon have to find a way to buy food and water. The cash and credit cards in his wallet were useless to him now, whenever now was, a question he'd have to answer soon, too. But he guessed it had to be sometime in the 1800s, only because Calico was an Old West ghost town . . . and it wasn't one now.

The 1800s. Shit. He supposed it could be worse. At least he didn't have to worry about being eaten by a dinosaur. He made a video diary entry of his thoughts, then spent the next couple of hours stacking rocks and brush in front of the cave to obscure the entrance and the tent-covered SUV, though he left space for himself to get inside and room to open the hatchback.

It was mindless work but it distracted him from his unbelievable plight. When he was done, he went down to the water barrel and used the dipper to take a drink. The water wasn't bad. He poured some into the tin cup and brought it to the donkey, who lapped it up.

It was nice to have the company, though he had no idea how to care for the beast or what to do with him. He glanced up at Calico. The pounding still continued and now he was seeing people, some on horseback and some on foot, moving between the town and another settlement to the south, by the railroad tracks.

He took a deep breath. It was time to see where and when the hell he was.

Owen changed into a clean blue Ralph Lauren polo shirt, put on sunglasses and a Tommy Bahama baseball cap with their blue marlin logo sticked on front, and reluctantly took along the bearded man's canteen for water. A bottle of Arrowhead drinking water, or an SOS Earthquake Emergency Water Packet, would be hard to hide or explain. He locked the car with his key fob then glanced at the donkey.

'I'll be back soon. Watch the car.'

He took a deep breath and set off towards Calico. As he made his way through the brush, he almost stepped in a pile of shit. Beside it was a corn cob. A few yards away, he came across a similar tableau. Was the bearded guy wiping his ass with a corn cob? Was he on his way to take a dump when he saw a lightning bolt and then a car speeding at him? Did he jump out of the way into 2019? That would explain why he hadn't come back.

Owen had never crapped outdoors, or given the possibility any thought, but he knew there was no way he was going to wipe himself with a corn cob. But what would he use? He doubted they had Charmin out here. He'd just have to go on a liquid diet, he thought. Good luck with that in a desert.

A long-haired, bushy-bearded man in a wide-brimmed hat rode by on horseback, trailing a pack-mule on a rope behind him, toward Calico. The pack-mule was weighed down with all kinds of packs, mining tools, and buckets. They left a foul odor as they passed, the man staring at Owen the whole time.

Owen smiled and gave him a polite wave. 'Howdy.'

The man looked away and rode on. Over the next half-hour or so, a few more men rode by, looking and smelling about the same as the first one, all of them studying him as they passed. Clearly, Owen stood out.

In daylight, the jagged, rocky mountains, riven with canyons and cliffs, sparsely dotted with dry weeds barely clinging to the parched landscape, struck Owen as a standing warning to every living thing to stay the hell away, there's only death here, although the sunshine also brought out the various shades of red in the dry soil, giving the range an improbable beauty.

The town of Calico, at least what he could see of it from two miles away, was crowded onto a narrow, steep ridge that sloped down from the mountains to the flats and dry lake bed below, where the interstate and Yermo were supposed to be. It was bordered on the west by a deep canyon that rose higher, and became more sheer, as it cut north and, to the east, by a shallower gulley, and what appeared to be a tiny hill dotted with more structures that he couldn't clearly make out yet.

He heard a rumbling behind him and turned to see two horses pulling a wagon that was basically a big wooden barrel laying length-wise on wheels. The driver, riding on a bench in front of the barrel, slowed the horses as he approached Owen. Like the other men Owen had seen, the driver was long-haired and bushy-bearded, with a deep tan, and wore a wide-brimmed, soiled hat. Unlike the others, his clothes weren't covered in dirt, they were just deeply sweat-stained. The wagon came to a stop beside Owen. The man holding the reins looked down at Owen.

'Heading to Calico, mister?'

'Yes, I am.'

'You want a ride?'

'I'd be much obliged.' Owen had never used that phrase in his life, but they were always saying that in Westerns. He studied the wagon for a moment, looking for a way to get on. He stepped on a spoke of the wagon wheel, then the rim, then grabbed the framing for the seat, and lifted himself up on to the hard wooden bench.

The driver's body odor was overpowering and his teeth, the few that he had, were crooked and yellow, dangling from swollen gums. Owen tried to hide his shock and disgust. The driver gave the reins a shake, and the horses started going again. Owen heard water sloshing in the barrel.

The man looked Owen up and down, his gaze settling on Owen's $200 Nike running shoes. 'I gotta say, mister, I've never seen an outfit like yours before.'

'I've just returned from a spell in France. It's what everybody wears there.'

'Is that so. What are them shoes made of?'

'*Cuir français*,' Owen said, pronouncing the words in French, so they came out in English as 'Queer Fron-say'.

'They certainly are. Can't imagine what them French cows must look like.' The man offered his callous-covered hand to Owen. 'Name's Virgil Urt.'

Owen shook his hand.

'Ben Cartwright.' Owen surprised himself with his answer. It was a name from a TV western. Some instinct prevented him from using his real name. 'Are you hauling water to Calico, Mr Urt?'

'Three times a day.'

'Where from?'

'Me and my brother Clive got two wells by the river.' It was hard to discern what smelled worse, the man's body or his breath. Owen tried to breathe through his mouth.

'What river?'

Virgil looked at him like he was stupid which, given the situation, Owen knew was a fair reaction. 'The Mojave.'

Owen looked over his shoulder. All he saw was flat desert and, further south, some train tracks and a collection of wooden buildings. And, of course, the butte and mountain behind it where he'd come from. 'I don't see any river.'

'It's there, but it mostly runs underground, unless there are heavy rains or a big snow melt in the mountains.' Virgil pointed to the deep canyon to the west of the town.

'The first Calico camp was in Wall Street canyon until last spring. There was a storm and a flash-flood washed it all away . . . at least seven men were buried alive under the mud and rock. So they moved Calico up there.' He gestured to the sloped ridge.

'You said "at least seven" men were lost. What does that mean?'

'Could be two, could be twenty more poor bastards under there. Seems like every time somebody sticks a shovel in the dirt, they find another body.'

'What's water cost in these parts?'

'Five cents a gallon,' Virgil said.

Owen had no idea if that was high or low price. He assumed it was high. He figured his barrel of water, which he was sharing with the donkey, and his earthquake water, might last him a week. And he hadn't even thought about water for washing himself or his clothes. He needed to get a job.

'I reckon that's a fair price,' Owen said. 'Affordable enough so after a man earns his pay, he won't have to choose between going broke or dying of thirst.'

He threw in the 'reckon' because it's what everybody said in Westerns.

'Got to leave a man enough for a chew and a poke.'

'Or he ain't living.' Owen threw in the 'ain't' for good measure.

'Guess that means I'm half-dead. Got me plenty of chew and no poke.' Virgil spit out a glob of tobacco onto the dirt. It was disgusting.

'Why's that? You're obviously a prosperous businessman.'

'There's not enough sporting women for all the men here,' Virgil said, 'and I don't like sharing a bowl of soup that thirty men have already slurped from, if you take my meaning.'

'I do. Vividly,' Owen said. 'What's a miner earn for a day's labor?'

'Three dollars but after paying for a room, food, water, and whiskey, and if they can stay away from cards, dice, and a poke, which no man can, they're lucky if they can pocket two bits.'

It sounded to Owen like the only people making money owned the mines, stores, restaurants, and whorehouses or brought in water and other supplies. The miners were simply subsisting.

The wagon was passing the wooden building where all the pounding was coming from; smoke rose out of two tall stacks.

'What is all that pounding?' Owen asked.

'It's the stamp mill,' Virgil said. 'They've got four coal-powered stamps going day and night.'

'What are they stamping?'

Once again, Virgil looked at him like he was a moron, which he absolutely was, so he took no offense, maintaining his genial smile. 'The ore. For the silver inside it.'

'Right. Of course,' Owen said. 'You'll have to forgive me, I don't know much about mining.'

'Then why are you going to a mining camp?'

'Curiosity. Everybody in Los Angeles is talking about Calico, so I had to see it for myself. When did the first guy strike it rich?' Owen braced himself psychologically and emotionally for the date.

'The camp's booming. It hasn't even been a year since Sheriff King opened the Silver King mine up there on King Mountain.'

No date.

Oh well, Owen thought, it was a nice try. 'I'm surprised the town isn't named King, too.'

Virgil smiled. 'King sold out early, before there was a town, to a mining company from Milwaukee. The big boys are the only ones who can afford to get the silver out of them hills. Pretty soon they'll dig their own wells and put me out of business.'

'You've got nothing to worry about, Mr Urt. People will always need water in a desert.'

And, it occurred to Owen, they'd also need food, which they certainly had. But was it any good? It gave him something to think about.

Now they were heading up the slope toward Calico and Owen got a good look down the deep canyon. The steep walls were comprised of distinct, undulating layers of earth, a totem pole of geologic history stacked and compressed over centuries, and pockmarked with man-made burrows. Some of the caves were open and were as narrow as morgue drawers, others had barrel lids, canvas awnings stretched between boulders, or stacked-stone facades that resembled huts.

Owen gestured to the canyon walls. 'What are those caves on the canyon walls?'

'Free rooms for enterprising miners.'

'How can people live like that?' Owen asked.

'It's no different than where they work. They're just laying in a hole instead of standing in one, which is fine, cause all they do there is sleep.'

Owen was glad he had his Mercedes for shelter, with plush leather seats and a carpeted floor; the bales of hay in the bearded man's stone hut seemed like a mansion compared to those burrows.

There was a rumble, and for a moment Owen thought it might be a stampede, and then it was. But a controlled one. Twenty tethered mules, stretching in a line about a hundred feet long, pulled two enormous wagons filled with rocks on steel-rimmed, wooden wheels that were taller than Owen, who was an even six feet. The mule team roared down the canyon toward the stamp mill, kicking up a huge plume of dust and, he thought, pulverizing the bones of any dead men that might still be buried in the dirt.

The water wagon started up the slope to the flattened ridge where the town sat and Owen was immediately hit by a horrid stench of rot and excrement, accompanied by an incessant buzz that was nearly drowned out by the pounding of the stamp mill. The buzz came from the gulley to Owen's right, which was alive with flies. He could see piles of shit down there and two men, standing on the embankment, peeing into the ravine, one of them raising his fist at the encampment of tents and stone cabins atop the opposite ridge.

The pisser yelled: 'Fuck you, you yellow sonsofbitches!'

Owen glanced at Virgil. 'What's his problem?'

'The Chinese. That's their camp on the other side of Jack Ass Gulch.'

Owen looked back at the opposite ridge. No one over there seemed to pay any attention to the pisser, though his voice carried across the ravine. 'Just being here made him angry?'

'They came here thinking there was silver for them, too.'

'There isn't?'

''Course not. They can cook our food, clean our clothes, lay our tracks, and dig our roads, but what comes out of those mountains, that's ours. Two days ago, a Chink brought rocks into the assayer . . . and nearly got strung up.'

'Nearly?'

'Lucky for him, there ain't no God-damn trees and nobody could spare the lumber to build gallows,' Virgil said. 'But he took a licking.'

They passed the pissing man and continued up into the town, where Owen got his first good look at Calico.

TEN

Calico wasn't much of a place. One-room cabins of wood or stone and false-fronted, one-story wooden commercial buildings were backed up against the two edges of the ridge, leaving a single steep dirt road that snaked up to the mountain. Main Street was the only street.

Owen saw animal droppings everywhere, scattered on the street and swept into piles, and damp spots where piss had soaked into the parched ground. Bearded men caked in red dirt carefully crossed the street, as if negotiating a minefield, and walked on the loose wood planks that served as rudimentary sidewalks between the tightly packed buildings, many of which had porches with benches or stools under shaded overhangs. Horses and mules were tied to hitching posts, tails swatting at the swarms of flies that were drawn to all the droppings. A few wagons carrying lumber, rocks, and black coal went up and down the street. There wasn't a woman or child in sight.

He saw a livery stable, a boarding house, a saloon, an assayer's office, a restaurant, and a doctor's office that doubled as a drug store, interspersed with individual tents and shacks that he assumed were homes. A few more tents, shacks, and stone huts dotted either side of the street towards the craggy mountains to the north, where he could see mining carts and men moving along narrow ledges in front of several levels of tunnel openings.

Virgil Urt stopped his water wagon in front of a one-story wood-plank building with the words 'Stoby's General Store & Post Office' painted on the high portion of the false front.

Owen turned to Virgil. 'Thank you again for the ride and the informative conversation.'

'Seems to me I was mostly jabbering to myself,' Virgil said.

That was no accident. The less Owen said, he figured, the less likely he was to say something that would make people suspicious of him.

Owen climbed off the water wagon as the rotund, rosy-cheeked storekeeper, a white apron straining around his profound waist, came out to greet the arrival and gave him a wide-eyed look.

Virgil noticed and said to Owen: 'This here is Purvis Stoby, one of our leading merchants. This gent Ben Cartwright just arrived from France.'

'I didn't know they were so colorful over there,' Stoby said. His teeth were as bad as Virgil's, but he had a carefully waxed mustache and clean, sunburned skin.

'They like to live boldly,' Owen said. 'So do I. Pleasure to meet you, Mr Stoby.'

Stoby gestured to his store. 'Whatever you need, Mr Cartwright, we sell it.'

Virgil said, 'Except a poke, at least until Stoby's young wife gets tired of him. Should be any day now.'

Stoby's round cheeks reddened. 'That ain't funny, Virgil.'

'Have a good day, gentlemen,' Owen said. 'I'm going to mosey along and get a look at this metropolis.'

Owen tipped his hat and walked up the street, careful to remain on the boards to avoid stepping in shit. He wished he had a bandana, or a hazmat suit, to protect himself from the execrable smell, which combined with the heat to make the air feel like a hot blanket soaked in urine.

Calico was nothing like the Western towns he'd seen on TV shows and movies, with nicely dressed, clean-shaven, freshly bathed people strolling on clean, shitless streets.

Of course, none of that was real. Anybody who gave a Western two seconds of thought, which he'd never had reason to do before, would realize that. All those horses had to relieve themselves somewhere. And so did the people. And without a sewer system, where else were they going to do it besides outside?

But did it have to be so close to where they were living? If they could dig caves to sleep in and tunnels to mine ore, couldn't they dig a sewer system instead of shoveling the shit into a gulley?

Owen thought Calico was a disgusting, unsanitary slum that made the homeless encampments he'd seen in Los Angeles seem like five-star resorts by comparison. Although, he figured the Los Angeles of eighteen-whatever-it-was probably wasn't much cleaner than this place. He'd have to adjust his expectations . . . along with everything else in his life. The important thing now was his immediate survival, and that meant securing a job so he could buy food and water.

At about that moment, he found himself standing outside 'Tuttle's Saloon'. A signboard by the open doorway advertised 'all the finest liquors', 'all the finest gaming', 'fine dining', and 'the finest haircuts and shaves in the latest continental styles'. A menu board advertised: Breakfast: pork, beans, biscuit – 15 cents. Dinner – steak, beans, biscuit, boiled potato – 25 cents. Beer – 5 cents, Coffee – 5 cents, pie – 10 cents. 'Our coffee is made from the purest, finest article and you only need a taste to prove its merits.'

Restaurants were his happy place, and he was curious, so Owen went inside.

It was a large wooden shack, dark and dingy, that smelled like a men's locker room in a fertilizer plant. The floors were uneven wood planks. Spittoons were everywhere, surrounded by dark globs that looked like duck crap all over the floor around them.

Men sat at tables, eating chunks of fatty bacon in a puddle of grease, hard biscuits and beans on tin plates. It didn't look appetizing at all. In another corner, a man sat in a chair, getting a shave from a barber. A desultory young woman in a low-cut dress sat on a bench in front of a small piano. She was asleep, snoring gently, her upper body slumped over the keys.

At the bar, in the back of the room, two men stood reading a newspaper over coffee and talking to the bartender at the simple wooden bar. One of the men was fat, wearing a pinstriped suit, vest, and a stove-pipe hat that reminded Owen of Abraham Lincoln. The man beside him wore a white-collared shirt and pants held up with suspenders. Neither man had the layer of red dust on them that every other man in the place, with the exception of the bartender, did. They were white collar in a time when that phrase was probably coined.

All eyes, except the sleeping woman's, were on Owen as he walked in. He approached the bar.

The bartender stepped up to greet him. 'Welcome to Calico.'

'How did you know I just arrived?'

'We definitely would've noticed you before and heard about you.' The bartender gestured to the man in suspenders. 'Overmyer would've written about you in his newspaper.'

'I'm hardly newsworthy.' Unless, of course, they knew he was visiting from the future and could tell them . . . *what?* His knowledge of nineteenth-century history wasn't that detailed. It wasn't like he'd appeared on the *Titanic* before it hit the iceberg, or in Pearl Harbor before the Japanese attack, or in Ford's Theatre before Lincoln got shot. But he was in the Mojave Desert where, as far as he knew, nothing had happened in a hundred and thirty years except, perhaps, that this town would die and be resurrected as a tourist attraction with actors playing residents.

The bartender picked up the newspaper on the bar. 'Here's today's big story – "we call attention to the full column advertisement in our paper by Mr Purvis Stoby. It is evident Mr Stoby understands the benefits to be derived from the representation of his business and that the men in our midst will naturally throw their patronage to those who demonstrably know their wants." If an advertisement is big news, imagine the write-up Overmyer would do if a skunk ever wandered into camp.'

The fat man with the stove-pipe hat said, 'We have plenty of skunks here, Mr Tuttle, all of the human variety, which can be far more odious.' He shifted his gaze to Owen. 'You, sir, don't appear to fall in that category.'

'Thank you kindly.' Owen glanced at the paper. It was called the *Calico Print.* The date was February 3, 1882.

1882.

Owen felt a little faint. He really had traveled back in time. The evidence was right in front of him.

Unless, of course, this was one giant, elaborate, outrageously expensive *Mission Impossible*-level con, or some new reality TV show he'd fallen into, scenarios which were even less believable somehow than driving through a rip in time.

'The camp is becoming duller and hotter every day, Judge,' Overmyer, the newspaper publisher, said to the fat man. 'We really need a decent robbery or killing before I go out of business.'

Owen took a seat on a barstool beside the Judge, afraid his legs might not hold his weight. 'Mr Urt told me a Chinese man was nearly lynched a few days ago for prospecting.'

'That's like saying the sun rising and setting is news,' the Judge said.

Owen was still digesting the fact he was in 1882. What did he know about the year? Or even the decade? He couldn't even say

who was President. The first historical thing he could think of was
the San Francisco earthquake, but that was decades from now. So
he clearly couldn't rely on future knowledge to survive. And he
didn't have special skills. He wasn't a surgeon, an engineer, or a
soldier. He'd never even been a boy scout. He was an ex-chef on
YouTube. All he knew how to do was cook.

'If he'd a been hung, at least you'd have something to do,'
Overmyer said. 'You're a judge with nothing to judge.'

'I'm kept plenty busy assaying rock samples, registering mining
claims, and staying abreast of the law.'

'You're staying abreast all right.' Overmyer and Tuttle shared
knowing grins and glanced over at the sleepy woman at the piano.
The Judge wasn't the least bit embarrassed over the impugning of
his character.

'It's a medical fact, gentlemen,' the Judge said, 'that regular
amorous congress keeps the blood flowing and the mind sharp,
which is a necessity for maintaining the wise counsel expected of
a man occupying my high office. Otherwise, I wouldn't bother. It
aggravates my back.'

Owen glanced around the room again, at the slop on everyone's
plates, and a thought occurred to him, a way he might be able to
make some money to get the food and water he'd need to live . . .
because he had no idea how to get back to his own time besides
waiting for the sky to open up again.

Tuttle snorted and turned to Owen. 'What can I get you, mister?'

'Nothing, thank you,' Owen said. 'Are you the proprietor?'

'Dave Tuttle, that's me. But if you're intending to gamble, you
aren't welcome to ply your trade here, even if you toss me a cut.
These are working men at my tables. I don't mind them losing
at cards—'

Overmyer interrupted. 'Especially to the house.'

Tuttle ignored the dig and kept talking. '—but I won't let
professional card-sharks cheat them out of their wages.'

Owen asked, 'What makes you think I'm a gambler?'

'Anybody dressed as fancy as you, soft bodied, with white
teeth, smooth hands, and clean fingernails is a swindler of some
kind, either a banker or a card-player,' Tuttle said. 'A banker
would wear a tie, long sleeves, and a coat to instill confidence,
convey sincerity, and project authority. A gambler rolls up his

sleeves, so you think there's no place he can hide a card, and appears colorful, fun-loving, and relaxed, so that you'll be charmed while you're being fleeced. You're all that and you don't even have sleeves to roll up.'

The Judge clapped a hand down on the bar. 'I had no idea you had such a keen eye and prodigious powers of deduction, Dave.'

'This isn't my first saloon in a mining camp, though it's my first in a God-damn desert. I don't know what I was thinking,' Tuttle said. 'I'm breathing, eating, and pissing dust.'

'I'm not a gambler, Mr Tuttle,' Owen said, 'but I will make you a wager.'

Tuttle grinned at his two friends. 'Here it comes . . .'

'I'll bet you I can go in your kitchen right now and make you the best meal you've had since you got to Calico out of whatever ingredients you already have on hand,' Owen said. 'If I do, you have to hire me as your cook at a fair wage.'

'And if I think your vittles are mule droppings?'

'I'll pay for whatever I've cooked. Seems to me you've got nothing to lose and everything to gain.'

It was a huge risk for Owen, since he had no idea what ingredients Tuttle had or how he'd pay for the food if he lost. But the challenge excited him.

The Judge said, 'He makes a compelling argument.'

Overmyer said, 'And I'll get a story out of it, which is free advertising for this establishment.'

Tuttle wasn't swayed. 'Except if I lose, I've got to pay for a grub-slinger when I've got a wife who does it for nothing.'

Owen offered a carrot. 'You'll make up the cost tenfold in extra business.'

Tuttle laughed and looked at his friends. 'This guy has some balls.'

'Of course he does,' Overmyer said. 'You see how he's dressed. He's obviously been prosperous before.'

A haggard woman, her graying hair tied back with a scarf, came out of the backroom by the piano. She wore a flour-dusted dress and a stained apron. 'Nobody asked my opinion.'

Owen stood up. 'Please forgive me. I meant no offense to your cooking, ma'am.'

'My cooking is an offense, sir, but that's nice of you to say.'

The Judge said, 'Your victuals are mighty fine, Dora. I've got the belly to prove it.'

He patted it for emphasis.

'I make a good apple pie, Judge, I'll give you that,' Dora said. 'But I got enough to do minding our working girls—' She kicked the piano bench, waking up the girl and giving her a scolding look. 'And keeping this place clean on top of my endless wifely duties.'

'I'm the easiest man in California to live with,' Tuttle said. 'I only beat you morning and night, hardly ever in between.' He winked at Overmyer.

Dora ignored him and smiled at Owen.

'We'll take you up on your wager.' She took off her apron and handed it to Owen.

'It would be a shame to stain those nice clothes. Kitchen's in the back, mister, get to it.'

Owen took the apron, tied it on, and headed into the kitchen, which turned out to be a tiny, stuffy room with a cast-iron coal-burning stove, a stone fire pit, a Dutch oven, butter churn, and some frying pans for appliances. All antiques. A piece of wood on two barrels was his cutting and prep surface. No running water. No refrigerator, beyond the contraption he'd seen in bearded man's hut . . . and inside it, he saw a few brown eggs and some iffy pieces of tough beef. That's when he noticed a ceramic lid on the dirt floor. He lifted it up and saw what appeared to be a clay pot within a larger clay pot, surrounded by a layer of moist dirt. The interior of the pot was surprisingly cool, and inside he saw a dish of butter.

There was a shelf of various canned and pickled vegetables, condensed milk, molasses, and bags of salt, beans, flour, and pota-toes. On another shelf sat a block of cheese. Some slabs of salted pork and ham hung from hooks. There was a small barrel of water, though he wasn't sure if it was for drinking or cooking or to put out a fire. Maybe all of the above. There was already some dough, presumably to make biscuits with all day, but he didn't want to use Dora's premade stuff. That would be cheating.

As far as utensils, he saw some knives, serving spoons, and a wheel spoke he assumed was used as a rolling pin. And, to his surprise, he spotted a can opener. He had no idea they'd been around so long. A pair of leather gloves, with blackened fingertips, appeared to be the hot pads.

He didn't know how to control the heat on the stove or Dutch oven, beyond tossing in hunks of coal from the pile in one corner. He felt a pang of panic, but then told himself: Grow the fuck up. This was no different than an episode of *Iron Chef* or one of those Guy Fieri cooking competitions on the Food Channel. Any half-decent, short-order cook can make something great out of cheap, lousy ingredients, using seasoning, grease, and sauces to hide the inferior quality, spoilage, and toughness. He could do this. He had to do this.

He remembered a trip to Italy, where an elderly Jewish woman told him how the poor made delicious pasta dishes when they couldn't afford eggs and could only get offal for meat. That would work here. So would some pizza bites, an Old West variation on a hot pocket, itself a variation on Cornish pasties eaten by miners in the UK in the nineteenth century . . . which was right now. And, if he had the time, there was one more dish he'd try.

Owen got to work. He started with the pasta, made the dough with flour, water, and salt, kneaded it on the wood, then wrapped it in burlap to let it sit for a half-hour. How would he survive without Saran Wrap and aluminum foil? While the dough rested, he diced some ham, pork, and potatoes and put a pan on the stove, tossing in a bit of bacon fat in for grease. He began to fall into a rhythm that felt natural. The cooking, despite the unfamiliar surroundings and new challenges, was ridiculously fun. It relaxed him, but it also gave him the sense that he had some control over the insane situation that he found himself in.

ELEVEN

An hour later, Owen brought the dishes out to Tuttle, his wife Dora, the Judge, and Overmyer, at the bar. The dishes were two entrees on plates and one egg dish in a tin cup, presented as best he could, given the primitive circumstances.

'The pasta dish is a Mojave *strozzapreti bolognese*, an eggless pasta with diced meat and other savories. Those tiny pies are Hot Pockets, an Italian variation on the classic Cornish miner's pasty

made with meat, cheese, tomatoes, and other scraps. And, finally
. . .' He gestured to the tin cup. 'A breakfast entree I'm calling the
Calico Frittata, a single egg, some meat, some oil, some cheese,
and some imagination cooked in a tin cup.'

His four diners stared at him.

Dora said, 'You're hired.'

Tuttle glowered at her. 'We haven't tasted anything yet, Dora.'

'Anybody who can make grub that looks and smells this tasty
out of our cheap ingredients deserves the job,' she said.

The Judge used a fork to taste the pasta and looked at the plate
in shock. 'Dear God.'

Overmyer popped a hot pocket in his mouth and his eyes
widened. 'Oh my.'

Dora tried the frittata and moaned. 'Now this is fine dining.'

Tuttle frowned at them all. 'Oh, for God's sake, stop your
tomfoolery, it's the same food we've always had, just served
differently.'

The Judge said, 'Two men can carve a statue from the same block
of marble but there can only be one Michelangelo.'

'I have no idea what you're talking about.' Tuttle tried a bite of
everything, and as he did, his expression turned from frustration to
pleasure and then bewilderment. He looked at Owen. 'You make a
decent grub pile, I'll give you that.'

Now they all began sampling the various dishes. Overmyer took
out a nubby pencil and a notebook. 'What did you say your name
was?'

'Ben Cartwright. But please, call me Ben.'

Overmyer noted his name in his pad. 'I'm Hank Overmyer, editor
and publisher of the *Calico Print*. This man beside me is the
Honorable Josiah Orville, our Justice of the Peace, Assayer, and
County Clerk, among the many hats he wears.'

Dora offered Owen her hand. 'I'm Dora Tuttle. Long-suffering
wife, whore-wrangler, maid, seamstress, dishwasher, and cook.'

Overmyer asked, 'Where did you learn to prepare food like
this, Ben?'

'I just returned from a culinary tour of Europe, which is why I
find myself financially adrift at the present moment.'

Dora glanced at her husband. 'He isn't any more, is he, Dave?'

Tuttle licked his lips and did some mental calculations. 'I'll pay you two dollars a day and you don't touch the liquor or the doves.' He gestured to the woman at the piano and another woman, considerably older than the other, who was chatting up a customer who had bacon grease in his shaggy beard. 'Milly and Esther.'

'How many meals do you serve in a day?' Owen asked.

'Sixty, maybe seventy,' Tuttle said. 'But mostly it's just biscuits, bacon, and coffee. Potatoes all the time. Some roast beef for supper. Pies for dessert.'

'That's going to change,' Owen said. 'I'll take four dollars a day to start, plus whatever I want to eat, of course, and we'll see how things go. Oh, and I decide what to make, nobody else.'

'Two twenty-five, and you can create the menu, but I set the prices and the food budget. And you wash all your dishes.'

'Three fifty, and I'll stick to your budget, but I buy all the food and ingredients on your credit and I can help myself to the liquor as long as it's strictly to flavor my cooking and I don't wash dishes.'

'Two fifty and I'll give you one poke a week with one of our doves at half-price, withdrawn from your weekly wages.'

'Three dollars, no poke, and wages paid at the end of each day. That's my final offer,' Owen said, 'or I'll see what the restaurant up the street wants to offer me.'

He watched Esther lead the shaggy-bearded miner out of a side door and to one of two tiny shacks visible outside located in the wide space between the saloon and the building next door. There were harder ways to make a living in a mining town.

'We have a deal.'

Overmyer was scribbling madly to chronicle the exchange.

The Judge said, 'I bear witness to the terms of the agreement and eagerly anticipate the fruits of it.' He turned to Overmyer. 'You can quote me on that.'

'I just did,' Overmyer said.

The Judge slid off his stool. 'Now that my basic appetites have been most satisfactorily met, it's time to lubricate my mind for the intellectual demands of the day with some convivial society with that young lady.'

The Judge wandered over to Milly, the woman at the piano, who took his hand and led him away to one of the two sheds out back.

Overmyer turned to Owen. 'The Judge means his morning poke

with Milly, followed shortly thereafter by his morning constitution in the privy . . . and then his morning nap . . . after which he'll look at a few rocks and scribble some mining claims in his ledger until there is finally something for him to adjudicate.'

Tuttle ignored Overmyer's remark. 'When can you get started, Ben?'

'If you'll let the butcher and grocer know I can purchase on your account, I'll come up with my menu based on what's fresh and available, gather the supplies tomorrow morning, and be ready for breakfast.'

'That'd be fine,' Tuttle said.

'But first, I'd like to familiarize myself today with the town and sample what the competition is serving.'

Overmyer said, 'That'd be Noel's Saloon, Mama's Bakery, and Roy's Chophouse, not counting the meals served at the boarding houses.'

Dora waved away the remark. 'You can forget the boarding houses. It's mainly biscuits, bacon, and coffee or cold mush. It don't count as food.'

'It's what you serve,' Overmyer said.

'That's my point,' she said.

Owen glanced at Tuttle. 'You'll have to stake me a day's pay to subsidize my competitive research, of course.'

Tuttle took a step back. 'You mean you want to go out on the town with my money.'

Dora said, 'Seems reasonable to me, Dave. We always visit the saloons before we decide to set up in an established camp.'

Tuttle glared at her. 'Don't you have dishes to wash or a floor to mop?'

She matched his glare.

Tuttle gave up, reached into his pocket, and handed Owen some coins. 'I better not hear that you've been gambling or pirooting with that money.'

Owen didn't know what *pirooting* was, but was sure he wouldn't be doing it.

Overmyer slid off his stool. 'I'll keep an eye on him and show him around.'

Tuttle pointed at Overmyer while looking at Owen. 'And don't spend a nickel on that mooch . . . he can pay his own way.'

Owen went outside, proud of himself for solving one immediate problem, his sustenance, but hoped there'd be a rip in time tonight so he wouldn't have to come back. But he knew in his heart that there wouldn't be. As he stood there, looking out at the dusty mining camp, he felt a tremor of panic.

Sure, now he could eat, but could he survive? And if he did, what kind of life would he have? He was trapped in a nightmare.

Overmyer stepped up beside him. 'Where are you staying?'

Owen took a deep breath, willed himself to stay calm and gestured to the valley floor. 'I'm camping down yonder, on a claim I purchased from a destitute miner in return for stage fare back to San Bernardino.'

He threw in the *down yonder* to sound authentic, though so far he hadn't heard anyone else say it, or *I reckon*, for that matter. Perhaps he was better off just talking in his time.

'You got swindled,' Overmyer said, 'but you don't strike me as someone so easily fooled.'

Owen shrugged. 'He gave me the claim papers and it came with lodging.'

'You don't strike me as the cave-dwelling type, either.'

'I'm full of surprises,' Owen said.

'You've already proven that.'

They walked up the street, but didn't go far when Owen stopped and examined a donkey tied to a hitching post. He was curious how the pack saddle was attached to the animal. The donkey he'd inherited could come in handy for transportation . . . if he could figure out how to ride him. And it hit him again how little he knew about the basics of living in the world he was now trapped in. A child here knew more than he did.

Overmyer studied Owen studying the donkey. 'Haven't you ever seen a donkey before?'

'I just acquired one. How are they to ride?'

'Like a stubborn turtle.'

That wasn't much help. They continued walking uphill. Owen tried not to notice all the stares he was attracting. Once he'd saved up some money, he'd have to get some clothes that didn't make him stand out.

As they strolled, Overmyer explained that Calico was quickly transitioning from a 'cave and tent camp' to a 'wood-frame and stone town' as mining expanded every day, and more silver was pulled out of the rock, drawing prospectors from California's gold country, and experienced miners from other states and as far away as England.

'A mining camp starts becoming a town when businesses arrive to serve every human need, virtue, and vice,' Overmyer concluded.

They passed the offices of the *Calico Print*, a one-room cabin where Overmyer lived and published his weekly paper with a printing press that he'd lugged all over the West. Owen vaguely remembered that building, recreated in the Calico Ghost Town as a place to have your picture taken in vintage Western clothes.

Next door was the Judge's cabin. It had two doors, Overmyer said, one for his living quarters, the other for the space that served as an assay office, county clerk's office, and his Judge's chambers. Trials were held on the porch, the Judge dragging out his desk for the occasion. Beside his cabin was a jail cell, made of stone, and some iron-barred doors and window openings.

'Where's the marshal's office?' Owen asked.

'We don't have one.'

'So, who enforces the law?'

'The community. They have a strong sense of right and wrong and don't tolerate bad behavior,' Overmyer said. 'But it's surprisingly peaceable here, which is good for daily living, but terrible for news. Most of the men are too exhausted or drunk to commit any crimes.'

That's when Owen realized that he hadn't seen a single person wearing a gun. All the Western movies and TV shows made it seem like everybody had one. It made him nervous. Not for his safety, but because if he couldn't believe anything he'd seen in a Western, he was totally unprepared for what life might be like for him here.

They passed the Calico Hotel, a boarding house, and the bakery and came to what was now the north-eastern edge of the ridge Calico was on. A flimsy wood slat and rope bridge stretched over Jack Ass Gulch to the Chinese camp to the east, where the same tent-to-board expansion seemed to be occurring that was happening in town.

Overmyer followed his gaze. 'The Chinese built that bridge so they don't have to climb in and out of that stinking ravine to get over here.'

Just before the town sloped up toward the mine on the mountain, there was a row of six wooden privies with half-moons or moons cut into the doors for airflow and so it was possible to see if they were occupied.

But the outhouses seemed reserved for defecation, with men lined up to use them, while other men at that spot went to the edge of Jack Ass Gulch to relieve their bladders.

Owen said, 'I haven't seen a church or a school.'

'They'll come when the women and children do. Right now, this place is just five hundred men digging into stone, but when they know the money is steady, they'll send for their families and Calico will become a real town. The question is: how long it will last?'

Not long, Owen knew, but he didn't know exactly when the end came. Ten or fifteen years, perhaps. He wished he'd paid more attention when he'd visited the tourist trap years ago.

They headed back down the hill. Owen stopped at the meat market and Overmyer introduced him to the butcher, a bushy-bearded rancher named Art Lebec, who wore a blood-splattered apron, was missing a fingertip on his right hand, and had already heard about Owen and his arrangement with Tuttle.

'News travels fast,' Owen said.

'It's hell on my business,' Overmyer lamented.

Owen tried not to show his disgust with the conditions of the meat market. There were plenty of cuts of beef and pork, but not much chicken. With no refrigeration, the meat was bloody and out in the open.

It was fresh, Lebec boasted, slaughtered that day at his nearby ranch along the Mojave. That was a plus, Owen thought, but he'd have to cook it or salt it right away.

The butcher also sold eggs, dipped in grease that kept them fresh for up to six months, and also a variety of salted and smoked meats that'd keep even longer, but Owen didn't trust someone else's meat preparation. Eventually, he'd have to salt and smoke his own meat. Maybe not now, but down the road.

And what was down the road? What was life going to be like for Ben Cartwright, a man from another time?

Owen must have looked a little distraught, because Overmyer said: 'I know the prices are a shock for outsiders, but we're used to it here.'

Overmyer explained that the prices were exorbitant because the environment, unlike the gold rush country, was so inhospitable to man. The only resources Calico had needed to be dug out, whether it was silver or water. Nothing grew out there. All the water that flowed was underground. Everything in Calico had to be delivered from somewhere else, from lumber and cotton to vegetables and meat.

'There isn't any decent game to hunt,' Overmyer said, 'unless you have a good recipe for scrawny jack-rabbit.'

Lebec said, 'Skin it, gut it, skewer it with a stick, and hang it over a campfire. That's all you got to do.'

Overmyer snorted. 'This is why you're a butcher and not a chef.'

Owen gave Lebec a list of cuts that he wanted and said he'd be back at sun-up to get them. They returned to Stoby's store, where the shopkeeper was already waiting outside for him.

'Back to do some shopping, Mr Cartwright?' Stoby said, beckoning him inside with a sweep of his arm.

Overmyer replied, 'He's spending Tuttle's money.'

'So I heard,' Stoby said. 'I'll gladly take anybody's money. In fact, I'd like to get some of yours one day.'

'Did you see the big write-up I gave your store?' Overmyer said as he walked in with Owen. 'That was worth far more than what I owe you. I'd say we're even.'

'Of course you would,' Stoby said.

Owen spotted a woman behind the counter. She was slim, with big brown eyes, and was the most beautiful woman he'd seen in Calico.

'Mr Cartwright,' Stoby said, 'this is my wife Evelyn.'

Owen immediately understood why Virgil's jokes about her leaving Stoby made the shopkeeper uncomfortable. She had to be twenty years younger and thirty pounds lighter than her husband.

'I'm pleased to meet you, ma'am,' Owen said.

She smiled with such warmth that he felt like he'd just been given a hug. 'What can I get for you?'

'I'm not sure yet.'

At the front of the store were mining tools, explosives, hats, shirts, pants, belts, boots, canteens, chewing tobacco, and just about anything else any man would need to do his work and to survive. The groceries were in the back.

He began by browsing the shelves of seasonings, of which there was a wide variety, cans of assorted fruit and pickled vegetables, and sealed tins of salted cod, corned beef, and other meats. There were dried peppers, boxes of baking soda, crackers, condensed milk, and raisins. There were hard biscuits and loaves of sugar. On the floor, there were barrels of molasses and sacks of potatoes, beans, corn meal, rice, and different grades of flour.

A menu of creative and inexpensive meals, much of it inspired by dishes he'd featured on his shows, immediately came to Owen's mind. There was plenty here that he could work with. He gave her a list of items and Stoby said he'd deliver the order to the Tuttle's saloon for him that afternoon.

That settled, Evelyn pointed to his Tommy Bahama cap. 'What is that fish?'

'It's a marlin.'

'Why is it on your hat?'

'I caught one down in Cabo San Lucas. I couldn't bring him home with me, so I had this made to remember him by instead,' Owen said, thinking fast. 'I like to wear my travels on my clothes rather than tattoo my skin.'

'Why do you have a man on horseback sewn on your shirt?'

She reached out and touched the Ralph Lauren logo, tracing the stitching.

'It's a polo player,' Owen said. 'It's a very popular sport in England, where I bought the shirt.'

'I've never seen anything like that before.'

Stoby rushed over and swatted her hand away from Owen's chest. 'Because you've never been anywhere.'

She blushed. 'That's true. I've only been on my poppa's farm in Wyoming and here . . . so I haven't been anywhere. But now I'm mighty knowledgeable about nowhere.'

Owen smiled. She was a clever girl. He said goodbye to the Stobys and headed outside with Overmyer.

'She's a mail-order bride,' Overmyer said. 'She arrived one day on a wagon with the rest of Stoby's stock. Every man in town would like to take her away from him.'

'Do they have a chance?'

'Hard to say. Stoby tosses every fella that tries into Jack Ass Gulch before anybody can find out.'

They headed across the street to Noel's Saloon. Owen looked

at the bill of fare mounted on the wall beside the door. The menu was nearly identical to Tuttle's. Next he went over to Chophouse, which was like Tuttle's bar inside, minus the bar. There were lots of tables, chairs, and spittoons. The customers were filthy, half of their food catching in their beards before it got to their mouths.

Owen went inside, stealing glances at the diners' plates as he headed for an empty table. Most of them were eating some kind of meat, slathered in gravy, with potatoes and beans and hunks of bread.

Overmyer introduced him to Roy, a gangly man in a proper suit, though it was ragged and stained.

Roy said, 'What can I get you gentlemen?'

Owen took a seat at a table. 'What everybody else is having, with cup of coffee and a slice of pie.'

Overmyer ordered a coffee and sat down across from him. 'They serve Arbuckles' Ariosa here, along with everybody else in town.'

'Of course.' He had no idea what Arbuckles' Ariosa was, but he assumed it was a premium brand of coffee bean. Before the reporter could ask him a question, Owen asked one. 'I just realized I didn't see a bank in town.'

'We don't have one, though the Judge doubles as a Wells Fargo agent if anybody has serious financial transactions to conduct.'

'Is there anything the Judge doesn't do?'

'Pay for his drinks,' Overmyer said. 'Or anybody else's.'

'What's his story?'

'He says he's from a rich, highly educated family of Boston lawyers and that he came out here because the California climate was better for his bad lungs. I'm sure that's true, but I also heard he had to skedaddle because his pecker got him in trouble with some married women. Then it happened again in San Francisco so he fled out here.'

That's when Roy brought the food. Owen looked past Roy and saw a Chinese man in the kitchen. The cook wore a mandarin shirt, his hair in a long braid that went down his back. Owen wondered what dishes the Chinese residents on that other ridge cooked for themselves. He was sure it was a lot tastier, and more creative, than what was served here.

Roy said, 'Enjoy your meal.'

Owen tasted the meat. It was very tough beef, heavily salted, slathered in a greasy but tasty brown gravy that hid a lot of sins.

The bread was a thick, dense, dry sourdough that sopped up the gravy nicely and was a meal unto itself. The potatoes were pan-grilled in bacon fat. Heart disease, Owen thought, must be the biggest cause of death in the West.

It was a satisfying, basic meal, perhaps because he was hungrier than he thought he was.

Overmyer watched him eat. 'So . . . how's it rank?'

'It does the job. But food can be so much more than just something to fill your stomach. It can be an artistic, cultural, and sensual experience without costing a penny more. All it takes is some passion and creativity.'

'You do that and you could put Roy out of business.'

Owen took a tentative sip of coffee, afraid it was going to be bitter sludge, but he was pleasantly surprised. It was thick, black, and very strong roast with a rich, robust, even slightly sweet flavor, with a strangely eggy aftertaste. He liked it. The only problem was that it was gritty, leaving behind a layer of coffee grounds on the bottom of the cup when he was finished.

'That's a fine cup of coffee.'

'That and a piece of hard-tack is what passes for a meal for most men here,' Overmyer said.

Owen pushed the cup aside and confronted the pie. He took a bite. The apples had a strange consistency, perhaps because they were dried and reanimated with some water and molasses, and the crust was made from the same dough as the biscuits, which gave the pie an unappetizing sweet-and-sour flavor.

He slid it over to Overmyer. 'Enjoy. I won't tell Tuttle.'

Overmyer picked up a fork and pulled the plate closer. 'Don't mind if I do.'

He dug in while Owen waved over Roy and paid him for the meal and their coffees. Owen assumed tipping was not required. They got up and walked out.

'Is that the best place in town?' Owen asked.

'It was,' Overmyer said.

Owen smiled. Maybe he'd survive.

TWELVE

Overmyer realized he still had a newspaper to publish and rushed back to his office, finally leaving Owen on his own.

He toured the town again, taking a few surreptitious videos with his iPhone, documenting everything without really knowing why. Afterwards, he bought some biscuits from Mama's Bakery to take back to his cave for dinner.

On his three-mile walk back to what was now his home, in the scorching heat of the mid-afternoon, with a dollar fifty in old-time money in his pocket, he recorded a selfie video, commenting on his experiences of the day. Somehow the act of talking to an imagined audience made him feel better, keeping the fear and sadness away for an hour or two.

Owen went over to the donkey, unhitched him, and took him for a walk, like a dog. He figured the animal didn't appreciate being tied up in one spot for the day. Then he rewarded the donkey with one of the biscuits, refreshed his water, hitched him to the other side of the wagon this time, and went inside the cave.

Seeing his Mercedes again brought back the enormity of his predicament. He started the engine, plugged his phone into the charger, and sat down in the driver's seat. He even indulged in some air conditioning, though he hoped there was enough circulation in the cave that he wouldn't die of carbon-monoxide poisoning. At least if he did, it would save the future from him accidentally doing something to mess it up.

It felt good to be swaddled in all that leather and future-tech, to be back in his time capsule. But it was also devastating, because he knew it represented a time and a daughter forever out of reach. He flipped through pictures and videos of his daughter Nicole on his phone, his vision blurring with tears.

Owen was bone-tired and could barely keep his eyes open. So he set the alarm on his phone for 1 a.m. He wanted to be awake at

2 a.m. in case another rift in time opened up in front of him and he could escape this nightmare.

He didn't have to wait for the alarm to rouse him. He was awakened at 12:25 by his stomach, the contents roiling, his sphincters barely holding.

He grabbed some napkins from the map pocket in the driver's side door, rushed out of the cave, went behind a boulder, dropped his pants, and did something he'd never done before: he had explosive diarrhea out in the open. Nobody saw him, except perhaps the donkey, but he was still embarrassed by what he'd done. The uncomfortable experience also taught him a lesson: he was risking his health if he ate anything in this backward time that he didn't prepare himself.

But now he was wide awake and didn't much feel like staying in his cave until 2 a.m. He washed his hands with a few drops from the tiny bottle of Purell he kept in the car, drank a packet of SOS water to replenish his fluids, and fed the leftover biscuits to the donkey.

He sat outside against a boulder and waited for the tears in time to come back. He was still waiting at 3 a.m. The skies had stayed infuriatingly clear and still.

Owen wasn't surprised. It had to be a freak occurrence that sent him here, not a nightly one. It was desperation to believe otherwise.

He was stuck.

Owen spent a good half hour or so crying over his plight, before he took a deep breath and considered his situation.

Feeling sorry for himself wouldn't change anything.

The best he could hope for now was to stay alive without doing anything that might prevent himself, and by extension, his daughter from being born. The way to that, he decided, was to stay right where he was, a place where he knew nothing would substantially change. It would remain largely desolate for the next hundred and thirty-seven years.

Instead of going back to sleep, he decided to get an early start on his day.

To conserve his clothing, he didn't bother changing. He pocketed his iPhone and the similarly sized solar battery in his jeans, and saddled the donkey which, to his surprise, wasn't as hard as he thought it would be.

Using the light from his iPhone, he led the donkey down to the trail that led to Calico, climbed on to the short animal, and gently nudged him with his feet. Owen hadn't been on a horse since he was a kid . . . and never on a donkey.

'Hi-yo Silver, away!'

To his surprise, the donkey started loping toward the town without any further prodding. It must have been a trip the donkey had taken before because he didn't need any direction from Owen, which was a good thing, because he wouldn't have known what to do. It wasn't a comfortable ride on the hard saddle. At times, it was like being gently but firmly slapped on the scrotum with a ping-pong paddle. But it was better than a three-mile walk uphill in a desert, even at night.

The stamp mill was still pounding away and he could see some miners on the town's single street, getting late supper or early breakfast from Roy's Chophouse, or heading to or from the mines or the mill.

He reined the donkey to a stop outside of Tuttle's Saloon, tied him to a post, and went around the back, passing the two huts in between the buildings where Milly and Esther, the prostitutes, slept and did their work. By prior arrangement, Dora had left the back door of the kitchen unlocked for him.

Owen took out the solar battery from his pocket, reached up, and slipped it into the low, flat roof, so he could keep an eye on it while it was being charged. It was a risk having the battery there, but less so than leaving it out in the sun unattended near the cave, where someone could find it and create a catastrophe in the time-space continuum. He opened the door into the dark kitchen and, unable to see a thing, dared to turn on his iPhone flashlight to find the box of matches near the cast-iron stove.

Owen struck a match, found the kerosene lantern hanging from a peg, then realized he had no idea how to light the damn thing. How hard could it be? He examined the lantern in the dim light cast by the match. It was cast iron with a glass globe. There was a wick under the glass, a key-like dial at the base, and some kind of lever. The flame burned his finger and he tossed the match with a curse. He used his iPhone flashlight again, pushed the lever on the lantern, and saw that it raised the glass so he could access the wick. He turned off his phone, struck another match, lifted the glass, and held it to the wick. It lit. He turned the dial and the wick rose more, the flame burning brighter.

Proud of himself for mastering the primitive technology, he set the lantern down and got to work churning his own European-style butter, which he'd use to make a rough puff-pastry dough, something he'd never tried before without refrigeration.

A couple of hours later, after he'd busied himself with some food prep for breakfast and lunch, Owen began layering his butter into the dough. Milly came in, dressed in a long loose-fitting pajama dress that kept slipping down over her shoulders. Her eyes were deep-set and blood shot, her skin pale.

'I hope I didn't wake you,' he said.

'I never sleep well,' Milly said. 'Is there anything I can do to help?'

'You could start up the stove for me.'

He hoped she could because he didn't know how to do it himself. She tore some pages from a catalog on the floor that he hadn't noticed before, wadded them up, and stuffed them into the firebox. He went back to work on his dough.

Milly said, 'I like being in the kitchen when someone is cooking. Feeling the warmth, smelling the smells, tasting things.'

'That's how I got hooked, watching my grandmother work in the kitchen, especially when she was baking cakes or cookies. She was an amazing chef. She knew all the recipes by heart and made them from there, too.'

Milly took some wood kindling from a box and laid them out in the oven's firebox to create a raft on the crumpled paper. 'I wish I was like that. I wanted to be. I never was.'

'There's still time,' Owen said. 'You aren't dead yet.'

'I died a long time ago. I just haven't been buried.' She scooped some coal with a hand-shovel out of a bucket and piled the pieces on the wood.

'Well, until that happens, I could teach you how to make something delicious.'

'I don't have the heart for it,' she said.

'Sure you do.'

She struck a match, lit the paper under the wood and, when it was burning, she closed the iron lid to the firebox. He began folding the layers of butter and dough into crescent shapes and placed them in the Dutch oven. 'What are you making?'

'Petite Croissants.'

'That tells me nothing.'

Owen picked up a bottle of vinegar that he'd ordered from Stoby and gestured to her to follow him to the door that led outside.

'Hold out your hands, palms up, out the door.' She did. He poured a little vinegar in her hands. 'OK, now rub your hands together.' She did. 'Stay there.'

He went back into the kitchen, got a dipper of water from a barrel, and emptied some of it on her hands.

She looked bewildered. 'Why did you do that?'

Owen was disinfecting her hands, and then washing the vinegar flavor off of them, but he didn't know if he'd break the future or simply insult her if he told her that. So what he said was:

'It's for good luck.'

'What for?'

'Our cooking.' He led her back to the table where the dough was laid out. 'Can you fold some of these for me? Like this . . .'

He showed her how to fold the layers into a crescent roll.

'What if I make a mistake?' she asked.

He smiled at her. 'You'll have to eat it.'

She smiled back. 'This is the first time I've ever wanted to make a mistake.'

They folded croissants in a comfortable silence.

The smell of fresh croissants, sizzling meat, and hot cheese soon drew Tuttle, his wife Dora, and Esther into the kitchen in their nightclothes.

Tuttle said, 'I didn't expect you in so early. It's not even sun-up.'

'I had a lot of prep to do for the first day,' Owen said. 'Plus I wanted to give you a chance to sample the menu.'

Dora went straight to the plate of croissants on top of the oven. 'What are these?'

'Croissants. Think of them as French biscuits.' He held up the plate of croissants for them. 'Give them a try.'

They each plucked one off the plate, took a bite, and moaned with pleasure.

Esther said, 'These are so light, flaky and buttery. I could eat a thousand of them.'

She started to reach for another one, but Tuttle swatted her hand away.

'You're lucky I'm not charging you for the one you just had,' Tuttle said, then gestured to a tin platter of pastry puffs that had bits of melted cheese along the edges. 'What are those?'

'Spicy Bacon & Cheese Feuilletée,' Owen said.

Tuttle tried the *feuilletée*, a mix of salt, cheese, bacon, and diced peppers in a buttery puff pastry. He rolled his eyes with delight. 'How can we afford to make these? More importantly, how can men afford to buy them?'

'It's actually cheaper than what you were making before,' Owen explained. 'This recipe uses diced bacon, so not only are you using less meat per serving but you're getting more meals out of what you buy. The only difference is flavor.'

Dora had one and said: 'It's like an entire breakfast in one bite, with kick to it.'

'That's to create an incentive for the customer to buy another cup of coffee,' Owen said. 'Or a whiskey.'

Tuttle wagged a finger at him. 'I like the way you think, Ben. It also scares me.'

'Why's that?'

'You're going to out-smart me one of these days.'

'He already has,' Dora said and turned to Owen. 'What can I do to help?'

'Milly can show you how to start folding some more croissants.'

Dora gave Milly a wary look. 'She can?'

Milly folded her arms indignantly across her chest. 'I haven't always worked on my back, Dora.'

'She's been a big help,' Owen said, 'and I'm going to need it today. Is that a fire pit I saw out back?'

Dora nodded. 'Sometimes the oven isn't enough.'

'You can use that to brew up the coffee and maybe some of your biscuits for the customers who don't want what I'm offering.'

'They'll want it,' Dora said. 'They just don't know it yet.'

Owen reached for the vinegar bottle. 'But first, I need to wish you luck.'

*　　*　　*

At sun-up, the saloon filled with tired, dusty men ready for their biscuits and coffees. Tuttle was at the bar with the Judge and Overmyer.

Tuttle said, 'The men are getting restless for their grub.'

The Judge said, 'I think I can hear their stomachs growling.'

Overmyer said, 'That's actual growling.'

At that moment, Owen, Dora, Milly, and Esther emerged from the kitchen carrying trays of small croissants and breakfast puff pastries.

Owen stood up on the piano bench. 'Can I please have everyone's attention? I am Ben Cartwright, the new executive chef, and today we'll be serving some French delicacies: *croissants* and spicy *feuilletées*. Your first taste is free, but if you want more, raise your hands and it'll be ten cents for the *croissants* and fifteen for the *feuilletées.*'

Owen stepped off the bench and the women began circulating with the samples.

Tuttle dashed over to Owen and grabbed him by the scruff of his shirt. 'Free? Are you out of your goddamn mind?'

'These men are creatures of habit with unsophisticated palates. You can't expect them to buy something they've never tasted before.'

'Why should they buy breakfast when you're giving it away?'

'Turn around,' Owen said.

Tuttle did and saw every hand in the place raised. The Judge had both hands raised, as if he was being held up. Tuttle released Owen and pushed him toward the kitchen. 'What are you standing here for? Get cooking.'

Owen returned to the kitchen and Tuttle made his way back to the bar. Overmyer and the Judge were finishing up their samples. The men in the saloon were smiling and perked up.

The business ended up being so brisk that Dora had to go out for more supplies to meet the demand. There was a lull mid-morning, giving Owen a chance to begin preparing his Hot Pockets, a dish which allowed him to use the cured meats and potatoes Tuttle already had on hand, livened up with peppers and cheese. They were as big a hit with customers as breakfast and, since they could be eaten by hand, cut down on dishes and created faster customer turn-over.

By late afternoon, the number of customers had thinned and

Owen came out of the kitchen for some air. He was exhausted and soaked with sweat. The Judge and Overmyer, to his surprise, were still at the bar.

'What are you two still doing here?' Owen sat down on the piano bench. He was tired, but he was also pleased. The day had gone even better than he'd hoped. Sally Ann sat on the bench beside him.

'We're waiting for supper,' the Judge said. 'And we don't want to lose our seats.'

'I'm strictly here as a reporter,' Overmyer said. 'But the Judge likes your food so much, he didn't even leave for a poke.'

'He couldn't if he'd wanted to,' Tuttle said, glowering at Owen, 'because you kept the working girls busy serving food. You're killing my hospitality business.'

Milly sat down on the bench beside Owen, who smiled at her and said to Tuttle: 'Those are champagne problems.'

Dora stepped out of the kitchen. 'Good idea.'

'What is?' Tuttle asked.

'We don't have champagne,' Dora said, going behind the bar. 'But I think whiskeys for the staff are called for.'

She grabbed a bottle from the shelf and began pouring glasses.

Tuttle shifted his glower to her. 'I don't recall being consulted.'

Dora ignored his objection, passed along shots of whiskey to everybody, and, when everyone had a glass, she raised hers in the air. 'To a great day . . . and a great cook.'

They all raised their glasses.

'Thank you.' Owen set his drink untouched on the piano and turned to face the keys.

He knew now that he'd be able to survive in this backward time, at least as long as possible in a world without antibiotics, vaccines, or even decent sanitation, when a mosquito bite could be fatal. But he was still a prisoner of time, never able see his daughter again, at least not in the flesh.

He began to play Jim Croce's 'Time in a Bottle' and sang the mournful lyrics.

He wasn't much of a singer, but by the time he was done, Milly and Dora were crying . . . and so was he.

Tuttle turned to his friends. 'If that's his idea of a celebratory song, I'd hate to hear his sad stuff.'

'You may have to hire him as a piano player, too,' the Judge said.

'Why don't I just give him the damn saloon and be done with it?'

Overmyer said, 'I wouldn't be surprised if you just saw the future.'

Only one person in the room was sure he'd seen the future and knew that, unlike any man before, all of his tomorrows would forever be in the past.

THIRTEEN

Thursday, February 7, 2019

Beth McDade stood on one side of the metal examination table in the morgue, looking down at Owen Slader's bones, which Amanda had laid out in their proper order.

'OK, walk me through it,' Beth said. 'First off, what killed Slader?'

'I have no idea. There are no indications of violent trauma on the bones,' Amanda said. 'But he could have been poisoned, or had his throat slit, and that wouldn't have left signs on his skeleton, either. He could also have died of natural causes, of course.'

'How? I have him on video, alive and healthy, driving away from Eddie's minutes before he disappeared.'

'A heart attack, a stroke, a pulmonary embolism, a ruptured abdominal aortic aneurysm, any number of things could have killed him.'

'Then where is his car?'

'I can't answer that question, that's your job. All I have to go on are the bones on this table, and the clothing he was buried in, and what they tell me.'

Beth held up her hands in surrender. 'You're right, of course. I'm sorry. It's just very frustrating. None of it makes sense.'

'That's for sure. We know from the dental and orthopedic implants that this is definitely Owen Slader, who disappeared a week ago. His clothes also indicate that.' She turned to the adjacent table and picked up a large evidence bag containing what remained of his clothes. 'Tommy Bahama shirt. Ralph Lauren pants. Louis Vuitton belt. Today's fashions, with labels. Also I found plenty of synthetic materials – plastics, polyester, etc. – in his clothing that didn't exist in the late 1800s.'

'So the only thing that dates him is the casket,' Beth said.

'And his bones are over a hundred years old.'

'How can you be sure?'

Amanda picked up a bone from his arm and held it up to Beth. 'The bones become brittle, as the moisture and proteins are leached out over decades of burial. And you can see that the iron in the soil has dyed the bones reddish, which also happens over a long period of time.'

She could see the red, but didn't buy it. 'It's been faked somehow.'

'These bones are over a hundred years old on a microscopic and chemical level,' Amanda said. 'I don't know how you fake that.'

'Clearly somebody has, because Owen Slader disappeared last week, not over a century ago. And what happened to his body? I mean, where are his flesh and organs?'

'He decomposed,' Amanda said. 'It's long gone.'

'I'm not a coroner, but I've seen enough death to know a body doesn't decompose to this degree in a week, even if it's left out in the open,' Beth said. 'Could someone have gutted and cleaned him? Then dried out and stained his bones?'

'There are no signs that any other process besides nature was applied to these bones.'

'OK,' Beth said, 'could we be looking at his recent bones mixed with somebody else's ancient ones?'

'That's highly unlikely—'

Beth interrupted her. 'It's more likely than his bones being over a hundred years old.'

Amanda went on. '—but I'll run DNA tests to be absolutely certain.'

'Good.'

'And let's say, for the sake of argument, that it's possible to artificially age bones to this degree.'

'Obviously it is,' Beth said.

'If somebody wanted to fool us into thinking this was a late-nineteenth-century grave site, why didn't they bury him in period clothes and remove his orthopedic implants, his dental implants, and his porcelain-capped teeth? It defeats the purpose.'

'We don't know the purpose yet,' Beth said. 'But I will find out.'

'And how does Motor Home Man fit in?'

Beth glanced at the bank of closed morgue drawers, knowing the miner was on one of them. 'What does he have to do with this?'

'You don't see the parallels between these two cases?' Amanda marched over to a morgue drawer and pulled out the shelf with Motor Home Man on it.

'Of course I do,' Beth said. 'Motor Home Man seems to have stepped out of the 1800s and while Slader stepped into the past, both on the same night and in the same area. But other than that, the cases are entirely different. For one thing, we know how Motor Home Man died.'

'We don't know why he had all of his other unusual physical issues.'

'We know they didn't happen overnight or even over a week,' Beth said. 'They were the result of years of bad luck and bad choices.'

'We also know what happened to Owen Slader's bones didn't happen over a night or even a week,' Amanda said. 'It was the result of decades of decay, not a single week.'

'Those are two entirely different deaths,' Beth said. 'One is natural, the other unnatural.'

'You're making an assumption not based on facts.'

'So are you,' Beth said. 'You're assuming that these two cases are connected.'

'Both men met their fate on the same night and the forensics connect them both to the late 1800s.'

'Or someone who knows about Motor Home Man's death wants us to think so to confuse things,' Beth said. 'And he's succeeding.'

Amanda shook her head. 'I think you're ignoring the Marty McFly in the room.'

'The what?'

'Marty McFly. The character Michael J. Fox played in the *Back to the Future* movies.'

'You think this has something to do with time travel?' Of course the notion had crossed Beth's mind, but she wouldn't have said it out loud if Amanda hadn't brought it up first.

'There was a lightning storm that night,' Amanda said, like that was meaningful. It wasn't to Beth.

'What does that have to do with anything?'

'When I was a kid, I saw this movie called *Final Countdown*. Kirk Douglas is the captain of a nuclear supercarrier that goes through a time storm and ends up near Hawaii, the day before the Japanese attacked Pearl Harbor, and he has to decide whether to use his superior aircraft and fire power stop it from happening.'

'You think a time storm in the Mojave last week sent Owen Slader back to the 1800s and Motor Home Man to the present.'

'That would explain it,' Amanda said.

'Those were movies. They have no basis in reality.'

Amanda gestured to the two dead bodies. 'Can you explain them?'

'No, I can't, but I'm sure the answer isn't Marty McFly or a time storm. These are your pregnancy hormones talking,' Beth said. 'Do you really expect me to base my investigation on a crappy Kirk Douglas movie?'

'Of course not, but the movie isn't as bad as it sounds and it had a great twist at the end but that makes zero sense if you think about it.'

'So does what you are saying right now.'

'You're right, I know. I'm sorry. I'm just bewildered, that's all,' Amanda said. 'I can't explain why Motor Home Man's body was in the state it was or how a man who disappeared a week ago can have century-old bones.'

'The only way to do this is by sticking to the facts and letting the evidence guide us,' Beth said. 'We can't let our frustration, or our imaginations, intrude. I'm going to get the crime scene investigators to sift through every grain of dirt around that grave for more evidence. Are there more tests you can do on Slader?'

'Oh, yeah,' she said. 'Hundreds.'

'Good, maybe the results will give us something more to work with than we have now.'

Or raise more questions. Beth started for the door.

'One more thing before you go,' Amanda said. 'Am I notifying the LAPD that we've found their missing person or are you?'

Letting Amanda do it would be the easy way out. But Beth knew she'd hate herself for it. 'I'll handle it.'

Beth walked down the long, dark hallway and called Carson Edlow, the construction foreman out in Newberry Springs, to tell him not to resume work, then she called and gave her captain an update, though she left out the time-travel stuff. She got his OK to call out CSU to the scene again. Then she called CSU, who weren't thrilled about going back out to the desert on what they called 'a scavenger hunt', and then, when she got to her car, she called Trent. He answered on the first ring.

'It's me, Beth. We found Owen Slader yesterday, buried in the desert.'

'How was he murdered?'

'We aren't sure that he was,' she said.

'He's dead and somebody buried him. That doesn't sound like natural causes to me.'

'Or to me,' she said, 'but forensically it's more complicated than that. We only found his skeletonized remains.'

'He hasn't been dead long enough to be a skeleton. Someone had to do that to him somehow. Doesn't that suggest a homicide to you?'

Of course it did.

'I don't investigate suggestions, Trent. I investigate facts and right now we don't have enough to know what the hell happened to him. There's no trauma to his bones.'

'Except that there's no flesh on them anymore, which is some freaky, freaky shit. There's a psycho out there.'

Yes, there probably was, she thought. 'We don't know that.'

'I do. He disappeared a week ago, Beth. No matter how he died, he shouldn't be just bones. Somebody did that to him and did it for a reason. Have you recovered his car?'

'Not yet.'

'The car may give us some idea what happened. I'll be out this afternoon.'

'No, you won't,' she said. 'His body wasn't found in LA. It was found here. This is my investigation.'

'You need our help. You don't have the resources in Barstow that we do.'

'I don't need any more help from the LAPD than I've already had,' Beth said.

'You know what I meant.'

'You want to help? Look into his life in Los Angeles and see if he was into anything there that might have ended here.'

'I can do that,' Trent said. 'But I can also do more.'

'Like what? You don't have the experience or the skills. We both know how you got the job. You'll be the first to know when I have the answers.'

She hung up and drove back to the station.

Parmalee, the crime scene investigator, was back at the Newberry Springs construction site with two other investigators, one going over the area with a cadaver dog, the other sweeping the lot with a ground-penetrating radar device.

Beth waited until they'd been working for a few hours before she went out there to give them a chance to get their work started. She approached Carson Edlow, who stood outside his trailer, watching the team work.

'Seems to me that you're going to a lot of trouble for nothing,' he said.

'Are you absolutely sure this site wasn't disturbed in any way before you started your work?'

'I told you before, nobody has stuck a shovel in this dirt in decades,' Edlow said. 'When can we get back to work?'

'It depends on what they find.'

'Time is money in my business,' he said. 'It's adding up.'

She nodded and went over to talk with Parmalee, who was crouched at the grave again, which still contained the rotting remnants of the wooden casket. Behind him was a pop-up tent over a card-table and their equipment and a box of bottled water.

'Found anything?' she asked.

'No other graves, if that's what you mean. Just some foundation footings from the house that used to be out here. But we did find this.' He led her over to the tent, where various rusted artifacts like kitchen utensils, coins, cans, and bottle fragments were laid out on the folding table. He picked up a plastic bag containing a rusted metal box, similar to a tobacco tin. 'We found the bones of a child's severed thumb in this box.'

'Is it recent?' she asked.

'At least a hundred years old.'

'You said the thumb was severed. How do you know?'

'The cutting edge leaves a mark. My guess is that it was done with the single swing of an ax. It was undoubtedly an amputation.'

'What a bizarre thing to find.'

'Not really,' Parmalee said. 'We find a lot of family members and dead pets buried in old home sites from the 1800s. It makes sense that they'd bury an amputated limb in their backyard, too. What else would they have done with it? Toss it in the desert for the vultures? That would've been cold. Imagine if it was your limb. You'd want it treated with respect.'

'I hadn't thought of that,' she said. 'I'll get out of your way so you can get back to work.'

'I can't promise we're going to be here much longer,' Parmalee said. 'If anything else comes up in the county, we're out of here. My supervisor told me this is his lowest priority.'

'Understood.'

Beth got back in her plain-wrap Explorer and got onto west-bound I-15, headed for Barstow. But as she was nearly at the Marine Corps Logistics Base, she thought about the mysterious explosion that happened there on Saturday morning.

She thought about Bill Knox, their security chief, showing up at the scene of the Motor Home Man's death, right outside their fence.

She thought about Owen Slader disappearing at the same time, around the same spot on the interstate where she was right at that moment.

She thought about the lightning storm, the fire at Fort Irwin the same night, and Amanda's outrageous 'time storm' theory.

And that reminded her of Alan Vernon, the ranting conspiracy nut on the radio, who warned that the lightning storm was a sign that the extraterrestrials at Fort Irwin were preparing for an imminent invasion of Earth.

Time travel. Alien invasions.

It was crazy.

But she couldn't shake all the coincidences or the feeling Bill was definitely hiding something. Maybe if she found out what his secret was, the connections between all the incidents would be clear.

So she got off the freeway at the Ghost Town Road exit, made a hard left, and drove east, past Peggy Sue's, to the entrance to the Marine base. She drove up to the guard gate and flashed her badge to the uniformed Marine inside.

'I'm Beth McDade, a detective with the San Bernardino Sheriff's Department. I'd like to see Bill Knox.'

'Is he expecting you?'

'Nope.'

The guard picked up the phone and made a call that she didn't hear. When he was done, he came back to the window.

'You can park right over there.' He pointed to a spot inside the gate, beside the fence.

'I know my way to his office.'

'Park over there,' he said.

They'd never asked her to do that before. She was sure it was because Bill didn't want her to see the damage caused by the 'dumpster fire'.

But she did as she was told. She drove through the gate, pulled over at the fence where the guard could keep an eye on her, and waited.

Ten minutes later, Bill arrived in an open-air Jeep and parked on her driver's side.

'Something up?' he said, not leaving his vehicle. That was a message to her in itself.

She flashed him a smile. 'I'm starving. I thought I'd hit you up for that burger you offered me last week. We could go across the street to Peggy Sue's.'

'I wish I could, but it's too late for lunch and too early for dinner.'

'My stomach doesn't know that and I work odd hours. It messes up your internal clock. You know how it is. We were both up at 2 a.m. last Saturday.'

'That was an unusual situation.'

'Sure was, especially for you. You had to deal with that dumpster fire at the same time there was a dumpster fire at Fort Irwin. I heard six men were medevac'd to the ER, four from Fort Irwin, two from here. What are the odds?'

He looked irritated. 'It wasn't a dumpster fire at Fort Irwin. They were doing night-training in the desert. A simulated IED went off too hot and too close to some men. But yeah, it was a rough night.'

'It was for everybody,' she said. 'A lightning storm, a bus accident on the I-15, a fatal car accident, a man disappearing on the freeway, a vehicle engine appearing in somebody's living room, and explosions at two military bases, all happening at precisely the same time. Makes me wonder if they were all connected somehow.'

Bill gave her a hard look. 'I wouldn't make assumptions.'

'Yeah, that's what my training officer used to say. "Just deal with facts, Beth. That's all that counts.'"

'Your training officer was right. Making bad assumptions can lead to terrible mistakes. It can destroy a career.'

That was a threat. She didn't like threats. And in this case, she thought, it was a weak one. Her career was ruined years ago.

So she returned his hard look. 'Here's a fact. Two men from your base were rushed to the ER with third-degree burns. But instead of being with them, or investigating what happened, your priority was checking out a car crash on the street at 2 a.m. outside of Peggy Sue's. I'd like to know why.'

'I told you why.'

Because he wanted to see her again, to set some more bed sheets on fire. 'If you were that hot for me, Bill, we'd be eating a cheese-burger right now and then you'd try go get me into a bed at the Holiday Inn Express.'

'I really like you, Beth. I want to see you succeed. The best way to do that is to keep your head down, do your job, and don't look for problems.'

She didn't like being mansplained. 'I'm a homicide detective investigating a traffic fatality, Bill. This is my job.'

'A transient ran into the street and got hit by a motor home. Is there any doubt that it was an accident?'

'Nope,' she said.

'Case solved. Move on.' He drove off without saying goodbye.

Beth watched him go. She'd never told him the victim was homeless.

How did he know that? How close an eye was he keeping on her case?

On the other hand, she thought, deputies were showing Motor Home Man's picture all around, maybe Bill just heard the scuttlebutt at Jack-in-the-Box or a gas station.

But she doubted it.

As she drove away, she wondered if she should have asked Bill if he'd ever seen that Kirk Douglas movie or if he was an alien possessing a human body.

She also wondered if she'd just made a big mistake.

FOURTEEN

Beth sat down at her desk and watched the video from Peggy Sue's, of Motor Home Man getting killed, and the video from EddieWorld, of Owen Slader buying his beef jerky and driving off into oblivion, hoping she'd see something new. She didn't.

So she thought about all the other strange things besides Motor Home Man's death and Slader's disappearance that she knew happened on February 2nd – the camper attacked by an extinct grizzly bear, the multi-car collision caused by a boulder on I-15, and the engine some guy found in his living room.

Was there more weird shit that happened that night that she didn't know about?

She logged into the station's incident report database, typed in February 2, and accidentally hit enter before she'd typed in the year, so she got far more data than she wanted, going back decades.

Last Saturday, there were the incidents she'd heard about, plus the usual domestic disputes, drunk and disorderlies, car thefts, break-ins, and arrests for shoplifting, drug-dealing, and prostitutions. But she did see some other unusual things happened on same day over the years.

On February 2, 2017, the tire from a Jeep smashed into a Las Vegas-bound tour bus on I-15 in Yermo. Sixteen people were hurt. It was never determined where the tire came from.

On February 2, 2011, a woman in Lenwood went outside to pick up her morning paper and saw a severed cow's head on her roof.

On February 2, 1999, a car in the Outlet mall parking lot was crushed by a boulder.

On February 2, 1992, a house in Barstow collapsed and the woman who lived there, Gwendolyn Hale, went missing. Her body wasn't in the rubble and no trace of her was ever found. Building inspectors investigating the collapse determined it was caused by the removal of a large section of an upstairs bedroom wall that supported the roof. All traces of the wall were gone, but they couldn't figure out how the wall was removed.

On February 2, 1983, several cow legs were found scattered in the playground of Barstow Elementary School.

On February 2, 1978, a soldier from Fort Irwin went missing on a night-training exercise in the Mojave.

Beth saw a pattern of incidents involving boulders, car parts, dismembered cows, and missing people occurring on February 2nd across several years. But she didn't understand what it meant. Or if she were seeing patterns where none existed.

Am I turning into Alan Vernon?

Is this how the insanity starts?

Her phone rang, startling her. It was a call from Russell Parmalee, out in Newberry Springs. He told her they were wrapping up their investigation at the site. They'd found nothing and had a triple homicide in San Bernardino. She asked him to send the severed thumb to Amanda, and he agreed to do that.

Beth hung up and put in a call to the San Bernardino County Clerk's office to see what they could tell her about the ownership of the Newberry Springs property. The clerk she spoke to, a man named Mel Deacon, told her that he'd have to pull the information from the archives, and they were about to close. But he would try to have the records ready for her to view the next morning.

That meant an hour on the road each way. But she decided a change of scenery might be nice.

She thanked him and hung up just as Hatcher came in, breaking her from her thoughts.

'I'm glad you're still here,' he said. She glanced at the wall clock and realized it was an hour past the end of her shift. 'Salem has made a deal with the DA and is going to give up his crew tonight. We're heading out now. You want in?'

'Hell yes.'

'Then suit up. This is going to be a silent running.'

Suit up meant Kevlar vests, and big guns. Silent running meant only a very small, select team of deputies would be involved in the arrest to keep word from leaking out to the targets.

'Walk me to my car,' she said. He did. When they got outside, she asked: 'How many people know?'

'Locally, besides us, just the Captain and the DA,' he said.

'Deputies from San Bernardino are already running surveillance of Salem and his three-man crew and will join us for the take-down.'

She thought it was still a smart move to keep the Barstow-based deputies out of the loop because there might be some unknown personal ties.

She opened her trunk and got out her Kevlar vest, night-vision goggles, and helmet. Out here, they weren't just their own forensic unit. They often had to be their own tactical assault team.

'What's the plan?'

'Salem and his crew are going to hit another house tonight, out at Hula Lake,' he said. It was another private lake neighborhood, this one even less attractive, and with fewer homes around it, than Lake Betty, where Grenlick had his place. 'We'll be inside waiting.'

She closed her trunk. 'Where are they meeting first?'

'At Salem's warehouse in Daggett,' he said, referring to a tiny collection of scattered desert homes and derelict storefronts a few miles south of Yermo.

'Why not take them at the warehouse?'

'All we have is Salem's testimony and video of three masked men,' Hatcher said. 'The DA says there's no evidence that directly connects anyone but Salem to the stolen toys on the property. She needs to catch them in the act to really tie the case up in a neat bow.'

But she knew a big problem with a desert stakeout was that there was nowhere to hide. Staging raids or maintaining surveillance were incredibly hard to pull off without the targets noticing. 'Easier said than done.'

'That's why we are keeping it small. Just six of us.' He gestured to a van across the parking lot. 'That's our ride. The operation will be coordinated from a mobile command center parked inside the derelict gas station on Yermo Road and we'll have air support.'

'How do you know the crew will show up or that Salem won't tip them off that they are walking into a sting?'

'He's at home now. We've got eyes and ears on him and tracking devices on his vehicles. I suppose Salem could slip them a note, or use a code word, or act out a message in charades. But one thing is for sure, he's going down no matter what happens.'

'If you put a man in a desperate situation,' she said, 'he's likely to do something desperate.'

'Yeah. I got that same fortune cookie once.'

They walked across the parking lot to the van.

It was a dark night. The deputies arrived at the lake house from the desert side in two SUVs. Hatcher and two deputies were in one vehicle, Beth and two deputies were the other. The six were all wired with radios and earbuds so they could talk to each other, as well as the airship and mobile command station, where the Captain and DA were overseeing the operation, on a secure frequency.

Hatcher and his team approached the target house on foot from the desert so they wouldn't draw the attention of any neighbors or potential look-outs. Beth and her team removed shovels from their SUV, and also approached the home, but didn't leave the desert. They took positions across from the house and began digging shallow holes the length of their prone bodies.

When Hatcher got to the house, a one-story cinderblock ranch, he punched in a special code he'd received from the alarm company to temporarily disable the security system. He unlocked the front door and went inside with the two deputies, locked the door behind himself, and reset the alarm in 'stay' mode.

He reported his status to the team. 'Unit one is inside and in position.'

Beth used the dug-out dirt to create a small berm around the hole that would hide her body from the sweep of headlights on the street. She laid down the shovel, covering the shiny handle and spade with dirt so they wouldn't reflect light, either, and settled in to wait, directly across from the house.

She clicked the radio mike on her headset to report in. 'McDade in position.'

The other two members of her team reported that they were in position, too. Now all they could do was wait. Thirty minutes later, their radios crackled. It was the Captain.

'Target vehicle is on the move, a truck and toy hauler, emerging from the warehouse in Daggett and heading your way.'

A few minutes later, the Captain radioed again.

'We don't have a visual on the occupants but we can confirm they are all in the vehicle. They all arrived at the warehouse and nobody stayed behind.'

Ten minutes later, Beth saw the headlights as the truck and toy hauler turned on to the street and headed their way.

Beth radioed in again. 'McDade. I have visual on the target, approaching the house.'

She ducked down before the headlights swept over her, then lifted her head as the truck passed and pulled up in front of the house, blocking it from view.

'McDade to Unit One. They are here.'

Something didn't feel right to her. On the last job, Salem backed the toy hauler up to the garage so they could easily load up the jet-skis and ATVs. So why was the truck parked in the street, *parallel* to the house?

Salem got out of the truck, but nobody else did, and walked towards the rear of the toy hauler.

As he did, she heard the roar of engines inside the trailer. If they were coming to steal toys, why would they bring some?

And then she realized what was coming.

Salem began to unlatch the back panel, which would become a ramp. Beth yelled into her radio, drew her weapon, and scrambled to her feet.

'Move in! Move in!'

She ran toward the rear of the toy hauler while another deputy approached Salem, ordering him to freeze.

But it was too late. The back door dropped and Beth turned to face it in firing stance, just as a four-wheeler ATV with two men inside burst out, coming right at her, flying off the ramp.

She planted her feet and fired twice at the left front wheel, blowing it apart, then leaned to one side, as if avoiding an irritating insect, as the vehicle flew past her, hit the road with one shredded tire, and tipped end over end, landing upside down.

A second later, a dirt bike with a single rider shot out of the toy hauler, clipped the top of the overturned ATV, and flipped the rider into the desert.

Beth whirled around and approached the ATV, her gun drawn. Both men had been thrown clear. One was lying on the asphalt, covered in blood, and screaming in pain. The other was in the sand, sitting up, clutching a broken arm and looking dazed. But they were alive.

A moment later, a helicopter streaked overhead, its searchlight illuminating the desert, where the dirt biker was limping away. He wouldn't get far. A deputy was already chasing after him.

Beth holstered her weapon and spoke into her mike. 'We've got three assailants down in need of immediate medical assistance.'

She figured Salem must have clued his crew in at the warehouse on the sting. He was screwed, but at least they still had a chance to escape and he'd help. But damn, she thought, what a stupid plan.

Hatcher appeared out of nowhere at her side. 'Jesus, Beth. That was insane.'

'Yeah, I don't know how they thought that was going to work.'

'I was talking about what you did, standing in front of them,' he said. 'You could have been decapitated.'

'I ducked,' she said.

'Brilliant strategy,' he said. 'Almost as brilliant as theirs.'

Dave Salem was the only member of his crew who didn't require surgery to repair multiple broken bones and wouldn't be walking with a limp for the rest of his life. The dirt-biker also lost an eye. But they were all lucky to be alive. And Beth considered herself lucky they were alive, too.

Between the reports she had to fill out, and the extensive interviews with the officer-involved shooting unit, Beth was up all night, but by the time daylight broke on Friday, she was unofficially told that her shooting was justified. Officially, she was assigned to desk duty for the next few days, pending the conclusion of the investigation.

She was too jacked up afterwards to go home, and a visit to Pour Decisions wasn't good idea, so instead she put on the fresh set of clothes in her locker and took the one-hour drive out to San Bernardino, arriving just as the county clerk's office opened up.

Deacon was a balding, bespectacled man with a bow tie. The look suited him. He set a big, dusty, leather-bound ledger on the counter between them.

'I had to go back into the basement archives after I got your call yesterday. I'd never been that far back before. There was a layer of dust on the floor you could grow crops in.'

'I appreciate the effort,' she said.

He tapped the book. 'These are the property records from the late 1800s. They were all handwritten in ledgers like this back then.'

'You haven't digitized them?'

'We don't have the money in our budget for that. These are basically historical records of interest only to scholars. This may be the first time this book has been opened in our lifetimes.'

She noticed two folded pieces of paper being used as markers in the ledger. He'd obviously taken a peek at the details before she arrived.

'What can you tell me about the property?'

'It's actually rather interesting. The original deed was recorded in Calico but those records were lost in a fire that leveled the town. The first known owner was in 1890, Ben Cartwright, who apparently had a ranch there, a desert Ponderosa.' He laughed, but she didn't understand the joke. 'The Ponderosa. You know, the Cartwrights. Ben, Little Joe, Hoss, and Adam? On *Bonanza*?' He started humming a piece of music that she didn't recognize. She was too tired to play games.

Instead of slapping him, she asked: 'Can you please just get to the point?'

'It was a TV Western,' he said.

'I don't watch television.'

'It ran for fourteen years and made Michael Landon a star,' he said.

'I have no idea who that is.'

'It must have been quite a home in its day. I asked some of my co-workers. Apparently, the ruins of the front steps and stone chimney were still there until as late as the 1960s.'

'What do you know about the subsequent owners?'

'There haven't been any,' he said. 'That's why I had to go so far back to find the original records.'

'You mean the Cartwrights still own it?'

'The Cartwright Family Trust. They've never stopped paying their property taxes. Or their descendants,' he said. 'The checks have been coming from an account at the Bank of San Bernardino that's almost as old as the bank itself.' Deacon opened the ledger and removed the paper he was using as a bookmark. He unfolded the paper and handed it to her. It was a list of dates and figures. 'In a hundred thirty years, they've never missed a payment on their two properties.'

'Two? Where's their other one?'

'I thought you might ask.' He opened the book where the other bookmark was and showed her what looked like a hand-drawn map on the page. She recognized it as Yermo, though according to the map, it was called Otis at the time.

'It's right here. Up against a butte, north of Elephant Mountain, which was then known as Table Mountain. I'm amazed that the property was never exploited for mining, given how much activity there was out there at the time. The Oriental Mining Company mill was on the other southeast side of that butte and pulled out quite a bit of silver in its heyday. The ruins of the stamp mill and low gauge railroad are still there.'

Beth knew the butte and the spot, along Yermo Road, south of the I-15, walking distance from Peggy Sue's diner. She'd driven by it a thousand times. There was nothing there but empty desert.

'I'm surprised nothing has been built on that Newberry Springs property,' she said.

'Because it was strictly prohibited.'

'By the county?'

'By the trust,' he said. 'I took some notes from the original document, which is too delicate to be handled. It dictated that the property could not be sold and that no development could occur before February 2nd of this year.'

Beth felt a jolt, as if she'd just touched a live wire. It even raised the hairs on her neck, a sensation she'd never felt before.

Nothing that happened on Saturday is a coincidence.

It's all connected.

But how?

'When did the trust pick that date?'

He glanced at paper he was using to bookmark that page. She saw a bunch of handwritten notes on it. 'The trust was created by the Cartwrights in the 1880s. When Ben Cartwright died on October 7th, 1912, control of the assets passed to his wife. On her death in 1933, it passed to their only son. The trust is presently controlled by their great-great-grandson, Christopher Cartwright, who was born in 1962.'

Beth had so many questions.

Why did the Cartwrights pick February 2nd, 2019?

What was the significance of that date to them 107 years ago?

And why start construction now?

But he wouldn't know the answer to any of those questions. So she asked him one he could answer: 'Does the trust impose the same restriction on the second property?'

'No, in this case, the sale and development of the land are prohibited forever, unless the trust ever stops paying the property taxes and the county auctions off the land. That said, given the desert location across from the interstate, probably the only people who'd be interested in developing it would be a fast-food restaurant, a gas station, or a motel. But the parcel isn't large enough to accommodate any of those businesses, at least not under the present building codes.'

So what's so sacred about that property?
What were they protecting . . . or hiding?

'What more can you tell me about the Cartwrights?'

'Ben was the widowed patriarch, and he had three sons, each born by a different mother, which is why they were so different in body and temperament. Hoss, the middle son, was a big lovable bear of a man,' Deacon said. 'The show was never the same after he died.'

She desperately wanted to smack this guy, but she needed his help. 'I was asking about the *real* Cartwrights.'

He grinned, having fun. 'I doubt the show was based on them. It was set in a big ranch in Nevada, near Lake Tahoe, not in a dry, empty desert. But if anybody can answer your questions, it will be Selma Neary at the San Bernardino County historical society.'

'Thank you.' Beth got up to go, but had a second thought. 'One more thing. What can you tell me about Desert Lake Ventures?'

'A first-class company. They've done a lot of work in Southern California, mostly exclusive gated housing tracts and high-end shopping malls in desert communities. They raise property values wherever they build. The county would love to see them build more projects here.' Deacon moved to a computer terminal further down the counter and typed in some commands. 'Their headquarters are in Los Angeles. Here's their contact information and corporate officers.'

He swiveled the monitor toward her so she could see the details on screen. Beth jotted down the company's address and phone number, then used the mouse to scroll up the page and get the names of the officers.

They were all named Cartwright.

FIFTEEN

Calico, September 1882

I n the seven months since Owen's arrival, the population in Calico seemed to double every week and he fell into a routine, riding his donkey into town in the morning, cooking all day, and returning to his cave at night.

For the first few weeks, he'd stayed up every night until 2 a.m., staring out at the desert and hoping for another tear in time to appear, before he'd finally accepted the heartbreaking fact that it wasn't going to happen and that there was no way to get back to 2019. It wasn't like he could build a time machine or convert his Mercedes into Marty McFly's DeLorean. So, he'd focused on just making it through each day.

He still wasn't used to the horrible smell that permeated Calico from all the excrement piled in the street and down in Jack Ass Gulch . . . or the overpowering stench and bad teeth of nearly every filthy, sweaty person he met. He'd have worn a bandana over his nose and mouth but was afraid he'd be mistaken for an outlaw. By far the best smelling people in town were Milly and Esther, Tuttle's Saloon's two prostitutes, who apparently doused themselves with perfume between their many clients. He imagined the other prostitutes in town also smelled nice, but he hadn't visited the other saloons or the new dance hall where most of the working girls plied their trade.

By local standards, Owen knew he was considered a successful man who lived comfortably. But the way he saw it, he was living in squalor. His home was a cave and what passed for civilization was a primitive, unsanitary shanty town in middle of a desert.

But he also knew that he was making the best of his plight. He thanked God every day for the car battery and solar charger that kept his iPhone and MacBook running. The two Apple devices were precious ties to his time, his music, and his daughter . . . and the key to maintaining his morale as well as his sanity. He also shot videos of Calico, took selfies, and recorded his thoughts. At night, he listened to music on his earbuds and scrolled through his photos and videos. Owen was living in 1882 but refused to totally commit himself to his new – or was it old? – time.

The benefits of living in the cave weren't just the technological and creature comforts of his Mercedes. He also enjoyed the fresh air and the total silence. Calico's stench didn't travel the three miles south and he wasn't disturbed by the 24/7 pounding of the stamp mills that were the incessant, discordant back-beat to daily life. But that might not last. Several new stamp mills had opened in the canyons and along the desert floor and more were coming.

He didn't pay for food or lodging, so he'd managed to save a few hundred dollars, which he stashed under the spare tire in his Mercedes. With his basic survival no longer an issue, Owen worried about the day he'd run out of toothpaste and dental floss . . . or when his running shoes finally fell apart and he'd have to buy a pair of antique shoes.

He also worried about his health and cherished his first-aid kit, particularly his limited supply of aspirin, ibuprofen, antacids, antihistamines, and even some Vicodin left over after the reconstruction of his broken elbow and the months of physical therapy that had followed. The thought of losing any of those drugs, or having them expire, was too terrifying to consider.

He used his electric razor, which he kept charged with the solar battery, to keep himself clean-shaven but had some disposable razors in a pinch. To bathe, he washed himself with a rag, a bar of soap, and water from the barrel he kept in the hut outside of his cave (and that Virgil Urt refilled on a semi-regular basis). He craved a hot bath or shower, but he refused to visit the Calico bathhouse in the Chinese camp and get into a tub of water that was already filled with the filth of several other men. Water was too scarce to waste on just one man's bath. He also kept a Sears Catalog handy for toilet paper. Just looking at a corn cob made him cringe.

Most of his clothing, with the exception of his underwear and socks, stayed in his suitcase. He'd purchased two shirts to wear over his T-shirts while he cooked because he didn't want to stain his twenty-first century clothing. The Tuttles laundered his 'work shirts', but he washed his own clothes by hand at the cave, using his water and soap, because he didn't want to risk them being 'lost' or examined too closely by whoever laundered them. He'd also bought a wide-brimmed hat to wear to and from Calico and only wore his Tommy Bahama baseball cap in the kitchen, though he didn't know why he bothered. Nobody would ever complain about finding a hair in their food if they had no problem with a full-time barber working in the dining room.

He'd been teaching Milly how to cook, but those lessons were brief and sporadic, usually conducted in the very early morning, because she was kept busy day and night with her main job and both she and the Tuttles earned more when she was on her back than when she was on her feet.

On this particular morning, already eighty degrees at sunrise, Owen was carrying a burlap bag of onions from Stoby's store when a wagon came charging up to Tuttle's saloon with a driver in front and two dusty bearded men sitting in the bed. As soon as the wagon came to a stop, the two men jumped off the back and lifted out a fourth man, who was lying unconscious in the bed, and quickly carried him into the saloon.

But Owen wasn't paying much attention to them. He was staring in shock at the wagon's driver, a craggy-faced, weather-beaten man. Or, to be more precise, what the man was sitting on.

It was the front seat of a car.

The low-backed seat was upholstered in green crackled vinyl and was welded on to the wagon's front bench.

Owen tried to sound casual when he spoke to the driver. 'That's some fancy seat you've got there.'

The driver spit a wad of tobacco in the street. 'Ain't it, though? I found it in the dirt a few weeks ago out by Bicycle Lake.'

'Where's that?'

'North of here, on the other side of the mountains.'

'Why's it called Bicycle Lake?'

'Because somebody once found a bicycle in the muck,' the driver said. 'It ain't really much of a lake, barely even a puddle. The trails heading west are littered with stuff like pianos, chairs, dishes, and stoves that settlers chucked out of their wagons to lighten their load.'

The car seat looked to Owen like the kind that would be in a jeep, a Humvee, or other off-road vehicle. He wondered what happened to the rest of the vehicle . . . or whoever might have been driving it. He'd have to find a way to get out there and have a look for himself.

The car seat felt like an omen, but of what he didn't know. 'Did you find anything else out there?'

'Just this. I'd have throw'd my wife and kid out of the wagon before this seat. My ass never had it so good.'

That's when Overmyer rushed over from his office, notepad and pencil in hand, and approached the driver.

'You charged in here like you were being chased by the devil. What happened?'

'A prospector got himself bit by a rattler. His friends were bringing him into town on a pack mule when I ran across 'em.'

In all the excitement about the seat, Owen had forgotten about the guy that had been carried into the saloon. 'And you brought him here for a drink?'

The driver gave him a bewildered look. 'To see the barber.'

'It's an odd time for a haircut and a shave,' Owen said. 'Shouldn't he see a doctor instead?'

Now Overmyer looked at him with bewilderment, too. 'We don't have one. He's damn lucky we've got a barber.'

The comment made no sense to Owen. 'Why? Is he cleaning himself up for the mortician?'

'That's not funny.' Overmyer rushed past Owen into the saloon.

'It was a serious question.' Owen followed him inside and was surprised to see the injured man laid out on top of a table, the barber and Tuttle examining the man's bloated, black leg.

Tuttle shared a few words with Dora, who rushed past them out the door, then he joined Overmyer and Owen in the doorway.

'Ledru says he's gonna have to amputate. I've sent Dora to fetch a hacksaw from the butcher.'

Owen was still deeply confused. 'Wait a minute. You're going to let the barber cut off the man's leg?'

'It can't be saved,' Tuttle said.

'I get that,' Owen said, trying not to sound patronizing. 'But he's a barber. What does he know about medicine?'

'Before he went into business for himself, Ledru was a barber in the cavalry,' Tuttle said. 'He knows what he's doing.'

Tuttle said it like it changed things, like it made any rational sense. But even if it did, which it certainly didn't to Owen, there was so much more that was wrong with this.

'So, based on that, you're going to let the barber saw off a man's leg right here, in the saloon, on a table where people eat and drink?' Owen looked around and, to his dismay, he saw the early breakfast customers didn't seem the least bit disturbed by what was going on. They were continuing to eat, barely paying any attention to the man on the table at all.

'We've got a blanket on the table and we've put some dirt on the floor to catch the flesh and blood,' Tuttle said.

'I can't believe you're letting this happen,' Owen said.

'What do you suggest we do, Ben? Let the poor man die?'

Overmyer said, 'It might already be too late if the poison and infection have spread past his leg.'

'At least this way he has a chance.' Tuttle grabbed two bottles of whiskey and brought them over to the barber.

Owen turned to Overmyer. 'Be reasonable, Hank. He's a barber, for God's sake. This is a saloon.'

'What's your point? Sometimes I don't understand you at all.' Overmyer went over to the table to watch the operation.

Owen hoped he'd never need a doctor or worse, the barber. Mining-camp medicine was absolutely barbaric. Was he the only one who realized that? He turned and saw Milly and Esther at the bar. They seemed as relaxed about the imminent amputation as everybody else. That answered his question. But he wasn't going to stand here and watch the human butchery.

He approached Milly. 'Would you like to help me prepare breakfast?'

'I can't,' she said. 'Business always picks up after an amputation.'

'You're kidding,' he said.

Esther piped in. 'It reminds a man how important all his appendages are and to take proper care of 'em while they're still attached.'

'Not me,' he said.

'You ain't normal,' Esther said. 'You haven't had a poke since you got here and we know you can afford it.' She tipped her head to Milly. 'She'd probably give you one for nothing.'

Milly gave him a warm look that confirmed that Esther was right.

'I'm saving myself for marriage,' Owen said.

'She'd be up for that, too,' Esther said.

Sally gave her a hard elbow in the side.

Owen went to the kitchen with his bag of onions. The amputation began a few minutes later but it didn't slow down the breakfast orders at all.

A little over an hour later, the now one-legged prospector was taken to a boarding house to recover or die, the bloody dirt and severed leg were tossed in Jack Ass Gulch, the table was wiped down, the barber went back to giving shaves, and business in the saloon resumed as if nothing had happened.

Owen was still shaken, but he had to accept that in the 1880s, it was normal that the barber, in the absence of an actual doctor, performed surgery in a dining room. He'd have to add it to the list of all things he didn't know.

So far, being from the future, with all the knowledge of things to come, hadn't given him any edge at all.

When business ebbed in mid-afternoon, he ventured into the saloon to have his customary cup of coffee with the Judge, Overmyer, and Tuttle. He was surprised to see three nuns in the saloon, along with a man in a pin-striped suit, mingling with the customers at their tables. Esther came in a side door with one of her satisfied customers and scowled when she saw the women.

Owen asked, 'Where did those nuns come from?'

The Judge replied, 'They aren't nuns, but they're just as pure.'

Overmyer said, 'I'd like to test that theory.'

Tuttle said, 'So would every man in Waterman Junction they serve food to at the Harvey House.'

Owen had heard of the Harvey House, but as a chain of roadside coffee shops along Route 66 that had largely disappeared, along with the mother road itself. He didn't know they existed in the 1800s. 'They're waitresses?'

'They are more than that,' the Judge said. 'They are refined single women, with at least an eighth-grade education, who've signed a six-month work contract in return for eighteen dollars a month in pay, room, and board.'

Owen scrutinized the women now. What he mistook for nuns' habits were long black collared shirtdresses with white dress-like pinafore aprons over them. The women were clean, pale, and prim, with severe black-and-white bonnets on their pinned-up hair that seemed more religious than culinary.

His gaze drifted to one woman, and was immediately struck by her bright smile and her curvaceous figure.

The smile.

The curves.

He felt a chill of recognition roll down his spine, a sensation that was both frightening and exciting because he'd never met or seen the woman before.

But he knew her secret.

The Judge prattled on. 'The women are trained in etiquette, live in a dormitory under the strict supervision of a matron, and agree not to fraternize with any men while under Harvey's employ. They can't even talk to each other in front of the customers. That man is their chaperone and the manager of the restaurant.'

Overmyer gave him an incredulous look. 'How do you know all of that?'

'I've dined there a few times in my travels, less for their food than the service. You can have an intelligent, informed discussion about literature, politics, and science with these women while you dine.'

Tuttle snickered. 'Since when do you want to have "informed discussions" with a woman?'

'I enjoy engaging in all manner of social intercourse with the fairer sex,' the Judge said. 'But this is a town predominantly of men and the few women here are either married, and therefore stuck in their cabins performing their menial labors and child-rearing, or are single entrepreneurs in too much of a hurry to conclude their business to have a satisfying conversation.'

At that moment, the man in the suit addressed the room in a loud, commanding voice.

'Good afternoon, gentlemen. My name is Ambrose Felder, and my staff and I are visiting Calico today to invite you to visit the Harvey House in Waterman Junction, where you will experience gourmet dining and exceptional service provided by gracious, well-mannered, and highly educated young women who will see to your every need.'

Esther shouted out: '*Every* need?'

The men chortled. Ambrose smiled, not the least bit flustered.

'Of a virtuous nature, of course,' he said. 'We are a respectable establishment of the highest order, ma'am . . .' And then, seemingly aware of how this might be taken, glanced at Tuttle and added, 'Where families with children, as well as the discerning single adult traveler, can dine in comfort and style.'

Tuttle nodded, as if to acknowledge no offense was taken. But Overmyer wasn't as easily mollified.

'In other words, not like this place,' Overmyer said. 'I'm surprised you let that prick in here, Dave.'

'We aren't competitors,' Tuttle said. 'In fact, the prick has agreed to recommend the saloon to travelers heading this way.'

Ambrose continued his pitch to the dining room of largely disinterested miners.

'When you visit our establishment, you can exchange the coupon we're giving you for a generous slice of pie with a cup of coffee, a twenty-cent value, free of charge.'

Owen hadn't heard a word anybody said since he'd laid eyes on the one, striking waitress. And now she approached the bar and handed them coupons. He looked at her bright, white, perfect teeth, and her full bosom, and whispered to her.

'I know where you're from.'

'Now that you do, I hope you'll come visit us soon. We're right in the train station.'

She smiled and moved on. Owen wasn't sure whether what he was seeing and feeling was real or wishful thinking, but he knew a sure way to find out.

Ambrose and the women started to head for the door. Owen hurried across the saloon to the piano, sat down on the bench, and immediately began to play, and sing, the *Gilligan's Island* theme, about a handful of tourists, including a professor and a movie star, who embarked on a three-hour sailing tour.

The striking woman he'd been talking to froze, then turned around slowly to face him, apparently in shock. He felt a thrill of excitement as he kept his eyes locked on hers and sang about the boat getting tossed around in a storm and everyone ending up shipwrecked on an island.

Overmyer turned to his friends. 'I don't know what possessed him to break into song, but this is much more cheerful than the last tune he played.'

Tuttle nodded in agreement. 'Yes, it is . . . but what's a movie star?'

'I think it's French for whore,' Overmyer said.

As Owen continued on to sing the end theme, hitting the part about the castaways being stuck on that uncharted isle for a long, long time, the woman seemed to snap out of her shock and appraised him from head to toe.

And that's when her gaze landed on his Nike running shoes.

Her eyes went wide. She dropped her coupons on the floor and started moving across the saloon towards Owen.

Ambrose called after her. 'Wendy, it's time to go!'

But Wendy ignored him, picking up her pace.

Owen kept singing, about how primitive life would be for the castaways without their modern amenities.

She let out a cry, akin to a war whoop, and launched herself at him, grabbing him by the collar and lifting him to his feet.

'Who the fuck are you?' she shouted. 'Why are you doing this to me?'

SIXTEEN

It wasn't quite the response Owen was hoping for, but close enough. He spoke quickly and quietly, choosing his words carefully in case he was overheard. 'I'm trapped here, just like you.'

Ambrose rushed over to her. 'Let go of him!'

Wendy whirled around and pointed a finger at Ambrose.

'Back off. We're talking.' She turned back to Owen. 'How many others are there?'

'You're the first one I've met.'

Ambrose said, 'Do you know this man?'

Owen smiled at Ambrose over the woman's shoulder. 'Give us a minute, please.'

Owen led Wendy off to a corner of the dining room, where they continued to speak in whispers.

'How did you know where, I mean *when*, I'm from?' Wendy asked.

'You have to promise not to slap me if I tell you.'

'I'll slap you if you don't.'

'Your teeth,' he said. 'And your boobs.'

She looked down at her chest. 'What's wrong with them?'

'Nothing. They're perfect. That's the tell. You've had orthodonture and implants.' He smiled and she studied his teeth. 'You wouldn't believe the headgear and rubber bands I had to wear in high school to get this smile.'

She smiled, too. 'I thought I was alone.'

'So did I.'

Ambrose stepped between them and faced Wendy. 'That's quite enough. Fraternizing with men is strictly forbidden. You know that. We're going now.'

He grabbed her left forearm, but she wrenched herself free.

'Let go of me. I'm staying.'

Her statement surprised Owen, but he was glad to hear it.

'Don't be absurd,' Ambrose said with a dismissive laugh. 'You can't. You signed a six-month contract with us, remember?'

She got in his face. 'I do and it expired three weeks ago. Or did you forget to keep track?'

The two other Harvey Girls laughed. Ambrose's face turned red with anger. He gave the girls a furious look that shut them up right away, then he turned back to Wendy, a cruel smile on his face.

'You want to stay in this hell-hole? Fine with me. But that uniform belongs to us and can only be worn by employees, which you no longer are.'

'No problem.' Without hesitating, she tossed off her bonnet at him, which he caught, then she untied her pinafore apron, letting it drop to the floor.

Tuttle turned to Overmyer and the Judge. 'Hell-hole? Is he talking about my saloon or this town?'

'It could be both,' Overmyer said.

'And the people who live here,' the Judge said, clearly offended but staring at Wendy.

She began unbuttoning the front of her black dress, staring defiantly at Ambrose as she did it. One of the miners began to whistle, and another whooped, but that didn't bother her at all. Wendy let the dress drop to the floor, then stepped out of it, wearing only her short-sleeved laced chemise and cotton bloomers that reached nearly to her knees.

'I like this woman,' the Judge said.

'What's not to like?' Tuttle said.

She kicked off her shiny black shoes at Ambrose, who had to dodge to avoid being hit by them. If he'd meant to embarrass her, he'd failed. She put her hands on her hips. 'You can send my accumulated salary to the Wells Fargo agent here.'

Ambrose laughed and gathered up shoes and clothes. 'As far as I am concerned, your depraved language and indecent conduct today broke both the terms and spirit of your contract, therefore your earnings to date are forfeited.'

The Judge spoke up. 'Your interpretation of the terms is meaningless, sir. You are contractually obligated to pay her.'

'Stay out of this,' he said. 'It's none of your business.'

'On the contrary. It's a legal matter, and therefore very much my business. I'm Josiah Orville, the Justice of the Peace . . . and the Wells Fargo agent. You'll send me this young woman's pay within seven days or I'll dispatch a deputy to arrest you.'

Ambrose looked at him in disbelief. 'On what charge?'

'Embezzlement. Fraud. Indentured servitude and overall despicable conduct unbefitting a civilized man or the manager of a Harvey House.'

The men in the saloon all applauded. Ambrose glared at the Judge, then motioned to the two other girls to follow him and stormed out of the saloon.

Wendy walked barefoot, and shamelessly, over to the bar and smiled at the Judge. Owen followed her, a bit dazed by the startling turn of events.

He wasn't alone. She was from the future, too. And if she was, how many others were there?

Wendy smiled at the Judge. 'Thank you, your honor.'

He removed his stove-pipe hat and gave her a slight bow. 'It was entirely my pleasure as well as my duty, young lady.'

Tuttle said, 'You can have a job here if you want it.'

'What kind of job?'

'Waitress. Card dealer.' Tuttle glanced at Esther, then added: 'Or movie star.'

Wendy sat down on a stool beside the Judge.

'Right now I'll settle for a whiskey.' She tipped her head towards Owen. 'The piano player is buying.'

Tuttle set a shot glass down in front of her and picked up a bottle of whiskey. 'It's on the house.'

He quickly poured her a drink. She knocked it back.

Owen said, 'We need to get you some clothes.'

'No rush. It's damn hot here and it feels good to be wearing less.'

'Yeah, Ben,' Overmyer said. 'No rush.'

The publisher gestured to Tuttle to refill her glass, which he did. She picked up the glass and looked at Owen.

'Is there somewhere we can talk?'

'The kitchen.'

He led her out of the dining room and into the kitchen, and when he was sure nobody was within earshot, he said:

'They are going to have lots of questions, so we need to get our stories straight. My name is Ben Cartwright.'

'The dad on *Bonanza*?'

'I don't think it's a good idea to use our real names here. It could mess up the future.'

'But why that name? Why not James Bond? Or Bruce Wayne? Or Indiana Jones?'

'They aren't cowboys,' he said.

'Nobody *here* knows that.'

'Stay focused,' he said. 'You and I had a relationship in San Francisco before I went off to Europe. That's all they need to know.'

'How come I didn't recognize you when we spoke at the bar?'

'It's been years and you've never seen me clean-shaven.'

'I can sell that,' she said. 'How can you make a living as a piano player?'

'I can't. I'm the executive chef. That was my profession in our time, too. What was yours?'

'Being beautiful but I mostly waited tables between modeling gigs. I was Miss Teen Route 66 and then Miss Barstow, which I hoped would lead me soon to Miss California, then on to Miss America and a career in fashion, or acting.'

'That explains how you got a job as a Harvey Girl.'

'I'm all about poise and etiquette,' Wendy said. 'How did you get here?'

Owen lowered his voice to a near whisper. 'I was driving from

Las Vegas to LA when a rip in time opened up right in front of me, down there where the interstate should be.'

'You have *a car*?' she said, her voice spiking with excitement.

'It's hidden in a cave. I also have this . . .' Owen stepped outside, looked all around, then reached up on the roof, and pulled down the solar battery. He held it out to her.

'What is it?'

'A solar battery.' He put it back. 'I use it to charge this . . .' He slipped the iPhone briefly out of his pocket to show her. 'Among other things.'

She looked bewildered. 'What's that?'

'An iPhone 10. I guess you're into Androids,' he said. 'I hope yours isn't with the stuff you left behind at the Harvey House.'

'You think I have . . . an android?' She stared at him. 'What was the exact date you drove through that rip?'

'February 2nd, 2019.'

'And people have androids. Wow. That happened sooner than I imagined. Oh well, one more thing I'll miss out on.'

She knocked back the shot of whiskey.

Now he stared at her as he came to a realization. 'It's the brand name of a cell phone, not a robot. When are you from?'

'Bet you never asked a girl that before.' She tossed the shot glass across the room. It broke against the wall. 'February 2nd, 1992.'

He let that sink in.

Wendy noticed. 'You think that's weird? Imagine what it's like for me. I'm stuck in the past meeting a man from the future.'

'How did it happen?'

'I woke up in the middle of the night and saw a portal to another world in my bedroom closet, like *The Lion, the Witch and the Wardrobe*, one of my all-time favorite books.'

'The Chronicles of Narnia. I read them, too.'

'I was obviously dreaming, so I got up and walked barefoot, wearing only a tank-top and panties, through the portal. But it wasn't in Narnia I stepped into,' Wendy said. 'It was shithole Barstow back when it was an even worse shithole called Waterman Junction.'

'Those are harsh words coming from a former Miss Barstow.'

'That's right. Who'd know more about Barstow than me?'

He felt a jolt of excitement. Of possibility. Of hope. 'Does that mean you know the history of this area?'

'I've visited this ghost town a dozen times and wrote a report about it in seventh grade. Got a B+.'

'That knowledge could be very useful,' he said.

'More than yours?'

'I've stopped here once and have driven past it many times,' Owen said. 'I know it's doomed in a few years. But beyond that, the earliest historical event coming up that I'm aware of is the San Francisco earthquake in 1903.'

'1906.'

'My point is,' he said, 'it's decades away and knowing about it is no help to us now.'

'What about your technology? Is time travel a thing in 2019? Is your car like the one in *Back to the Future*?'

'No, it's not a time-traveling DeLorean,' he said. 'And nobody has hoverboards, either.'

'That's disappointing,' Wendy said.

That's when Dora Tuttle marched in, holding a dress and a pair of boots.

'I'm Dora Tuttle, my husband Dave and I own this saloon. I heard what happened to you. Actually, the whole town has by now.' She held out the dress and shoes to Wendy. 'I can loan you this outfit today so you can go shopping. We can't have you running around Calico half-naked with that body. It could cause a riot. You won't find dresses here, but you'll do fine in men's clothes until you can order something from a catalog.'

'That's very kind of you,' Wendy said, 'but I don't have any money.'

Owen said, 'I'll pay for it.'

'That's not necessary,' Dora said. 'Her credit is good in Calico. Thanks to the Judge, everybody knows that your salary is on the way. Ben needs to start cooking dinner and you need clothes, so come along.'

Wendy looked back at Owen, who waved her off. 'I'll see you tonight.'

The two women left. Alone in the kitchen, Owen let the momentous events of the day sink in. He wasn't alone in this nightmare anymore.

The men's clothes didn't do anything to diminish Wendy's beauty, not even in the dark of a desert night. Owen met her in the saloon

after the supper rush and walked with her to the northern edge of
town, where they settled on a rocky point with a sweeping view of
moonlit Calico and the dry lake beyond.

'At night, this town looks a lot better,' he said.

'Smells better, too. The past really stinks,' she said. 'You'd think
that would have made it into the history books.'

'Maybe here it's worse because water is in such short supply.
Nobody wants to waste it on washing anything.'

'I've made my own toothpaste out of baking soda, water, and
some sugar. What about you?'

'I've still got some Crest in my shaving kit.'

'Lucky you,' Wendy said. 'You wouldn't happen to have any
tampons?'

'Afraid not.'

'Being a woman in 1882 is a living hell.'

Owen shook his head. 'This is not how it's supposed to be.'

'What do you mean?'

'The heroes in time-travel stories never worry about toiletries
. . . or toilets. They have detailed historical knowledge and
superior skills, like being a surgeon or an engineer, that gives
them a big edge over everybody in the past. But me? I can make a
soufflé. Not much of an edge.'

'It's not an accident that I'm in Calico today,' she said. 'I
volunteered for this marketing trip, though I didn't plan on ending
up in my underwear in a saloon.'

'What was your plan?'

'To see how far along the silver boom is here. It's still early days,
Ben. A year from now, there will be two thousand people here,
dozens of mines in the mountains, and a hundred stamps pounding
ore. But today only a tiny fraction of the silver that's out there has
been found.'

'Do you know where it is?'

'I know the general area where some of the big strikes will be. I
want to find one of them first, stake a claim, and lease it back to a
mining company for some big, upfront cash that will set me up
nice for life, because unless you have the blueprints to build a
time machine, I'm stuck in the past until I die.'

'You may know roughly where the mines will be, but there are
a lot of experienced prospectors crawling over these mountains right

now, hunting for signs of ore. What makes you think you can find the silver before they do? Are you a geologist?'

'No, I'm not, but I've got a community college education, which is like a Master's degree in quantum physics compared to the education these prospectors have,' Wendy said. 'I'm also a beauty queen from the future.'

'Aren't you worried that what you do will change it?'

'There was a woman prospector who struck it rich in Calico. Why can't she be me?'

'Because she wasn't you,' Owen said.

'She's not in Calico yet, never had kids, and died a penniless drunk. So she had zero impact on the future.'

'How do you know all that?'

'My seventh-grade report was about her,' Wendy said. 'Besides, even if I find silver, how do we know she still won't show up, strike it rich, and completely fuck up her life?'

We don't, he thought. 'Good point. What will you need?'

'A burro, saddle, and harness, prospecting tools, and money to live on while I look around. It could take a few weeks, maybe even a few months, before I discover some silver. But I will.'

'How can you be so certain?'

'Because people dumber and less attractive than me did. I learned in my report that the great thing about the silver here is that it's shallow, and the veins run horizontal, close to the surface, so miners tunnel for it at different levels of a mountain or canyon rather than dig shafts. It also means you can sometimes spot the veins of silver in plain sight on a canyon wall, or on the ground, or in scattered rocks rich with ore as you stroll along. How hard could it be?'

He liked her confidence. And at least she had some historical knowledge that could give them an edge. 'We'll get you equipped tomorrow.'

'I don't have that kind of money. A good mule alone costs fifty dollars.'

'I've already got some of what you need and enough money saved up to buy the rest,' Owen said. 'Plus, I'll keep working while you prospect, so there will be cashflow.'

'Why would you do that? You don't even know me.'

'Because we time-travelers have to stick together, and I want half of whatever you find in return for my investment.'

'It could be fifty percent of nothing,' she said.

'Then I won't be much worse off than I am now.'

She held out her hand. 'You have a deal.'

They shook on it. 'Great,' Owen said.

'I'd like to see your cave and your car.'

'We'll do that tomorrow. I talked Tuttle into letting me have the day off to settle things with you.'

'What is there to settle?'

'We have a complicated past,' he said.

'Technically we have the future, though my future was in your past, unless I would have outlived you, which is possible, since I'm guessing I am about ten years younger than you are, which would have made you part of my future and my future past. But now you are my future and my present while I am your past and present.'

'Like I said, it's complicated,' he said. 'Do you have a family?'

'My parents, my grandparents, and some aunts and uncles,' she said. 'I'm an only child.'

'I am, too,' he said. 'But my parents have both passed away.'

They sat there, staring out at Calico, taking in the view in silence, the pounding of the stamp mills like a shared heartbeat they both felt and heard.

After a time, Wendy said: 'What do you miss most from your time?'

'My daughter Nicole. She's twelve and lives with my ex-girlfriend in Silver Lake. All I can give her now is the certainty of her existence.'

She looked at him. 'How can you possibly do that?'

'Calico will be abandoned, and fall into ruins, decades before it's recreated as a tourist trap, so I know there'll be no trace that I was ever here. And this desert barely changes over the next hundred and thirty-seven years,' he said. 'So this is where I'm going to stay, and try not to do anything that will prevent me from being born and fathering her, though for all I know, maybe I already have just by being here.'

She nodded. 'At least you have something to live for besides yourself. I'm just trying to make it through each day . . . just like I was doing in the future.'

'What do you miss the most?'

She looked at him again and smiled. 'Tampons.'

SEVENTEEN

The next morning, Owen met Wendy outside of the boarding house and gave her Mr Ed. The donkey was outfitted with the rig and all the prospecting tools Owen had inherited, though he knew she'd need more. So they went to Stoby's store, where the shopkeeper gladly set her up with a canteen and other equipment that she'd need . . . including a gun for protection. A woman alone in the mountains, especially a beauty queen from the future, would be vulnerable. She didn't argue with him.

They left Mr Ed and her prospecting supplies at the livery stable and went to see the Judge, who explained to them how to legally stake a claim, and mark the actual spot with a monument of stones, if she was lucky to discover ore.

Afterwards, Owen and Wendy made the three-mile walk to his cave, where she was wowed by his car, especially the flat-screen monitor mounted on the dashboard, though it wasn't very impressive without any satellites and cellular networks to connect with.

He lit a campfire and prepared beef burritos for lunch, which she devoured, then he opened up his MacBook and showed her some of his personal travel videos, and episodes of his cooking show, so she could see what the future looked like . . . which both excited and depressed her, since she knew she'd never live to see it with her own eyes.

To make her feel better, he let her brush her teeth with his toothpaste, which she seemed to enjoy more than sex, not that they had any.

Over the next few months, Wendy and Mr Ed became a familiar and much ridiculed presence among the prospectors working the steep, craggy mountains and narrow, twisting canyons of the Calicos.

Every morning Wendy and Mr Ed would venture out at sun-up, spend the day collecting rock samples from promising spots, and bring them back in the afternoon for the Judge, in his role as assayer, to examine for silver content. He found little or none, but she wasn't discouraged.

She and Owen would get together almost every night, in his SUV in the cave, or in her room at the boarding house, share a set of iPods, and listen to music on his iPhone or watch one of the many bootleg movies and TV shows stored as .mp4 or .avi files on his MacBook. He also let her shoot some movies, and take some photos, of her own with his iPhone. Owen became more attracted to her with each passing day, but was afraid if he acted on his feelings, or spoke of them, he'd scare off the one person who knew his secret, understood his fears, and saved him from feeling utterly alone.

One morning, after Wendy had breakfast with Owen at the saloon, and headed off for another day of prospecting, Tuttle stood at the bar and watched her go, then said to Owen:

'There are cheaper ways to get into a woman's bloomers than grub-staking her rock-hunting.'

'It's not like that,' Owen said, finishing a cup of coffee.

'What is it, then?'

'There are people making fortunes out there and I'd like to be one of them. Thanks to her, I can be in two places at once, because I'm sure as hell not going to strike it rich cooking here all day.'

'That's where you're wrong. Unless you're a mining company, this is where the only fortunes are made.'

'What about the prospectors who lease their claims to the mining companies for huge sacks of money?'

'Sure, there are maybe a dozen lucky bastards like that at each camp. But then there's the thousands of other men who work themselves to the bone, pounding at rocks deep in the earth, and if they're lucky, they can keep two bits in their pockets each day after paying the cost of living, which is what they give to us,' Tuttle said, picking up the coffee pot behind the counter and refreshing Owen's cup. 'Most of the miners and prospectors end up broke and broken in the same ground they've been digging in. And we merchants move along, fat and happy and flush, to the next mining camp to do it all over again . . . until we're ready to retire on a nice ranch somewhere.'

'The companies are mining silver and you're mining the men.'

'That's how you strike it rich,' Tuttle said.

'It's a depressing way to become wealthy.'

Tuttle shrugged. 'It's even more depressing if you don't.'

That afternoon, a Thursday, Wendy returned to the saloon from her prospecting as dirty and smelly as any miner, and headed straight for the kitchen, drawing stares as she always did. She was dressed in a man's cowboy hat, a man's shirt opened to a hint of cleavage, and denim pants worn tight with gun belt around her hips. It was such an effective outfit with the men that Esther and Milly were thinking of dressing the same way themselves. Wendy found Owen making pasta.

'How'd it go today?' he asked. She walked up, pulled him to her, and gave him a deep, hungry kiss that jacked up his heart rate like he'd been zapped with defibrillator paddles. 'What was that for?'

'The Judge says each milligram of silver derived from twenty-nine grams of rock reflects the presence of one troy ounce of silver in two thousand pounds of ore.'

He didn't know what she was talking about. 'OK . . . so what does that mean?'

'The silver value of the samples I brought in today from a spot way up in Odessa Canyon is $200 a ton. I'll dig up a few more stones . . . and if they are as rich in ore as the sample today, then we've struck it rich. We could lease the claim to a mining company for $30,000 which, by my reckoning, is close to $1 million in future money.'

'How do you figure that?'

'The price of shoes today compared to what they cost in our time,' Wendy said.

'I've never heard of the shoe standard in calculating inflation.'

'You don't have my keen financial mind.'

'We should celebrate,' he said.

'We will, quietly, just the two of us, because right now, it's our secret. I filled out the claim and made the Judge promise to keep his mouth shut. Tomorrow, I'll go back up the canyon, stake the claim with three piles of stones, and make it official. Until then, the claim is vulnerable to being jumped if word gets out.'

'What do you want to do tonight?'

'Have a hot bath with soap and first water. You should, too. We deserve it,' she sniffed around him and made a sour face. 'And need it.'

First water meant water that nobody else had used before, which he knew cost extra, and having it heated cost even more, as did the soap. It would easily cost $3 for each of them. He'd never done it since he'd arrived in Calico.

'Then what?' Owen asked.

'Come to my room and we'll figure something out that won't draw attention.' She kissed him again, tenderly, and left.

Owen had heard the best bathhouses were in Chinatown, so that's where he went. He had his half-hour bath, in a wooden tub, with hot water poured on him by a Chinaman, who then brutally scrubbed him with a bar of soap and a stiff brush. It felt like he was being sanded down, but after the sting had passed, his skin felt smooth and clean.

Afterwards, he dressed in a fresh shirt, underwear, and pants that he'd bought at Stoby's that evening because he didn't want to put on dirty clothes after a $3 bath, so he ended up spending three times as much as the bath by itself. But he figured he was a rich man now, he could afford some extravagance. As he was getting dressed, he saw the dirt-caked miner come in who'd be bathing in his soapy water. Owen had seen him in the saloon, but didn't know him by name.

'Were you first water?' the miner asked.

'Yes, I was,' Owen said.

The miner broke into a big, nearly toothless smile. 'Then this is my lucky day.'

'Why's that?'

'You're one of the cleanest men in camp. Last time I got a bath, I was the second man, but I still came out dirtier than when I went in.'

Owen stuffed his dirty clothes into a burlap sack and left before the miner undressed. He hurried through the Chinese camp, the air thick with the intoxicating aromas of grilled fish, Asian spices, and oils coming from the meals being prepared outside the shanties and tents. As he crossed the rickety bridge over Jack Ass Gulch to town, he thought about coming back to the Chinese camp one day and buying some of their ingredients to add an Asian flair to his own cooking. But on second thought, he decided his clientele might not be ready for fusion cuisine. Then again, he didn't have to tell them that's what they were eating.

He went to the boarding house, which was one-story row of a dozen individual rooms that reminded him of a small motel, with a few burros parked out front instead of cars. He knocked on Wendy's door and she told him to come in.

Owen opened the door into darkness, though he knew from past visits that there was only a single bed, a chest of drawers that doubled as a table, two chairs, and a chamber pot. It took a moment for his eyes to adjust and then he saw her, standing naked in front of the bed. His breath caught in his throat. She was like a ghost. A beautiful ghost. A memory of something he once had, once felt, and thought he never would again.

'Are you going to just stand there gawking at me,' Wendy said softly. 'Or are you going to take off your clothes?'

He dropped the burlap bag on the floor and undressed.

They made love fast and hard the first time, slow and gentle the second, and even slower the third, lying languidly afterward, wrapped around each other, as much to be close as to keep themselves from falling off the narrow bed.

Wendy said, 'I think we've done some things they haven't discovered here yet and that might be considered immoral, if not illegal, if anybody knew about it.'

'On the other hand,' Owen said, 'we could make a fortune as sex educators if your claim doesn't pan out.'

'You pan for gold,' she said. 'You dig for silver.'

'I stand corrected.'

She reached between his legs. 'Not yet, old man. I fear if we teach women today about the clitoral orgasm, or instruct men about how to induce it, we could radically change the future.'

'You're right. We should keep this powerful erotic knowledge to ourselves.'

'Isn't that why you've remained celibate until I came along?'

'What makes you think I have?' he said.

'Esther told me. You haven't been with her or any of the other women in town. She asked around.'

'Why would she do that?'

'Because she couldn't figure out why you weren't interested in sex. But once I showed up, she had her answer,' Wendy said. 'You were just waiting for the right woman to come along.'

'One from the future,' he said.

'That's right. A woman who wouldn't be shocked by your sexual techniques and wouldn't tell other people what she'd learned.'

'I like the idea that here and now I'm a Sex God,' Owen said. 'I certainly wasn't in my time. But there is another, simpler explanation you haven't considered. Maybe I was waiting until I fell in love.'

'The only thing you were waiting for was me to make the first move.'

'But I didn't resist,' he said.

'Of course you didn't, you're a solitary man who hasn't had sex in months and I'm a beauty queen.'

'So you don't think I love you.'

'Oh, I know you do. You've loved me from the moment you saw me,' Wendy said. 'You were just afraid of scaring me off.'

'Have I?'

'I'm in love, too, you idiot. I waited until now to throw myself at you because I didn't want you to think that I'm desperate or settling for the first man from the future that comes along.'

'But you are.'

'Wholeheartedly.'

And then she kissed him.

EIGHTEEN

The next day, Wendy went up into the mountains to stake their claim and collect more rocks, returning to town in time for the Judge to do another assay before his Friday night trial.

With the rapid expansion of the mines, and the massive influx of new miners, the Judge finally had plenty of legal disputes and crimes to adjudicate, which he did each Friday night on the front porch of his cabin.

The trials were big entertainment events, the equivalent of a concert or play, and drew a sizeable crowd that usually liked to have a good meal beforehand, so it brought a lot of business to Tuttle's Saloon and all the other eateries in town. All those mouths to feed, and all at once, kept Owen too busy to meet and talk with Wendy. So he didn't find out that her new rocks assayed as highly as the first samples until after supper service, when they met outside on the street on their way to the Judge's cabin for court.

'That's fantastic news,' Owen said. 'So what's the next step?'

'I'll approach some of the local mine operators, show them the Judge's assays, and offer them the first chance at leasing our claim, maybe get a bidding war going,' Wendy said. 'If they turn me down, then I'll wire some of the East Coast mining companies that haven't got a toehold here yet.'

'I like the way you think.'

'That's not all you like.' She squeezed his hand and didn't let go as they continued walking.

Wind blew southwest through the town, kicking up the dirt, but it was a welcome relief from the oppressive desert heat. It was a pleasant evening to be out. Just about everybody who would otherwise have been patronizing Calico's businesses, as well as the merchants themselves, were attending court, except for the soiled doves, who used the time to get a good nap.

The Judge sat on his porch behind a table with a gavel, a couple of law books, and one book of Greek fables on top as props to add some legal decorum to the frontier setting. He referred to a sheet of paper with a list of the disputes to consider and read the particulars of the first case to the audience of easily two hundred onlookers. Overmyer stood at the edge of the crowd, taking notes.

The first case involved a miner named Gould who was charging shopkeeper Stoby with assault for throwing him into Jack Ass Gulch, which everybody knew was Stoby's favored method of dealing with men who chatted up Evelyn, Stoby's young mail-order wife. Stoby had also banned Gould from ever entering the store again. Gould was demanding damages to cover the injuries to his person, the various abrasions sustained in his fall, and the subsequent shame of walking through the streets covered in human waste and garbage.

The Judge looked up from his notes and addressed Gould, who

stood in front of the audience, along with all the other people with cases before the court. 'Is this an accurate summation of your complaint, Mr Gould?'

Gould took off his hat and held it in his hands as a sign of respect for the Judge. 'Yes, sir. And I am most aggrieved.'

The Judge looked at Stoby. 'Did you toss this fellow into the Gulch?'

'Hell yes, I did, and I had every right to do it,' Stoby said. 'He was making improper advances to my wife. He's lucky I didn't bust his jaw, too.'

The Judge looked out into the audience. 'Were there any witnesses to this altercation?'

Another man stepped forward, clearly a miner as well, the fine layer of red dust on him from head to toe showing he'd come straight from the tunnels for this.

'I saw him chattin' up Miss Evelyn,' the miner said.

Stoby pointed a finger at him. 'That's Mrs Stoby to you.'

The Judge ignored Stoby's interjection. 'And you are, sir?'

'Earl Pudney.'

'Do you know Mr Gould?' the Judge asked.

'I've seen him around some but no, we aren't friends,' Pudney said. 'We aren't enemies, neither.'

'So you're stating, under penalty of perjury, that you didn't collaborate with him on your testimony.'

Pudney nodded. 'That's right, your honor.'

'Very well. Were Mr Gould's comments to Mrs Stoby lewd or suggestive in nature?'

'I couldn't say, but he was telling her how pretty she is . . .' Pudney's gaze drifted over to her and stayed there. '. . . and how everything she wears fits her so nice and how she smells better than a bunch of flowers and that seeing her each day is like seeing the sun rise.'

She smiled at him and Stoby's face turned bright red. He wagged a finger at Pudney again.

'You watch your mouth, Pudney, or I'll toss you too.'

The Judge ignored Stoby's remark and addressed himself to Pudney again. 'Did Mr Gould's comments involve unwanted physical advances?'

'He tipped his hat to her and followed her around the store a bit.'

Stoby said, 'The drooling animal was chasing her for a grope.'

The audience laughed and the Judge hammered his gavel on the table. 'Order in the court! Order in the court!'

When things died down, the Judge returned to his questioning of Pudney:

'Did it appear to you, Mr Pudney, that she was trying to evade him?'

'Naw, she was just going about her business.'

'Did she appear irritated, offended, or frightened by his comments or attention?'

'She smiled, thanked him kindly, and that's when Stoby grabbed him from behind, carried him out of the store, and heaved him into the ravine,' Pudney said.

The crowd roared with laughter. When it abated, the Judge turned his attention to Evelyn, who was clearly embarrassed by the attention.

'Mrs Stoby, did you feel harassed or endangered by Mr Gould?'

Evelyn said, 'No sir, Mr Gould is nice man.'

Stoby rolled his eyes. 'You ain't never been off the farm, Ev. You think all the men who come in the store are nice.'

'They are to me,' she said.

'Because they're trying to court you,' he said.

'How can that be if my husband is standing right there?'

'That's why I have to toss 'em,' Stoby said. 'If I didn't, they'd just be encouraged to do more.'

The audience laughed again. The Judge banged his gavel until the laughter died down.

'I've heard enough and am ready to make my ruling.' He cleared his throat and waited until he had everyone's full attention before he continued.

'Flirtation is one of the great pleasures of civilized life and so is appreciating the beauty of a fine woman. Even the theologians and scholars of Greece waxed poetic about it.' He tapped the thick book of Greek fables. 'Mr Stoby, what your wife is doing by allowing it, perhaps even enjoying it, is called courtesy. I dare say it's also shrewd salesmanship. There are other general stores in Calico. You should be delighted that men still prefer yours over the others, despite the ever-present threat of violent physical expulsion, just to experience your wife's cheerful, friendly service to enliven their souls before descending into the dark, cruel depths of the earth to endure their brutal, pitiless labors.'

His description of the miners' toils drew agreeable grunts from the appreciative audience. The Judge stole a sideways glance at Overmyer, who was taking down every word and gave him a subtle nod of approval.

Wendy whispered to Owen. 'The Judge should be a politician.'

'The Justice of the Peace is an elected position.'

'Ah-ha,' she said.

The Judge addressed himself to Stoby. 'Does Mr Gould presently have a debt in your store?'

'Seven dollars and two bits,' Stoby said.

'It's hereby erased,' the Judge said. 'And if you eject another man into the gulch, it better be for a serious violation of decency or I'll get some men together to toss you in there and then lock you up in this cell for a week. Do I make myself clear?'

Duly chastised, Stoby lowered his head in acceptance. 'Yes, your honor.'

Gould cleared his throat and stepped forward. 'One more thing, Judge. I'd like to be able to go back to his store.'

The Judge looked at him, incredulous. 'Why would you want to patronize the business of a man who tossed you in excrement?'

'To visit with Miss Evelyn, of course. She's the prettiest thing in Calico.'

Stoby practically roared with fury. 'See! *That's* exactly what I'm talking about!'

As if to underscore Stoby's rage, that's when the back of Roy's Chophouse exploded in a ball of flame and cinders that the wind blew out across the town.

Everyone hit the ground, although the building was down the hill, about twenty-five yards south of them.

Roy ran out of his burning restaurant, unharmed but terrified. 'My damn oven blew up.'

Some men ran down to him and one of them asked, 'Was there anybody inside?'

'No,' Roy said. 'Just me.'

Owen sat up and saw embers blowing in the wind and landing like flaming arrows on the buildings downhill, instantly igniting the dry, baked wood. Within seconds, Tuttle's Saloon, Stoby's store, and the boarding house were aflame, their embers igniting even more buildings, which might as well have been soaked with gasoline. The speed of the fire was astonishing.

The Judge yelled: 'Get some buckets! Start a water brigade!'

Men ran off to do so, but Owen knew it would be like spitting in the wind. There wasn't enough water in Calico to save one building, much less the entire town, even if they could organize a bucket brigade in time, which they obviously couldn't.

The flames were already inside Tuttle's Saloon, flickering behind the windows, and he had a horrifying realization: His solar battery was still on the roof. If he lost his battery, he wouldn't be able to power his iPhone or MacBook once the gas tank in his Mercedes was empty and he'd never see or hear Nicole again.

Without a word to Wendy, he dashed across the street to the blazing saloon, ignoring her frantic calls to him to come back.

He ran between the burning saloon and the two huts where Milly and Esther did their business and had gone off to nap through the trials. He was nearly at the kitchen door when it occurred to him that the sound and fury that accompanied the explosion of Roy's Chophouse was tepid compared to the almost daily blasts of dynamite from the mines.

What if the two women had slept through it? What if they had no idea of the immediate danger they were in?

Owen doubled back and threw open Esther's door. She was naked and actively engaged on top of a naked man in her bed, both of them grunting and huffing along, oblivious to the fire outside their door.

'The town's on fire,' Owen yelled. 'Get out!'

Esther didn't waste an instant. She dismounted from her customer and ran nude out the door without looking back. The man, dazed by the sudden and unwelcome change in his situation, slowly reached for his pants.

'There's no time,' Owen yelled. 'Go, you fool!'

He yanked the man out of bed and kicked his bare ass to get him going. The man ran out tender-footed and in a high state of excitement.

Owen stepped out, saw the saloon fully engulfed in fire, and moved quickly into Milly's hut. She was asleep in her underwear on her tiny bed.

He shook her awake. 'Milly!'

She smiled when she saw him. 'About time.'

She drowsily reached up for him and he lifted her from the bed.

'There's a fire,' he said.

'I feel it, too, baby.'

'Not that kind.' He put her down on her feet and that's when she saw the saloon aflame outside her door. She gasped and ran out with Owen, but he stopped and she kept going, ducking under the flames and reaching the safety of the street just as the front of the saloon collapsed, taking Esther's hut down with it.

Owen staggered away from the searing heat, and turned towards the back half of the saloon, which was still standing and ablaze, flames licking out of the kitchen doorway and up around the solar battery resting on the roof. The heat and flames were too intense for him to step into the doorway and reach for the battery.

There was a barrel of water nearby, the one used to wash dishes. It was half-full but still too heavy to lift. He tipped it over into the doorway, the murky water diminishing the flames for an instant, long enough for him to jump up and make a grab for the battery.

He snatched the device off the roof just as the inferno reached the saloon's supply of kerosene or whiskey or both because that's when the remainder of the building exploded, the force of the blast hurling Owen off his feet and into Jack Ass Gulch in a spray of burning wood.

He tumbled down the jagged slope, smothering the embers on his clothes as he rolled, and bounced, and then landed hard on his back in the sewage at the bottom.

Owen lay there for a moment, dazed and sore and mildly burned, the battery clutched in his hand, the smell of smoke in his nose, killing the stench of whatever he was covered with. The ridge above him, where the lower end of the town stood, was a solid wall of flame, embers blowing over the gulch like red-hot snowflakes, and he knew he was lucky to be alive. He felt the sharp sting of cuts and burns all over, particularly his head, and his body was sore where he'd banged against rocks, but it was nothing serious. No broken bones, no third-degree burns, no gaping wounds. No need to see the barber for stitches or an amputation.

He crawled up the ravine, through the muck, toward King Mountain, in the opposite direction of the wind and fire. As he reached the bridge to the Chinese camp, he was met by some Chinese men, who lifted him to his feet and doused him with buckets of water. He thought it was because he was covered in shit, but then realized they were dumping the water on his head. He reached up, felt around, and discovered that much of his hair was gone, burned away. Maybe he'd see the barber after all, for a haircut, to even things out.

He thanked the men for their help, stuffed his battery in his back pocket, and staggered across the rickety bridge to the high end of Calico, where everyone had gathered, watching helplessly as the town burned. The Chinese camp, upwind and across the gulch, had been totally spared.

Owen weaved through the crowd until he found Wendy, standing with the Judge, the Tuttles, Milly, and Esther, who'd wrapped herself in a horse blanket. Overmyer stood writing in his notebook beside his Washington hand press – an iron contraption resembling the frame of a recliner – and several cases of movable type, some of the individual letters, like amputated typewriter keys, spilled in the dirt in his haste to rescue his business.

Milly spotted Owen first and ran to him, her arms outstretched. 'Ben!'

He held up his hands to fend her off. 'Don't. I fell in the gulch.'

But she didn't care. She wrapped him in a tight hug. 'You saved my life.'

'Then you must not be as dead inside as you thought.'

He looked over her shoulder and saw Wendy scowling at him. Milly let go of him and followed his gaze.

'I hope I didn't get you in trouble,' she said.

'You didn't.'

'I'll tell her it's not what she thinks.'

'Don't worry. Everything is fine.' He walked away from her and over to Wendy with a sheepish smile on his face. 'Now I know how Mr Gould felt . . . and smelled.'

Wendy glowered at him. 'You're a damn fool.'

He shrugged. 'I don't know what came over me.'

'I do.' She patted the battery in his back pocket. 'Was it really worth dying for?'

'I didn't,' he said, 'so it's moot.'

She slapped his face so hard that he would have lost his balance if she hadn't grabbed him and pulled him close.

'You're a selfish prick. How am I supposed to live in this damn, backward world without you?'

His eyes were tearing up from the slap, but it might have been more than that.

'I'm sorry,' he said.

She stomped away from him to the others and, after wiping the tears from his eyes, he followed after her.

The townsfolk watched in silence as the wind-blown firestorm roared downhill towards the desert floor, torching every structure in its path, growing hotter and more fierce until it finally ran out of wood to devour and burned itself out two hours later.

All that remained standing afterwards were the outhouses, the Judge's cabin, and a boarding house on the highest end of town. It was sheer luck that most people who were in town that evening were out in the street to watch the trials when Roy's stove blew up. As a result, nobody was killed and all the animals were released from the livery stable before it burned.

Owen and his friends, sad and sullen, looked down at the smoldering remains of Calico.

Overmyer put his notebook and pen in his pocket. 'The fire didn't touch the tens of millions of dollars in silver waiting to be mined. I guarantee you that Calico will be rebuilt within weeks and endure for years to come.'

Wendy whispered in Owen's ear. 'I forgot to tell you, Calico burns down twice. It happens again in 1887.'

He whispered back, 'Do you know which day?'

'I'm not even sure I have the right year.'

Tuttle sighed. 'I'm done.'

The Judge clapped him on the back to reassure him. 'You'll go back into business and be even more prosperous than before.'

'Maybe so, but not here,' Tuttle said. 'I hate this Godforsaken desert. It's inhospitable to life. We're leaving on the first train out of Daggett.'

Tuttle started shaking hands and saying goodbye to everybody. When he reached Owen, he said: 'Our stove was a big iron bastard. You can have it and anything else that survived.'

'Thanks for taking a chance on me when I needed the job,' Owen said.

'It's the only smart decision I made here, though you really ought to come with me. We could make big money together somewhere else, where there's plenty of water and wood, but no decent places to drink, gamble, and eat.'

'I'm going to stay,' Owen said. 'My future is here.'

'I'm going to miss your cooking.' Tuttle turned to face the townsfolk. 'Good luck to you all.'

Dora gave Owen a hug, and then she and her husband walked down the ash-covered street, hand in hand.

Overmyer turned to the Judge. 'You're the luckiest man in Calico.'

'How do you figure that?' the Judge said.

'Your office is still standing and Tuttle didn't ask you to pay off your credit debt before he left, though it would've been nice if you'd offered.'

'You owed him more than I did.'

'But you actually have the money to pay him,' Overmyer said.

'He's a proud man,' the Judge said. 'He would have taken offense.'

'You can soothe your guilty conscience by finding space in your shack for my printing press,' Overmyer said. 'I have a paper to publish this week.'

'There's room as long as you don't mind sleeping on the porch.'

Wendy grabbed Owen's hand and pulled him over to the Judge. 'Marry us,' she demanded.

The Judge's eyebrows shot up into his stove-pipe hat. 'What?'

'Marry us right this God-damned minute.'

Owen looked at her, pretty shocked himself. But also deeply touched. 'I don't recall proposing or being asked.'

Wendy looked him in the eye, daring him to oppose her. 'Are you saying no?'

'No. I mean no, I'm not saying no,' Owen said. 'But is this really the right time?'

'It's never going to be the right time for either of us,' she said. 'Unless we are together.'

The Judge looked confused, but Owen knew exactly what she meant.

Owen said, 'But half of my hair is burned off and I'm covered in shit.'

Wendy smiled. 'You never looked better.'

He gave his shirt a tug, as if that would somehow improve his appearance. 'OK then.'

She turned to the Judge. 'What are you waiting for? Get to it . . . and don't be too wordy.'

The Judge cleared his throat. 'Do you, Ben, take Wendy to be your lawfully wedded wife, to love and to cherish, to have and to hold from this day forward, for better or for worse, for richer or for poorer, in sickness and in health, until death do you part?'

Owen took her hand. 'I do.'

'Do you, Wendy, take Ben, to be your lawfully wedded husband, to love and to cherish, to have and to hold from this day forward, for better or for worse, for richer or for poorer, in sickness and in health, until death do you part?'

'What a dumb question,' Wendy said. 'Look at him. If I'll take him now, I'll keep him no matter what.'

Owen smiled. 'Gee, thanks.'

Laughter rippled among the townsfolk who were, only moments ago, united in their sadness and misery.

But the Judge was frustrated. 'This is an official, legally binding ceremony. Is that an "I do" or not?'

'I do,' Wendy said.

'Very well,' the Judge said. 'By the power invested in me by the people of Calico and the County of San Bernardino, I now pronounce you man and wife.'

Owen and Wendy kissed and the townsfolk applauded, even Milly, despite her sobbing.

NINETEEN

Friday, February 8, 2019

Beth met Selma Neary, head of the San Bernardino County historical society, in her office at the county museum in Redlands. The tiny office was filled with books, overflowing from sagging shelves and in stacks that had collapsed into a giant pile. There was barely room for a desk, two chairs, and the two women.

'You're a homicide detective?' Neary asked.

'That's right,' Beth said. 'We found a dead body in a hundred-year-old grave on land in Newberry Springs that was once home to the Cartwright family.'

Neary smiled, her pearl necklace disappearing in the folds of her neck. 'It's a little late to bring the felon to justice.'

'This man was killed a week ago and buried in an old casket,' Beth said. 'I'm wondering if there might be some connection between the victim and the Cartwright family or at least that bit of land.'

'Unfortunately, Calico burned to the ground twice, destroying most of the legal records, and almost every issue of the *Calico Print* newspaper, so much of the town's history, outside of the mining activity, is lost. What little we know about the daily lives of any individuals comes from letters, a few diaries, and a dozen surviving issues of the *Calico Print*.'

'Anything you can tell me will be helpful,' Beth said.

'Well, we know that Ben Cartwright owned a popular restaurant in town called Denny's, though it appears their menus were very different from the coffee shop chain that we know today,' she said. 'The Denny's in Calico was considered a very fancy place to eat, full of European delights that Cartwright learned about in his world travels.'

Beth was momentarily speechless. It all seemed to her like one big practical joke. The nicest restaurant in Calico was Denny's . . . and the cook who owned it had the same name as a character in a Western TV series. Not only that, but Owen Slader was a chef . . . and his dead body was found buried on the Cartwrights' land, where development had been legally forbidden for over a hundred years . . . until the same day in 2019 that he disappeared.

It was all tied together. It all meant something. But she had no idea what it could be.

Neary reached out a hand to her. 'Detective? Are you all right?'

No, she wasn't. Not at all.

'Yes, I'm fine, just tired, I had a long night. I keep zoning out,' Beth said. 'Do you know when Ben Cartwright first arrived in Calico?'

'The first mention of him was in early 1882, in a tiny item in the *Calico Print*, when he began working as a cook at a saloon as the result of winning a wager with the bartender. Miners were lined up out the door to sample his cuisine.'

'Early 1882? How early?' Beth had a frightening feeling that she already knew the answer.

'The *Calico Print* was a weekly. The news item mentioning the bet was published in their Saturday, February 4th issue.'

Beth was glad she was sitting down, because she was suddenly very light-headed. She was beginning to half-believe Amanda's crazy time-travel theory. Or maybe she was just so sleep-deprived that she was losing her grip on reality, entering some kind of dream-fugue state.

'Do you have any pictures of the Cartwrights?'

Neary opened up a large book in front of her. 'Only this one of Mrs Cartwright, standing outside Lane's General Store with John & Lucy Lane, the proprietors.'

It was a grainy, fuzzy, black-and-white photo taken on the wooden front porch of an adobe building. The Lanes weren't smiling and looked homely to Beth. But Mrs Cartwright, dressed like a man in a denim shirt and jeans, was radiant and sexy, looking directly into the camera, and she intuitively struck a confident yet casual pose that accentuated her shapely figure and offered the perfect angle on her face so that the sunlight would highlight her striking features. She was as poised as a fashion model, knowing her body well and playing to the lens and the light with expertise, as if she'd been photographed a hundred times before.

Beth took out her phone and snapped a picture of the photo. 'She was beautiful.'

'She certainly was,' Neary said. 'Wendy Cartwright was also a savvy prospector or just very lucky. She discovered one of the earliest and richest silver mines out there and sold it to a big East Coast mining company. It made them rich.'

'So why did they stay in the desert and keep running that restaurant? Why not move to a mansion in LA or San Francisco or anywhere else?'

'I think they deeply loved Calico.'

'Why do you say that?'

'Ben Cartwright never left and in the early 1900s, years after the town went bust and her husband died, Wendy continued to wander through the ruins like a ghost. People say they even heard Ben's voice in the wind, following her through the dusty canyons. It's said that she's the reason why they started to call Calico a ghost town.'

'Where was Cartwright buried?'

o, but all the burial records were lost in the
d the town into ashes,' Neary said. 'Not only
loods through Wall Street Canyon washed
..eadstones and graves. They couldn't have put
...d in a worse spot. We aren't entirely sure how many
..c are or were buried out there.'

'Do you know what happened to Wendy?'

'In 1916, a naturalist studying the Calicos mentioned that Mrs Cartwright allowed him to camp overnight on her ranch. He reported a bizarre experience in his journal. He says there was a "ghostly light" emanating from her home. And when he crept to the window, he saw her talking to a "ghostly head" floating in her hands. We also know her son Nicolas and his family came to stay with her during the Spanish Flu in 1918, basically living in self-imposed quarantine.'

Smart move, Beth thought.

Neary said: 'She went back to Los Angeles with them, leaving the property to rot. What was left of the house burned down in the 1920s, likely from a vagrant's campfire, though some ruins remained until the 1960s. Now there's no trace that the Cartwrights were ever there.'

Beth wasn't so sure that was true.

Beth drove back to Barstow, intending to head straight home and get some sleep. Maybe in the morning, she thought, when she was refreshed and could think clearly again, everything she'd learned today would make some kind of sense.

But as she neared her exit she changed her mind and kept on driving until she rolled into Yermo, slowing to glance out the passenger window at the butte and the undeveloped property below it that the Cartwrights had owned for over a hundred years.

There was nothing remarkable or memorable about the land, Beth thought. It was just another dull patch of desolation passing in the blur of travel on the interstate. If anybody noticed it at all, it was in their peripheral vision, which was really all it merited. Which was probably exactly why Peggy Sue had to put dinosaurs all around her place to get any attention.

She got off at the Ghost Town Road exit, turned right and then right again at the Jack-in-the-Box, heading back on the two-lane

road in the direction she just came, driving parallel to the ii
on her passenger side and the butte to her left.

The Cartwright property was small and had no visible comi.
cial or residential appeal that she could see. It was a sliver of desc
tucked tightly between the steep side of the butte and a two-
lane crumbling asphalt road to nowhere, facing a big, wide, noisy,
polluted interstate. It was bleak and pitiful, strewn with trash that
people had thrown out of their cars as they sped by.

Beth made a U-turn on the empty road and parked in front of
the low barbed-wire fence that surrounded the Cartwrights' property. Bits of trash, mostly shreds of plastic and paper bags, were
caught on the sharp barbs, fluttering like tiny flags in the breeze
created by the interstate traffic.

She popped the trunk of her car, found a tarp, and draped it over
the fence so she wouldn't catch her clothing, or cut her skin, on the
barbs as she climbed over it.

The ground was covered with rocks, garbage, and desert scrub
leading to a natural curtain of creosote and saguaros along the
base of the butte. Or perhaps, Beth thought. it wasn't natural at
all. It was intentional. Because as she got closer, she saw the
thick row of plants hid the entrance to a cave, which was sealed
with rocks and boarded up with wood. The rotting wood was
covered with yellowed 'No Trespassing', 'Private Property', 'No
Entry – Extremely Dangerous', and 'Abandoned Mine Shaft. Stay
Out and Stay Alive' signage, all illustrated with plentiful skulls
and crossbones.

It was overkill, which only made Beth curious if there was
something more inside the mine than certain death.

She turned toward the valley and saw how close the property
was to Peggy Sue's and the spot where Motor Home Man was
killed. In fact, she realized that if she were to run straight out from
where she stood, it would be the same direction that Motor Home
Man appeared from in the restaurant's security camera video, looking
over his shoulder in terror.

For a moment, she wondered if this cave was Motor Home Man's
home, but she closely examined the opening and didn't see any
indication that the boards had ever been breached or disturbed. So
much for that theory, she thought with a yawn.

What was she doing out here anyway? This was a waste of time.

She trudged back to her car, tore her tarp yanking it off the barbed-wire fence, and stuffed it in her trunk to throw out later.

She drove back to Barstow with her windows rolled down, hoping that being buffeted by air would keep her from nodding off at the wheel. It did, but barely.

When she got home, she walked straight into her bedroom and flopped down on her bed without bothering to get undressed, her car keys and her phone still in her hands. Thirty seconds later, she was asleep.

She awoke later that Friday afternoon, with a dry throat and a pounding headache, her clothes sticking to her sweat-damp skin. Remnants of her dream still flitted across her mind. The dream was mash-up of time-travel movies, with Michael J. Fox, Arnold The Terminator, and Kirk Douglas all making cameo appearances.

She picked up her phone from her bed and trudged into the kitchen, grabbed a beer from the refrigerator, and sat down at her kitchen table. The nap hadn't made her feel any better. If anything, it made her feel worse. She wasn't tired anymore, but she felt hollowed out and raw, mentally and physically.

Was it the shooting? Or what she'd learned in San Bernardino? Maybe it was both. Maybe it was all too much. Maybe what she needed was a week in Hawaii.

She glanced at her phone and saw that she'd slept through a text from Chet and calls from reporters at the *Desert Dispatch* and the *San Bernardino Sun*, who were probably looking for quotes about the shooting. They wouldn't be getting any quotes from her. It would just be an invitation for them to resurrect the scandal in Los Angeles.

But thinking about the botched stake-out at Hula Lake made her think about Newberry Springs again, and the lake the Cartwrights wanted to build on their property, the one that couldn't be developed until February 2nd, 2019 . . .

The same date that Owen Slader disappeared . . . and the same place where his bones were found buried and aged over a hundred years.

She pulled up her photos of the Cartwright property in Newberry Springs and scrolled through them, looking at Slader's bones in the grave, the dry dirt, the construction trailer, the well-drilling equipment, and the bulldozer. Nothing stood out. Flat and bleak for as far as the eye could see.

It must have been a horrible place to live, especially a hundred years ago. There was no scenic beauty. No shade from the relentless heat. All the dry land had going for it was that it wasn't in Calico and there might actually be some water underneath it to live on.

Beth finished her beer and was about to get up from the table, maybe take a shower and go out for something to eat, when she felt something flitter across her mind, just out of reach, like a song she couldn't quite remember. Or a familiar face in a crowd that she couldn't quite place.

It had something to do with water, that was the thought that caused her mental hiccup.

She sat down again and scrolled through the grave site photos, zooming in on the grave, and the bones, but nothing clicked. The rest of the photos were of the undeveloped construction site. But there was even less to see than in the grave. They hadn't done any grading or even drilled an exploratory well.

The water.

Beth zoomed in on the drill and the company name on the truck.

Herbert George Well Drilling.

And there it was, right in her face.

Beth was sure that the Cartwrights owned that company, too. Because it was another joke, just like their name, just like Denny's restaurant.

Only *this* one was on the nose.

The drilling company was named after H. G. Wells, author of *The Time Machine*. She'd never read it, but she'd seen the movie, and now that she thought about it, she took another look at the name of the contractor.

Morlock Construction. She wasn't sure, but weren't the Morlocks the monsters in the movie? They had to be. Because someone was trying to send a message.

Owen Slader and Ben Cartwright were the same person.

Somehow, last Saturday, Owen Slader drove into the past and Motor Home Man ran forward into the future, and it had something to do with that lightning storm and the explosions at the two military bases.

Or at least that's what someone wanted people to believe.

The odds were better, and it was more realistic to assume, that the emerging picture was some big, elaborate con rather than time travel.

But if it wasn't a trick, if it really was *fucking time travel*, she'd need overwhelming, undeniable proof before she, or anybody else, would believe it.

And she didn't have it.

Yet.

Beth went shopping at the Home Depot in Barstow and drove back that night to the sealed cave in Yermo with work gloves, a sledge-hammer, a pick-ax, and a bad temper. In her car, she had cinderblocks, plywood, nails, a bucket, a trowel, and some quick-mix mortar.

She yanked off the boards with the pick-ax and used the sledge-hammer and pick-ax on the rocks. It took her two hours of hard, sweaty labor, but she managed to clear away enough rocks to create a hole large enough for her to crawl through . . . if the remaining rocks, loosened by her work, didn't collapse and crush her to death.

She crouched down, turned on her flashlight, and aimed the beam through the hole, but all she could see was a cave wall and the edge of a dusty canvas tarp. At least there wasn't a big, gaping shaft on the ground on the other side of the rocks.

It was a tight fit, but she managed to scramble through the hole without the whole thing crumbling down on her.

Yet. She still had to crawl out again.

She got slowly to her feet without hitting her head on anything, and swept her flashlight beam over the space. The cave was actually the very narrow mouth of a tunnel that only went back a few yards, as if someone had given up digging very early. The tunnel was almost entirely occupied by whatever was under the tarp.

And she had a hunch what it was.

Beth yanked the tarp off, revealing a black 2018 Mercedes GLC.

Slader's car.

The tires were rotted away, the paint was oxidized in spots, and the leather interior was cracked. The vinyl dash was solid, and the dust-covered iPad-like computer screen seemed whole, but the burled walnut stripes were blistered. The Mercedes had either decayed incredibly fast over a few days or was in amazing condition for a car that was over a hundred years old.

Either way, it was unbelievable.

Her hand, still in a leather work glove, was shaking as she reached out to open the door, which gave easily, without even a creak. She half-expected the dome light to turn on, too, but it didn't. She lit it up with her flashlight.

Beth leaned in and opened the center storage unit. There was a leather wallet, a set of house keys, the ignition key-fob, and a thick stack of hundred-dollar bills. Inside the wallet, she found Owen Slader's driver's license, credit cards, and some more cash, and a photograph of a young woman that she assumed was his daughter.

She took pictures of it all with her phone, then walked around to the rear of the car, lifted the hatchback, and saw two suitcases, which were already unzipped. There were some clothes inside, but no toiletries.

She photographed the suitcases, the contents, and the rear license plate of the car, then walked around to the front passenger side, opened the door, and opened the dashboard glove box. There wasn't much inside, just some faded documents that appeared to be the registration, original sales sticker, and service invoices. She took pictures of that, too, then stood back and considered what she'd learned.

This was definitely Owen Slader's car.

The facts, if she could call them that, suggested to her that *he* hid it here . . . and eventually bought the land to ensure that it would never be developed.

Because he didn't want the Mercedes found.

Unless, she thought, this car and everything inside it was just a prop in a brilliantly elaborate trick of some kind.

Which it had to be. Didn't that make more sense than time travel?

But if it was a trick, what was the point of it?

The one thing that was true in both of the unbelievable, crazy scenarios was that Owen Slader was dead.

There was no doubt about that. She had his bones and his implants.

That left two big questions. *When* did he actually die . . . and was it a crime?

That's when she realized she was missing something important. Trent told her the LAPD learned when and where Owen Slader disappeared by tracking the last GPS pings on his car and his cell phone.

His car was here, but where was his cell phone?

And now that she thought about it, where was his laptop? Surely he had one with him for the trip.

So she thoroughly searched the car, at least the obvious places, but couldn't find any personal electronics.

It was possible that they were hidden somewhere more secure, where they couldn't be stumbled upon, but she didn't have the tools or knowledge to dismantle the engine, doors, or anything else. She'd leave that to the crime scene investigators . . . if she ever called them, or anyone else, about this.

It certainly wouldn't be today.

How could she explain herself, or what she thought this all meant, without coming off as insane?

Besides, if this actually was a crime scene, she knew that she'd rendered any evidence she'd found inadmissible by breaking in without a warrant, not that any judge would have granted her one.

She had no legal grounds for a search. Not even *rational* ones.

There was only one thing she could do, and if she was being honest with herself, she'd known it even before she'd come out here, or she wouldn't have brought the cinderblocks, mortar, and wood.

She'd keep Slader's wallet and house keys, but otherwise she'd leave everything where it was, and seal the cave up again. It was the best way, she believed, to keep the evidence secure until she could figure out what happened to him; if he'd really traveled back in time, or if he was the victim of some bizarre charade.

And what, if anything, she was going to do about it.

TWENTY

Calico, 1885

Calico was booming. Or so it seemed. The main street on the butte was bustling with seventy-five businesses serving the 3,500 people, primarily single men, living and working in the mountains, canyons, and valley floor. There were hundreds of mines and dozens of stamp mills pounding the silver out of the rocks. The mining companies were extracting millions of dollars' worth of silver from the mountains, but most of that wealth was going to the owners back east.

The slim percentage of profits being invested in the community went toward satisfying the basic needs of the inhabitants – which were food, water, and sex, and not necessarily in that order. Nothing was spent on things that would enhance the quality of life, or create anything of permanence, that would allow Calico to evolve from a mining camp to a town.

Wells were drilled, tanks were built, and pipe was laid to get running water to the mines and most of the businesses on Main Street, but there still wasn't any kind of sanitation system. Waste continued to pile up on the street and spill unfiltered into Jack Ass Gulch, creating an unbelievable stench.

The whore population had swelled to fifty and there were dozens of professional gamblers lurking among the bars and gambling halls. There was a post office, but no banks. There was a jail, but no sheriff or deputies.

Luckily, the population was generally peaceable, but when a serious offense or crime was committed, such as cheating at cards, theft, or murder, the people were quick to rise up in fury or indignation, restrain the miscreant, and drag him to the jail to await Judge Orville's ruling, though mob justice did, at times, prevail before he had a chance to adjudicate anything. There might have been more hangings if there had actually been an old tree in town. But sturdy trees wouldn't grow on the inhospitable landscape and wood was too valuable to waste on hangings or on erecting gallows when it could go towards building a whorehouse, privy, or saloon instead.

Despite the fire that had decimated Calico, half of the buildings were still made of wood, the rest were made of stone or adobe.

A school was being built for the camp's thirty children, that would also double as a 'town hall' for community meetings, dances, and trials. But there wasn't a single church in Calico and preachers rarely visited, because they knew there wouldn't be a nickel donated for their collection pot when it could be better spent on a bet, a beer, or a biscuit.

The way Owen looked at it, Calico wasn't a place where people wanted to live. It was a place people had to endure. People working outdoors, or in the businesses on Main Street, had to suffer the scorching desert heat by day, often in the triple digits, and bone-chilling cold on winter nights. The only relief was in the mines, where it was a constant sixty-five degrees, but it was hard to enjoy the subterranean climate while doing back-breaking labor, breathing dirt and facing the ever-present danger of a cave-in or being blown up by the dynamite used to burrow deeper.

There was also the inescapable stench of excrement, coal smoke, and human sweat in Calico, though the general population became nose-numb to it after a while. The same was true of the constant noise – the loud crashing of ore tumbling down long chutes from the mountain mines to the valley below and the incessant pounding from the dozens of stamp mills.

The only reason people were there at all was to earn enough money to live well somewhere else. But only the mine operators, and some of the shopkeepers, were able to achieve that goal. Owen and Wendy were in that rarified group.

The Cartwrights lived on a ranch in Newberry Springs, sixteen miles away, far enough from Calico not to hear it or smell it or drink its water, but close enough to keep an eye on business. Owen went back and forth every two days, sleeping in the bedroom above the restaurant where they'd lived until their home was built.

The Newberry Springs home was single-story, with a large balcony in front, facing the Calicos. The ranch had a well, a melon patch, and an alfalfa field, mostly to supply hay for the family's horses and milk cows. There was a small barn, a chicken coop, and a bunkhouse for the handful of men who worked for them.

On this particular day, Owen got up at sunrise, hours earlier than he ever did in the twenty-first century, to an empty bed, which wasn't unusual. Lately, Wendy was an even earlier riser. He got dressed, trudged outside to the outhouse to relieve his bladder, then went to the barn to find Wendy, eight months pregnant, sitting on a stool, milking the cow. For some reason he couldn't understand, that was a task she enjoyed. She looked up from tugging teats when he came in.

'Soon you'll be doing this to me,' she said, a spray of cow milk loudly hitting the bucket for emphasis.

'That's a sexy thought,' Owen said. 'We need to go if you're going to make your train in Daggett.'

'I could stay.' But even as she said it, she reached out her hand to him and he helped her to her feet.

'Unfortunately, there's no Zillow or DocuSign yet.'

'What are they?' she asked.

Owen kept forgetting she wasn't exactly from his time. 'The point is, we can't really buy land in Los Angeles today without going there to do it.'

He picked up the bucket of milk and carried it out to the horse-drawn buggy, where she already had her suitcase. There were also several large empty glass jars in a box loosely packed with hay. She'd thought of everything, as usual.

'You say *we*,' she said, 'but it's *me* who has to go.'

'You should be thrilled. You're the one who always complains about how boring and remote it is out here.'

'We live in a desert.' Wendy unscrewed the jars and he filled them with milk.

'And now you can enjoy the culture and excitement of the big city . . . it will be a vacation.' Owen began pouring milk from the bucket into the jars.

'You're bored, too. That's the only reason you're still running the restaurant. We're filthy rich, thanks to the mine leases. We could live anywhere we want to or just travel the world.' She screwed one jar shut as he moved to fill another.

'I have to live here,' he said.

'One trip to Los Angeles won't kill you.'

The bucket empty, he set it aside and they both began screwing the lids on the jars. 'Not now. But maybe in a hundred years if I'm not born.'

'You don't know that will happen if you leave this desert.'

'You might be right, but I can't take the risk.' They'd talked about this many times. He felt like he should just record his argument on his iPhone and play it for her. This was one of the few places on Earth where he knew that virtually nothing had changed between 1882 and 2019. If he didn't leave, if he lived and died right here, he believed it was unlikely that he could do anything that would prevent himself, and more importantly by extension his daughter, from being born. 'It's also not safe for you to be here right now.'

'There's cholera in Los Angeles, too, Ben.'

'Not as bad as it is in Calico,' he said. 'You'll be staying at the Nadeau House, the cleanest, most luxurious hotel in the city. They also have a doctor on call.'

'We have a doctor in town.'

'Phineas Walsh is nearly deaf and rarely sober. All he knows how to do is amputate. At least when the barber does it, he throws in a nice haircut, too. You'll be much safer in LA.'

'You're just as likely to get infected here as I am.'

'But I'm not pregnant.' It was the one point she couldn't refute and he knew it. He led her to the front of the buggy and helped her up into the buckboard seat.

'I can't wait to have this baby so I can start winning arguments again,' she said.

'That's the only reason I knocked you up,' Owen said. 'I may keep you pregnant just to maintain my masculine authority in this relationship.'

'You'd have to sleep with me again to do that, and the odds of that happening is diminishing with each word you say.'

Owen climbed up on the buggy and took the reins. God, how he missed his Mercedes. He even missed the Kia he had as a teenager.

Rico emerged from the bunkhouse, scratching his belly. He was their ranch hand, a former miner and Mexican immigrant in his thirties, who appreciated the steady income and sunlight over his previous job. He tended their cattle, chickens, and alfalfa crop.

Owen called out to him. 'I'll be back in a few days.'

'So will I,' Wendy said.

Rico nodded and waved as they left. 'Have a safe trip, Mrs Cartwright. Don't worry about nothing here. Rico's watching over things.'

Owen and Wendy used the three-hour ride into Daggett as an opportunity to listen to music on Owen's iPhone, using shared earbuds he'd bought for himself and Nicole. It made the time pass and distracted them from the numerous discomforts on the road. They might have moved a bit faster if not for Wendy's frequent stops to relieve herself.

He also missed gas station restrooms.

Daggett was six miles from Calico and a place most people only passed through on their way to the mines, or to stock up on supplies or spend their wages on entertainment and booze.

Like Calico, it was a man's town. The few women there were mostly prostitutes. The brothels, gamblers, and thieves preyed on visitors but were smart enough to recognize locals and leave them alone. So Owen and Wendy felt reasonably safe there.

The train station was the usual hub of activity, the prostitutes, the pickpockets, and the hucksters from the saloons and hotels swirling around arriving passengers from east and west. Owen pulled the buggy to the front, helped Wendy down, got her suitcase for her, and led her to the platform, where the train was already waiting. They'd cut the timing close, thanks to the many pee stops. He had no idea how she was going to deal with her bladder on the train and didn't want to ask.

Owen led her to the first-class car. 'Send me a telegram when you arrive at the hotel so I know you got there safely.'

'I will.' She gave him a kiss. 'I should be back in two or three days. Is there anything you'd like me to bring you from LA?'

'A son or a daughter.'

She stopped and stared at him. He handed her bags up to the porter, a black man in a uniform, to avoid her glare.

'You expect me to stay there until I've had the baby?'

'Maybe a few weeks longer, at least until this outbreak has cooled down,' he said. 'I'll send you a telegram when it's safe.'

She planted her hands on her hips. 'We had hours to talk about this on the ride here and you waited until *now* to bring this up?'

The porter wisely disappeared inside with her bag.

'I only want what's best for you and the baby.'

'Maybe I won't come back at all. Maybe I'll run off with all of our money to New York or Paris.'

Owen shrugged. 'Now's your chance. You know I won't chase you.'

'You would if you loved me.'

'I won't *because* I love you,' he said. 'And because I love Nicole. I'm a prisoner of the women in my life.'

He thought that sounded very noble. It was also true. And self-serving, but still true.

'God, I hate you sometimes.' She kissed him again, but it was more like a head-butt, and got on the train.

Owen waited until the train left, then went back to his buggy. Nobody had dared steal it since everyone in town knew it belonged to him, so a thief wouldn't get very far. And the penalty for horse theft ranged from flogging to branding and death, depending on whether the assailant was captured by vigilantes or tried by an actual court.

Big Stan, named for his enormous belly, was waiting for Owen at his buggy. The man owned the largest saloon in Daggett and had an ownership interest in one of the livery stables and two of the brothels. He was a frequent diner, and big spender, at Denny's.

'Morning, Stan,' Owen said.

Big Stan hooked his thumbs around his suspenders. 'Have you given any thought to my proposal?'

Big Stan had offered to build a Denny's, Owen's up-scale restaurant, and a McCartwright's, his 'take-out' operation catering to price-conscious miners looking for a fast, tasty, cheap meal, in Daggett, right across from the train station.

'I'm not ready to franchise Denny's or McCartwright's yet.'

'Franchise?'

'I don't want to take on a partner and open a restaurant in another town,' Owen said.

'Are you against making money, Ben?'

'I'm already rich.'

'You have something against being richer?'

'It's too much work,' Owen said.

'I'll do all the work. Just send me the hooker who does your cooking.'

'Milly is my sous-chef, maybe the best chef in Southern California, and I depend on her to run my kitchen when I'm not around.'

'So train another hooker. There are plenty of them,' Big Stan said. 'Think of all the Big Bens you could sell here.'

He was referring to the Double Cheeseburgers Owen sold at McCartwright's, his 'walk-through' kitchen, where he had a low-price menu limited to hamburgers, hot pockets, fries, and beer to go. Owen even sold reusable 'lunch boxes' that the food could be carried in to the mines or back home. Everyone who bought a lunch box was entitled to half-price French fries.

'If people can eat my food here,' Owen said, 'they won't come to Calico for it.'

'Or you'll double, maybe triple your business,' Big Stan said. It was a sensible argument, but Owen didn't want to be partners with Big Stan or in business in Daggett, a hell-hole he tried to avoid.

'I appreciate the offer, Stan, but I'm going to pass.' Owen climbed up onto his buggy, but Big Stan didn't get the message that he was being politely brushed off. Or he did and decided to ignore it.

'Milly knows all your recipes,' Big Stan said. 'Somebody could come along and offer Milly her own restaurant . . . then you'd be cut out completely. Doesn't that bother you?'

It was a not-so-veiled threat, but Owen chose to keep smiling. 'She'll definitely open her own restaurant and when she does, I'll be very happy for her.'

'Even if it's in Daggett?'

'Hell no. It will be in Los Angeles or San Francisco. She's too good for Daggett.' Owen started to pull away.

'We got lots of women like her here, Ben. For two bits, you can have any of them for a half-hour.'

'So build one of them a restaurant.' Owen rode off.

TWENTY-ONE

On his way to Calico, Owen passed the cave where his Mercedes was hidden behind rocks and still had a half a tank of gas. He'd stopped spending time in his piece of air-conditioned, leather-upholstered heaven months ago. It only reminded him of all the creature comforts he could never have again and made it harder to face the cruel reality he was living in. So, he'd basically buried the car as a time capsule for the future.

He was in Calico in an hour, though he heard it, and smelled it, long before that. It was one of the reasons why he'd chose to raise his new family in Newberry Springs and not there.

As he passed the cemetery, he saw men digging new plots for a row of tiny crudely made caskets. He could tell from the size of the caskets that three more children had died. It was another reason to keep his family away from Calico. The plagues raged through the town far too often, taking mostly the young and the very old. But in the 1880s, the very old was anybody in their forties. He hoped one of the vaccines he'd had in his lifetime had immunized him against cholera and typhoid, or at least gave him stronger resistance.

There was a big line outside McCartwright's, his 'take out' restaurant, where his mostly Chinese staff were grilling burgers, the intoxicating smell overcoming the general stench of the town and making people salivate. It even worked on him, since he'd forgotten to eat breakfast in his rush to get Wendy to the train. The beef for his hamburgers was ground to his specifications and seasoned with his own version of Lawry's Seasoned Salt. His cheese slices and sesame-seed buns were all home-made.

He said hello to some of the miners in line that he knew by name and saw Virgil's water wagon park in front of Denny's, his 'upscale' restaurant built on the site of Tuttle's old saloon. Owen had figured that as the town grew, a key clientele would be the well-off mining execs and their families who'd want, and could afford, a dining experience that was more than basic nourishment. There wasn't one until he opened Denny's.

Owen imported ingredients from Los Angeles and San Francisco and his Denny's menu was full of creative dishes mixing European, Asian, and Central American influences to cater to the international mix of people in Calico. It worked. His place was packed with Calico's rich and powerful almost every night.

Owen tied up his buggy beside Virgil's wagon and carried in the box of milk jugs, now churned into butter by the natural rocking and bumping of the road. Inside Denny's, the waitresses were laying out tablecloths and dishes for the evening service.

Virgil Urt was sitting at the chair by the door, as he was most afternoons, wearing his Sunday best clothes, not that he ever went to church, and holding a bouquet of flowers in his hands.

'How's it going, Virgil?' Owen asked.

'Same as always.'

'Where I come from, they have a word for what you're doing.'

'Courting?' Virgil said.

'Stalking,' Owen said.

'I ain't hunting her like some Indian. Flowers never hurt no one.'

'I don't think your strategy is working.'

'Why do you say that?'

'Well, has she ever shown you any encouragement?'

Virgil smiled, which wasn't a good look for him, given the poor condition of his teeth and gums. 'Every time she looks at me.'

'It's an angry glare.'

'I've lived in this desert all my life and I've never seen anything as beautiful as her. Just seeing her, any expression on her face at all, is enough to make my day.'

'What about her day?'

Virgil held out the flowers. 'That's what these are for. So she always knows that somebody loves her.' He stood up from his chair and laid the bouquet on top of Owen's milk bottles. 'Can you take these to her? I'll be back tonight, after my deliveries. I don't want them to dry up.'

'Sure.'

'How's your well doing?' Virgil asked. He and his ornery brother Clive had found the water and dug the well on Owen's ranch, which was counter-productive, since it meant they'd have one less customer for their water deliveries. Virgil had also refused to take a dime from Owen for their work because, he said, you don't take money from friends. Perhaps, Owen thought, that was why Clive was ornery and didn't make friends.

'The well is great,' Owen said. 'We couldn't live there without it. When are you and your brother going to come to the house and let me make you that nice dinner that I owe you?'

'I have supper with that smelly bastard Clive every night. When I come to your table, it will be with Milly.'

Virgil walked out. Owen continued on to the kitchen, where he had several cast-iron stoves, including the one left for him by Tuttle. Milly was at the cutting board, her back to him, chopping vegetables.

'I started buggy-churning some fresh butter for tonight,' he said, then held up the bouquet. 'And I've got more flowers for you from Virgil. The man doesn't give up.'

He set down the jars, took yesterday's flowers from Virgil out of a vase by the window, and put in the fresh ones.

'He should,' Milly said, without looking at the flowers. 'Virgil can do a lot better than me.'

Owen noticed tears running down her cheeks. 'Did you hear what he said about you?'

She nodded. 'It was sweet but he's a fool. How could he ever love me knowing that any man he sees could be someone who's had me once, twice, maybe a dozen times?'

'That's not you anymore.'

'It's always going to be me, Ben.'

'Is that why you're crying?'

She shook her head. 'Of all the men I've had in this camp, only one really saw me as somebody and treated me with affection, in bed and out, and I'm terrified I'm going to lose him.'

Owen was confused. 'Virgil?'

Milly looked him in the eye. 'Of course not. You and Virgil are among the few men in town who've never been with me.'

Now Owen knew who she was talking about and felt his heart drop. 'Has something happened to the Judge?'

Her eyes went wide. 'Oh God, I thought you knew. He's sick, Ben. Bad sick. It's the blue death. The doctor doesn't think he's going to make it.'

That changed everything.

'What Walsh thinks means nothing,' Owen said, his anger flaring. 'You're better off asking the butcher for his medical opinion.'

He rushed out the door and went up the street to the Judge's house, assay office, and courtroom, all under one roof. One door led to his home, the other to his offices.

Overmyer was pacing on the porch when Owen got there. The reporter had a bandana over his nose and mouth. The first thing Owen noticed was the smell was as bad as the gulch.

Owen slipped a bandana over his nose and mouth, too. Overmyer looked very tired and pale. 'I just heard about the Judge. How is he doing?'

'Horribly. The doctor has been with him all night. He's taken every measure he can, but he thinks it's hopeless.'

'Walsh is an idiot,' Owen said. He was also deaf and drunk. Even a competent doctor in this era was still practically useless, as far as Owen was concerned. His biggest fear was him or Wendy, and now their future child, getting sick in this backward time.

'You don't need to be a doctor to know the miasma is bad here,' Overmyer said. 'You can smell it.'

Miasma? Jesus, he thought. They might as well blame evil spirits.

Sometimes the ignorance of the people around Owen was infuriating, though he couldn't really blame them for it. They didn't have the knowledge yet, and filled it with bullshit. Like the idea that a smell itself spread disease, rather than whatever was causing the odor.

Owen made an effort not to sound patronizing when he spoke.

'John, it's not the air that's causing the outbreak, it's the shit and piss everywhere that's contaminating everything. It's the people and everything they are touching. Nothing and nobody are clean in this town.'

'That's what I'm saying. The odor is going to kill us all. It's everywhere. We can't escape the sickness.'

Yes, they could, Owen thought, if the town invested in a sewer system and if the people just washed their hands and clothes, boiled water, and disinfected surfaces. Instead, they were tracking the shit on the streets into their homes, food, and water. Even taking a bath was deadly. As many as four or five men might use the same water at a bathhouse before it was changed. But Overmyer wouldn't understand what he was talking about. People didn't know about germs yet.

'Maybe the Judge can escape it,' Owen said. 'He's a wily fellow.'

Overmyer shook his head. 'What you're smelling now is from his cabin. He's been vomiting and shitting his guts out for two days. I don't know how the doctor can take it in there.'

'Whiskey,' Owen said.

'I'd be a drunk, too, if I had to do what he does.'

As if on cue, the door opened, and Dr Phineas Walsh came out, wearing a dark overcoat covered with stains of all kinds, carrying a bed pan filled with excreta, and tossed it over the side of Wall Street canyon, only furthering the outbreak.

Walsh turned to face the two men, a grim expression on his face. 'He can't stop purging fluids. I don't know where it's all coming from because he hasn't kept anything inside. I've done the best I can . . . but I fear it won't be enough.'

Owen stepped up to him. 'Which is what, exactly?'

'What?' Walsh asked.

Owen repeated and clarified his question, louder this time, into his good ear. 'WHAT TREATMENT HAVE YOU GIVEN HIM?'

'I've put socks filled with hot sand around his body to encourage profuse perspiration,' Walsh said authoritatively. 'And I've applied a body rub of mustard, salt, turpentine oil, and cayenne pepper.'

Owen couldn't believe what he was hearing. 'Are you treating him or marinating him?'

'What?' Walsh asked.

Owen raised his voice again, shouting at the doctor to be heard. 'WHY DID YOU PUT THAT STUFF ON HIM?'

Overmyer put a hand on Owen's shoulder. 'Settle down, Ben.'

Owen ignored Overmyer and waited for Walsh's answer.

'The Judge is desperately lethargic,' Walsh said. 'That rub will energize him.'

It was worse than putting salt in the wound, Owen thought. It was salt *and* hot peppers. 'Because he'll be so damn angry about his burning skin?'

Walsh didn't hear what he said, but apparently caught the gist. 'The rub excites the nerves and encourages more perspiration, the sovereign remedy for this malignancy.'

'Let me get this straight,' Owen yelled into Walsh's ear. 'He's dehydrated . . . and you're sweating him?' He could smell the whiskey on the doctor's breath.

'I'm changing the direction of fluid expulsion away from the stomach, and the injurious rush through the intestinal tracts, to the vascular system, giving the internal system a chance to recover while also cleansing the body through the natural, external filter of skin.'

It was one of the dumbest things he'd ever heard. 'What medications are you giving him?'

'What?' Walsh asked.

'WHAT MEDICINE ARE YOU GIVING HIM?'

Walsh took a bottle of pills out of his overcoat pocket. 'Five anti-spasmodics every half-hour, followed by a half-glass of undiluted whiskey.'

Owen examined the pills, which were imperfectly shaped, made by hand. 'What's in the pills?'

'Opium, chili pepper, camphor, spirits of wine, and conserve of roses.'

'You're giving him Vicodin and Jack Daniel's?' Owen said. 'Do you think this is a frat party?'

'What?' Walsh asked.

Owen yelled, 'HOW MUCH OF THIS MEDICINE HAVE *YOU* BEEN TAKING?'

Walsh shifted his gaze to Overmyer, seeking a sympathetic ear. 'Enough to fortify my body against the miasma, which I believe is prudent, given the risk.'

'Of course you do,' Owen said. 'That's why you're constantly fortified, even when there is no outbreak.'

'I face a lot of illness,' Walsh said.

'If you were less fortified, and more sober, maybe you'd remember that alcohol is a diuretic.'

'What?' Walsh asked.

Overmyer put a hand on Owen's shoulder again. 'The doctor is doing his very best and at great personal risk.'

Owen ignored him and yelled at Walsh: 'ALCOHOL MAKES YOU PISS. IT DEHYDRATES YOU. YOU SHOULDN'T DRINK WHEN YOU'RE TRYING TO RETAIN FLUIDS.'

Walsh sighed, wearied by Owen's ignorance. 'Whiskey is a cordial stimulant that assists the opium in restoring the tone and energy of the nervous system, which contracts the blood vessels, diminishing all secretions and excretions, with the exception of perspiration, which it increases.'

'You mean it gets him high faster so he won't notice the misery he's in.'

Walsh looked past him to Overmyer. 'The Judge's purges have become incessant, odorless, and have the consistency of egg whites. That means he's on the precipice of collapse, the final, deadliest stage. So I've bled eight ounces from him, which I believe could change the disastrous course he's on.'

'YOU DID . . . *WHAT*?' Owen yelled, this time not to be heard, but out of pure rage.

'I bled him,' Walsh said.

Owen lunged at Walsh, but Overmyer pulled him back before his fists made contact.

'What's wrong with you?' Overmyer said, pinning Owen's arms behind his back.

Owen wanted to tear Walsh apart. 'The Judge is dangerously dehydrated, so what does this fucking imbecile do? He drugs him into a stupor, then sweats and bleeds buckets of fluid out of him. It's the exact opposite of what he should be doing.'

Walsh glowered at Owen.

'I am a graduate of the University of Pennsylvania School of Medicine. I know that's not the same extensive training as a cook receives, but I believe it gives me a slightly better understanding of the body and digestive system than someone who prepares food.'

He shifted his gaze to Overmyer. 'If the Judge gets worse, give him ten more pills, another whiskey, and send for me immediately. I'll bleed six more ounces from him'.

Owen said, 'The hell you will, you fucking barbarian. Why not just slit his throat and be done with it?'

Walsh ignored Owen and continued to address Overmyer. 'I have to go now. I have other, seriously ill patients who need and appreciate my care.'

Owen said, 'At least change your coat first.'

The comment puzzled Walsh enough to earn Owen his attention. 'I only have one overcoat.'

'How can you wear that into a sick person's home?'

'Because I don't want to stain my good clothes. I would think that's obvious, even to you. Don't you wear an apron in the kitchen?'

Walsh went away. When the doctor was safely out of reach, Overmyer released Owen, practically pushing him.

'What the hell is wrong with you?' Overmyer said.

'This is a nightmare,' Owen said. 'It's like I'm back in medieval times instead of the 1800s.'

'I know you're worried about the Judge. So am I. But that's no reason to take it out on the doctor. He's a good man, doing heroic work against impossible odds.'

Owen pointed at the retreating deaf, incompetent drunk. 'He's a killer, spreading illness everywhere he goes. I'll bet you he doesn't even wash his hands between here, the saloon, and the next patient he's going to murder by bleeding them to death.'

Overmyer sighed. 'You're being ridiculous and making a fool of yourself. Walsh was an army doctor during the Civil War and saved countless lives.'

'Everyone would be better off if he stuck with amputations, removing bullets, and setting broken bones.' Owen paced on the porch, trying to walk off his anger and frustration. 'He obviously knows nothing about infections, bacteria, and viruses.'

'And you do?'

Yes, he did. It was clear to Owen that an average, educated person in 2019 had more medical knowledge than any doctor in the 1880s. But that wasn't an argument he could make to Overmyer for his behavior.

'I've never been to medical school, but I've spent hours watching

Dr Gregory House, Dr Meredith Grey, and Trapper John M.D, three world-famous physicians, doing their work so I know that Walsh's remedies are worse than useless, they're deadly. They defy common sense.'

'I thought you were a smart man,' Overmyer said. 'I can't believe that you don't trust science or medicine.'

'I do, which is why I object to Walsh's insane treatments.' Owen gestured to the cabin. 'I want to see the Judge.'

'That's not safe,' Overmyer said.

Owen wasn't worried about getting infected. Cholera wasn't spread through the air. It was caused by ingesting contaminated food or drink. He'd frequently and thoroughly washed his hands. 'I'll be careful.'

Overmyer sighed. 'Prepare yourself, Ben. He's unrecognizable.'

'Don't exaggerate. I saw him two days ago. He couldn't have changed that much in so short a time.'

Owen took a deep breath and went inside the door leading to the Judge's humble living quarters.

TWENTY-TWO

It was a tiny living space, better suited to a monk. There were stacks of law books everywhere, a simple table and two chairs, a roll-top desk, and a small iron oven which doubled as a stove and a room-heater. The room was lit by a lantern on the table.

The Judge was wrapped in blankets and lying on a narrow, sagging, single bed that was pressed against one wall. But even swaddled like a baby, the Judge appeared to be a shriveled, deflated version of his former self. Overmyer hadn't been exaggerating. There was a bucket of water, some towels, and several empty pans, presumably to catch whatever else came out of the Judge, though he didn't look like he had anything more left of anything in him.

The Judge's sweaty skin was a frightening shade of blue, his lips were chapped, one arm was bandaged where he'd been bled, and his body was surrounded by socks bulging with hot sand.

The Judge regarded Owen with bloodshot eyes.

'You presented a compelling case, Ben.' The Judge's voice was weak and thready, barely more than a whisper.

Owen approached the bed. The smell was horrible, like an unflushed toilet. 'You heard all of that?'

'The dead could have heard you. I am not among them yet, but I am convinced that I will be with great haste if Dr Walsh has his way.' The Judge glanced at Overmyer. 'You're my witness. I refuse any further treatment from the doctor.'

Overmyer gave him an imploring look. 'You're full of opium and whiskey, you aren't thinking clearly.'

'I am of sound mind, if not body. I don't want to see Dr Walsh again.'

'You could die,' Overmyer said.

'At least it won't be in agony and from blood loss. Write up a document expressing my wishes, which we will all sign, so there's no dispute over who made this decision. Be quick about it, while I am still coherent.'

Overmyer sighed with defeat. 'If that's what you want.'

He went to the Judge's desk, found a sheet of paper, a quill, and an inkwell, and sat down to write. The Judge looked at Owen.

'Can you get this seasoning off of me?'

'Gladly.' Owen pulled a chair over to the bed. 'I'm staying with you until you're back on your feet.'

'Or dead.'

'Let's be optimistic,' Owen said.

'Just keep up the opium and whiskey regimen. It may not be curative, but it's stopped my cramps and dulled my misery.'

'I'm sure it has. It's amazing to me that you're even conscious.'

'I don't see why. I'm a man with a powerful intellect who is accustomed to prodigious and habitual use of spiritous beverages.'

The Judge's humor gave Owen hope. The three men signed the document that Overmyer wrote up. Then Owen sent Overmyer away to get more water and fresh rags, and to ask Milly to prepare Owen's own version of Gatorade: one cup of juice from the sealed tins of fruit, several tablespoons of honey, and a teaspoon of salt, mixed together, heated in a saucepan until the honey and salt dissolved, then poured into six cups of water, shaken and allowed to cool. In the meantime, while Overmyer was away, Owen removed all the hot socks, wiped the Judge's body down with wet towels, and covered him with a fresh blanket he found in the cabin.

Overmyer returned with the supplies, then had to excuse himself to get some sleep and publish his newspaper, leaving Owen alone with the Judge.

Owen gave the Judge a teaspoon of Gatorade every half-hour, the way he used to do when Nicole had stomach flu and couldn't keep anything down.

The Judge dozed and Owen browsed through some of the law books. But after only one hour, and two teaspoons of Gatorade, the Judge was wracked by a horrifying series of spasms, culminating in a massive and disgusting purging of clear, odorless fluid that filled a bed pan. It was like the Judge's insides were melting. Owen emptied the bed pan into the ravine because he had nowhere else to do it.

He gave the Judge another teaspoon of Gatorade a half-hour later, but it provoked the same explosive result. It brought tears to Owen's eyes, but at least he didn't vomit again. When Owen came back in the cabin, the Judge whispered to him.

'Give me one of those opium pills.'

Owen did, which the Judge swallowed dry.

'Nothing more to drink,' the Judge said hoarsely.

'You'll die without fluids.'

'I'm already dying. I'd like to do so with some dignity left.'

'You haven't lost any of yours,' Owen said.

The Judge slipped into sleep. Owen kept checking on him over the next few hours. His body became increasingly cold, his breathing more shallow, his skin a deeper blue. But at least the spasms and purging had stopped. His skin was sticking to his bone. Owen knew the Judge wouldn't be coming back from this. At one point, late into the night, the Judge awoke again.

'I'm afraid,' he said feebly.

'Don't be. What lies ahead is wonderful.'

'I wish I could believe that,' the Judge said, closing his eyes.

Owen made a sudden decision. He took out his iPhone, placed the earbuds in the Judge's ears, and played Judy Garland singing 'Somewhere Over the Rainbow', one of Nicole's favorite songs. The Judge's eyes fluttered open, looking at Owen in wonder.

'Do you hear the music?' His voice was a barely audible rasp.

Owen nodded. 'Have you ever been to Paris?'

'Only in my dreams.'

'Let's go together, right now.' Owen stopped the music, pulled up a video he took on a trip to Paris and held the iPhone screen in front of the Judge's face. 'This is Notre Dame . . . the Palace of Versailles . . .'

The Judge's eyes were wide now, full of wonder. 'It's the opium. None of this is real.'

'Have your dreams ever looked like this?' Owen asked. The Judge was mesmerized. 'Shall we visit Venice?'

Owen didn't wait for an answer. He showed him some movies he'd taken in Venice, then some from Rome. 'This is the Vatican . . . and this is Michelangelo's painted ceiling in the Sistine Chapel. Would you like to see the future?'

The Judge nodded.

'Have you been to San Francisco?'

The Judge nodded again.

'Well, this is Union Square in San Francisco in the twenty-first century.' Owen showed him some videos of himself and Nicole at the cable cars in Union Square. The Judge pointed a shaky finger at the image in Owen's palm.

'That's you. In the future.'

'Yes, it is.'

The Judge tapped the image of Nicole. 'Who is she?'

'My daughter Nicole.'

'But you haven't aged.'

'Because that was two years ago. I miss her every day.'

The Judge looked up from the iPhone and into Owen's eyes. 'What are you doing here and now?'

Owen smiled. 'To show you there's more to life than what we know or can explain and it's magical. You don't need to be afraid of what lies ahead.'

'I believe it now.' The Judge smiled and took Ben's hand. 'Can I hear that song again?'

Owen pulled up 'Somewhere Over the Rainbow' and played it. The Judge closed his eyes and before the song was over, he said softly:

'You can go back to her now.'

And he drifted off into unconsciousness.

Owen almost said, I wish I could. But now he had a wife he loved, and a child on the way. If a hole to the future opened up now, could he step through it and leave them behind?

No, he couldn't.

He realized that what he'd said to the Judge was true. There was magic in the unknown.

What happened to him on February 2nd, 2019, wasn't a tragedy. He'd been given a second chance at life. To get it right this time.

He was the luckiest man in the world. This was his home and his time now.

Owen pocketed his earbuds and iPhone and fell asleep. He awoke a few hours later to find the Judge still, and more sunken than before. There were no signs of breathing. He felt for a pulse . . . and found none.

The Judge was dead.

Owen pulled a sheet over the Judge and went back to his room at Denny's to sleep.

Shortly after dawn, Owen was awakened by the sound of activity downstairs. He dreaded having to tell Milly and Overmyer about the Judge's death. He went down to the dining room and found Overmyer and Milly having coffee, all smiles, which only made the task at hand worse.

Overmyer raised a coffee mug to Owen in greeting. 'You should start selling that elixir of yours, Ben, though the doctor is convinced it was that final bleeding that did the trick.'

Elixir? Magic trick?

'What are you talking about?' Owen asked, sure he was still suffering the mental fog from his short sleep and the fatigue from his long, emotional night.

Milly said, 'The Judge is going to be fine.'

'The Doc says the worst is over,' Overmyer added.

Owen was very confused and sat down at the table. 'Hold on. I don't understand. The Judge died. That's why I left.'

Overmyer poured Owen a cup of coffee from the pot on the table. 'This will clear your head. Walsh came by this morning to check on his patient, pulled away the sheet, and he was awake, thirsty as hell, though. The doctor gave the Judge some of your medicine and it immediately energized him.'

Milly said, 'I've been making more of it for him. If the Judge keeps improving, the doctor says he might be able to have soup tomorrow.'

None of this was making any sense to Owen. He held up his hands in a halting gesture. 'But he didn't have a pulse. He wasn't breathing. He was dead.'

'You made an understandable mistake,' Overmyer said.

'I did?' Owen said.

'You were tired and you're not a doctor,' Overmyer said. 'Walsh says some patients fall into a coma so deep it's like death, their pulse is so slight it can't be felt. That's why it's common practice to wait a day before burying the dead from cholera.'

'It is?' Owen said.

Milly grimaced. 'It's horrifying to think how many poor souls might have been buried alive.'

'Don't worry,' Overmyer said. 'All is forgiven and forgotten between you and the doc, too. In fact, he'd like more of that remedy you gave the Judge for his other patients.'

'Sure. Of course. Whatever he needs. No charge,' Owen said. He took a sip of his coffee and let the news sink in. He was happy the Judge was alive but terrified about what he might remember.

Milly gave him a kiss on the cheek and stood up. 'It's a miracle. I've got to get back to work or the boss might fire me.'

She went to the kitchen. Owen had some more coffee, sitting with Overmyer for a moment in a comfortable, and much appreciated, silence while he thought of all the horrible things that could happen as a result of revealing his true situation to the Judge.

'Oh, I almost forgot,' Overmyer said, reaching into his pocket. 'This came for you from the telegraph office in Daggett with the morning mail.'

Overmyer handed Owen an envelope, which he opened. It contained a note from Wendy, letting him know that she'd arrived safely in Los Angeles.

Owen poured himself another cup of coffee and thought about spiking it with something stronger. 'Has the Judge said anything?'

'No, but he keeps humming a beautiful ditty. Very catchy.'

Overmyer hummed 'Somewhere Over the Rainbow' and Owen felt a pang in his stomach. He hoped it was anxiety and not cholera.

*   *   *

Owen visited the Judge the next day with a pot of soup. It took that long for Owen to work up the courage.

The Judge was sitting up in bed now, the color restored to his skin, and some of the wrinkling was gone, but he still looked weak and shrunken. His eyes, however, were sharp and alert. Like a hawk, Owen thought.

'How are you feeling?' Owen said, setting the bowl down on the tray on the Judge's lap.

'Thankful. You saved my life.'

'I doubt that.' Owen pulled a chair over beside the bed. The room smelled a lot better, but hardly fresh.

'You kept the doctor away from me.'

'And nature did the rest,' Owen said. 'I was just company.'

'You stopped my fever, gave me nourishment, and sang me lullabies.'

'It's what my mom used to do for me when I was sick.'

'Maybe that's why it's her voice singing that I remember,' the Judge said. 'And not yours.'

Oh, shit.

'Your mind was playing tricks on you,' Owen said. 'You were on a lot of opium.'

'I still am. It's amazing the dreams you have in your delirium. I traveled the world and saw places I've never been.'

'That's why opium is so popular and addictive.'

'It can also be enlightening,' the Judge said. 'The Indians are big believers in sweating themselves, fasting, and smoking peyote to communicate with spirits. They come back with new understanding and purpose.'

'Is that what happened to you?'

'I prefer to see this as a moment of enlightenment rather than a brush with mortality.'

The conversation, much to Owen's relief, then shifted to the politics of the community, the economics of the mining industry, and other local issues.

When Owen left, he was convinced his secret was not only safe, but that the Judge wasn't even aware of it. What little the Judge remembered was just fragments of a dream.

It wasn't until a few weeks later, after the outbreak had passed, and Wendy returned to Calico with their baby boy, that something happened that shook that belief.

Owen and Wendy brought the baby to the restaurant one afternoon and introduced him to Milly, and then to the Judge and Overmyer, who were dining at a table. The Judge still hadn't regained his weight and walked with a cane, which he lifted to point at the baby.

'What a handsome child. What's his name?'

'Nicolas,' Wendy said.

The Judge smiled and winked at Owen. 'Of course it is.'

And as Owen and Wendy walked away from the table, the Judge began joyfully humming his new, favorite tune.

'Somewhere Over the Rainbow'.

TWENTY-THREE

Saturday, February 9, 2019

Beth woke up early on Saturday morning, feeling sore all over her body from the previous day's hard labor. She had the weekend off, assuming there weren't any homicides that Hatcher couldn't handle. But she wasn't going to stick around the house, cleaning up, doing laundry, or thinking of artwork she could hang on the walls to convince the men she brought to bed that her personal life wasn't barren.

Instead, she made the two-hour drive out to Silver Lake, the northeast Los Angeles neighborhood where Owen Slader lived in a Craftsman bungalow on an extremely steep hill overlooking the reservoir and its concrete shoreline.

Going back to Los Angeles after her years in her desert purgatory felt sneaky and forbidden, as if she'd been officially exiled and was breaking the law by returning, in broad daylight, no less. She half-expected to be greeted at the city limits by armed sentries, who would order her to turn around or be shot.

You have nothing to feel guilty about.

Although she wasn't breaking any law, she was knowingly

violating procedure. She was supposed to inform the LAPD that she was investigating a case in their jurisdiction.

But ignoring that rule didn't bother her at all.

She decided what she was really feeling was shame, not over what she'd done, but for not being able to live up to her father's memory. This was his city. It was his badge that she'd lost. Coming back here meant confronting his disappointment in her.

He can't be disappointed, she scolded herself. He's dead.

And he was buried years before two cops on patrol, responding to a homeowner's complaint, caught her having sex with Trent in a parked car in a Studio City neighborhood . . . and her life unraveled.

Why couldn't they have waited to fuck until they got in his house?

Beth pushed the thoughts out of her head as she took the Glendale Boulevard North exit off the Angeles Crest highway into Silver Lake. She had work to do. Police work. Because she still had a badge.

It might not be LAPD, but it was the same job. Her dad's job. His legacy she was continuing, no matter where she was.

Silver Lake had a grungy, liberal, bohemian feel that reminded Beth of Berkeley or Seattle, full of clubs, coffee houses, thrift stores, hookah bars, vinyl record stores, and ethnic cafes, on the major streets and an eclectic mix of Art Deco, Craftsman, Streamline Moderne, Victorian, Tudor, and Spanish-Colonial homes and apartments tightly packed and stacked in the hills above. But that youthful, cash-strapped, student vibe seemed too carefully curated to her, more style than a lifestyle, belied by all the expensive Mercedes Benzes, BMWs, and Teslas she saw on the streets amidst the mint-condition, self-consciously appropriate old Volvos, Subarus, and Volkswagens on display.

Her 1970 Mustang, which she'd inherited from her father and meticulously maintained, fit in with the neighborhood and didn't call attention to itself as a cop's unmarked car, but she was afraid the parking brake might not hold on the insane, nearly vertical incline in front of Slader's bungalow.

The front yard landscaping was a drought-resistant mix of succulents, cactuses, and pea gravel that was attractive but still not as water-saving as the parched, unplanted, sandy-dirt that surrounded her Barstow home. So she could congratulate herself on being environmentally conscious and water-wise.

She took out Slader's keys, unlocked the front door, and, to her relief, walked inside without having to deal with deactivating an alarm. It wasn't the alarm itself that worried her. In her experience, people were lazy with alarm codes, opting for significant birthdays and anniversaries, and she'd come armed with some of his. What she wanted to avoid, by inputting a code, was creating a digital trail indicating that someone had visited Slader's house after his death. She didn't know who might be waiting and watching.

His place was clean and orderly, with comfortable, hand-made-looking furniture that reflected the same Craftsman style as the home's exterior. The walls were decorated with art-deco prints and framed posters of old foreign films. The open kitchen was huge, befitting a professional chef, with the latest appliances, wide counters, and rustic pots, pans, and utensils artfully hanging from ceiling racks. It looked too good, like a movie set, and that was by design. In front of the kitchen was a professional digital video camera on a tripod, and several key lights were positioned on the edges of the room, ready to turn the space into a brightly illuminated set for his YouTube show. She wondered how much of his mortgage he was writing off as a business expense on his taxes.

Beth opened the refrigerator, which was filled with wine, meat, cheese, fruit, and vegetables, though much of it was already beginning to go bad. The nearby pantry had enough spices, flour, sauces, cooking oils, and different types of rice to supply a restaurant or two. But she also spotted boxes of Frosted Flakes, Cocoa Puffs, and Captain Crunch, presumably favorites of Slader's daughter.

There were three small bedrooms. One was clearly for his daughter, with a child's bed and desk, YA books on the shelves, and some of her clothes in the closet. The master bedroom was divided into an office on one end, with his desk, a computer, file cabinets, and bookcases filled with cookbooks and memoirs by famous chefs. The other side of the room was a makeshift TV studio, with a floor-to-ceiling green backdrop for superimposing images, key lights, a boom microphone, and a video camera outfitted with a teleprompter on a tripod. The remaining bedroom was his, with a king-sized bed squeezed in tight and nearly touching three walls.

She spent the next several hours searching first Slader's desktop computer (the password was a combination of his daughter's name and her birthday) and then his house for anything that might tie him to Newberry Springs, Yermo, Calico, or the Cartwrights. She didn't find anything. The only evidence of criminal activity she found was a hard drive of pirated music, theatrical films, TV series, and porn downloaded from the Internet that made him guilty of copyright infringement. Among the movies she discovered on the hard drive was the *Back to the Future* trilogy, but she avoided the temptation to watch it.

Her visit to the house gave her a sense of Owen Slader's personal and professional life, and his prurient interest in lesbian sex, but nothing that would help her solve the mysteries surrounding his disappearance or his death.

Or his time travel.

That was an insane theory, and one she couldn't prove, and shouldn't even allow to intrude into her thoughts or influence her work.

For now, she told herself, she had to approach this like any other investigation of a suspicious death, until the evidence suggested . . . no, *proved* . . . otherwise.

Sabine Denier, Slader's ex-girlfriend and the mother of his daughter, owned a French-Vietnamese fusion café, coffee house, and LGBTQ bookstore called The Outlit in Atwater Village.

Beth met her at The Outlit and they sat down at a table in the middle of the narrow, brick-walled storefront with two iced *cà phê đá*s, a Vietnamese coffee.

Sabine was a slim, fine-boned woman in her thirties who appeared to Beth to be a French-Vietnamese fusion herself. Her hair was colored deep black, and was cut in a short, very masculine style. She wore a tank-top that allowed her to display the intricate sleeve of tattoos on her left arm, from her fingertips to her shoulder.

Sabine saw her studying it and said: 'It's the history of the French occupation of Vietnam. It takes a few hours to truly appreciate the whole arm and the story it tells.'

Beth took a sip of her iced coffee, an intensely dark roast mixed with condensed milk that had a bold taste that was refreshing and packed a surprising caffeine jolt. She really needed it.

'Why all on one arm?'

'Because it only represents part of who I am, my ethnicity. My right arm will express my omnisexuality, which I've only recently come to understand and celebrate, so I am still researching the imagery I want to use. I thought Owen would mock my plans, but he surprised me by being supportive,' she said. 'He was an unfaithful, undependable, irresponsible, infuriating boyfriend . . . but he never stopped being my closest friend. Does that make sense to you?'

No, it didn't, but she said: 'Of course. We all have relationships like that.'

'I never doubted that he loved me, or Nicole, but for a long time, he loved himself more. Then, over the last couple of years, Owen really changed. He truly cherished his time with Nicole. He never missed one of his weekends with her and kept in touch with her every day with a call, a text, or by sharing a photo of something interesting he saw, or some unusual dish that he ate. Sometimes it was just a simple emoji. But there was always something to let her know he was thinking about her. That's how I knew, when he didn't show on Saturday, when he didn't even call me or text her, that something terrible had happened to him. Do you know yet how he was killed?'

'We know that he's dead,' Beth said. 'We don't know that he was killed.'

'What's the difference?'

'Dying isn't a crime. Killing can be, if it wasn't an accident. Usually, a killing is characterized by signs of physical trauma, like broken bones, gunshot, or stab wounds, that kind of thing. He doesn't have any.'

'What about poison, suffocation, or electrocution?'

'The coroner hasn't found any evidence of that,' Beth said, not mentioning it would be hard to find in century-old bones, though she hoped Trent only told her they'd found his decomposed body, not how truly decomposed it actually was.

'Someone buried him,' she said.

'Burying a body isn't necessarily a crime, unless you were responsible for the death or intentionally covering up for whoever was. But we're treating his death as a homicide until we know for sure what happened,' Beth said. 'That's why I am here.'

A woman squeezed behind Sabine's chair to reach for a book on a shelf in the Alternate Worlds & Alternate Sexes section, which Beth assumed would translate to Science Fiction & Fantasy in a Barnes & Noble.

Sabine scooted closer to the table to give the customer room to move and said to Beth: 'I'll help in any way I can.'

'Did Owen have any personal or business connections to Yermo or Newberry Springs that you know about?'

'No,' she said. 'I'd never heard of either place until Owen disappeared.'

'What about Calico?'

'What's Calico?'

'An old mining town and tourist attraction in the mountains north of Yermo,' Beth said. 'They have mine tours, a mystery shack, gold-panning for the kids, and a train ride.'

'Owen hated places like that,' she said. 'He was always looking for authentic experiences, in life and in food. What's Calico have to do with anything?'

'It's in the same general area where he disappeared,' Beth lied, figuring that was much better than saying one of her theories was that Owen went back in time and opened a fine-dining restaurant in a mining camp. 'I'm not leaving out any possibilities.'

Including time travel. Which was absolutely insane and something she wouldn't say out loud, certainly not to this woman.

'An open mind is a good thing. It leads to meaningful discovery,' Sabine said. 'It's what this bookstore, café, and my life are all about now. Free-thinking, free-living, and free-loving, without being bound by inhibitions, self-doubt, and arbitrary definitions. You have to believe that anything is possible.'

'That's not easy for me,' Beth said. 'I need to be able to prove what I believe.'

'Maybe in court,' Sabine said. 'But how about to yourself?'

'Me, too.' Perhaps there was a book in the Alternate Worlds & Alternate Sexes section that might help her do that.

'But there's so much in this life, in this world, that's real, that you can feel, that you can know is true, but can't be proven. Does that mean it's false?'

'It does in my job,' Beth said. 'Did Owen ever mention the Cartwrights?'

'No,' she said. 'Who are they?'

'They own the patch of desert where Owen's body was buried, but it's probably meaningless. It wasn't fenced in or anything. There's no way anybody could tell that sand apart from anywhere else in the desert. I'm just looking for something, anything really, to go on.'

Beth knew that made her appear desperate and lost, and that didn't inspire much confidence in others, but she wasn't ready to share the truth. Sabine must have sensed how pathetic the admission made Beth look, because she reached out and patted her hand reassuringly.

'I appreciate your effort,' Sabine said. 'I don't get that same sense of commitment from the LAPD. At least you're trying and that means everything to me.'

'I'm not going to give up,' Beth said.

'Keep that open mind,' Sabine said.

The Cartwrights lived in a massive contemporary home on a Bel-Air hill high above the Los Angeles basin.

Beth drove up to their imposing wrought-iron gate, identified herself on the intercom, held her badge up to the camera, and was allowed inside.

It was like driving through a botanical garden, full of mature trees, lush vegetation, burbling creeks, and serene ponds that Beth assumed required an army of gardeners to maintain, though they were nowhere in sight.

The home was a cantilevered wonder of white stucco and floor-to-ceiling glass that seemed to defy gravity, floating above the garden, a stream, and the city below. It was nearly transparent.

She parked her car and walked up to the huge glass doors where Christopher Cartwright waited for her in a loose silk shirt, linen slacks, and loafers. Only a light dusting of gray in the brown hair at his temples hinted that he was in his fifties. Otherwise, he looked to her like one of those well-off, middle-aged male models in an advertisement for men's cologne, reverse mortgages, or pills for erectile dysfunction.

Cartwright looked worried, which was a typical reaction to a homicide detective showing up at someone's door, but she'd been hoping for an unexpected reaction, something to arouse her suspicions, especially given all the odd ways the family was connected to Owen Slader's bones. It was a disappointment.

'You're a long way from home, detective,' he said nervously. 'The news must be pretty bad if you came all this way to deliver it personally.'

'Don't worry, Mr Cartwright, I'm not here regarding a member of your family or a close friend, at least I don't think so. Perhaps you heard about the old grave found at your construction site in Newberry Springs?'

'No, I didn't,' Christopher said, taking a deep, relieved breath. 'We have hundreds of projects going on in California and uncovering a fossil or an old grave isn't unusual. That's why we employ a full-time team of archeologists.'

'I would have thought this project was special,' Beth said, 'since it's on land that's been in your family for generations.'

He smiled, beckoning her inside with a sweep of his arm. 'That doesn't really narrow it down. My family has been purchasing land in Southern California since the 1880s. You'd be surprised how much property we've acquired over the last century that still remains undeveloped, waiting until just the right moment or opportunity. We have thousands of acres in Kern County, for instance, that could become an entire town someday. Being visionary is part of our DNA as a family and as a company.'

Or they already knew what was coming, she thought. At least until February 2nd, 2019.

Beth stepped past him into an enormous two-story great room. A free-standing, transparent plexiglass cat-walk crossed the space, connecting the two second-floor wings of the house. There was even a plexiglass opening in the floor, offering a view below of Cartwright's subterranean garage and his collection of new and old sports cars.

'The body I'm investigating was found on what was once your great-great-grandmother's ranch,' Beth said.

'Ah yes, the Desert Lake resort. We're so excited about that project. We just broke ground on that one last week.'

'Because you couldn't do it any earlier under the terms of your family trust,' Beth said, walking to the far window. Outside was an infinity pool that spilled out to an astonishing view of the entire Los Angeles basin, east to the cluster of skyscrapers downtown, south to the Inglewood Hills, and west clear out to the Pacific. There were two women in the pool, a middle-aged woman in a one-piece suit and a younger version of her in a bikini, both floating on air cushions, sipping cocktails and when they got bored, Beth imagined, tossing bolts of lightning down on the mortals in the city below.

'You've been doing your research,' Christopher said.

'I've never heard of a hundred-plus-year prohibition against developing a particular property.'

'Actually, property protections in a trust aren't that unusual. My great-great-grandparents' hearts and souls were obviously invested in that land and I respect that. What's unusual is that they allowed it to be developed at all.'

'What was the significance of February 2nd, 2019 to them?'

'I don't know,' Christopher said. 'I mean no offense, detective, but what does any of that have to do with the bones that were found?'

'Because that date is significant to us. That's when a man named Owen Slader disappeared on his way back to Los Angeles from Las Vegas,' Beth said. 'It's his body that was discovered a few days later, buried in an old grave on your great-great-grandparents' land.'

'That's a startling coincidence.'

'So you can see why we are wondering if there is a connection.'

'Yes, of course, I am wondering about it now, too, but I can't imagine what it could be,' Christopher said. 'I've never heard of Owen Slader.'

'That's frustrating,' Beth said. 'I was really hoping to leave here with something to go on for my investigation. His grieving family is desperate to know what happened to him.'

'I wish I could help,' Christopher said.

Beth gestured to the women in the pool. 'Perhaps they know him?'

'That's my wife Elinor and my daughter Britney. I doubt they knew him, either. But you're welcome to ask them.'

'Can we?'

He led her out to the patio. The pool had vanishing edges on all side, a design trick involving a narrow overflow channel that made the patio seem flush with the water and continued the illusion that the sky, the water, and the home were all floating together over the city.

'Ellie, Britney, this is Detective McDade, she's here from Barstow investigating a skeleton that was found during work on one of our construction sites,' Cartwright said. 'She'd like to ask you some questions.'

'Just one, actually,' Beth said. 'Do either of you know a chef named Owen Slader?'

'I haven't met him,' Britney said, 'but I like his YouTube show. He knows where to find all of the best food trucks in the city.'

'You eat out of a truck?' her mother said.

'They are kitchens on wheels,' Britney said. 'Owned by some terrific chefs.'

'If they are so terrific, they would be working in restaurants, not in a parking lot or on the side of some road,' Elinor said.

'Besides watching his show,' Beth said to Britney, 'have you had any other interaction with him?'

'I left a comment on one of his videos,' she said. 'But he didn't respond, so I guess my interest was unrequited.'

'*Unrequited* suggests some love or affection was involved,' Elinor said. 'I think you mean *unreciprocated.*'

Britney gave her a sour look. 'I'm having a conversation, not writing a term paper, but thanks for the correction, Mom.'

Elinor smiled at Beth. 'I was a high-school English teacher in a previous life.'

'Is that where the family interest in H. G. Wells comes from?' Beth asked.

'*The Time Machine* is Christopher's treasured heirloom, not mine,' Elinor said. 'It's one of the terms of the pre-nup I signed twenty-six years ago.'

Cartwright looked at Beth. 'How did you know that I own a first edition of the book?'

'I didn't,' Beth said. 'But when I saw trucks from Herbert George Well Drilling and Morlock Construction at the Newberry Springs property, I figured somebody in the family must be a big fan of H. G. Wells.'

'That was Ben and Wendy Cartwright, my great-great-great-grandparents,' Christopher said with a smile. 'The book has been handed down in the family for generations. Ben and Wendy were also the ones who established those two companies.'

'Why do you think *The Time Machine* meant so much to them?'

'They probably just thought it was a wildly entertaining book,'

Christopher said. 'They were very well-read. There wasn't much else to do for entertainment in the middle of the desert. They had an extensive and impressive library that included first editions of books by Mark Twain and John Muir. In fact, Muir's daughter Helen lived in Daggett for her health and he visited her often. They were regular dinner guests at the Cartwright ranch. John Muir died of pneumonia on one of his visits to the desert.'

'Maybe his bones are on Dad's land, too,' Britney said.

'He's buried near his home in Martinez, California,' Christopher said.

Elinor smiled at Beth. 'California history is one of Christopher's passions.'

'It's so unbelievably boring,' Britney said. 'He can go on for hours and hours and hours about obscure stuff nobody remembers.'

'There's no future without the past,' Christopher said. 'We owe everything this family has to the investments Ben and Wendy Cartwright made over a hundred years ago. The land they bought in the San Fernando Valley, Beverly Hills, and Santa Monica built our company. They foresaw the future of Los Angeles.'

Or Ben Cartwright was from it, she thought, and used his knowledge to make investments that were guaranteed to pay off.

She wondered if Christopher already knew or suspected that, and if she'd finally solved for him the mystery of who Ben Cartwright really was. She had the uncomfortable feeling that she was a puppet, her strings being pulled from a hundred and thirty-seven years in the past.

'Which brings us back to H. G. Wells,' Beth said.

Christopher appeared bewildered 'It does?'

'The impact of the past on the future, and I suppose vice-versa if we aren't careful,' Beth said. 'Isn't that the message of his book?'

'Actually,' Elinor said, 'I think the message of *The Time Machine* is in the quotation from Robert Browning on the title page, "All that is all lasts ever past recall."'

Britney said, 'Sounds like bullshit to me.'

'It means that what we do, and what we create, outlasts us all, long after we are forgotten,' Elinor said.

'Then why didn't he just say that?' Britney said.

'It's not as poetic,' Elinor said. 'Or beautiful.'

'Maybe to you,' she said. 'To me, it sounds like a confusing, idiotic way of saying something that's dull and obvious, so why bother saying it at all?'

Beth turned to Christopher. 'What happened to Ben and Wendy Cartwright's personal library?'

'Some of it was given away to friends and neighbors, some was lost or damaged,' Christopher said, 'but I'm pleased to say that most of it, particularly the truly valuable books, was donated over the years to libraries, universities, and museums.'

'Except for *The Time Machine*,' Beth said. 'That book made such a lasting impression on Ben and Wendy Cartwright that it's remained in your family to this day. Don't you wonder why?'

Christopher shrugged. 'I guess we'll never know.'

'Don't be so sure,' Beth said to him, then turned to his wife and daughter in the pool. 'Thank you both for your time.'

'Are we suspects?' Britney asked.

Beth smiled. 'Everyone is a suspect.'

'Cool,' Britney said.

Her mother gave her a sharp look. 'Why would you want to be a suspect in a man's death?'

'It makes me feel like a femme fatale,' she said. 'Sexy and dangerous.'

'Why would you want to feel like that?'

'Because I'm not a withered old prune,' Britney said.

Christopher smiled at Beth and took her gently by the arm. 'I'd better see you out before this turns into a crime scene.'

'A drowning,' Elinor called after him as he and Beth walked away. 'That's absolutely not an accident.'

Christopher led Beth back through the house and out the front door before speaking again. 'I'm curious, detective. What's next in your investigation?'

Beth turned to him, standing in his doorway, and looked him in the eye. 'I don't believe in coincidence, Mr Cartwright. I am going to prove what happened to Owen Slader on February 2nd, 2019, and why your ancestors decided over a hundred years ago not to let anyone dig on their land until that date.'

'I was hoping you'd say that,' he said. 'Don't give up.'

Christopher smiled and closed the door.

And once again, she felt the distant tug of a puppeteer's strings.

TWENTY-FOUR

On the way back to Barstow, Beth followed Sabine's advice about keeping an open mind. She decided to accept, at least for the length of the drive, that Owen Slader was Ben Cartwright and to consider everything she knew about his disappearance, and the events surrounding it, from that standpoint.

Sabine had also stressed how much Slader cherished his daughter Nicole, and that he'd always found a way to remain in touch with her. When Beth factored his devotion into her thinking, everything seemed to fit together so naturally, and so quickly, that it took her breath away.

Beth understood why Slader had stayed in the desert, despite their wealth, and why he'd protected the land he was buried on with an iron-clad trust that didn't expire until the day, over a century in the future, when he would disappear.

He didn't want to do anything that would prevent himself, or his daughter, from being born.

But as soon as she had that thought, she realized there was more to it than that.

Slader must have desperately wanted Nicole to know that he hadn't abandoned her, that he loved her, something he couldn't do from 137 years in the past.

Or could he?

That's why he directed that, upon his death, his body would be buried in an unmarked grave on his ranch, not in a cemetery plot. And it was why he established a trust that would guarantee that if his body was ever found, it would be after there was any chance that the discovery would alter the future he'd lived in from happening.

That was February 2nd, 2019 . . . because after that, he'd already be in the past and his daughter's future would be safe . . . and still yet-to-be, unknowable to him.

There was no way, of course, that Slader could predict how long after that date his body would be exhumed, but at least he'd created the *possibility* that his daughter might someday learn the truth about his disappearance.

And to point whoever was looking in the right direction, he'd left some obvious clues.

He named himself after a character in a TV Western. He named his restaurant after a national chain of coffee shops. And he named a company after the author of *The Time Machine*.

If that wasn't enough, he'd even left his 2018 Mercedes intact in a cave as a prize for a truly persistent investigator.

And that's me.

Owen Slader was speaking to Beth from the past, telling her that the responsibility for finding that truth, the explanation of his fate, for his daughter was now in her hands.

In that moment, she knew something else.

She believed it.

Owen Slader went back in time.

It was the only explanation that made sense.

But crazy people always think what they believe makes perfect sense. That's what makes them crazy.

She knew in her gut that Slader being hurled back in time, and Motor Home Man into the future, had something to do with the freak lightning storm, the explosions at the Marine Corps Logistics Base and twenty-five miles away from there at Fort Irwin, and all of the other strange incidents that happened in San Bernardino County at the same moment.

Somehow, she'd have to find tangible evidence that would not only explain what happened, but undeniably prove it, too, or she'd be treated as a lunatic for the rest of her life.

Like Alan Vernon, the guy on the radio. Alone in the desert, screaming into the wind about wild, extraterrestrial conspiracies that nobody believes.

What evidence did she have so far?

Owen Slader's ancient bones with modern-day implants. Motor Home Man's body scarred with nineteenth-century afflictions and dressed in period clothing. A 2018 Mercedes missing for only a week but showing decades of erosion. An impossibly prescient trust document written over a hundred years ago. And the confirmed existence of a fresh, bullet-riddled carcass of a California grizzly bear that had been extinct for nearly a century . . . until it magically reappeared on February 2nd.

It wasn't enough evidence to convince people that time travel had somehow actually occurred and that there wasn't some other, more believable and rational explanation for what happened to Owen Slader and Motor Home Man.

She needed much, much more.

But she knew where to start.

Beth went directly to the Barstow Sheriff's station, rushed to her desk, and printed out the name and address of the man who'd found a car engine in his living room on February 2nd. His name was Nate Retchel and he lived on Lombardy Avenue in Skyline North, an island of fifty-year-old tract homes surrounded by open desert.

She got back in her car and headed north, passing Pour Decisions on 1st Street, where she'd overheard the engine story from two cops and where, she guessed, she might not be very welcome any more after putting three of their colleagues in the hospital jail ward.

Oh well, she could always go back to Baker.

Beth went over the old iron bridge, past the Harvey House train station, and up into the desert below the craggy Waterman Hills.

There were about a hundred sun-bleached homes in Skyline North; some were well maintained on nicely landscaped properties, but most of them were on barren land and looked like terminal cancer patients in their final days of chemotherapy.

She went to the address, at the south end of Lombardy where the asphalt road just petered out into the sand, and was surprised to see only a sickly palm tree lurching over an empty lot where Retchel's house should be.

Beth double-checked the address she had on paper with the number on the curb, and they matched.

She got out of her car, walked up to the lot and noticed, as she got closer, that it was recently graded, the boundaries marked by the tread marks of heavy earth-moving equipment. It gave her a queasy feeling.

'Are you looking for the Nate Retchel place?' a woman asked.

Beth turned and saw a heavy-set woman in a T-shirt, shorts, and flip-flops, standing in the backyard of the neighboring home and holding a tiny diapered baby boy like a sack of groceries in her arm. There was a picnic table, a swing set, several bikes, an inflatable baby pool, several cats, and the stripped carcasses of two cars on blocks in her yard.

'Yes, I am,' Beth said. 'I guess I am not the first person who got the wrong address.'

'You got the right address,' she said. 'But you missed the house.'

'I don't understand.'

'They paid Nate off and took it away,' she said.

'Now I am really confused.' Beth walked over to her and flashed her badge. 'I am Beth McDade, a detective with the Barstow Sheriff's Department. I came here to follow up on a deputy's report that someone broke into Mr Retchel's home and dumped a car engine in his living room.'

'Nate, the old fool, thought Dale, that's my husband, might've done it, since he's a mechanic like Nate used to be and has killer sense of humor, but Dale says there's no way you'd get Caterpillar C6.6 engine in Nate's house without taking out his front door and most of the wall around it. And that engine is for military trucks and Dale doesn't work on those. Mostly he works on pickups and American cars, your Detroit-made Ford and Chevys, none of those Japanese or German shit cans 'cause his grandpa fought in World War II, lost an ear and supposedly one of his balls, but nobody dared ask him if that was true for fear he'd shoot 'em. The man liked his guns, rest his soul.'

'That's all very interesting,' Beth said, and some of it was, especially the part about the military trucks. 'But what I really need to know is where I can find Mr Retchel and his house so I can begin my investigation.'

'Nate's out at his son's place in Lake Havasu for now,' she said. 'I don't know where his house is. On Thursday, some rich real-estate investor showed up, offered Nate a dump truck of money for his place and everything inside it. The catch was he had to go that night and sign a contract promising not to say nothing more about it. So that's what he did. Next morning, they came, tore the entire house down, and took it all away.'

Beth's throat went dry, which wasn't unusual when standing outside, in ninety-degree heat. But this time it wasn't from the heat.

'Who was this investor?' she asked.

'I don't know. But his crew was all out here wearing them space suits in case of any asbestos. That's what the guy said who came to our door. He said we weren't in any danger, but just to be absolutely sure we'd be safe, and to apologize for our inconvenience, he offered us and the Nickersons across the street $1,000 in cash to go away for the day.' Her baby started to wail, so she casually lifted up her top and offered him a nipple to suckle, which immediately quieted him down. 'I asked if he'd like to buy our house too, but he said it didn't fit into their development plans, whatever they are. So we took the cash, went to the Outlets, lived large at I-Hop, bought clothes for the kids, and when we got back, Nate's place was gone. Like it was never there.'

Beth looked back at the empty lot. *They* had to be the military. But they didn't just come for the engine. They took the entire house. Why would they do that?

'You must be happy,' the woman said.

Beth turned back to her. 'Why is that?'

'Now you don't have to figure out how that engine got in Nate's living room.'

That was probably the idea, she thought. And then it occurred to her that if they'd take an entire house, not just the engine, they wouldn't let any evidence remain of whatever the hell had happened.

Any evidence . . .

Beth ran back to her car without a word to the woman and peeled out, her tires burning rubber, her V-8 roaring to match her own rage.

It only took her eight minutes, driving at seventy miles an hour and blowing through every red light she hit, leaning on her horn, to get to the Old Barstow hospital. She came to a screeching stop and ran up to the hospital doors.

They were chained shut.

Beth walked back to her Mustang, popped the trunk, took out the tire iron, and marched up to the first ground-floor window that she saw.

She smashed the glass out with the tire iron, climbed inside the vacant office, and marched down one shadowy hallway after another until she reached the morgue.

The doors were closed and locked.

Beth pried them open with the tire iron, splintering the wood, and went inside the dark room.

The morgue was completely gutted. Down to the studs.

TWENTY-FIVE

Beth went back outside, threw the tire iron back in the trunk, and called Amanda Selby. The coroner answered on the first ring and Beth could hear children playing, and circus-like calliope music in the background.

'Good news, you just proved there's cell phone reception in hell,' Amanda said.

'What's hell?'

'Chuck E. Cheese,' Amanda said. 'A kid's birthday party. I'd rather be doing an autopsy of a corpse that's been in a lake for a week. In fact, that's what the pizzas here remind me of. What can I do for you?'

Beth thought about how to say it without sounding crazy. 'The morgue in Barstow is gone.'

'Oh, yeah, I'm surprised they didn't inform you guys, too. I got a text about it yesterday. Apparently, an inspection found asbestos or something in that old hospital, so they decided to immediately shut the temporary morgue there out of an abundance of caution, which I appreciate as an expectant mother, and bring everything back to San Bernardino until the remodel of the field office in Needles is done.'

'When I said gone, I mean gone,' Beth said. 'Down to the studs.'

'Of course, morgue freezers, exam tables, and equipment are expensive and we have a tight budget. They aren't going waste that stuff. The hospital is being torn down soon, anyway.'

Probably a lot sooner than anybody expected, Beth thought. It was obvious that Amanda didn't find anything ominous about the shut-down. But Amanda didn't have the context, she didn't know about Retchel's house, the Mercedes in the cave, or anything else, and Beth wasn't about to share that right now.

'What happened to all the files, bodies, and physical evidence?'

'I'm sure it's all waiting for me downtown to deal with on Monday,' she said. 'I'm just glad they didn't haul me in to help with the move. Not having a field office is good for me, it means

I'll be closer to home, but a pain in the ass for you. You're going to be spending a lot more time on the road the next few months if you want to attend any autopsies.'

'Yeah, that's going to be a pain,' Beth said. 'Sorry to bother you on your day off. It was just a shock to find the morgue gone.'

'What were you doing there?'

It was a good question. If she'd been called to the morgue now for a case, it would have been to San Bernardino. Amanda had some good cop instincts of her own.

Beth thought about how to answer her and, perhaps, give her a warning at the same time. 'I was looking for Marty McFly.'

There was a moment of silence, when all Beth heard was the calliope music and the excited shrieks of children, then, softly: 'I thought you were ignoring him.'

'Not anymore,' Beth said.

'I might go into the morgue tomorrow and get a head-start on sorting things out from the move,' Amanda said, trying to sound casual, 'so all of that crap doesn't get in the way of my day-to-day work.'

'There may not be as much to do as you think,' Beth said.

'I'll call you if I find myself with time on my hands,' Amanda said and hung up.

Beth was certain Amanda got the message. They were entering into uncharted territory now, somewhere in the Twilight Zone, and Beth was lost. She didn't know where to go next. And then it occurred to her.

Find an experienced tour guide.

TWENTY-SIX

Newberry Springs, 1887

Owen had gotten up before Wendy for a change so he could begin prepping food for the big supper he'd agreed to cater in Borate, the borax-mining camp deep in Mule Canyon, for Nelson Dumetz's potential investors.

Over the last year, borax mining had become almost as big a business for Calico as silver and Owen knew it was what would support the town in its dying days, after the price of silver plummeted.

Dumetz needed a cash infusion to build a refinery in the valley floor instead of sending the ore to Alameda, up in Northern California, by rail to be processed.

A local refinery would cut his costs considerably but would also require a huge capital expenditure, which was a problem for Dumetz, despite the success of the mine. He'd already borrowed half a million dollars to buy out his partner, build out the Calico mines, and acquire the plant in Alameda.

Owen wished him success. The refinery would be a boost to the Calico economy and his own wallet. He had to do what he could to support it. But he also had another agenda.

Wendy came in, carrying Nicolas, and gave Owen a kiss on the cheek as he checked how the pork he'd been marinating was doing. 'Morning, Future Man.'

'There are fresh croissants on the table.'

'It was the smell that woke me up,' she said. 'I don't see why you are going all the way out there to cook for those scumbags. We don't need their money. We're rich.'

'Calico needs it, but that's not entirely why I'm doing it,' Owen said. 'These investors have come from all over the country to see Dumetz's borax operation. This is my chance to speak directly to the decision-makers.'

The mine was deep in wind-whipped Mule Canyon, where temperatures were scorching during the day and freezing at night, forcing many of the mine workers to live and work underground. The workers were paid $3.50 a day, but a dollar of that went to room and board (with Chinese cooks, of course) and any other niceties had to be bought from the company store at exorbitant prices, the profits going to the mine. Only fresh fruit and mail were brought in from Calico, and the men had to pay for that, too. The men worked ten hours a day, seven days a week, with only four hours off a week on Sundays, which made it unlikely they'd ever leave the camp. And when they did, few had much money saved up to show for their labors. Owen thought that was unconscionable.

Wendy put Nicolas in his high chair, gave him a piece of a croissant, and began eating the rest herself.

'It's pointless, Ben, you know that. History shows he exploited his workers, sucked the mountains dry, then dismantled everything and moved on to the next mother lode.'

'Maybe this is some history I can change without endangering my future.'

'You're dreaming.'

Rico came in with a snake draped over his arm like a shawl. Wendy gasped, and Owen put himself protectively in front of the baby's high chair, until they both realized the snake was headless.

Rico grinned, showing off five of his few remaining good teeth. 'I found a huge rattlesnake dozing on the porch, so I chopped off his head with my shovel. Now you have meat for your kitchen and a new toy for little Nicky.'

He shook the still-bloody amputated rattle in front of the chubby, joyful child, who squealed with delight.

Wendy was clearly repulsed but forced a smile. 'That's a really lovely thought, Rico, but I want him to be afraid when he hears a rattler, and not think of it as something to play with.'

Owen saw how crestfallen Rico was, so he jumped in to say: 'But I will take that meat. It will make an exotic ingredient for those stuffy money men I'll be feeding.'

Rico removed the dead snake and handed it to Owen.

Wendy shook her head. 'You should take the venom for them instead.'

Rico shook the rattle again and stuffed it into his pocket. 'I will keep the rattle as a good luck charm. Your horse and carriage are ready, Mr Cartwright.'

'Thank you, Rico.' Owen offered Rico the plate of croissants.

Rico took three. 'For the other men.'

'Take the whole plate.'

Rico did and hurried out before Owen could change his mind. Wendy looked after him. 'I'll bet you he eats them all himself.'

'It's a small price to pay for all the work he oversees for us.'

Owen relied on Rico and his men to tend the alfalfa, cows, chickens, cantaloupe, and watermelon, and to kill the rabbits that ravaged everything they tried to grow. The goal was for the ranch to achieve self-sufficiency by the time Calico died in a few years and Owen didn't have the farming or ranching skills to do it on his own.

Owen began packing up his food into a wooden crate. 'I'm going back to Calico tonight for the big dance. The town will be filled with a lot of hungry people. Is there anything you'd like me to bring back on Sunday?'

'Check to see if we have mail at Stoby's. I'm expecting a copy of *Dr Jekyll and Mr Hyde* by Robert Louis Stevenson.'

'Since when are you into horror stories?'

'I'm into owning first editions. Do you know what that book is going to be worth someday?'

She gestured to the bookcase in their front room. She already owned first editions of all of Mark Twain's books.

'No, I don't,' he said. 'Do you?'

'I'm sure it's a lot. We know what all the classics are going to be. It would be a crime if we let the opportunity to grab them go by. I'm buying *Dracula, The Wizard of Oz*, and the first Sherlock Holmes novel as soon as they come out. Someday our library will be worth a fortune.'

Maybe not for them, he thought, but for their descendants.

'I hadn't thought of that,' he said, picking up the crate.

'You are so lucky to have me.'

'I certainly am.' He kissed Nick on the cheek, too, and headed out for his long ride.

Back when he lived in the future, Owen used to complain about the long, dull five-hour drive between Los Angeles and San Francisco on Interstate 5 through bleak, endless farmland, not a town or city in sight, just a cluster of gas stations and fast-food places, like patch of weeds.

The only benefit of taking the five was that it was essentially a straight shot through flat land. The Highway Patrol cops had no place to hide. In his view, anybody who didn't spot the CHP planes or patrol cars deserved to get a speeding ticket.

He'd had no idea in the twenty-first century how luxurious and wonderful that drive was, gliding on cruise control at a hundred miles an hour, listening to podcasts and music in air-conditioned comfort on the plush leather seat of his Mercedes GLC. He didn't appreciate what he had.

Now he was in the outdoors, sitting on a buckboard bench, riding on wooden wheels across twenty miles of rutted desert, the sun pounding down on him, facing the active assholes of two horses on an hours-long trip that would have taken a few minutes by car, from his home in Newberry Springs to Mule Canyon, three miles east from Calico. The only joy he had was his iPhone, and being able to listen to music on his earbuds.

Steering a carriage across the deserts was mindless, the horses pretty much going on their own. But once he got into the narrow, steep-walled, wind-whipped canyon, things got tricky for him. He ended up relying on the horses to press on and not to kill themselves and him finding their way to Borate.

The mine itself was tucked into a crease in the canyon, the cave openings covered with wooden, fake facades, like a Hollywood set. But there were a few detached wooden cabins for the senior staff and their families, who occasionally came into Calico to dine at his restaurant.

But dominating it all, on a hill overlooking the canyon, was Nelson Dumetz's Victorian-style one-story house, which was staked to the ground with iron cables like a hot-air balloon so the fierce wind, shrieking up from the canyon, wouldn't blow it away. From there, Dumetz could look down on his domain and his workers could gaze up at him in the heavens, the mighty roar of the wind like his own voice, commanding them to continue their labors. It made a powerful statement.

The wind shook Owen's carriage as he branched off from the canyon and up onto the steep trail to the house. He gripped the reins, terrified that a sudden gust would send the carriage, horses and all, onto the jagged rocks below. But somehow he made it to the top, where he was greeted by Nelson Dumetz and his uniformed black butler as he pulled up to the wide front porch.

Dumetz was a round man in a suit and top hat, with a bushy mustache that reminded Owen of the cartoon character on the Pringles potato chips canister. He had round glasses that only accentuated his overall roundness. He leaned on a silver-handled white-tipped walking stick that looked like a prop from a Fred Astaire dance sequence.

'You're right on time, Mr Cartwright. I admire punctuality.'

'You can thank the horses. I was just along for the ride.' Owen's ass and lower back were killing him, and he was covered in a layer of dust.

'I also admire modesty. You can come on down from there. Black Charlie will tend to your horses and bring your things around back to the kitchen.'

'Black Charlie?' Owen climbed off the carriage.

Dumetz gestured to the butler, who climbed up to take Owen's place.

'We have four Charlies, Mr Cartwright. Yellow Charlie is our cook. He'll be helping you today. Mex Charlie is the head house boy, though he's forty if he's a day.'

Owen stretched and slapped some of the dust off himself. 'What about the other Charlie?'

'He's Charlie, the mine supervisor.'

'Not White Charlie? Or American Charlie?'

Dumetz laughed and clapped Owen on the back. 'I also admire a good sense of humor. It seems you have many admirable qualities, in addition to your renowned culinary expertise.'

'I'm bound to do something you don't admire, so you'd better brace yourself.'

In fact, Owen was sure of it.

'As long as it's not the meal. I have some big investors to impress, one from as far away as Scotland.'

Dumetz led him into the house. The walls must have been reinforced with stone, because the sound of the wind instantly became a dull rumble.

The interior was elegant for its time, with fine paneling, imported furniture, beveled mirrors, and leather-bound books on the shelves.

Five businessmen, in similar attire to Dumetz, were in the living room, being served drinks by another uniformed black man, and were smoking fat cigars.

Dumetz paused to introduce Owen to them. 'Gentlemen, this is Ben Cartwright, owner and chef of the finest restaurant in Calico and, in my opinion, one of the best chefs in California. I'm delighted that he's agreed to prepare our supper today.'

Owen smiled at the guests.

'I apologize for being so dusty, gentlemen. I promise none of it will be in your food.'

An investor with huge ears, and enough hair sticking out of them to make a fake mustache, said: 'That already makes you a cut above the other cooks in the West. Dirt seems to be their main ingredient.'

'Especially in the coffee,' said another investor, the first real person Owen had ever seen wearing a monocle.

'What are you serving?' asked an investor with substantial goiter that Owen tried not to stare at.

'A frontier gourmet menu, using mostly locally sourced ingredients. An appetizer of cold Vichyssoise soup and tea-poached eggs with honey and sage over a warm dried fruit compote,' Owen said, realizing he was staring at the man's goiter. He forced himself to look at Monocle man instead. 'The other courses include Cuban-style whiskey-soaked Mojo pork, and Mojave-grilled rattlesnake chili.'

Big Ears said, 'Did you say . . . rattlesnake?'

'It's the catch of the day,' Owen said.

'We're in the desert,' Monocle said.

'Exactly,' Owen smiled. 'See you in a couple of hours.'

Dumetz gestured to one of the houseboys, who led Owen into the kitchen, which had an iron stove, a butcher board, and all the finest cookware for the time, all clean and perfectly organized. There was a vast array of spices, clearly labeled, all within easy reach for food preparation. It was impressive.

All of Owen's ingredients and supplies had been unloaded and carefully set out on the wooden counters, presumably by the Asian cook who was examining everything, his hands clasped behind his back. The Asian man wore a spotless white apron over a uniform similar to the one worn by the other staff. He smiled when he saw Owen and gave him a slight bow.

'I'm Yellow Charlie. Mr Dumetz's personal chef. He asked me to assist you.'

Owen bowed in return. 'I'm Ben. Thank you for allowing me to be a guest in your kitchen, Charlie.'

'It's *Yellow* Charlie,' he said. 'And it's Mr Dumetz's kitchen, not mine.'

'I'll call you Yellow Charlie only if you call me *Gweilo* Ben.' Owen knew that *Gweilo* was a derogatory term for whites among the Chinese. He'd heard it muttered a thousand times in Calico.

'That will not happen,' Charlie said.

'Then we have an understanding. Dumetz may own this kitchen, but it's yours in every way that matters. Your personality, and the pride your take in your work, is reflected in every detail. I don't have to taste a thing to know you are an excellent chef.'

Charlie bowed again. Owen meant every word he'd said, but it was also crucial to gain Charlie's support. The man could easily, and catastrophically, sabotage his dinner if he felt slighted in any way, unless Owen banned him outright from the premises, which he wouldn't do.

'You are very kind, Ben. How may I help?'

He handed Charlie the decapitated rattlesnake.

'You can start by skinning and deboning this, then coat it with two tablespoons of olive oil, one tablespoon of chili powder, and one teaspoon of salt and one of pepper . . . if you don't mind.'

'Not at all.'

Charlie didn't hesitate, which was a good start. And with that, Owen changed out of his dusty travel outfit into the fresh set of clothes he'd brought with him . . . and began preparation of the rest of the dishes. His first task was getting the pork in the oven.

He'd been marinating the meat for twelve hours, putting his travel time to good use. Most of the meat served in Calico, and throughout the West, was dry and stringy. But this pork was a bone-in, butt cut with a nice fat cap that would keep the meat moist as it cooked for the next three hours. He'd supervised the butcher's cut himself.

While he worked over the next few hours, and gave instructions to Charlie, he mentally practiced his speech imploring Dumetz to treat his employees better and his argument to the investors on why they should insist upon it, too. Perhaps he'd make some history today.

Two hours later, the investors were seated at a long dining room table, with fine china and silver cutlery. Dumetz sat at the head of the table and discussed the precise, technical details of borax mining and refinement.

Owen started by serving a *tarte soleil*, a buttery pastry with layers of cheese arranged to resemble a flat sun on the plate, and the tea-poached eggs. When that appetizer was done, and those dishes were cleared and replaced with soup bowls, he emerged from the kitchen again with a soup pot and ladle to personally serve each guest.

But as he stepped out in the dining room, announcing the cold, Vichyssoise soup, a fancy name for creamy mix of chicken broth, cream, pureed leeks, and potatoes, he noticed there was a new guest in the room.

A man in his late thirties, perhaps early forties, stood at the far end of the table, facing the guests. His face was black with soot, his clothes were caked with dirt, and he wore a miner's head lamp cap – a canvas cap with what looked to Owen like a tiny brass teapot resting on the leather brim, a kerosene and lard-fueled flame flickering from a wick stuffed in the spout.

But the most striking thing about the man were the sticks of dynamite that he clutched in his raised hands, letting the wicks dangle frighteningly close to the flame on his head.

TWENTY-SEVEN

Dumetz stood up and looked angrily down the length of the table at his unwanted, dynamite-carrying, guest.

'What is the meaning of this intrusion?'

'My name is Bufe Sibley and I've had it. This has to end.'

'What are you babbling about,' Dumetz said, seemingly blind to the dynamite in the man's trembling hands. 'Spit it out, you idiot.'

Perhaps, Owen thought, Dumetz hoped to subdue the man by sheer force of his personality. Or was too arrogant to take the threat seriously. Not Owen. He was terrified. However, he simply ladled soup into Dumetz's bowl, hoping that continuing his menial labors would make him invisible, or at least harmless, to the crazy man. He didn't want to die here today.

Bufe said: 'My only crime is being poor and wanting more. I don't deserve a life sentence of hard labor.'

Dumetz laughed, and looked around the table, apparently seeing his amusement shared in his mind when, in reality, his guests were all frozen in fear.

'This isn't a prison,' Dumetz said. 'There are no walls or guards. The door is right there. You can walk out and keep on going. In fact, we'd be delighted if you would.'

He waved Bufe away, pointedly ignoring that the man was holding explosives, and sat down to enjoy his soup. Owen did not see that as a winning strategy. Did Dumetz have a death wish? Why wasn't he as frightened as Owen was?

Bufe stepped closer to the table, where Owen was now serving soup to the Monocle.

'You want me to walk into a desert without food, water, or a nickel in my pocket? That's a death sentence. If I'm gonna die, I'm taking you bastards with me.'

Big Ears said, 'I see why you might be angry with him, Mr Sibley. But why us? We have nothing to do with this dispute.'

Owen kept ladling out the soup, moving from man to man, trying hard to look oblivious to the tension, merely a waiter unobtrusively serving food during the floor show. He hoped when he was done serving, he could simply walk out without Bufe noticing or caring. But his heart was pounding so hard in his chest he was afraid everyone could hear it.

'You're paying for all this,' Bufe yelled at him, 'and reaping all the profits off our backs.'

Dumetz set down his spoon. 'Oh, stop whining, you fool. We pay you a decent wage. It's not our fault if you squander it.'

Goiter looked at Dumetz, then at his fellow investors. 'We? Why is he saying we?'

Bufe drilled Dumetz with his eyes and waving his dynamite in his fists. 'You pay me three dollars a day to spend ten hours in the world's hot, dirty, dry asshole . . . seven days a week . . . and you take two-fifty of that for room and board . . . you even make us pay you for the bar of soap to wipe the grime off our faces and the candle to light our bunks while we do it. What kind of life is that?'

So much for my speech, Owen thought, continuing to move around the table, getting closer to Bufe. A plan for saving himself began to form in his mind.

Dumetz shook his head in disgust. 'The kind that got me from where you are to this table. But I had more grit than you.'

'They can put that on your tombstone.'

Bufe touched the dynamite wicks to the flame on his cap.

The men around the table rose up from their seats, but there was no time to run before the explosion.

Owen heaved the bowl of soup at Bufe, dousing most of the wicks, and tackled him, a few remaining lit sticks scattering across the floor.

The other men rushed about, frantically stamping out the wicks on the dynamite. But one rolled into the fireplace. There was no time to get to it.

I'm going to die, Owen thought.

Dumetz overturned the dining table, the top facing the fireplace, and dove to the floor.

The explosion blew a hole out the back of the chimney and the remaining force sent the table sliding across the floor, slamming into Owen and Bufe.

It took a moment for the smoke to clear. Owen's ears were ringing, but otherwise he was fine and lying on top of Bufe, who looked up at him and licked his lips.

'That's delicious. Did you make that?'

'Yeah,' Owen said, barely able to hear him. He couldn't believe he was still alive and in one piece.

'Best meal I've had in months.'

Owen got up, offering Bufe a hand. 'It's hardly a meal.'

'You haven't seen what I've had to swallow.'

At that moment, the two Charlies rushed in – the butler and the cook – followed by several houseboys and miners.

Dumetz stood up, took stock of the room. The investors seemed shaken, but otherwise unhurt and, despite the gaping hole in the fireplace and some shattered windows, the house stood firm. He gestured to Bufe.

'Get this lunatic out of here and shoot him,' Dumetz said.

'You can't do that,' Owen said. 'It would be murder.'

'Fine,' Dumetz said. 'Drag him out of here, point him toward the canyon, give him a firm kick in the ass. But if he comes back, shoot him.'

Bufe looked at Owen. 'Seems like a reasonable compromise to me.'

Charlie the Butler said, 'There's a fire, sir.'

Dumetz noticed a corner of the rug by his feet was burning. He stomped it out as if it was an irksome insect. 'It would have been much worse than that if not for Mr Cartwright's quick thinking. Waste of a good pot of soup, though.'

The butler looked confused. 'Out in the desert, sir. I think it's Calico. Least that's the direction the smoke is coming from.'

Owen ran past the butler and the men and out to the porch. A dark plume of smoke was rising from the west. He'd known for a couple of years that the town would burn a second time, but it didn't make the sight any less disturbing. He turned back to the butler.

'Where are my horses and the carriage?'

'Round back, sir,' the butler said.

Owen looked past the butler to Bufe, who got to his feet unsteadily. 'You want a ride out of here, Sibley?'

'You'd give me one after I almost blew you up?'

'You saved me from making a bad speech.'

Owen headed outside. Bufe staggered after him.

Dumetz bellowed: 'Wait. You can't leave. You haven't served dinner yet.'

Owen turned on his heels and faced the man. 'Calico is burning. That's where my restaurant and my friends are.'

'It will be ashes by the time you get there,' Dumetz said. 'You can go back in the morning.'

'People are going to need help. You should come, too. Bring your men, food, water, clothes, anything you can spare. That would be the decent thing to do.'

Owen didn't wait for an answer, he ran to the carriage, quickly climbed up and, once Bufe was on board, got going. He steered the horses past the house and down the steep trail, moving them as fast as he dared, hitting the canyon only moments before the chimney of Dumetz's house crumbled, toppling into the yard.

It wasn't until they were out of the canyon, and safely on the flat desert floor, heading toward the plume of dark smoke in the distance, that Bufe spoke.

'What was your speech gonna be?'

'Roughly the same as yours, only without the despair, the dynamite, and the destruction.'

'That wouldn't have been very exciting or convincing. Why would they have listened to you? You're just a hired cook.'

'I was hoping to appeal to their reason and humanity.'

'They don't have any,' Bufe said. 'That's why I was going to blow them up.'

'And me, too.'

Bufe shrugged. 'Yeah, well, sorry about that.'

'What kind of name is Bufe?'

'It's short for Buford.'

Owen nodded. 'Would you really have killed yourself?'

'I still might,' he said.

'How? You're out of dynamite, and you don't have a gun, a knife, a rope, or poison or the money to buy any of them, though I suppose you could just dive in front of the horses and hope I run over you good.'

Bufe looked at him. 'Do you think the best way to talk me out of suicide is to remind me of how pathetic my situation is? It's a good thing I stopped your speech. You'd have convinced them that paying his workers three dollars a day was a dollar fifty too much.'

It was nightfall when Owen and Bufe finally reached Calico, the embers of the ruined town glowing eerily in the darkness. Only a few buildings remained standing, chiefly the livery stable (because it was at the southern end of town and separated from other wooden structures by a corral), and Stoby's store and Denny's, both buildings made of stone and adobe. Even Chinatown was in ashes.

Owen pulled his carriage up in front of his fire-licked restaurant, where most of the townsfolk seemed to be gathered, standing in a daze, staring at the smoking ruins. Many were quietly sobbing. One tearful woman stood apart from the rest, holding a duck in her arms, a donkey at her side. She was clearly ostracized.

Owen climbed off his carriage and approached a dejected Overmyer, who sat on the ground by his printing press and several drawers of loose type. Some letters had fallen in the dirt in his haste to save them from the flames.

'What happened, John?'

Overmyer gestured to the woman with the duck. 'Daisy was getting ready for the dance tonight when her goat came into her room, got startled by his reflection in her mirror, and went crazy, knocking over her lantern and setting the room ablaze. She was lucky to get out alive.'

Owen didn't need to be told how fast the fire spread after that. He'd seen it happen before. 'Was anybody hurt?'

'No and it's a miracle. Everybody was out on the streets again . . . heading for the dance.'

Bufe looked at Daisy, then back down at Overmyer. 'What's with the duck?'

Overmyer noticed Bufe for the first time. 'That's her pet, the only thing she was able to grab in her escape. He didn't lose a feather. I, however, have lost everything.'

Owen patted the printing press. 'You got away with what's most important to you. Your life and your printing press.'

'Twice,' Overmyer said. 'I'm not pushing my luck again. I'm leaving Calico and going somewhere with plenty of water . . . and decent sanitation. At least with all this smoke you can't smell the shit. There's an upside for you.'

'You'll feel better about things in a few days,' Owen said. 'You can stay with us in Newberry Springs while you rebuild.'

Overmyer shook his head. 'It's decided. I'm done here. I should have left when Tuttle did. I'll print one last issue tonight to memorialize this tragedy and then I'm going.'

Owen didn't know Overmyer's future, but he knew the printing press ended up on display at Knotts Berry Farm's fake Western town.

'Does that mean you saved some blank paper?'

'Not a single piece. All of my back issues were lost, too. My work was all for nothing.'

'So what are you going to print your newspaper on?'

'Stoby is giving me some bedsheets,' Overmyer said.

'That's got to be a first.'

'Lots of news has been made on bedsheets,' Overmyer said. 'Just never reported on them before.'

Milly and Virgil came over, hand in hand. They'd been courting for a few months now. Her eyes were tear-streaked.

'I can't believe it happened again,' she said.

'That's why I know Calico can and will come back from this,' Owen said. 'Bigger and better than before.' At least for a few more years, he thought, until the price of silver plummeted and the slow death that followed. 'But for now, anybody who doesn't have room and board at the mines can eat here for free. No one is going hungry in Calico . . . and that includes the Chinese.'

Virgil said, 'Or thirsty. I'll make sure there's water.'

Milly gifted both men with a smile. 'That's mighty kind of you both, but we don't have enough hands to prepare the food and feed so many people.'

Owen gestured to Bufe. 'I brought some help. Meet Buford Sibley.

He'll serve food, peel potatoes, wash dishes, or whatever else needs doing.'

Bufe looked back at him. 'What do you pay?'

'Two dollars a day, but I'll be charging you three dollars a day for room and board.'

Bufe grinned. 'Sounds fair to me.'

Milly said, 'He's not too good at math, is he?'

'Just keep him away from any rope or sharp objects,' Owen said.

'I'm past that,' Bufe said.

Virgil said, 'I ain't too good with numbers, neither. But I'll lend a hand. I know Stoby and the others will pitch in, too. This town sticks together. I'll start organizing the volunteers.'

'Anybody seen the Judge?' Owen asked.

'He's over at what's left of his place,' Milly said.

Owen left them to walk up the street and check on the Judge, who was sifting through the ashes of his cabin and examining the charred remains of a leather-bound book.

'I'm sorry, Judge. I know how much you loved your law books.'

The Judge tossed the leather binding aside. 'They can be replaced. It's the lost property records and land surveys that I'm worried about. It will lead to chaos and years of lawsuits.'

'Sounds to me like the town is going to need you more than ever before.'

The Judge straightened up and leaned on his cane for support. 'You always see the bright side.'

'It's how I get through the day.'

The Judge eyed him. 'I suppose that makes sense for a man in your position.'

What position was that? Owen was afraid to ask for fear of hearing what the answer was and what the Judge might actually remember.

'You're welcome to use the restaurant as your home and courtroom until you can rebuild,' Owen said.

'I finally have a legitimate excuse not to leave my barstool.'

'Now you're seeing the bright side,' Owen said.

'I accept your offer, but rest assured, the county will pay you a fair rate for my room and board.'

'That's not necessary.'

'I insist. I don't want anyone suggesting that you've bought yourself a judge's favor if you're ever in a dispute that ends up in my court,' the Judge said, 'especially if my bench still happens to be your bar.'

'Makes sense.'

The Judge glanced back at the restaurant. 'When we rebuild, I'll see to it that the building code requires that at least every other building is constructed of stone or adobe like yours to prevent a fire from spreading so fast or Calico is destined to burn again.' He looked back at Owen. 'Will it?'

Yes, it would, or so Wendy had told him, but it wouldn't be as catastrophic as the first two fires. Once again, Owen worried about how much the Judge remembered, and believed, from his feverish night.

'I hope not. But if it does, I'm sure it won't be as bad as this.'

Owen walked away before the Judge could pursue his line of questioning any further.

TWENTY-EIGHT

An hour after Owen's return to Calico, Charlie the Cook arrived outside of his restaurant with a wagon full of flour, potatoes, and other goods, which he said were all courtesy of Mr Dumetz in the town's time of need.

'Really? I'm shocked,' Owen said, surveying the supplies in the wagon's bed. He didn't expect such generosity from Dumetz, especially after he'd given a ride to the disgruntled miner who'd nearly blown up his house with everyone in it.

'Or it's possible I am only a few hours ahead of a posse that will hang me for horse theft,' Charlie said. 'I am hopeful Mr Dumetz will choose the more charitable version.'

'He will after the town express their heartfelt appreciation,' Owen said. 'I'll spread word of his good deed to the community. It will make the front page of the final issue of the Calico newspaper. He'll have a hard time challenging the story after that without looking like an asshole.'

'The man does love publicity,' Charlie said. 'Could you use another cook while we wait to see if I will be hung or not?'

'Now more than ever before,' Owen said. 'I've got the homeless of Calico and Chinatown to feed.'

'I can take care of Chinatown for you.'

It was also the safest place for him to be if Dumetz was unreasonable and sought his neck.

'Good plan.'

Owen stayed up all night preparing for the massive breakfast he served that morning to hundreds of men, a few women, and even fewer children, who lined up for food.

Dumetz and his posse did arrive the next day, causing both Bufe and Charlie to go into hiding, but after the appreciation he received from the grateful townspeople for his aid, he forced a smile, accepted their thanks, and quickly claimed that he'd arrived to personally oversee distribution of his supplies and to lend a hand.

Charlie's theft was never mentioned nor were any charges pursued against him or Bufe. Dumetz left with the horses and wagon Charlie borrowed. A few days later, news came that Dumetz secured the investment he needed to open his refinery, providing a much-needed economic boost to Calico when the town desperately needed it. Dumetz was a hero.

After breakfast was served, Owen accepted a copy of the final, bedsheet issue of the *Calico Print* and took Overmyer and his printing press to the train station in Daggett in his carriage. They said their goodbyes, then Owen headed back to Newberry Springs, falling asleep on his buckboard. Luckily, he didn't fall out of his seat and the horses guided themselves back to his ranch on their own.

Owen awoke shortly before reaching his home, where he found Wendy waiting for him on the porch, teary-eyed and pale. She'd obviously seen the smoke from Calico and, later, his slow approach across the open desert.

He climbed down from the carriage, every bone and muscle in his body aching.

'The town is ashes, but don't worry, Wendy, nobody was hurt and our restaurant is still standing,' he said. 'But Overmyer has given up and left for good, and you won't believe how things went in Borate . . .'

Wendy embraced Owen with surprising fervor and started sobbing on his shoulder. He patted her back, not sure what to make of her reaction. Was it relief?

'It's OK,' he said. 'We came out fine and so did everyone we care about.'

That seemed to provoke even deeper sobs and a tighter hug. Finally, she sniffled, took a deep breath, and looked up at him.

'We're far from fine, maybe we never will be again,' she said. 'Nicolas is going to hate me forever and so will you.'

What was she talking about? Owen looked around the ranch and everything seemed as he'd left it, though he didn't see Rico or his men. Had they quit for some reason? Surely she wasn't crying about that.

'Where are Rico and his crew?'

'They left last night. Rico couldn't live with the guilt of what we'd done. I don't think I can, either.'

What did *that* mean? He could only think of one explanation. Owen held her away at arms' length and looked her in the eye. 'Did you sleep with Rico? Did Nicky see you?'

Wendy shoved him away. 'No, of course not. How can you even *think* that?'

'Then what are you talking about? Just say it.'

She shifted her gaze, unable to look him in the eye.

'After you left, Nicky and I came out on the porch. I was reading while Nicky crawled around and played with his toys, babbling the way he does, and then he screamed. I looked up and saw the rattle-snake's amputated head stuck around his thumb like a ring . . .' She stopped, choking up.

'I can see how that was scary, but the snake was dead. It was harmless.'

Wendy shook her head. 'The fangs were still full of venom and pierced Nicky's skin. His thumb swelled up fast with the poison.'

Owen remembered what happened to the man who was bitten by a rattlesnake and brought into Tuttle's bar to see the barber.

She said, 'There was only one thing I could do to save him.'

Now he noticed a key detail he'd missed when he'd rode in, half-asleep and in his first, quick glance of the property: a meat cleaver stuck in the upturned log they used for a chopping block in front of the house.

He took two steps away from her in horror. 'No . . .'

'Rico offered to do it, saying it was all his fault, but I insisted that it had to be me. Rico held down Nicky's hand on the stump and I chopped off his thumb with the meat cleaver . . .'

Owen jerked, hearing the chop as if it had just happened.

Wendy went on, still unable to face him. 'Nicky passed out from the horror of it, thank God. Rico used a hot poker to cauterize the wound . . . and I took Nicky, limp in my arms, inside to treat it with the antiseptic and bandages from your first-aid kit. Rico buried Nicky's thumb in a tobacco tin and left some time during the night.'

It was a nightmare.

Wendy was crying again. She looked at Owen now. 'Do you want me to go, too?'

Yes, he did. He could barely stand to look at her, even though he knew that she'd done the right thing . . . the only thing . . . and doubted he would have had the courage to do it if he'd been in her position.

He forced himself to look at her, to take a step towards her, to offer forgiveness he didn't yet feel.

'Of course not. If you'd taken him to Calico for help, even if you'd managed to get there before the fire, the poison in Nicky's thumb would have spread during the journey. Walsh would've cut off Nicky's entire arm, though it still might have been too late to save him. You did what needed to be done.'

But now she stepped back, shaking her head.

'I should have been watching him. If Rico hadn't left that snake head on the porch . . . and if I'd been watching Nicky while he played, he wouldn't be maimed now. It's my fault.'

'It was an accident. Nobody is to blame.'

'Nicky will be terrified of me,' she said. 'Until he grows up, and then his fear will become pure hate.'

'He's two. He won't remember.'

'You don't forget your mother hacking off your thumb with a meat cleaver.'

'He's too young to comprehend what happened, but as Nicky grows older, he will be grateful for what you did and for your bravery. Because you saved his life. That is what he won't forget.'

Owen was telling her that to convince himself, too. He pulled her into an embrace and she cried. So did he.

Intellectually, he knew what she did was right, but in his heart, he hated her right now . . . and himself for not being there when they needed him. It took some time, but when they were both cried out, he spoke.

'How is Nicky now?'

Wendy wiped her nose on her sleeve. 'He's sleeping now . . . and crying some. There's no fever or anything. When he was up, for an hour or two, I ground some Advil in apple sauce and fed it to him for the pain and swelling. But he wouldn't look at me.'

'You're imagining that.'

'He probably never will again. I can't even look at myself in the mirror.'

Owen held her by the shoulders. 'Look at me.'

She did.

'Look into my eyes,' he said. 'What do you see?'

'Lots of little blood vessels,' she said. 'You need Visine.'

'Look deeper and you'll see yourself as I do: a strong, wonderful, loving mother who fought for her child's survival.'

'No, I just see bloodshot eyeballs.'

Maybe she would have seen the image if it was true, if he'd really felt that now. But he didn't. He'd get there. They both would.

'I'm trying to help you here,' he said. 'I'm trying to help us.'

She smiled and gave him a kiss, which became a hug. 'I know you are. But come on, did you really expect me to see myself in your eyes? To look into your soul? That's stupid. What movie did you steal that from?'

Probably some maudlin trash on Hallmark, but he thought women loved that stuff. 'At least I made you smile.'

'I can always count on you for that.'

'We'll get through this together, I promise.'

Owen took her hand and led her into the house. In his heart, he knew that he'd forgive her. But it wouldn't be today. There was still tomorrow . . . for him and, thankfully, for Nicky, too.

And as the years went on, Owen was proved right.

Nicolas didn't remember what happened, remained devoted to his mother, and, once he understood how he'd lost his thumb, was grateful for her quick thinking.

In fact, decades later, Nicolas had reason to thank her again.

When World War I was raging in 1917, the US Government drafted men between the ages of twenty-one and thirty-one and sent them into battle in Europe. But not Nick. His missing thumb disqualified him from military service, perhaps saving his life for a second time.

At least, that's the way Nicolas looked at it.

TWENTY-NINE

Saturday, February 9, 2019

P our Decisions was aptly named, Beth thought, because it accurately represented just about every choice she'd made there, including stepping through the door that night. The place was packed with first responders, all of them radiating resentment her way as she came in. But thankfully, their animosity wasn't shared by Sally, who greeted her with a smile and a mug of beer at the bar.

'Don't mind those assholes,' Sally said. 'You did your job. It's not your fault the crooks wore badges.'

'I'm glad you feel that way, because I need a favor.' Beth beckoned her to the far end of the bar, out of earshot of the other customers, and lowered her voice to a whisper. 'I'd like to talk to your ex-husband.'

'Which one?'

'Alan Vernon, not because he's in any trouble, but because I could use his insight,' Beth said. 'I'm working a case that's got some strange twists to it. I think he might be able to help me see if there's any truth behind the crazy.'

'There usually is,' Sally said. 'But most of the time, it's something harmless that can be made out to be anything you want it to be. A neighbor's new satellite dish might mean he's communicating with outer space to get an Italian soccer game. Or it could mean he's calling his Klingon overlords to say, "Come on down, it's time to conquer Earth."'

'I've got a situation like that,' Beth said. 'I'd like to see Alan tomorrow. Can you tell me how to reach him and put in a good word for me?'

Sally looked past Beth at her other customers. 'Shooting and arresting some dirty cops won't win you much love in this room, but it will win over Alan. Give me your card and I'll let you know what he says.'

Beth slid her card across to her. 'Thanks, Sally. Just so you know, I didn't shoot any cops. I shot the ATV two of 'em wanted to run me over with. The other cop tried to jump over the wreck with his dirt bike. It's stupidity that put them in the hospital, not me.'

'But it's you who put them in jail.'

'It's my job to arrest crooks.'

Sally nodded toward the rest of the room. 'Are you going to stick around for a cheeseburger just to show them you aren't intimidated?'

'That's right,' Beth said.

Sally put a shot glass on the table and filled it up with whiskey. 'Then you're going to need this, too.'

'I'd need it anyway.'

'That kind of day?' Sally asked.

'And then some,' Beth said.

Sally went into the kitchen to prepare the burger and Beth worked on her drinks, doing her best to think about anything but what she'd learned today.

It wasn't easy.

Beth was just beginning to feel the alcohol soften the edges of her tension, when two men approached her, one on each side. They were big guys, with big muscles, but she figured if it came down to it, she could still hurt them, though probably not as much as they could hurt her. She prepared herself mentally for battle, casually covering a fork with one hand, ready to grab it in an instant.

'We wanted you to know something,' Muscles To Her Left said. 'If you're ever out on the desert alone, facing a bunch of hyped-up tweakers with guns who want to gang-bang you to death, and you call for backup, don't expect any Barstow cops to come running.'

No shit, she thought.

'Except us, day or night. This is my personal number,' Muscles To Her Right said, passing his BPD card to her. She glanced at it. His name was Officer Jim Smith and he'd handwritten a phone number under his name. The gesture was so unexpected that it startled her. Muscles To Her Left sensed her surprise.

'Crooks are crooks,' he said, passing her his card, too. Officer Phil Weslyn. 'With or without badges. My number is on my card, too.'

Beth smiled and moved her hand away from her fork. 'Can I buy you two a drink?'

Smith said, 'On the contrary. We told Sally that yours are on us tonight. What you did took guts and integrity.'

Weslyn said, 'If you'd like some company to your car when you leave, you just let us know. Our friends call us Smith & Wesson.'

'I truly appreciate the offer but I can take care of myself.'

They nodded and went back to their table. A moment later, Sally showed up with a cheeseburger and set it down in front of Beth. 'Smith and Wesson are good guys. Both Mormons. They go to that church up in College Heights.'

'I thought Mormons couldn't drink,' Beth said.

'They don't. They come here for the fine cuisine and lively camaraderie.' She handed Beth a slip of paper. 'Alan is expecting you tomorrow. His place is in the desert, through the Jackhammer Gap, just north of the Calico Mountains, between Fort Irwin Road to the lower end of Coyote Dry Lake. I wrote down the GPS coordinates but you can see his radio antenna for miles. Head for it once you get off the road and you'll be fine.'

'You want me to bring him anything from you?'

Sally shook her head. 'Just come back and tell me how he is.'

'Will do,' Beth said.

Sally walked away to serve other customers, Beth took a bite out of her burger, and her phone vibrated with the arrival of a text. She checked the screen. It was a message from Chet.

'I heard what happened. Do you want to get together and talk?' She texted back:

'I want to fuck. My place in half an hour.'

It aroused her just to type that.

He gave her a thumbs-up emoji.

Oh, God, how she needed that.

For her, there wasn't a drink, a pill, a quart of ice cream, a sermon, or anything else that could match great sex to ease her pain, to clear her mind, restore her soul, and give her the strength to face whatever challenges or obstacles confronted her.

Accepting the existence of time travel, because that's what the evidence proved, had left her feeling alone, unmoored from reality, and even questioning her own sanity.

But after two hours of exhausting, desperate coupling with Chet, and three intense orgasms, Beth lay naked and physically spent in her dark bedroom, centered in herself again, her anxieties gone, her mind focused on the only thing that mattered.

Discovering the truth.

If doing that meant she had to transform her understanding of what was possible, and what was real, then that's what she would do.

The truth was that Owen Slader and some anonymous miner had passed through a crack in time, so that was what she'd prove, and nobody would stand in her way.

That wasn't crazy.

That was her job.

No, *that was her mission*. The same one her father died pursuing, and so would she, if that's what it came down to.

Because that's who I am.

She knew it with absolute clarity of purpose now.

'Are you OK?' Chet asked, lying on his back beside her, catching his breath.

'Better than OK,' she said. 'Clear-headed. You were just what I needed.'

'Glad to be of service,' he said. She hopped naked out of bed. 'Where are you going?'

'Eskimo Pies,' she said. 'I have a sudden urge.'

'I can't believe you have any urges left.'

Beth went to the kitchen, opened her freezer, and took two Eskimo Pies from the box. Light peeked out of the bedroom. She walked in to see that Chet had turned on the desk lamp on the gun safe. 'Why did you turn on the light?'

'I like to see what I'm eating,' he said.

'That didn't bother you a few minutes ago.'

'Don't be crude,' he said.

As she came into the bedroom, she spotted the two Eskimo Pie sticks on the floor, where they'd tossed them the last time he was over.

One of the sticks, at the base of the wall, was crushed into pieces. At least with the lights off, he couldn't see what a slob she was.

She handed him an Eskimo Pie and got into bed beside him. 'When did you get so prissy?'

'I'm a choirboy at heart. God, country, and family, that's me.' He took a bite out of his Eskimo Pie, eating almost half of it at once, then: 'You seemed awfully tense when I got here. Was it the incident with the Barstow cops that has you all knotted up?'

She started eating her ice cream. 'I'm not feeling any stress about that case. It was straightforward and very satisfying.'

'You get off on the action?'

'Not like I do from what we just did, if that's what you mean. But I definitely get a lot of satisfaction out of resolving a case with direct, decisive action.'

'Does that happen often?'

'I've got other cases that are a lot more muddled.' The A/C kicked on, a cool breeze blowing directly out of the high vent on the wall across the room. The air was especially refreshing combined with the cold Eskimo Pies.

'Are you talking about the guy that got hit by the RV?' Chet asked.

'I wish it was as simple as that.'

'What's complicated about it?' Chet asked. 'Seems about as clear-cut as you can get. What's left to investigate besides who the victim is?'

That was the part that was complicated. There was no way she was going to tell him the guy ran out of the past, that time travel was real, and she was going to prove it.

'Never mind.' She finished up her Eskimo Pie and licked the stick. She thought about going and getting another one.

'Clearly it's bugging you. I'd like to help,' he said, looking at her earnestly, the chocolate beginning to drip from his forgotten Eskimo Pie onto his hand. 'Talk it through with me. Use me as a sounding board the way you just did as a sex toy.'

'If I talk about it, I'll just get tense again.' Beth tossed her Eskimo Pie stick against the wall. It landed beside the crushed stick from the other day. She felt a chill, and it wasn't from the ice cream, or the cold air coming out of the vent on the wall above the sticks. It was from a realization. She'd been betrayed, in the most humiliating and debasing way. It was infuriating, degrading, and heartbreaking all at once. But she tried not to show any of what she was feeling.

'No problem,' Chet said. 'In ten minutes, I'll be ready to relieve it for you.'

'You're a real man of action,' she said, taking his half-eaten Eskimo Pie from him, which made him notice the melted chocolate on his fingers.

'Always ready to serve,' he said, and licked the chocolate off his fingers. She tried not to cringe with revulsion.

'Speaking of that, do you still keep in touch with any of your old army buddies?' she asked, finishing off his Eskimo Pie, working hard to sound casual, to keep her emotions in check.

'Not really,' he said, examining his hand for more chocolate. He'd gotten it all.

'None of your friends are stationed out here on one of the bases?'

'Nope,' he said.

'I have a friend at the Marine base. Bill Knox. I don't know his rank, but he's in charge of security. Have you ever run into him?'

'I don't know anybody out there.'

'In fact, funny you should mention the guy that got run over. Bill came out to see me at the scene outside Peggy Sue's.' Beth met his eye. 'He had *lots* of questions.'

'You say that like you think there's a connection between him and the case.'

'I'm the connection.' She licked the chocolate off the stick. 'He wanted to see me again. Bill is a married man, but he fucks around. He assured me that he and his wife have an understanding, but I doubt it.'

'You're sleeping with him?'

'Not anymore. The last time we were together, he freaked me out.' Now she tapped her anger for what to say next. 'I think he has PTSD. I'm not just saying that because he can't get hard. Bill started sobbing, and told me that he has a recurring dream where he walks into an elementary school with an AR-15, dressed as a clown, and kills every kid he sees. He said it was a *dream*. Not a nightmare. Think about that, Chet, because it haunts me. That's why I'm tense. Every morning, I wake up and wonder if this is the day that Bill makes his dream real.'

Chet stared at her. She tossed the Eskimo Pie stick across the room, higher this time, hitting the air vent. He saw her do it, and realized what it meant, what she *knew*.

'But that's not all,' she said. 'What Bill told me about the command staff over there was sickening.'

'Stop,' Chet said.

Oh no, she was just getting started. 'For instance, he walked in on a general masturbating while watching an Abu Ghraib video of a guy being waterboarded.'

'Stop, God damn it!' Chet shouted and glanced at the wall.

She couldn't see a camera behind the vent, but she knew it was there. The tip-off was the broken popsicle stick on the floor that she saw when Chet turned on the lights and that she noticed again when he started asking questions about her cases. It took a lot of weight to crush that stick. Like the weight of a man standing on a ladder to reach the vent above it. That would also explain why Chet wanted more light, for a better picture. So, she set out to prove her theory, by humiliating the man that she was sure was watching. After what she'd just said, Bill would have to destroy the tape.

'I'm curious, Chet. What did Bill tell you to get you to do this?'

Chet shook his head, got out of bed, and reached for his clothes on the floor. He started to put on his underwear, his back to the wall. She stayed where she was, not even trying to hide her nakedness.

'Don't be bashful now, Chet. They've seen it all.'

She'd been filmed unwittingly, betrayed by a man she'd trusted, but she didn't understand how he could allow himself to be watched like this, to be used in this way, and without showing any hesitation or self-consciousness. It was amazing to her that he'd been able to get it up. Or maybe he'd liked it. Maybe he got off on being watched, on showing his sexual prowess like some kind of porn star.

Chet pulled on his pants and looked over his shoulder at her as he buckled up. 'I love my country, Beth. When I am asked to serve, I do. No questions asked.'

'What did they tell you? That I'm a threat to the country?'

'I don't know,' he said, and slipped his bare feet into his shoes. 'Are you?'

'Go fuck a flagpole,' she said.

Chet put on his shirt, snatched up his socks, and walked out. She'd actually liked him until tonight, which showed what a horrible judge of character she was. She wanted to cry, but she'd be damned if she was going to reveal any pain to them. Instead, she took a moment to think things through.

She figured that they didn't just bug the place. They'd thoroughly searched for anything that might be related to her investigation. They'd probably copied the hard drive on her laptop, too. But none of that worried her. There was nothing here or on the computer of significance to the case. Slader's keys were in her pocket with her all day and his wallet was in the gun safe in the trunk of her father's Mustang. The photos on her iPhone could be a problem if they could somehow get remote access to her device or hack her iCloud backup. She had some work to do tonight.

Beth got dressed, found a gym bag in the closet, and stuffed some fresh clothes into it before going to her gun safe.

'I'm going out for the rest of the night,' she said, opening the safe and taking out her gun and her badge. She turned and faced the air vent. 'I want all of the surveillance equipment out of my house by morning, or I'll invite some reporters over for breakfast, show them all the devices, and tell them why I think they were planted. Don't make a mess and lock up when you leave. Oh, and you'd better get Chet out of California tonight, Bill, because if I ever see him again, I will immediately pay a visit to your wife and tell her in explicit detail everything that's happened between us . . . including this.'

She snatched her phone off the top of the gun safe, grabbed her shoulder bag off the kitchen counter, and walked out of the house, leaving the door unlocked behind her.

THIRTY

Beth drove to the Outlets, west of Barstow and south of the interstate, and went first to the Flying J Travel Center, a popular market, gas station, and sleep-over stop for long-haul drivers.

She bought four burner phones, more than she thought she'd need just to be on the safe side, and a Snickers bar in the Flying J store, then went next door to the Comfort Suites, got herself a room for the night, then went to their business center, where there were three desktop computers, along with FedEx and UPS mailing supplies.

She opened up one of the burners, powered it on, got the phone number, and wrote it down on one of her business cards, which she stapled to the package for another burner phone that she put into a FedEx Express Priority delivery box. She addressed a label to Amanda Selby's home, ticked the 'First Overnight Delivery' option, attached it to the box, added her credit card number, and delivered it to the middle-aged female clerk at the front desk.

'When does the FedEx guy come in next?' Beth asked the clerk.

'Run it out to the FedEx mailbox at the Flying J now and it could be picked up tonight and delivered tomorrow,' the clerk said. 'The FedEx drivers stop by the J often, outside of the posted hours on the mailbox, for a nap or a coffee, and make unscheduled pickups. They're there anyway and know truckers rely on those drop-off boxes to get stuff back home in a hurry. Otherwise your package will go out first thing tomorrow and arrive Monday.'

Beth thanked the clerk, ran next door to the Flying J, and dropped the package into the FedEx box, which was in a row with UPS and USPS mailboxes in an island of trees and picnic tables between the gas pumps and the overnight parking area.

When she returned to her Mustang, she removed Slader's wallet from the gun safe and, on an impulse, crawled all around the vehicle with her flashlight, looking for a tracking device. She was relieved not to find one. On the other hand, it was hardly necessary to put one on her car. Her cell phone served the same purpose. She hoped her phone hadn't led the military to the Yermo cave and Slader's Mercedes. But she certainly wasn't going back there now to check.

Instead, she went to her room at the Comfort Suites, ate her Snickers bar, and went to bed.

She woke up at 7 a.m. Sunday on the dot, as if she had an alarm clock in her head, showered, checked out, and devoured a Grand Slam breakfast at the Denny's next door (the irony not lost on her) before turning off her iPhone and driving out to the desert to see Alan Vernon.

The drive was a bore. The desert on the other side of the

rocky, jagged Calicos was bleak, barren, flat, and hot, seemingly inhospitable to life. It was the perfect place to train for a desert war, a Moon walk or Mars landing. Or to bury a body.

The advantages of living out there, she supposed, were solitude and privacy. Nobody could ever catch you by surprise. The wide-open space meant that Alan Vernon saw the dust trail of her Mustang approaching long before she arrived at his remote, but not hard-to-find compound.

Sally was right, his radio antenna was easy to spot from Fort Irwin Road. It resembled an oil derrick and stood out amidst the vast emptiness. As Beth got closer, she could see there were two large satellite dishes erected near the antenna.

The rest of the compound consisted of a 2,000 square foot, double-wide mobile home with siding, a peaked roof, and a front porch, which was much nicer than Beth expected, two prefab outbuildings, a large water tank, a solar power array, and a backup gasoline-powered generator. A spotlessly clean Range Rover Discovery was parked out front, gleaming in the sun. It was not the rundown, preparing-for-the-end-of-the-world, off-the-grid, crazy-white-trash survivalist compound she'd imagined at all.

She got out of her car and was met by Alan Vernon on his porch. He, too, defied her preconceptions. He was a short, clean-shaven man in his fifties, wearing tortoiseshell glasses, a wrinkle-free, navy-blue Lacoste polo shirt over a slight paunch, a pair of pleated khaki cargo shorts that showed off his knobby-kneed legs, and slip-on loafers with no socks.

Alan isn't a prepper, she thought. He's a preppy.

'Detective McDade,' he said. 'I hope you had no trouble finding me.'

'I didn't think people who live out here wanted to be found.'

'I'm not in hiding,' he said. 'I'm in exile.'

'I know the feeling.'

'The difference is, I chose it,' he said, economically conveying that he'd learned her entire past history. 'We'll go inside in just a moment, but first I need to confirm that you're human.'

'How are you going to do that?'

'It's very quick and simple.' Alan took an ophthalmoscope, a common diagnostic tool used by doctors during regular check-ups, from a cargo pocket on his shorts. 'This tool allows me to shine a beam of light through your pupil and examine the interior of your eye. It's harmless. May I look in your eyes?'

'The gateway to my soul? Sure. Is that what you're hoping to see?'

'You could say that.' Alan stepped up to her and, like a doctor, peered into her left eyeball. 'Look at the light. Thank you.' He shifted the device to her next eye. 'Again. Thank you.'

He pocketed the ophthalmoscope and took out a tiny plastic egg-shaped device. 'This is a lancet. I'd like to prick your finger and examine a drop of your blood. This is the same, harmless procedure diabetics use to check their blood glucose levels.'

Beth presented her left index finger to him. 'What levels are you checking?'

He pricked her finger with the lancet, drawing a droplet of blood. 'If I tell you that, and you're an alien, you'll go back and try to develop countermeasures to beat it.'

She watched as Alan captured the drop of blood on a test strip. 'Are you going to use my DNA to create a clone of me to take my place in the Sheriff's department?'

He inserted the bloody end of the strip into the bottom of a device that resembled a cell phone. 'The aliens can do that, but it's beyond my meager capabilities. I had a dog once I wish I could clone. I've kept some of his hair and blood to keep the possibility open.' He glanced at the reading and smiled. 'Congratulations, you're human.'

'That's a relief,' she said.

'You'd be surprised how shocked some people are when they find out they aren't.'

'They don't already know?'

'That's the truly insidious nature of the invasion,' he said. 'Come inside, I have the A/C on. It's hell out here.'

She stepped past him into the house. The air temperature was in the seventies, she guessed, which felt close to freezing compared to the heavy, dry heat outside. The decor was farmhouse contemporary, with sliding barn doors between some rooms. There were faux distressed wood floors, faux heavy wood ceiling beams, and faux shiplap and faux bricks on the walls. Beth wondered if Alan appreciated the irony that a man seeking the truth lived amidst so much that was fake.

He smiled at her and gestured to the barstool around the center

island in the open-concept kitchen, which had butcher-board coun-
tertops and a farmhouse sink.

'Can I offer you something to drink?'

'No, thank you,' she said. He opened the refrigerator and took
out a platter of grapes and melon balls, which he set on the island
in front of her. The melon balls were speared with toothpicks to
make them easy to eat. 'This is quite a spread. You shouldn't have
gone to so much trouble.'

'I don't get many guests, so this is a big deal for me.'

'I appreciate the hospitality, Mr Vernon.'

He popped a grape into his mouth, and sat down on the stool
beside her. 'How can I help you, detective?'

She picked up a cantaloupe ball and ate it to be polite. 'First, I
want your assurance that this entire conversation is off the record.
I don't want to hear it on the air and, in return, I pledge not to share
what you tell me with anyone else.'

'You have my word.'

'I can't go into detail, but I am investigating some strange
incidents that occurred on February 2nd at the same time as the
lightning storm and the explosions at the Marine Corps Logistics
Base and Fort Irwin.'

Alan smiled at her. 'The *simultaneous* explosions. I haven't reported
about that incident yet. I'm glad to have secondary confirmation.
Good for you, detective. You've made a meaningful discovery.'

'I have reason to believe these events are all connected.'

'You certainly do, because they are. In fact, they are aspects of
one single event.'

'How do you know?'

He ate another grape. 'From years of research, which allows me
to make educated guesses, and what my sources within the US
military have divulged to me. Are you familiar with the Philadelphia
experiment?'

'No, I'm not.'

'It was a botched attempt in 1943 by the US military at the
Philadelphia Naval Shipyard to use reversed-engineered alien
technology, recovered from a crashed UFO, to make one of their
destroyer escort ships invisible. It worked. For several minutes, the
ship was gone. Not because it was invisible. But because it truly
wasn't there.'

He paused for dramatic effect and to have another grape. 'They didn't know what they were doing and accidentally teleported the ship and its crew to Norfolk, Virginia. But moments later, it disappeared there, reappearing in Philadelphia again, only now it was badly mangled, and some of the crew members were merged, on a cellular level, into the steel bulkheads. The horrific, deadly incident was successfully neutralized by the alien-controlled entertainment complex, of course, but that's standard operating procedure.'

'What do you mean by "it was neutralized by the entertainment complex"?'

'*Alien-controlled* entertainment complex. In the early 1950s, a team of US Navy admirals, led by Vice-Admiral Leslie Stevens III, who was in charge of the navy's psychological operations division, worked with the aliens to use movies, TV shows, and novels to psychologically and emotionally groom humanity to accept a future where we are led by extraterrestrials. To launch the secret program, Stevens recruited his own son, Leslie Stevens IV, a TV writer and producer who was also a former navy intelligence operative. Leslie Stevens IV created *The Outer Limits*, and then he recruited Gene Roddenberry, who created *Star Trek*, to further disseminate propaganda dictated by the Galactic Federation of Worlds. But they also used Hollywood, and New York publishing, to minimize leaks that prematurely exposed the level of alien infiltration of our world.'

Beth was sorry she'd asked, but now that she was down the rabbit hole, she couldn't help herself. 'I'm still not clear on this. How did they cover up the Philadelphia experiment and other incidents like it?'

'By taking a real event and dramatizing it to a ridiculous extreme, radically altering the facts for novels, TV shows, and movies, the aliens and their human enablers transform the truth into mainstream fiction, rendering it totally inert, so it has no power to motivate people to action, specifically to rise up and fight the invasion that's happening right in front of their eyes,' Alan said. 'It's devious and brilliantly effective. *The X-Files* alone has done catastrophic damage to humanity.'

During his long diatribe, Beth devoured nearly all of the melon and most of the grapes. 'I take it the Philadelphia experiment became a book and a movie?'

'Several of both,' he said. 'All abominations.'

She pointed a toothpick at him from the pile in front of her. 'How does the Philadelphia experiment relate to the lightning storm on February 2nd, that proves, as you said on your show, that the invasion plans are moving into the next phase?'

He took a grape from the platter and set it on the counter in front of him. 'Think about it. The job of a logistics base is to get equipment and supplies from here to there.' He moved his grape in front of Beth. 'The job at Fort Irwin is to train soldiers and deploy them for battle. The challenge in an invasion is getting men, equipment, and supplies rapidly to key locations and, if possible, without alerting the enemy. Imagine the advantage the aliens would have if they could teleport equipment, supplies, weapons, and even an entire army anywhere in the world in an instant?'

'You think the electrical storm and the explosions were a result of the military trying to transport something from the logistics base in Yermo to Fort Irwin on the other side of the Calicos?'

'I do,' he said. 'Do you know how NutraSweet was invented?'

Beth sighed and ate a melon ball. It was baffling non sequitur. Her first thought was, of course, *extraterrestrials*, but what she said was: 'No, I don't.'

'In 1965, a scientist was trying to develop a drug to battle ulcers. He licked his finger to pick up a piece of paper, and it tasted sweet. It was the harmless drug residue on his fingertip. The ulcer drug went nowhere, but Aspartame, an artificial sweetener marketed as NutraSweet, has made billions of dollars,' Alan said. 'In 1943, while trying to create invisibility, the military stumbled on teleportation instead, something even better. Just like NutraSweet. But they had no idea how it happened and, after the horrible deaths in Philadelphia, they were afraid to experiment any further to find out. That terror lasted for seventy years.'

She had another melon ball. 'What changed?'

'Now they aren't toying with appropriated alien technology that they don't have the instruction manual for. Today the aliens are working with them. We've also come a long way technologically on our own since then. The timing was right. But something still went very wrong on February 2nd when they tried to teleport a loaded truck.'

It certainly did, she thought, and it led to yet another NutraSweet. *Time travel.*

She didn't believe the government was working with space aliens, but the notion of trying to teleport a truck from the logistics base to Fort Irwin wasn't outside the realm of possibility, especially if she was willing to consider that time travel might be real.

'What went wrong?' she asked.

Alan slapped his hand on the grape in front of Beth. He lifted his palm to show the smashed grape. 'The truck arrived like that.'

'What was the truck loaded with?'

'All I was told was "a mix of organic and inorganic cargo".'

Alan either had an incredible imagination or some well-placed sources in the military willing to risk prison to share classified information with him. She figured the only reason he wasn't already in prison was because the government believed that arresting him would lend credibility to his theories. Instead, they probably figured that his rants were so crazy that there was virtually no risk of anybody taking him seriously.

And yet, she was.

Not all of it. But a teleportation accident actually fit all the evidence she'd seen and the unusual events she'd learned about. If the truck somehow disintegrated in transit, that would explain the truck parts, boulders, and dismembered cow fragments strewn across the county, and across the years, on February 2nd.

But how many years back . . . or even forward . . . in time was the wreckage spread? And did the military know about the rifts in time? Did Alan? Or were she, Amanda, and perhaps Christopher Cartwright the only ones?

'Were any human beings on that truck?'

Alan shrugged. '"Organic material" sounds to me like a catch-all phrase for plants, or animals, or even innocent civilians abducted for alien experimentation. It certainly wouldn't be the first time.'

But she didn't think either Owen Slader or Motor Home Man were on that truck. So how did they get tossed through time?

Alan studied her. 'Does this help you, detective?'

'Yes, thank you, it explains a lot,' Beth said.

He smiled, full of hope. 'Does this mean you believe me?'

'I believe that you're telling me the truth as you know it. But I don't believe the whole story you're telling.'

'What doesn't ring true to you?'

'Almost everything,' she said. 'Except the teleportation, but that's enough.'

'Enough for what?'

Beth got up from the barstool. 'For me to do my job. Now I just have to go out and prove it.'

He walked her to the door. 'Will you share the proof with me when you get it?'

'I'll share it in a court of law,' she said.

'Then it will be buried and no one will ever know the truth.'

'We'll see,' Beth said.

'I've seen this before,' Alan said. 'I just hope you aren't buried with it.'

As Beth drove back across the open desert, she thought about what she'd learned from Alan Vernon. The teleportation-gone-wrong explanation actually sounded reasonable to her. It fit the facts that she had. But the Philadelphia experiment story struck her as far-fetched and she certainly didn't believe UFO technology or extraterrestrials had anything to do with what happened. The military was perfectly capable of making horrible, deadly mistakes with catastrophic, unintended consequences on their own, without alien intervention.

Alan Vernon's parting comment, though, was nagging at her at about the same time that she became aware of an aircraft coming her way from the north.

From Fort Irwin.

As it got closer, she saw it was a helicopter gunship, seemingly on a direct intercept course.

She was right.

Within a few seconds it was coming down low, its machine guns, Hellfire missiles, and Hydra rockets aimed right at her, blocking her path.

There was no point trying to flee. She was out in the open. An easy target.

How did they know she was out here?

Beth supposed they could have been tracking her with a satellite or a drone, not that it mattered now.

It didn't take long for Alan Vernon's worry to come true. Only a few minutes. She wondered if he was next, if there would only be a crater left where his mobile home once stood.

Beth stopped her car and waited for hot, blazing death.

The gunship hovered ominously in front of her for a long moment, whipping up an enormous cloud of sandy dirt, then it slowly landed and its blades stopped spinning. The dust settled. A man wearing camo gear and pitch-dark sunglasses hopped out of the chopper and strode toward her car.

Bill Knox.

She stepped out of the Mustang to meet him, doing her best to seem casual, like this happened to her every day and she hadn't just braced herself to die.

Beth leaned against the grille of her car and crossed her arms under her chest. 'Gee, Bill, if there's something you'd like to know, you don't have to send a guy to fuck me silly or scramble an Apache attack copter to stop my car. You could just ask me.'

'I'm not asking, Beth. I'm telling you.' His face was rigid with anger and implacable determination to get his job done. 'Your investigation is closed.'

She'd seen a variation of that look when he was on top of her in bed, pounding away at her, focused on completing his mission. The expression revealed both his emotional detachment and total physical commitment. There had been something arousing about it then, but not now.

'Or what?' she asked. 'You shoot me with your gunship, blow up my car, and say I strayed into a desert war game?'

'I don't have to shoot you. You've already shot yourself. You have zero credibility. You got thrown out of the LAPD because you're a drunken sex addict who can't control herself. It's only gotten worse since you arrived in Barstow.'

'I fucked you, that was certainly a mistake.'

'You're in that bar every night, drowning in a bottle then picking up any guy you can find, and now you've joined a dangerous, lunatic fringe who believe space aliens are taking over the world. You're obviously mentally unstable. Nobody is going to believe any story you tell. And if you tell this one, you'll never wear a badge or carry a gun again. Hell, you'll be lucky if you aren't locked up in an insane asylum. But if you walk away from this, and keep your mouth shut, you can go back to your life as it was. Nothing changes, though I'd make some if I were you, Beth. You've been trying to flush your life down the toilet for a while now, but there's too much shit clogging up the drain.'

Beth nodded her head, considering what he'd said. He'd made

some good points. 'Yikes, you really didn't like being called an impotent clown who fantasizes about killing kids.'

'This isn't a joke.'

She stood up from the car and got in his face.

'No, Bill, it isn't. One man is dead, at least one has disappeared, and many others were injured. Their families aren't laughing. They're crying.'

'It was an accident,' he said. 'No crime has been committed. That's all you need to know.'

'Then why are you all so afraid that I'll discover the truth?'

Bill took off his glasses and looked her in the eye. This was his hard sell move. 'I've told you the truth.'

'Convince me. Tell me what really happened.' But then she saw something, a split-second of doubt in his resolute, angry expression, that changed her whole take on the situation. She took a step back from him and smiled. 'You can't, and it's not because you've been ordered not to. It's because nobody knows, not even the people who were there, who were part of it. *That's* what's terrifying you.'

Beth knew she was right. She'd won this battle, and he knew it, too.

'This was your last warning,' he said, put his glasses on, and went back to his gunship.

The pilot fired up the rotor blades. The gunship rose slowly, hovering for a moment in front of her, as if wrestling with indecision.

One missile and Beth wouldn't be a problem anymore. That's what someone was thinking.

She stared at the gunship and gave it the finger.

The gunship roared towards her, nearly close enough to scratch the car's paint, then flew low and angry over her into the horizon.

THIRTY-ONE

Beth turned on her phone again, since Bill knew where she was anyway, and the burner, in case her package to Amanda was delivered, and went back home. She thoroughly searched the house for listening devices and cameras, but whatever was there before was gone now, along with the Eskimo Pie sticks on her bedroom floor, which she thought was a nice gesture. She checked to see if maybe they'd also cleaned her shower, or mopped the kitchen floor, or did a load of laundry, but no such luck.

So, as long as she was home, she decided to clean the place up, a task she hated, do her laundry, and maybe cap the big day off with some grocery shopping. She was tempted to burn the sheets after Chet's betrayal, rather than wash them, but then she'd have to go shopping for sheets, so that settled that.

The truth was she was just killing time with domestic drudgery, settling her nerves after her encounter with Bill, and trying to figure out, in the back of her mind, what her next move would be.

Her iPhone vibrated with a text. She checked the screen. It was from Amanda.

Marty McFly isn't in the room anymore.

That didn't surprise her, but it only added to the helplessness she was feeling. Beth texted her a thumbs-down emoji. She wasn't going to communicate with her on this phone anymore. She'd wait until they had their burners.

I sent you a baby shower present. It's a little early, but it was so adorable, I couldn't wait. Call me after you get it.

Beth transferred her laundry to the dryer because it seemed more productive than wallowing in anger, frustration, and despair.

She went into the Barstow station on Monday morning like it was just another shift, like she hadn't learned that a rip in time had swallowed up Owen Slader after a military teleportation experiment went wrong and that the government was threatening to ruin her if she didn't forget the whole damn thing. She had Slader's keys and his wallet in her pocket to keep them safe, but instead they served as a reminder of the secret she was carrying and needed to prove.

Hatcher wasn't in, she could tell because his Mr Rogers cardigan was draped over the back of his chair and his slippers were under his desk. There were some files on her desk. They were patrol reports from deputies on some residential and commercial burglaries over the weekend that the watch commander thought might merit investigation. That looked exciting.

There was a knock at the door. It was Captain Brobeck announcing his arrival. He was a fat man in his fifties who refused to buy a new uniform even though he'd clearly outgrown it long ago. The buttons were straining so hard against his bulge that she was afraid they might pop off at any moment, and become deadly projectiles. She could lose an eye.

'I've got some good news for you,' the captain said. 'The review of the shooting last week is over and the official determination, as we hoped, is that it was an appropriate use of force and within policy.'

'I'm glad to hear it, sir. I'm eager to get back out in the field, doing my job.'

'About that. The watch commander says you spent Friday out in San Bernardino. What was that about?'

'I was doing a records check on the property in Newberry Springs where we found Owen Slader's body.'

The captain nodded. 'That began as a missing person case in LA.'

'That's where he lived. He was heading back to Los Angeles from Las Vegas when he disappeared in Yermo, which makes it our case now.'

He nodded again. It seemed more like a nervous tic to her than repeated sign of agreement. 'Is it a homicide?'

'The coroner hasn't been able to determine the cause of death, but he didn't bury himself out there.'

'Burying a corpse isn't a crime or, if it is, it's not worth the time and resources we're spending on investigating it. Not every mystery gets solved.'

She was getting a very bad feeling. 'It's early days, sir. I'm still working on it.'

He nodded again. Definitely a nervous tic, a tell. She knew she wouldn't like what he was going to say next.

'No, you're not. Let the LAPD run with it if they want to. We have plenty of cold cases you can work on if things are slow. Pick one.'

'Yes, sir, I will.'

He nodded one last time and walked out. The military, or some-body, had told him to shut her down, she was certain of that. But working a cold case instead of Slader's was fine with her.

Beth turned to her computer, logged in, and pulled up the details on a Gwendolyn Hale, the twenty-six-year-old woman whose home collapsed on February 2nd, 1992, but her body wasn't ever found in the rubble.

The case file was archived in San Bernardino and hadn't been digitized, so she decided to start by doing a simple Google search to see what articles came up about Gwendolyn Hale and her disappearance.

And in the second it took for Google to produce the search results, Beth solved Hale's disappearance with such a startling jolt that she nearly screamed, not in terror, but in shock.

Several photos appeared of Gwendolyn Hale, as an adult, but also during her teenage years, when she won several local beauty contests, including Miss Barstow, Miss Route 66, and Miss Teen Alfalfa Queen. Her striking beauty and her confidence in front of the camera were familiar to Beth because she'd seen that face before.

It was Wendy Cartwright.

But just to be sure her memory wasn't fooling her, she took out her phone, found the picture she'd taken of the old Calico photo at the San Bernardino County historical society, zoomed in on Wendy's face outside, and held it up to her computer screen.

It was the same woman. Even the expression was the same.

Gwendolyn Hale was sucked back in time from her own bedroom on February 2nd, 1992, decades before Owen Slader's disappearance.

That was a fact, Beth knew it.

Somehow Owen and Wendy, two accidental time-travelers, found each other, got married, and started a family. And their latest descendant, Christopher Cartwright, had dug up Owen's grave, prompting the investigation that led to this discovery.

It was no accident, Beth knew now. It was an investigation set in motion over a hundred years ago when Owen Slader and Gwendolyn Hale, aka Ben and Wendy Cartwright, established the trust.

This was the proof.

But she knew the photos wouldn't stand up to scrutiny. Photos were too simple to fake now. Beth was sure Knox could find hundreds of experts to say the historical society photo of Wendy Cartwright was a clever fraud. Forgery would be easier to believe than the existence of time travel.

Her burner phone vibrated, startling her. The timing was uncanny. She took it out of her pocket and looked at the screen.

It was a text from Amanda. GPS coordinates and a time, followed by a question mark.

Beth sent back: OK

The rendezvous spot was a patch of open desert north of Apple Valley, off an unpaved road a few miles west of the High Desert Juvenile Detention Center, at the base of the hills around Turtle Mountain. Not quite the middle of nowhere, Beth thought, but where nobody could see them without a satellite or a drone, which was certainly something Bill Knox was capable of doing.

Amanda got out of her coroner's van and joined Beth in her Mustang.

'Why are we meeting here?' Beth asked.

'I had a body to pick up at the detention center. A teen OD'd on drugs someone smuggled in for him. Since I was going to be out here anyway, this seemed like a good spot to meet. We'll see if anybody followed us or is watching.'

Beth decided not to argue the point, especially since she had no facts to the contrary, just a healthy paranoia. 'I assume it's not just the bodies of Owen Slader and Motor Home Man that are gone but everything, including your notes.'

Amanda nodded. 'Of course I went straight to my boss about it, and he told me the Feds came in with a court order and took it all. It's their case now and I should move on.'

Beth turned to her. 'Is that what you are going to do?'

Amanda met her gaze. It was a challenge. 'Are you?'

'No, but I wouldn't blame you if you did. You have a family. I don't.'

'You say that like you've been threatened,' Amanda said.

'I have,' Beth said. 'Forcefully.'

'By whom?'

'I'm not sure I should tell you,' Beth said. 'Or that you really want to know.'

Amanda took a deep breath, thought something over, then said: 'They didn't actually take everything I had because it wasn't all at the morgue in Barstow or in my files in San Bernardino. Remember I warned you out in Newberry Springs that I'd broken the rules and was running some tests on Motor Home Man that could get me in trouble?'

'Yes, I do.'

'Well, I doubled down on it. I sent bone and tissue samples from both bodies to a physicist at UC Irvine who has access to an accelerated mass spectrometer, which enables him to detect the radioactive isotopes in organic and inorganic materials to determine their age,' Amanda said. 'The testing and detonating of nuclear devices since World War II changed the levels of carbon-14, strontium, cesium-137, and other elements in the environment. Those elements degrade at a certain rate over time. Someone who died before the 1940s, for example, wouldn't have the higher elevations of these isotopes in their bodies than people born afterwards do. Are you following me?'

Beth nodded.

'What I am about to tell you is fact, not speculation, based on objective, isotopic analysis. Motor Home Man, who was killed on February 2nd, 2019, was born sometime in the mid-1800s. That's impossible. Owen Slader's bones were a hundred years old but belong to a man who was born in the 1980s. That's also impossible. The only way these contradictions *are* possible is if both men traveled in time, one backwards and one forwards. Those two bodies prove time travel is real. One of the greatest achievements in science, or one of the biggest catastrophes in human history, has occurred, intentionally or unintentionally, and I won't let that go unacknowledged or uninvestigated. The consequences of ignoring it are too grave, for the world and for my kids. So, no, I am not walking away from this. I never will. There, I said it.'

Amanda waited, as if she expected Beth to argue with her. Instead, Beth nodded and held out her phone.

'These are some pictures of Gwendolyn Hale, a woman who disappeared from her home in Barstow on February 2nd, 1992. Take a good look at them.' Beth scrolled through them for her, then took the phone away for a moment and found another picture that she hid for a moment. 'This is a picture of a woman named Wendy Cartwright, taken in the 1880s in the Calico mining town.'

Beth held the phone out to Amanda, who gasped when she saw the picture. Amanda looked at Beth with wide eyes, showing excitement, not fear. 'It's the same woman. She went back in time, too.'

'Wendy was married to a chef named Ben Cartwright who ran a fine-dining restaurant in Calico called Denny's.'

'Those are twentieth-century cultural references made in the 1880s. That's not a coincidence or an inside joke. That's a specific message sent through time,' Amanda said. 'It's Owen Slader telling anyone in the future who was looking for him that he was Ben Cartwright.'

'That's not the only message he sent us.'

Beth then told Amanda everything she'd learned and the conclusions that she'd made. It was an incredible relief for her to finally be able to share what she knew with someone but also, in the telling, she became more convinced than ever that she was right.

'Something went explosively wrong when the military tried to beam a truck from MCLB to Fort Irwin and the collateral damage was that they blew a bunch of holes in time that at least three people fell through,' Beth concluded. 'I think they're trying to cover up the accident, to keep their teleportation technology a secret, but they have no idea what they've actually done. You and I may be the only people still alive who know that time travel has happened.'

'And Christopher Cartwright,' Amanda said.

'That's just a gut feeling I have about him.'

'I have it, too, but it might be gas,' Amanda said. 'Pregnancy does that to me.'

'The problem is, I don't think your unsanctioned and unsupervised isotope tests, some old photos, an ancient property trust document, and Owen Slader's rotting 2018 Mercedes in a cave will be enough to convince anyone else that time travel has happened,' Beth said, 'though I am not sure who we'd be trying to convince anyway.'

'Nicole Slader would want to know what really happened,' Amanda said. 'I'm sure the Hales and even the Cartwrights would want to know, too. It's not about science for them, like it is for me. Or about justice, like it is for you. It's about knowing if you were abandoned or loved. It's about knowing who you truly are. It's about easing the unending pain for their grieving families.'

'I wish we could tell them that Owen and Wendy went back in time and lived long, presumably happy lives together,' Beth said.

'The military has the bodies, their personal items, my autopsy reports, and the forensics. If they accept what the evidence is telling them, they will eventually discover that time travel occurred.'

'They just won't tell anybody,' Beth said. 'Without irrefutable proof, there's nothing we can say, either. The truth, and perhaps the danger, will be buried.'

'It already has been,' Amanda said.

'So we're done,' Beth said.

'Just the opposite. When did Wendy Hale-Cartwright die?'

'1933,' Beth said.

'About thirty years before she was born,' Amanda said and smiled. 'I'll bet the Cartwrights know where her grave is.'

Wendy Cartwright is evidence.

Beth smiled at Amanda, picked up her phone, googled the number of Cartwright's company, and called him, putting it on her speaker. She got a secretary, identified herself, and then asked to speak to Christopher Cartwright.

A moment later, he came on, upbeat and cheery. 'Detective McDade, what can I do for you?'

'I'm hoping you can answer some questions about the Cartwright family tree. Do you know when Ben Cartwright died and where he is buried?'

'He died in 1912 in Newberry Springs. I believe he's buried in the Calico graveyard, but there's no marker. The burial records are lost and the headstones were washed away in a flood.'

So Beth had heard. The question was just to get confirmation and as a little misdirection from her true interest, which was her next question.

'What about his wife?' she asked.

'In 1920, after the Spanish Flu pandemic, Wendy Cartwright came to live with her son Nicolas and his family in their magnificent Victorian mansion on Bunker Hill in what is now downtown Los Angeles.' Even the name of Ben Cartwright's child was a message, Beth thought, undoubtedly named for Owen's daughter Nicole, lost in time. 'The house is long gone now, but we made a fortune on the land it was on. And not just their estate, either. It's not common knowledge, but we owned a large number of properties on that hill. It was unimaginable to others, but somehow my great-grandfather anticipated that the expansion of downtown would inevitably demand the taking of even the city's wealthiest and most prestigious neighborhood.'

'It's uncanny,' Beth said, sharing a look with Amanda that

confirmed they both wondered if perhaps the whole family was gaming the future with inside knowledge.

'Wendy Cartwright died in 1933 at seventy-six years old and is buried at Forest Lawn Memorial Park in Glendale. In fact, all of my ancestors since Ben Cartwright passed away are buried out there,' Christopher said. 'You'd think, being in real estate, we would have bought a family plot, but it never occurred to us. I certainly haven't reserved one for myself. I suppose our own deaths are too morbid to contemplate. Or perhaps everyone in my family grew up with the mistaken belief that, for us, time doesn't run out. So the family is scattered around those beautiful rolling hills.'

'Thank you for your help,' Beth said. 'Aren't you curious why I'm asking?'

'It's not the investigation into the mystery that interests me, detective. It's the solution. Good luck.' He hung up.

Amanda smirked. 'It's definitely not gas.'

'Good to know,' Beth said.

'I have a good contact at Forest Lawn. There won't be any issues with Wendy Cartwright's exhumation. State law gives me the authority to do it without requiring a warrant, court order, or the family's permission.'

'So we won't be announcing our intentions, if anybody is watching.'

'I'm sure they are, but I think you're way ahead of them.'

'At least for now,' Beth said, though it was more of a hope than a strongly held belief.

'Meet me at Forest Lawn tomorrow at about noon. I should have the casket up by then. There's no point in you standing around while they dig. I'll text you on the burner if things go faster than I expect.'

Amanda got out of the car, which took some effort.

'Are you sure it's not twins?' Beth asked with a grin.

The coroner gave her the finger and went back to her van.

Beth desperately wanted to stop by Pour Decisions for a drink, and even more desperately wanted to pick up a man. There was a fire-fighter who was great at starting her fire who hung out there and wouldn't resent her arresting those Barstow cops.

But then she thought about Bill Knox out in the desert, reciting her character flaws. There was some truth to what he'd said, but they were all traits she shared with most of the cops and first responders she knew, male or female, married or single. It was the nature of the job and what it did to a person. Her father had been the same way. She knew it was probably a big reason why her mother had left them. But Beth never blamed her dad for it and hated her mom instead. That hadn't changed with time or perspective.

Even so, somehow the thought of going back to the bar tonight seemed wrong. So she found another way to satisfy her desires and relieve her stress. She brought home a pizza and a six pack of beer for dinner and then, after searching her house one more time for surveillance cameras, had a date with her vibrator.

It wasn't quite as satisfying as a fiery fireman, but it did the job.

THIRTY-TWO

Beth called in sick Tuesday morning, searched her Mustang for tracking devices, turned off her phones, and drove to Forest Lawn Memorial Park in Glendale.

She'd heard Forest Lawn described as 'the Disneyland of Cemeteries' because of all the replicas of famous art, statues, and churches spread across multiple 'themed lands' ('Slumber Land', 'Lullaby Land', 'Court of Freedom', 'Wee Kirk of the Heather', 'Graceland', 'Memory Slope', etc.) and the founder's mission statement, etched in marble, dedicating himself to creating the happiest place on Earth, full of flowers, splashing fountains, and chirping birds. Zip-a-dee-doo-dah! But Forest Lawn predated Disneyland by decades and Walt Disney himself was buried there. So, in reality, Beth felt it was more accurate to say that Disneyland was 'the Forest Lawn of amusement parks'.

The cemetery's three hundred acres of rolling hills, wedged above the southern crossing of the Golden State Freeway to the west with the Glendale Freeway to the east, was virtually free of tombstones, the lawn-carpeted slopes lined with flat granite or bronze grave markers and dotted with mature sycamore, pine, and oak trees. There was nothing to obscure the sensational views of the Verdugo Mountains to the north, or the skyscrapers of downtown Los Angeles to the southeast, except the smoggy haze that still hadn't burned off by noon when Beth arrived.

Wendy Cartwright's open grave, a mound of dirt and sod on a tarp beside it, was atop a steep south-facing slope, under the shade of an old tree. Her displaced grave marker, set against the pile of dirt, read:

Gwendolyn Cartwright
'There are no secrets that time doesn't reveal'
March 16, 1856 – September 21, 1933

With the marker, Gwendolyn Hale revealed her secret to anyone who might come looking for her. She was born on March 16, 1966, a date that, combined with that quote, would only encourage someone like Beth to literally dig further.

Beth felt the hard tug of those puppet strings again and was certain that Wendy Cartwright, and perhaps even Owen Slader, wanted her . . . or someone like her . . . to be here right now, putting the clues together, discovering the truth that had been buried for over a century.

Or just a few weeks, she thought, depending on who was looking at it . . . and when.

The coffin had already been raised and moved into a tent erected behind Amanda's San Bernardino County Coroner's van on Freedom Way, which ran along the top of the hill. Two muddy Forest Lawn workers milled around the back-hoe, checking their phones. Beth presumed they were waiting for instructions from Amanda.

Beth went into the tent and found Amanda, in a white hairnet, jumpsuit, and blue gloves, crouched over a dirt-caked concrete box, snapping photos with a digital SLR camera that was slung around her neck.

'Perfect timing,' Amanda said. 'We got lucky.'

'In what way?'

'Every way, starting with that grave marker. Pretty cheeky of her, as if she knew somebody would come along wondering if she was Gwendolyn Hale. She took extra steps to make things smooth for us, starting with this concrete vault the coffin was buried in. It protected the coffin from the elements and made it much easier to raise. The coffin itself is copper, which doesn't deteriorate like wood, and keeps the skeleton whole and in relatively good shape. It must have cost the family a fortune.'

'They certainly had the money.'

'It was money well spent and did the job.' Amanda stepped away so Beth could take a look. 'The evidence she left for us is remarkably preserved.'

Beth stepped up and peered inside. The floral dress that the body was buried in, along with the red lining of the coffin, had hardly deteriorated. Wendy's arms were crossed over a slim padlocked metal box on her chest, as if she was clutching it for the journey into the afterlife. But beyond the box, two things stood out, both perfectly intact and seemingly unaged.

'Are those breast implants?' Beth asked.

'Silicone gel. Implants existed in the lifetime she lived prior to her own birth, but not like these.' Amanda closed her eyes for a moment. 'Well, that was something I could never have imagined saying, or that would have made sense to me, until today. But here's the kicker. The serial numbers match the pair that Gwendolyn Hale, who died in 1933, had surgically implanted in 1988.'

'How did you already match the serial numbers?'

'Gwendolyn was missing and assumed dead, so her dental records, X-rays, and other significant medical records have been in our system for years in case her bones ever turned up. I've got them all right here.' Amanda picked up an iPad from a nearby folding table. There was an X-ray on the screen. 'She broke her right wrist when she was thirteen. The healed break is visible on the bone. All of her fillings and crowns match her dental records, too. And even if they didn't, her porcelain crowns are fused with metal, a technique that didn't exist until the 1950s. This is, without a doubt, Gwendolyn Hale.'

'Have you photographed everything?'

Amanda nodded. 'What do we do with the body now? If I take it back to the morgue, it will only be a matter of time, no pun intended, before the military comes for it and she disappears forever.'

'OK, let's take a bone, a breast implant, and that box, and then put her back in her grave,' Beth said. 'Let's hope she'll be safe there until we figure out what our next move is.'

Amanda reached into the coffin, gently removed the box from

Wendy's arms, and handed it to Beth. 'I can't wait to see what's inside.'

'Me, too. I've got a pair of bolt cutters in my trunk.'

'You do?'

'Doesn't everybody?'

Beth walked out of the tent, carrying the box, and glanced out at the view as she headed for her car. Something caught her eye. She stopped and looked at the view again.

A helicopter was hovering over the Golden State Freeway and she could see one black-and-white CHP cruiser parked on the shoulder in each direction, their light bars flashing so nobody would rear-end them.

She assumed she was watching a police pursuit in progress, coming this way, the two CHP cars waiting to pick up the chase when the bad guy's car hit their stretch of freeway. Car chases like this were a daily occurrence in Los Angeles and, ever since OJ's mad dash in his Bronco, TV news viewers never got tired of watching them.

She also noticed two LAPD black-and-whites speeding up Glendale Avenue, toward the front gate of Forest Lawn, in case the bad guy got off the I-5 and they needed to pick up the chase on city streets.

She looked to her left, southeast to the Glendale Freeway, and noticed there were also CHP patrol cars waiting there in case the driver merged on to I-5 at the interchange.

They had every option covered. Good for them. They'd certainly had enough practice at it.

Beth started back to her car when a thought occurred to her.

If the car they were pursuing was coming this way from the south, why would they have CHP cars waiting in *both* directions? Perhaps in case he got off the freeway and doubled back. OK, but where were the news choppers, following the chase?

That's when she noticed something else. She was all alone outside. The two Forest Lawn workers were gone.

She had a bad feeling.

Beth turned around, hurried past the tent, stood on Freedom Way, and looked eastward and saw a helicopter in the distance, streaking towards her from downtown LA.

The cops weren't in the middle of a pursuit, she realized. They were preparing a dragnet.

For us.

She looked down the steep, eastern slope of grave markers, to the ivy-covered fence below and the row of homes along the perimeter on the other side, and then shifted her gaze up the residential street to downtown Glendale to the north. There were no police cars in sight and she knew why.

There was only one way in and out of Forest Lawn, and it was on Glendale Avenue, behind two 5,000 pound, 25 foot tall, 80 foot wide wrought-iron gates, the heaviest in the world, larger than the ones at Buckingham Palace by five feet, and if they weren't closed now, they soon would be, trapping her, Amanda, and Wendy Cartwright's bones inside.

Beth ran back to her car, popped the trunk, and stuffed the metal box, and the bolt cutters, into the gym bag of clothes she'd packed for her night at the Comfort Suites. She opened her gun safe, removed her Glock, her ammo, and Owen Slader's wallet, and stuffed them into the bag, too.

She grabbed her bag, slammed the trunk closed, and ran into the tent, where Amanda presented her with the evidence baggies containing the silicone breast implant, and a finger bone.

'Give me those and the memory card from your camera,' Beth said, holding open her gym bag. 'Hurry.'

'What's wrong?' Amanda dropped the evidence into the gym bag.

'They're coming for us.'

'Damn.' Amanda plucked the tiny card out of her camera and tossed it in the bag, too. 'Ride like the wind.'

'Great, now I'm gonna have Christopher Cross in my head.'

Beth bolted out of the tent, looked down the west-facing slope, and saw three LAPD patrol cars snaking up Cathedral Drive. They were in no particular hurry. The cars were blocking the only road out and the front gates, taller and wider than the gates of Heaven or Hell, were definitely closed. She was boxed in, so why should they rush? They had her.

Fuck you, Bill. This isn't over yet.

She got into her Mustang, tossed the gym bag onto the passenger seat, fired up the engine, and floored it, charging across Freedom Way toward the east-facing slope. In the instant before her car barreled down the sharp incline, she saw the chopper in front of her and was relieved it wasn't armed with machine guns and Hellfire missiles.

The Mustang picked up speed and momentum. Beth gripped the wheel and braced herself for the imminent, head-on impact with the ivy-covered fence that separated the cemetery from the line of homes at the bottom.

Sorry about the car, Dad.

She smashed through the fence, crumpling the Mustang's hood, and burst into the driveway between two homes, clipped a trash dumpster, and careened into the narrow two-lane street, her mangled front bumper dragging on the asphalt, trailing a shower of sparks, before it ripped free, cartwheeling through the air.

Beth wrestled with the wheel for control, the Mustang fishtailing until it pointed north, and then she floored it again, weaving between cars and into oncoming traffic, the LAPD chopper right above her, its rotors whirring so loud that they nearly drowned out the chorus of screaming car horns all around her.

Ride like the wind.

The damn 1980s song was in her head now, thanks to Amanda, the sirens of the police cars closing in behind her providing a shrill underscore. She glanced in the rear-view mirror at the black-and-whites trailing her, their light bars flashing, but they were keeping their distance.

She wasn't worried about the cars in pursuit. The police wouldn't try to disable her with a pit maneuver or stop her with spike strips on a residential street. It was too dangerous. Because if she lost control, she could plow her car into someone's living room on live TV, which would be very bad press. At any moment now, she was sure that TV news choppers would join the chase, putting a million eyes on the police.

And on her.

That was why few people ever got away in a car chase with police. They had nowhere to hide.

But they weren't Beth McDade, an experienced detective with plenty of practice chasing cars through busy urban streets when she was a patrol officer herself.

The street dog-legged across the intersection ahead, creating a traffic bottleneck as drivers waited for the light or tried to negotiate the awkward turn. To avoid getting trapped, or veering instead into the southbound lane and dodging oncoming cars, Beth made a sharp right into Adams Square, a restored 1930s-era gas station converted into a tiny park.

She plowed through a low hedge, obliterated a picnic table, and shot across the intersection, leaving the patrol cars knotted in traffic behind her, unwilling to follow her brazen path.

But the chopper easily tracked her from above as she raced up the eight small residential blocks to East Colorado Boulevard, blew through the red light, and barely avoided being T-boned by an MTA bus.

She made a hard left, swerved briefly into oncoming traffic to dodge a woman in the crosswalk, then veered back into the westbound lanes, weaving fast through the slow-moving cars, sheering off her passenger-side mirror against a Prius.

Oops.

Four patrol cars were waiting for her at the Glendale Avenue intersection, one at each corner, and they fell into line behind her as she blazed west, her speedometer needle trembling at seventy-five miles per hour.

Up ahead was Brand Avenue, the city's major boulevard. The Americana shopping center was on the northwest corner and looked like a small rust-belt factory town that had been gentrified by young Apple, Facebook, and Amazon executives. It even had its own trolley. She blasted past the Americana to the Glendale Galleria behind it, a vast three-story indoor shopping mall, a 1970s relic that was like an aging, once popular actress who'd had too many facelifts in her terrified descent into irrelevance.

Beth turned right into the four-lane road that separated the Galleria's three-story parking structure from the mall it was beside. Several open-air pedestrian bridges crossed overhead, linking the two buildings. She waited until she was under one of the bridges, hidden from the helicopter's view, to make a sharp left into the parking structure, racing up the ramp to the second floor.

The helicopter, and cars chasing her, had lost her for a few precious moments.

She stopped near a bridge without setting the brake, grabbed her gym bag from the passenger seat, and hopped out of the Mustang, letting the car roll backward down the ramp behind her.

As Beth ran across the bridge to the J.C. Penney, she heard the metal-crunching, glass-shattering sounds of a vehicle collision and the eruption of dozens of agitated car alarms behind her.

Sorry again, Dad.

She burst into the second-floor men's department, startling a young saleswoman who happened to be standing there, folding some shirts.

Beth flashed her badge at the woman. 'Tell the other police officers who come in that the woman we're chasing is in the food court and has changed into a denim jacket. I'm in pursuit.'

The stunned woman simply nodded.

The mall entrance was to Beth's left. She dashed that way, grabbing a man's hoody off a table on the fly. To her surprise, no alarms went off as she ran out of the department store and into the mall with her shoplifted hoody.

Directly in front of her was a children's play area, a dozen strollers parked along the walled perimeter, the gleeful kids climbing on the play equipment inside while their tired mothers checked their emails. She dropped the gym bag into a stroller, covered the bag with a baby blanket, and kept on going, pushing the stroller.

Beth quickly rounded the next corner, a Zara on one side of her and an Abercrombie & Fitch on the other, and headed to the bustling center of the mall.

She took off her blazer, pulled the oversized man's hoody over her head, and stuffed her blazer in the first trash can she passed.

That's when she spotted the fire alarm on the wall and yanked down on the emergency lever. Instantly a siren wailed throughout the mall, lights flashed, and startled people started running towards the escalators.

Beth walked fast towards the large Macy's that anchored the north end of the mall and resisted the urge to look behind her to see if any cops had rushed in.

She went into the Macy's, took their crowded center escalator to the ground floor, and was carried along with the tide of frightened customers through the department store and out the door onto the sidewalk on Broadway.

Police cars seemed to be converging on the mall from all sides and a half a dozen helicopters, a mix of law enforcement and TV stations, circled in the sky.

Beth pulled the hood over her head and calmly crossed the street with her stroller to the bus stop, just as a westbound bus arrived.

It was almost as if she'd planned it that way, the end result of days of rehearsing with a stopwatch.

She ditched the stroller, grabbed her gym bag, and stepped on board, dropped some coins in the fare box, and scored a window seat to herself. The bus pulled away, chugging down Broadway, then turned left, going south on Pacific Avenue.

Beth felt the tension easing in her body, though she had no idea where the bus was taking her. The important thing was that she'd escaped with the evidence.

She glanced at a route map on the wall and learned that she was on the 201 Line, heading to the Wilshire/Vermont metro station, with a stop at the Silver Lake reservoir, down the hill from Owen Slader's home.

It felt like fate.

THIRTY-THREE

Calico, February 4, 1888

Virgil and Milly got married in Denny's. Owen was the best man, Wendy was the maid of honor, and the Judge officiated. The guest list was small, and included Virgil's brother Clive, Purvis and Evelyn Stoby, Lebec the butcher, Bufe Sibley, Dr Walsh, and Milly's former co-worker Esther, now Calico's most successful Madam.

Owen catered the reception, though he left most of the actual work to Charlie so he could enjoy the event purely as a guest. He sat at the main table with the happy newlyweds and Wendy, Clive, and the Judge, while little Nicolas concentrated on eating, and pretty much wearing, a huge slice of cake.

'Wendy and I have a wedding present for you,' Owen said, and passed an envelope on to Virgil, who opened it in front of Milly. The envelope contained a check for $2,000.

Milly let out a gasp. Virgil put the check back in the envelope and gave it back to Owen.

'Your gift is far too generous,' he said. 'We thank you, but we can't accept it.'

'It's not a gift,' Owen said. 'It's an offer to buy your fifty-percent share of your water business, so you and Milly can move somewhere else and open a restaurant.'

Wendy added, 'The only condition is that it can't be in Daggett or San Francisco.'

Virgil glanced at Milly, but she didn't say anything. This was Virgil's decision. He faced Owen and Wendy again.

'I understand why you'd be against Daggett,' Virgil said. 'It's a hell-hole. But why San Francisco?'

Because Wendy and Owen knew that an earthquake would level San Francisco in eighteen years.

'Personal reasons,' Owen said.

Virgil's brother Clive scratched his scraggly beard, which contained a good portion of everything he'd eaten that day and the day before, and studied Owen and Wendy. 'You want to go in business with me?'

'We'll be passive partners, relying upon your expertise for the day-to-day work,' Owen said, 'but we would like to change the name to reflect the change in ownership.'

'To Cartwright & Urt, I expect,' Clive grumbled.

Wendy said, 'Herbert George Wells.'

'Who is Herbert George?'

'You could say he's our godfather,' Wendy smiled at Owen, sharing a private joke. The publication of H. G. Wells' *The Time Machine* was still seven years away, so Owen felt safe that the name wasn't going to tip off Clive, who couldn't read anyway, or confirm any of the Judge's suspicions that what he'd seen in his cholera delirium was real.

'Is this George fella gonna want a say in things?' Clive asked.

'He'll only be here in spirit,' Wendy said. 'We'll handle the financial and strategic sides of the business.'

'We don't have them sides,' Clive said. 'We just dig wells and deliver water.'

'That's a problem we're going to fix,' Wendy said. 'The business needs to evolve to meet the demands of the future if you're going to remain prosperous.'

'I'd listen to her if I were you,' the Judge said to Clive. 'They see the future better than any of us.'

The comment made Owen nervous. It was too on-the-nose for comfort.

Virgil took Milly's hand. 'You haven't said a word. Is what they're offering something you want?'

'It's my dream to have my own restaurant and we could have a fresh start, where nobody knows us,' Milly said. 'Or who we were.'

Virgil turned to his brother. 'How do you feel about it?'

'I'll be glad to see you go,' Clive said. 'It won't be so awkward between us and you'll be less likely to kill me.'

'I haven't killed you yet,' Virgil said. 'Or even tried.'

'You know I poked Milly plenty when she was at Tuttle's and it's a burr under your saddle,' Clive said. 'You can ignore it, but the irritation will just get worse until you can't stand it no more.'

'You're hardly the only man she's known.' Virgil tipped his head towards the Judge, who acknowledged the point with a slight nod. 'I'm peaceable about it or I'd be killing men every day.'

'But I'm the only one of 'em that's your flesh and blood,' Clive said. 'Speaking truthful, Virg, I'll always have the itch for her. And you know I'm a drinking man who don't think straight when he's had too much.'

Virgil thought about that a moment, glanced at Milly, then offered Owen his hand. 'We have a deal.'

The two men shook on it.

Milly gave Virgil a big hug and a kiss. 'I've always wanted to live by the sea. How about you?'

'I'd live in Jack Ass Gulch as long as I'm with you.'

That's when a man covered in trail dust and sweat burst in from the street. It was Harry Knief, the superintendent of the Waterstone Mine in Odessa Canyon. Bufe sat nearest to the door, and stood up in front of Knief.

'Hold on, mister. Can't you see we're closed?' Bufe said, gesturing to the bride and groom. 'On account of a wedding?'

'I'm sorry, but this is an emergency, and we got to move fast.' Knief pushed past Bufe to the Judge. 'I was robbed coming back from Daggett with the monthly payroll for the mine, stamp mill, and refinery. That's $4,500 in gold coins.'

That got everyone's attention. There was plenty of vice in Calico, but robberies were rare, and there had never been one remotely as big as this one.

Wendy said, 'Does he look like the sheriff to you, Harry? What do you expect him to do, strap on a gun belt and go after them now?'

Knief ignored her, keeping his attention on the Judge. 'You're the only law around here, so you've got to do something. That money is important, not just to the Waterstone. There's a lot of men who'll go without pay and all the businesses in the town will feel the hurt, too.'

The Judge finished his beer, pulled the napkin out from his collar, and tossed it on the table. 'What exactly happened, Mr Knief?'

'I rode out from the Waterstone to Daggett yesterday, stayed the night, picked up the payroll from the Wells Fargo office at sun-up, meaning to get back in time for lunch . . .'

The Judge waved his hand, indicating he wanted Knief to speed it up.

'Anyways, I was halfway across the dry lake when the desperado rose up from the ground with his gun and told me to stop or he'd blow my head off.'

Virgil said, 'It's a wide-open desert. How is it possible you didn't see him until the last moment?'

'His outfit made him look like he was part of everything around,' Knief said. 'Damn near made him invisible.'

'Must've been an Indian savage covered in dirt,' Clive said.

'No, he was a white man and it was his clothes that was dirt-like.'

'Then he must've learned it from the Indians,' Clive said. 'They like to snatch white babies and raise them as their own.'

The Judge brushed that argument aside with his hand, as if it was hanging in the air like smoke. 'We haven't had any Indians around here in years. It's too crowded and noisy for them. It's a wonder we all aren't deaf.'

Bufe nudged Knief. 'Why didn't you pull your gun as soon as you saw him rise up? You could've got the drop on him easy.'

Knief turned to look at him. 'Because I don't have a gun.'

Bufe was astonished. 'You were carrying $4,500 in gold coins without a gun?'

'We're in the desert. There's no place to go. Who'd be stupid enough to rob me?'

'Maybe me,' Bufe said. 'If I'd known.'

The Judge glowered at Bufe. 'Let the man continue with his account.'

'The desperado told me to raise my hands and get off the horse,' Knief said. 'Then he told me to empty my pockets. He took my two $5 gold pieces, a gold nugget, and my tobacco. Then he got on my horse and rode off fast.'

'Which way did he go?' Virgil asked.

'Northeast, out toward Mule Canyon.'

'Were you riding that dappled gray?'

'I only got the one horse,' Knief said.

Clive tugged on his beard. 'The damn fool might as well be riding naked and firing his gun into the air.'

'He's clearly deranged,' the Judge said.

'I was walking for an hour before I hitched a ride here with the stage,' Knief said. 'So the robber couldn't have gone far.'

The Judge sighed. 'We can't have a crazy desperado like that running wild out there, terrorizing people. And if he gets away, it will only encourage more lawlessness.'

Virgil kissed Milly, stood up, and faced the Judge. 'Me and Clive'll get heeled and go after him presently.'

'Heeled?' Owen said. 'What does that mean?'

'Guns,' Virgil said to Ben. 'Sometimes I think you're from the moon.'

'You're not too far off,' the Judge said.

Milly bolted up and shook Virgil. 'Are you crazy? You can't go. You just got married.'

'We know the Calicos better than anybody,' Virgil said. 'We've lived here all our lives.'

'Virgil's also a fair tracker,' Clive said.

Stoby stood up at a nearby table. 'I'll meet you boys at the livery stable with six-shooters, a Winchester repeater, and provisions.'

'What about our wedding night?' Milly said.

'It'll have to wait until tomorrow,' Virgil said. 'If that desperado kills someone, it'll be on me for not catching him when I know I could've.'

Virgil kissed her, and walked out with Clive and Stoby.

Milly grabbed Owen by the collar and lifted him to his feet. 'Get up. You're going with them.'

'I don't know anything about tracking or shooting,' Owen said.

'You are going to make sure Virgil comes back to me alive,' Milly said. 'I won't bury another husband.'

'You were married before?' Wendy said.

'In Kansas. We came to California for the gold, to strike it rich,' she said. 'Andy died two months after we got here and left me with nothing but my body to live on. If Virgil gets killed, I will slit my throat.'

Wendy looked at Owen. 'You heard the woman. Get changed and get going.'

Over the next few hours, Owen didn't see much evidence of Virgil's tracking skills. Virgil made a show of studying horse tracks in the dirt, but mostly he just asked whoever they passed if they saw Knief's dappled gray and, if they had, to point them in the right direction.

The Urt brothers took the lead, with Knief and Owen bringing up the rear, all of them on horses provided by the livery stable.

Owen was the only one who wasn't carrying one of Stoby's guns, because he didn't know how to use one and didn't want to shoot himself by accident. But he didn't say that. Instead, he'd argued that his job was to keep his eyes out for danger.

'In other words,' Clive said, 'you're useless.'

'That's no way to be talking to your new business partner,' Owen said.

'Seems to me it's gonna be your woman,' Clive said. 'Not you.'

'She's not my woman,' Owen said. 'She's my wife.'

Knief said, 'I hope you're not taking marriage advice from this man, Virgil. He's lucky he's still wearing pants and not a dress.'

The tracks and witness accounts led them up Mule Canyon, towards Borate, then on a trail that branched off east, toward the vast dry lake on the eastern edge of the Calicos, not far from where Fort Irwin would eventually be located.

They traveled a rocky serpentine path through crevices and around huge boulders that had been trod, Virgil said, by animals and man in search of water for centuries. But the most recent tracks he saw belonged to Knief's horse and they weren't far behind.

'The desperado ran him through here hard,' Virgil said, studying the ground. 'It's a good way to kill a horse.'

'And yourself,' Clive said, taking another pull from a flask he'd been drinking from for hours. He'd begun to wobble a bit in his saddle.

'That would make things easier,' Knief said. 'But it would be a damn shame to lose that horse.'

Virgil looked up at the sky. 'It's gonna be dark soon. If we don't find him by then, we'll have to bed down for the night and go out again at sun-up.'

'It's a lousy way to spend your wedding night,' Owen said.

'A man's got responsibilities,' Virgil said.

'He's glad to be out here,' Clive said. 'He was looking for an excuse.'

Virgil turned his horse so he could look at his brother. 'What is that supposed to mean?'

'You haven't had a poke since Daddy took you to the whores in San Bernardino,' Clive said. 'You're afraid you forgot how it's done. Or that you won't measure up to all the others Milly's had. Especially me.'

'Shut up,' Virgil said.

'I can give you some pointers about what she likes,' Clive said, grinning. 'From experience.'

Virgil pulled his gun and aimed it at his brother's head.

'That didn't take long,' Clive said and took another pull from his flask. Owen rode up, placing himself between the two men.

'Put that gun away, Virgil,' Owen said. 'You go to prison, and what do you think will happen to Milly?'

'She'll come running to me,' Clive said.

Owen slapped the flask out of Clive's hand. 'Stop being an asshole. Do you want to get shot? This man is your brother. Why can't you be happy for him?'

'I was just joshing,' Clive said. 'Don't you have a brother?'

'No, I don't,' Owen said.

'It's what brothers do.'

Virgil holstered his gun. 'He wants to get shot, Ben. He's afraid because he's never been alone before. He's always had me around.'

Clive sucked on his beard, capturing the last drops of whatever he'd been drinking. It smelled to Owen like paint thinner. 'How is it a woman can be so troublesome?'

'Life wouldn't be very interesting if they weren't,' Virgil said and they rode on.

A few minutes later, they came upon Knief's dappled gray under a rocky outcropping, still saddled but missing the bags of gold coins.

It wasn't until Owen saw the horse that he understood how the breed got its name. The horse's white coat was splotched with gray rings.

Knief dismounted from his bay mare, went over to the dappled gray, took his reins and walked him in a small circle, studying how he moved.

'Your horse has gone lame,' Clive observed.

Knief nodded and stroked the horse. 'He'll be fine, he just needs some rest.'

Virgil got off his horse and checked out the tracks in the dirt. Even Owen could see the footprints heading off through the boulders that spilled down to the flatlands. 'The desperado set off on foot toward Coyote Holes. Wasn't too long ago.'

Now Clive got down, removing his rifle from its scabbard. 'Best go after him and get this over with while we can still see our feet.'

'What's Coyote Holes?' Owen asked.

'You'll see,' Virgil said.

They left their horses and set off on foot. They'd only gone about thirty yards when the trail opened up to a large mud puddle, about the size of a high-school baseball field, ringed with boulders, cactus, and tall grass.

They stood still, watching and listening.

Virgil looked at the ground. 'He's wily after all. He wiped his footprints, but he's around this hole somewhere. Probably watching us now.'

Knief drew his gun. Clive hefted his rifle.

Virgil turned to Owen. 'You stay here and try not to make yourself a target. I'll go left, Harry you go right. Clive, you find yourself a high spot back the way we came so you'll see if we flush him out into the open.'

The three men moved out, melding into the deepening shadows as the sun began to set. Owen crouched down behind a boulder, feeling useless. His ankles ached, so he got down on his knees, placing a hand on the ground to steady himself.

His fingers touched fabric.

Owen looked down and saw a set of clothes, neatly and precisely folded, as if they'd just been delivered by a professional laundry. He wouldn't have seen them if his fingers hadn't brushed them. That's because the fabric was tan, with splotches of brown and green dotted with black and white spots that looked like pebbles casting shadows, so it blended right into the landscape.

That was the intention.

Owen scrambled around further on his hands and knees and found a matching camouflage helmet and tan boots nearby.

It was a camouflage uniform, the kind that soldiers wore for desert warfare. And in training exercises at Fort Irwin, which in a hundred years wouldn't be far from where they were now.

It had only been two days since February 2nd, the sixth anniversary of the day Owen and Wendy had stepped through time. They'd stayed up until 2 a.m., as they always did on that special day, waiting to see if the sky cracked and showed them glimpses of tomorrow. A few times, in prior years, they'd seen sparkles in the darkness, but they weren't sure if it was real or stars or wishful thinking. But two nights ago, they saw flashes of light in the distance, north of the Calicos, and wondered if it was lightning or something more.

Now he knew.

The robber was a soldier from the future.

But was he here by accident? Or had he come hunting for them, like Arnold Schwarzenegger in *The Terminator*?

Owen rose up behind the boulder and peered out across the mud hole, searching for signs of movement. He saw Virgil's silhouette on the shore to his left, moving cautiously among the rocks, and he saw Knief to his right, slogging through the weeds, gun at the ready. Somewhere behind and above him, presumably, was Clive Urt.

But where was Arnold?

Owen stood up, to get a better look around him, and saw something odd, a shifting of shadows in middle of the mire.

A man sat up into a sitting position, dripping mud, like a corpse rising from the dead.

It was Arnold.

He'd been lying there, face up in just a foot of water, waiting for them. He slowly raised his right arm, pointing his gun at Virgil.

Owen yelled: 'Don't!'

Arnold whirled around and fired off two shots at Owen, the bullets glancing off the boulder inches from his head.

Owen ducked and heard a barrage of gunfire, seemingly from every direction, bullets whizzing over his head.

And then there was silence.

Owen risked a peek over the boulder and saw Arnold floating in the water, darkness falling over the murky pond like the curtain closing on a play.

He ran out to the body, sloshing through the muddy water, and saw a young man, maybe in his twenties, lying naked and face up, a bullet hole where one of his blue eyes used to be, and a lot of bullet holes everywhere else, all leaking blood.

There were dog tags around his neck. Owen yanked them off, stuffed them in his pocket, then looked for the man's gun, as he heard the sloshing of Virgil and Knief approaching. He only had seconds to act.

The gun was still in the dead man's hand.

Owen didn't know much about guns, but he knew it was a semi-automatic, that the bullets were loaded into a magazine that slid into the grip, and that it was nothing like the firearms in the 1880s. He feared that if it was found, and reverse-engineered, it would change the future more dramatically, and violently, than anything Owen had brought with him.

If he did nothing else in his life here, it had to be making sure this gun was never found.

Luckily for him, that was the moment Knief stumbled over something and fell hard into the water with a loud cry and an even louder splash, distracting Virgil long enough for Owen to take Arnold's gun, jam it under his waistband, and tug his shirt over it.

Knief rolled over in the water and crawled back to examine whatever he'd tripped over. He lifted up a mud-covered gunny sack. 'Looks like I found our stolen gold.'

Now Virgil regarded Owen. 'That was a damn stupid thing to do, calling out like that.'

'I promised Milly I wouldn't let you get killed,' Owen said. 'Especially not on your wedding day.'

'There's some truth to what Clive said about me.'

'You've got nothing to worry about,' Owen said.

Virgil nudged Arnold with the toe of his shoe. 'I'll be damned.'

'What is it?' Knief asked.

'Clive was right about him riding naked,' Virgil said.

Knief looked down at him. 'He was wearing clothes when he robbed me, but they looked like dirt.'

'Because it was dirt,' Virgil said.

'I didn't see his willy,' Knief said. 'I'd have noticed.'

'Maybe there isn't much to see.' Virgil lifted his head and spotted Clive on the shore. 'Don't expect any help from Clive carrying the body out of here or slinging him over a horse. He won't muddy himself for that. We're going to have to do that ourselves.'

'Can't we just leave him here?' Knief said.

'No sense fouling a good watering hole,' Virgil said. 'Besides, the Judge is going to want to see the body. Where's his gun?'

'Probably flew from his hand,' Owen said. 'You want search through the muck for it?'

'Might help us prove self-defense,' Virgil said, 'and avoid the noose for cold-blooded murder.'

'The Judge will take our word for it,' Owen said. 'I sure as hell don't want to spend all night in the mud looking for it.'

'I don't, either,' Knief said. 'It must be some gun, though. It sounded like he fired a dozen shots.'

'That was just the echoes playing tricks on you.' Virgil holstered his gun, crouched down, and slid his hands under Arnold's armpits. 'You get his legs, Ben.'

Owen grabbed Arnold by the ankles and they carried the body, which was astonishingly heavy, toward the shore.

Nobody thought to go back and look for the man's clothes and, as far as Owen knew, they were never found. The man was buried in the Calico cemetery, his grave marked by a simple wooden cross.

Owen dismantled the gun and, over a period of weeks, widely disbursed the pieces by burying them in the desert, dropping them into the outhouse 'toilets', and tossing them into the sewage of Jack Ass Gulch.

He didn't know if the soldier arrived in 1880s by accident or intent, but he kept the dog tags so the question might be answered, along with all the others, by someone in the future.

The dog tags would join the iPhone videos he'd been making in a 'time capsule' that he planned to somehow leave behind after his death so that his daughter might learn what had really happened to him.

The tricky part would be coming up with a way to control how and when the capsule would be discovered so that the secrets it contained wouldn't change the future and prevent himself, or Nicole, from being born. And now he also didn't want to do anything to endanger his past, and his family here, from happening, either.

His future was his past . . . and his past was his future.

He was living two lifetimes and he had to protect the people he loved in both of them.

Owen didn't know how to do that yet, but he had plenty of time to figure it out . . . more than his share.

THIRTY-FOUR

Silver Lake, California
Tuesday, February 12, 2019

The hike from the bus stop up the outrageously steep hill to Owen Slader's bungalow nearly killed Beth McDade. It wasn't that she was too old, or too out of shape for a decent hike, it was just that the stress of being chased across Glendale by half of the LAPD had wiped her out.

At least that was what she told herself as she struggled to catch her breath in Slader's living room and worried that the pain in her chest could be a heart attack.

She hoped it wasn't, because there was no way she was calling 911 after evading a police dragnet. She'd die first.

But the pain ebbed, and she didn't die, so she made sure all of the drapes and blinds were closed, took off her sweat-soaked hoody and shirt, and her pants and shoes while she was at it, and helped herself to some European beer she'd never heard of from his fridge.

She walked with the beer to the master bathroom, stripped out of her underwear, and stood under the cold shower, careful not to get any water in her beer bottle. The combination of a cold shower and cold beer refreshed her and cleared her mind, not quite as effectively the combination of beer and sex could, but it did just fine.

She set the empty bottle on the toilet tank, dried herself off, put on a terrycloth bathrobe that was hanging on the door hook, and realized she was ravenous. So she walked barefoot into the kitchen, opened the refrigerator, found some eggs and an unopened package of imported French sausage, an onion, some mushrooms, and some butter, and whipped up an omelet on his gourmet stove.

Beth devoured the delicious omelet, and washed it down with another beer, while warily eyeing her gym bag, which she'd tossed on the couch. Now that she'd outrun the police, revived herself with alcohol, a shower, and a meal, her curiosity asserted itself.

What was in that metal box that was so important to Wendy Hale-Cartwright that she locked it up and took it to her grave?

Perhaps a better question to ask, Beth thought, was what did Wendy want to keep safe until the right person put together all the clues and exhumed her grave?

Beth got up, went over to the gym bag, took out the box and the bolt cutters, and brought them over to the kitchen island.

She then went to one of Owen's mounted cameras that were aimed at the kitchen for his cooking show, hit record, and stepped in front of the lens, where she introduced herself, stated the date, the time, and her location.

'I retrieved this box from Gwendolyn Hale's grave, which I'm sure isn't news to you and is an event that's well documented,' she said. 'I apologize for the property damage, by the way.'

Beth went over to the island, picked up the bolt cutters, snapped off the padlock, and opened the box's lid. Inside was a zippered blue neoprene carrying case that looked as if it could have been bought yesterday. She turned the box toward the camera to document the contents, then lifted out the carrying case, unzipped it, and removed an iPhone 10.

Holy shit.

Beth glanced back at the kitchen camera. 'I don't believe this. It's an iPhone. It's a little scuffed around the edges, but otherwise it looks like it's in better shape than mine.'

She reached into the case and pulled out the next thing her fingers touched.

A MacBook Pro laptop.

It, too, seemed to be in remarkably good condition, especially considering it had been buried for decades. She showed it to the camera.

'This 2019 MacBook is over a hundred years old,' she said. 'I wonder if it's technically still under warranty.'

She laughed, giddy at the wonder of it all.

There were also two wall chargers, a solar battery charger, earbuds, and various cables inside the case.

And something else . . . a set of military dog tags. She glanced at the information stamped into the tin:

GRUBER, BERTRUM

174631503

A POS

CATHOLIC

Beth held the tags up to the camera and read aloud what was engraved on them.

She knew from experience it was a soldier's name, social security number, blood type, and religion, important information for identification and burial. But who was Bertrum Gruber? And why were his dog tags in the box?

Beth glanced at the box again and spotted a folded piece of paper. She unfolded it to reveal some faded handwriting that read:

020219

It was the date that Owen Slader disappeared. But she realized it could also be something else.

The numbers to unlock an iPhone.

She just stood there staring at everything for a long moment. This box, and particularly the devices it contained, was her lost Ark of the Covenant. What she had here was conclusive proof of time travel.

But only for her.

By taking the box from the cemetery, she'd destroyed the chain of evidence. Sure, she had this video documenting the unboxing, but she couldn't prove the box on camera was the same one she took from Hale's grave. Or that she'd recovered these devices from a coffin buried for eighty-six years and not in the last week from somewhere in Yermo or even from this bungalow.

She'd screwed herself.

Unless the devices aren't the evidence. It's the files on them.

That raised a big question for her. Could she still power up the phone and the MacBook?

There was only one way to find out.

But instead of using the chargers that were in the grave, she chose instead to use an iPhone charger that she'd spotted earlier plugged into a kitchen outlet and a MacBook charger that she'd seen on Slader's office desk.

She brought the two chargers to the kitchen island, plugged them into an outlet underneath the counter, inserted the appropriate power cords into the two devices, and then took a step back, watching them warily, as if they might burst into flames.

They didn't.

An image of an 'empty' battery icon appeared on the iPhone screen and the word 'charging' appeared underneath it, but she doubted that it actually was. She didn't expect the lithium batteries to still be capable of holding a charge after decades and didn't know if the devices would work off the juice from the wall outlets alone.

Beth picked up the phone, turned it on, and waited to see what happened.

The six empty spaces came up for the passcode.

A miracle.

She typed in 020219.

A picture of Nicole came up as the backdrop and an assortment of app icons filled the screen. She touched the camera icon.

The camera opened, showing the kitchen table. In the bottom corner, she saw a tiny thumbnail of an elderly Wendy Hale-Cartwright.

Beth's finger was shaking as she tapped the photo.

Wendy's face reappeared, larger now, looking directly into the camera. Her face was sunken, her sallow skin deeply lined, her hair sparse and grey, but Beth could still see the young woman she once was. There was a wall of books on ornate shelves behind her, the room dimly lit by a couple of reading lamps.

Below her photo, there was a scroll bar of tiny versions of the other videos and pictures on the phone.

That's when Beth realized that it wasn't a photo of Wendy she was looking at.

It was a video.

Beth glanced over her shoulder at the mounted camera in the kitchen.

'Can you believe this? The iPhone still works and the last recording is a video.'

Evidence.

Beth angled the iPhone so the screen could be seen by the mounted camera and then she tapped the image of Wendy. The video began to play.

If you're watching this, then you probably know or suspect what happened to me and to Ben, or you wouldn't have dug me up. And for you, it must be some time after February 2nd, 2019, because otherwise you wouldn't know what to do with these devices. At least I hope so, or I've really screwed things up.

This cell phone and laptop computer were supposed to be buried with Ben, to keep them safe for his daughter Nicole, and I promised him on his deathbed that I'd do that. But I was selfish and broke that promise, as I knew I would when I made it. I couldn't bear not seeing his face, or hearing his voice. I wanted to keep him alive the same way he wanted to keep his daughter, and the future, alive for himself and for her.

I didn't want to be trapped alone in the past.

Ever since Ben died, I've yearned for the night, and the cover of darkness, to put in my earphones, turn this on, and see him again. And each time I did, I knew I was putting our story and these magical devices from the future at risk. But it gave me so much comfort to know that he'd live again and so would I, and if there is such a thing as fate, we would be together all over again.

I've been sloppy in my selfishness. I know some people have glimpsed me watching the videos, or heard me listening to his voice, and didn't know what to make of it. They thought they were seeing or hearing ghosts. I suppose they were. But my secret – our secret – wasn't revealed.

I guess there's still a chance someone might steal these treasures from me or my grave, before they end up in the right hands. But that would have been a risk even if I'd kept my promise and buried them with Ben in Newberry Springs.

But if you're watching this, that means that, despite my selfishness, you managed to follow the clues we left, and things worked out the way Ben wanted them to.

What was it he wanted?

Owen Slader, the man I always knew and loved as Ben Cartwright, wanted his daughter Nicole to be born, to be safe, and to eventually know the incredible thing that happened to him. He also wanted his new family – the Cartwrights – to know our shared story, though I'm sure they've guessed some of it, if they've kept and followed the List and honored our wills and trust.

I'm certain that they've often wondered how the List could be so incredibly and accurately prescient . . . and why that helpful and cautionary foresight ends in 2019. And I'm sure they've puzzled over the significance of February 2nd, 2019, in our trust.

Well, now you know.

Or you soon will.

I also hope my parents, if they are still alive when you are watching this, are able to learn how I disappeared and to know that I lived a good, long life, and that the knowledge finally gives them some peace.

I wish Ben and I could have known how the cracks in time to 1882 opened up in front of us, on the same date, decades apart. But the answer to that mystery stopped mattering once we accepted our fate, fell in love, and had our family . . . because we knew that we never would have found each other, or had our son and grandchildren, if not for that cosmic event, or cruel experiment, or catastrophic accident.

We never forgot, of course, who we were and where we came from, and all of the conveniences, medicines, and technology from our times that would have made our lives in the past easier and healthier.

The important thing was that we were happy.

Oh God, were we happy.

So very, very happy.

What happened to us, in the end, was a blessing.

Except, perhaps, for Nicole, who I feel I know from all the videos and photos I saw and through her father's love, and who I grew to love as well. She needs to know the truth about her father's disappearance . . . and I hope she hasn't been wondering about it for long, that it has only been days or weeks rather than years or decades.

And then there's our Cartwright family, the descendants of our son Nicolas and his wife, who deserve to finally solve the mystery of their past and of the List that has guided them for so long.

That day has come.

The future is now yours to discover for yourselves.

I hope it is as great an adventure as the lives we lived.

Beth used her thumb to scroll through the photos and videos, hundreds of them, until she saw the Las Vegas Strip, then she went forward again until she spotted Owen's first video.

She played it.

Owen stared into the iPhone's camera. He was outside, in the dark. He looked tired and terrified.

I am so cosmically, titanically, biblically fucked. I'm stuck in the past. Can you believe it? I can't, but here I am. What am I going to do? All I know about time travel is from TV shows and movies, which is all bullshit, because nobody has ever done it before. Until now. Hurray for me. I remember a story where a guy goes back to prehistoric times to hunt dinosaurs, steps on a butterfly, and destroys mankind. God, I hope that's bullshit.

He glanced down. She assumed he was lifting up each foot to check his shoes. When he looked back into the camera, there was some relief on his face.

Mankind is safe for now. But the sun is about to come up, and I'm in the open desert, so soon people will be able to see my 2018 Mercedes. That's got to be worse than stepping on a butterfly . . . it's certainly a violation of the prime directive. Looks like I've got some work to do.

She scrolled forward and saw his first pictures and videos of Calico, images of mining-camp life from over a hundred years ago, but in high-def and with perfect sound, as vivid as if they'd been shot that day.

Beth set the phone down, her hands trembling, and looked at the kitchen camera.

'Holy shit,' she said.

She got up, turned off the camera, and then found Owen's liquor. She poured herself some Scotch, spilling some on the counter, drank the shot, and poured herself some more.

What she'd discovered wasn't simply the solution to the mystery behind two disappearances, or proof that the military was covering up a deadly accident that created collateral damage with extraordinary consequences. This was also a scientific milestone, a turning point for humanity, and a true Pandora's box.

The ramifications of her discovery could change the world, if the accident hadn't already done that in thousands of ways, both significant and subtle, from the instant it happened, sending ripples forward and backward in time. It gave her a headache just to wrap her mind around all the possible consequences that might already have occurred without her doing a thing yet.

Time is too fucking complicated.

She finished the second shot of Scotch. Her trembling was subsiding. So she poured herself another.

What's the right thing to do with this discovery?

But she didn't need to grapple with that question just yet. First, she had a more immediate priority.

Save the evidence.

Beth was able to power up Owen's MacBook and open the files it contained using the iPhone's password. The files on the laptop included backups of all the videos and photos that were on the iPhone. There were also lots of family and work-related videos and photos taken prior to his time-travel accident, as well as music, TV shows, movies, and porn.

Using Owen's MacBook, and working in total darkness so she wouldn't draw the attention of any neighbors, she went on the Internet, created new Gmail, Flickr, and other free online accounts. She uploaded as many of Owen's files, from his last few days in Las Vegas through Wendy's final recording in 1933, as she could to an account until she hit the point that required payment, then she went on to the next account, until she had backed up everything to the cloud. She couldn't risk using her credit card, checking, or PayPal accounts or Owen's to pay for any storage because she was certain the government or law enforcement was watching them for any new activity.

While her data was uploading, she browsed the web, looking to see if her car chase had generated any news stories. But car chases were almost a nightly event in Los Angeles and unless a celebrity or major shooting was involved, they didn't get any real journalistic attention beyond the brief live shot on the TV news.

She found a tiny item on the KNX 1070 news radio site. All it said was that the LAPD chased a stolen car from Forest Lawn to the Galleria, but the suspected thief got away. Her name wasn't mentioned. It was a relief to know that everyone in Los Angeles wasn't on the lookout for her, but that didn't mean there wasn't an APB out for her among law enforcement agencies. And it certainly didn't mean the military weren't hunting her down. She was certain they were and, if anything, intensifying their efforts. It would only be a matter of time, days at the most, before they figured out that she got on a bus, found out which one it was, pulled the surveillance video, and deduced her location.

It took hours to upload everything, and while the bytes flew, she washed all of her clothes, removed the memory card with the video of her unboxing from the kitchen camera, and poked around Owen's office. She found FedEx shipping supplies and a box of small, portable hard drives that she could see, from the hard drives on his desk, he used to back up video for his YouTube program.

Once everything was uploaded, which was at about 4 a.m., she copied Amanda's camera data card, her own iPhone photographs, and the files from Owen's iPhone and MacBook to several hard drives. While that final copying was going on, she went to bed, unable to keep her eyes open another second.

Beth awoke at 10 a.m. on Wednesday, had a bowl of dry granola and a cup of coffee for breakfast, then sat down to start looking at fifty years' worth of videos and photographs, from Owen's arrival in 1882 to Wendy's last recording before her death, so she'd know exactly what evidence she had and the whole story that Owen and Beth had to tell.

Owen shot hours of video, and took hundreds of photos, in the first few months after his arrival in Calico, but Beth noticed the quantity of material dropped dramatically after Wendy came into his life, when he no longer needed the psychological and emotional crutch that his imaginary audience provided. At first months, and later years, went by between new photos and videos, but it was enough for Beth to easily follow the course of Owen's life and also the boom and bust of Calico.

It was compelling, and at times awe-inspiring, to see the past so vividly alive, to see and hear places, like Calico, that she knew from her daily life as they were over a hundred years ago but with the vividness of photos and videos that could have been shot an hour ago.

It took her a full day to watch it all, pausing only to nap and prepare meals. By the time she got to Wendy's video again, she felt like she truly knew Owen and what he'd endured, and the peace he'd made with his situation.

She was glad she'd watched it all, because when it was over, she knew what she had to do.

THIRTY-FIVE

On Thursday morning, Beth put most of her fully-loaded, password-protected hard drives of Owen's files, and her own, into several FedEx boxes addressed to her friends or relatives. She added a personal note in each box asking the recipient to hold on to her drives for safekeeping, sealed the boxes up, and put them into a gym bag that she stole from Owen's closet. She put everything else she'd brought with her into her own gym bag and called a taxi to pick her up at Owen's bungalow.

It seemed old-fashioned to use a taxi, but she couldn't order an Uber or Lyft without a credit card. Taxis still took good, old-fashioned cash, and she had plenty of that, thanks to Owen's wallet, which contained several crisp one-hundred-dollar bills, along with some small bills.

She had the taxi driver take her to the Century City office building where Christopher Cartwright's real estate development company was based. It took forty minutes to get there in LA traffic. She stopped at the FedEx office in the building's lobby, paid cash to have the boxes delivered by overnight priority, and then approached the security guard station in front of the elevators.

Beth flashed her badge at middle-aged guard and told him that she was going up to see Christopher Cartwright. She pointedly did not ask for permission and the guard, probably a retired cop himself, was wise enough to just nod and remind her that the office was on the top floor.

She went to the elevator, hit the button for the 44th floor, and the car shot up so fast, her ears popped.

The elevators opened into a lobby much like the entry hall of Cartwright's home, offering a spectacular view of West Los Angeles, clear to the Pacific. The waiting area was outside a glass-walled conference room, where even the table and chairs were made of clear Plexiglas, so there was nothing to obstruct the view from hitting each guest like a bracing wind. From here, the Cartwrights could look down upon the city, and much of their real-estate empire. It seemed like they never wanted to take their eyes off of it.

The receptionist, a beautiful woman in a black dress wearing a thin headset microphone, was to Beth's left, behind a low counter. Beth flashed her badge, identified herself, and asked to see Cartwright. The woman typed something on a keyboard, spoke into her headset, and told Beth that he'd be right out.

Cartwright strode out moments later, a warm smile on his face, which immediately faded when he saw Beth's serious expression. 'What's wrong?'

'Nothing, Mr Cartwright. Is there somewhere we can go where we won't be on display and can have some privacy?'

'Of course.' He led her into the conference room, which seemed to be the opposite of what she'd asked for. But once he was inside, he picked up a remote control from the table and pressed a button. The transparent glass around them clouded with an opaque white haze. 'It's electrochromic glass. Nobody can see us or hear us, unless you're planning to shout at me.'

'You don't want me shouting this,' she said. 'I know everything you know and everything you've always wanted to know.'

'About what?'

'Your family and why that first edition of *The Time Machine* is such a treasured heirloom.'

'It's a rare book,' he said.

'It's a message. What you've always suspected about Ben and Wendy Cartwright is true, and I can prove it,' Beth said. 'But first, I'd like to see the List.'

Christopher started to say something, then changed his mind. He seemed at a loss for words. She could understand why. For over a century, they'd honored the promise to keep the List absolutely secret. It was the key to the family's fortune, their safety, and their future.

She said, 'I understand your hesitancy. But it can't do you any harm now to show it to me. Time has finally caught up to it. There's nothing on it that isn't common knowledge, which means for the first time in your life, you're like the rest of us. You don't know what to expect.'

Christopher met her gaze. 'It's frightening.'

'It's life, Mr Cartwright.'

'The List is at home,' he said. 'In a vault.'

'I want you to take me there and then I'll tell you the whole story, but it isn't only yours,' Beth said. 'Ben Cartwright's daughter is alive today and still grieving.'

'He died over a hundred years ago,' Christopher said.

'For Nicole, he's only been dead two weeks.'

Christopher sat down heavily in a chair, as if he'd suddenly gained more weight than his legs could hold, and stared out at the view. 'My God, it's really true. My ancestors were from today. But how is that possible? How did it happen?'

Beth crouched down in front of him. 'I can show you.'

'Show me?'

'Yes . . . and Nicole and her mother Sabine. They are your family, too. They need to know everything. It's what Ben and Wendy Cartwright wanted. It was as important to them as the List.' Beth smiled and took his hands in hers. 'You will be amazed, believe me. And when I'm done, we have some big decisions to make.'

'We?'

'I'm part of the story now.'

He met her gaze, and then nodded. 'Yes, of course, you are. Tell me where Nicole and Sabine live and I'll send a car for them.'

'Let me call them first,' Beth said. 'But there's one other thing we're going to need after you all know the truth.'

'What's that?'

'Your best lawyers. You need to make sure they are on standby tonight for your call,' she said. 'You'll understand why soon, but for now, let me put it in a way you'll appreciate: we're all on borrowed time.'

*   *   *

'You told me to keep an open mind and I did,' Beth said to Sabine, talking to her from a phone in Christopher Cartwright's conference room. 'Now I'm asking you to do the same thing for me. I also need your trust.'

'What's going on?'

'I know what happened to Owen. I want you and Nicole to come right away to a home in Bel Air, where I will explain it all to you.'

'You want Nicole there?' Sabine said. 'She's a child. Are you sure she's old enough to deal with this?'

'Age doesn't matter. We're all going to have trouble dealing with this, but not because what happened to him was violent or horrifying. I promise you the story of what happened won't traumatize your daughter. If anything, it might end her grieving and give her hope. But most of all, it's what Owen wanted.'

'How can you know what he wanted?'

'Because he left a message for your daughter and that's what I want to share.'

'Why do we need to go to Bel Air to get it?'

'For privacy, for security, and because the family who lives there, the Cartwrights, are an important part of the story.'

'I've never heard of them,' she said.

'They've never heard of you, either. But you are connected in ways you can't imagine.'

'That's mysterious,' Sabine said.

'I don't mean to be, but it's too complicated to explain everything over the phone. You need to be there, all of you, together, when I present the evidence. I can only do it once.'

'That's even more mysterious.' There was a moment of silence, then: 'All right. We'll be there. But I have to pull Nicole out of school first.'

'The Cartwrights will send a car for you,' Beth said.

'I can drive,' Sabine said.

'I know, but I don't want you driving home afterwards,' Beth said. 'You'll be too distracted to do it safely.'

'The news is that unsettling?'

'It's more like a revelation,' Beth said.

Your life will never be the same, she thought.

And neither will mine.

* * *

Christopher Cartwright drove Beth to his home in his Rolls-Royce Cullinan, an SUV that cost more than most homes in America. It felt like they were floating to Bel Air.

'Do your wife and daughter know about the List?' Beth asked.

'They'll find out today,' Christopher said. 'They will find out a lot of things. We all will. How much trouble are you in?'

'Did you see the car chase on the news last night? The one in Glendale?'

'Yes, I did,' he said.

'They were chasing me.'

'Why?'

'To stop me from telling anyone what I know or sharing what I've found,' she said. 'So you can assume they'll be coming for you soon, too.'

'They?'

'The US military,' she said.

'How much do they know?'

Beth shrugged. 'Enough to be excited . . . and scared shitless.'

Bel Air was only a few miles north of Century City, and to get there, they were traveling on narrow, traffic-clogged residential roads in Beverly Hills, and yet it still felt to Beth as if they moved with unnatural speed in the Rolls, the automotive Staff of Moses parting the Red Sea of traffic congestion in front of them. They arrived at Cartwright's house in ten minutes without even breaking the speed limit.

He drove down a ramp into an underground garage. The floor was polished concrete, the walls were marble, and it was brightly lit, making the polished sports cars and luxury sedans sparkle like diamonds to be admired from the great room upstairs, visible through the Plexiglas ceiling, as she had on her first visit. It must be nice, she thought, having cars that doubled as home decor.

They got out, Beth carrying her gym bag, and he led her to a free-floating staircase up to the first floor, where his wife Elinor waited to greet them in the living room with an anxious look on her face.

'I don't understand what your investigation has to do with us,' Elinor said to Beth. 'Nothing about this situation or you being here makes any sense to me.'

'It will very soon, but in the meantime, you have nothing to worry about,' Beth said. 'You aren't in any trouble and you aren't about to hear any bad news.'

Christopher took his wife's hand. 'She is actually doing us an incredible favor.'

'It doesn't feel like it.' Elinor took her hand away from her husband's grasp. 'It feels like I'm about to find out that you're having an affair. You look guilty of something.'

It was true, Beth thought. He did.

'I haven't been unfaithful, but I do have a secret,' Christopher said. 'One I've wanted to share for a very long time.'

Elinor shifted her gaze to Beth. 'Do you know what it is?'

Beth nodded. 'Don't be concerned, Mrs Cartwright. It's not a crime or a betrayal.'

'I'll decide that,' Elinor said, her voice tight.

Britney came up behind Beth with a Gatorade. She was in a sports bra and high-waisted neon-bright workout leggings. 'Finally, something exciting is happening in this house. You wouldn't believe how boring it is around here.'

'You need to get dressed,' Christopher said to her. 'We have guests coming.'

'Who?' Elinor asked.

Beth said, 'Owen Slader's ex-girlfriend Sabine Denier and their twelve-year-old daughter Nicole.'

'He's the chef whose bones you found in the desert,' Britney said.

'That's right,' Beth said.

'Why is his family coming here?' Elinor asked.

'Because I've solved the mystery of his disappearance and death,' Beth said. 'And the solution involves your family and its history.'

'Cool,' Britney said. 'This is like all those old TV shows where the detective invites all the suspects together in a room to expose which one of them is the killer. Is that what you're going to do? Is it one of us?'

Elinor sighed. 'For God's sake, Britney. Do you ever think before you speak? None of us is a murderer.'

But Beth saw a shadow of doubt cross Elinor's face.

'I am not here to unmask a killer,' Beth said, eager to change the subject. 'Do you have a TV that I can plug a laptop into?'

'We have a home theater downstairs with a multimedia system that can handle just about any file you might have,' Christopher said.

'Perfect. That's where I'd like us all to meet when Nicole and Sabine get here,' Beth said.

'I'll take you down now,' he said, seemingly as eager as she was to end the conversation with his family. He took her back down the staircase and across the showroom. Beth could feel Elinor's angry gaze on them as she watched them through the glass floor at her feet. He said, 'Elinor isn't going to be happy about the things I've withheld from her.'

'She might understand why after she's learned everything,' Beth said.

They went down a short hallway that led into a movie theater lobby, complete with popcorn machine, candy counter, soft-drink dispenser, and framed vintage movie posters on the wall.

'I'll take you into the theater in a moment,' he said, went to the snack bar, and pressed something under the counter. The entire bar slid away, revealing a lighted staircase underneath, the walls lined with thick concrete. It was like something out of a James Bond movie. 'These are the stairs to our safe room, which can be used to hide in a home invasion or to survive a nuclear apocalypse. It's built into the bedrock.'

He led her down to a huge steel door that looked like a bank vault. Christopher punched a code into a keypad, Beth heard the clank of something unlocking, and then he turned the wheel-like latch and pulled open the heavy door, which Beth guessed was a foot thick. The halogen lights inside automatically flicked on.

She stepped into what looked to her like the interior of a high-end, contemporary home. There were hardwood floors, leather furniture, and a gourmet kitchen. All of the appliances, fabrics, and finishes were top of the line. There were no windows, but in their place were huge flat-screen monitors that played different perspectives of the same ultra-high-definition video of a tropical beach. It created the illusion that they were in a beachfront home. She could even hear the crashing surf, the seagulls, and the gentle breeze rustling the palm fronds in the trees outside.

Christopher noticed her admiring the view. 'There are fifty different natural landscapes that can run in uninterrupted, one-hundred-hour loops to simulate views and even the sounds of the environment. It won't stop us from feeling trapped, or going stir crazy, but it's better than nothing.'

He walked her down a narrow corridor past several luxurious staterooms and bathrooms, each with their own flat-screen windows simulating a view, to a library she guessed was removed from a castle somewhere and rebuilt here. The shelves were filled with rare books, including *The Time Machine*, which was displaced face out in a special glass case.

Christopher picked up the *Time Machine* case, set it carefully on a leather easy chair, then pulled out, seemingly at random, two more books from various shelves. The action was like turning two numbers on a combination lock. One of the shelves slid away to reveal a hidden safe with a biometric pad. He pressed his thumb to the pad, which scanned his fingerprint, while he leaned forward and a beam of light scanned his eye.

'If I die, this vault can only be opened by my daughter,' Christopher said. 'She doesn't know that yet. She doesn't even know the vault is here. I'm the first Cartwright without a male heir to pass the List down to. But that won't be an issue any longer.'

The door opened, and he reached inside. He came out with another glass case, this one containing four handwritten sheets of paper that he handled as if they were the original, hand-written US Constitution.

'This is the List,' he said, presenting it to her. 'You are the first person outside of a direct descendant of Ben and Wendy Cartwright to ever see it.'

THIRTY-SIX

The List was written in a man's inelegant handwriting, hardly befitting such a meaningful document.

Beth read the first paragraph.

This list of events, warnings, and advice is confidential, should be shared with absolutely no one except your direct descendants, and followed more religiously than the Ten Commandments. Doing so will keep you safe and prosperous well into the twenty-first century. We know how ridiculous it sounds, and the huge leap of faith we're asking of you, but soon you will learn to respect the accuracy of our foresight. We know there are items on this list that don't make any sense, that read like gibberish, but as you get closer to the time when they are relevant, their meaning will become clear. It's also very important that you don't take any sudden, obvious actions based on this list that will make others suspect you have any knowledge of things to come . . . or you will be persecuted, or prosecuted, or worse . . . and all will be lost, not just for you, but for the future of our family. It's because of these very real concerns that we can't tell you how we've acquired our knowledge. Don't waste your time trying to figure out the answer to that question. Just accept what we have given you for what it is. Think of this list as our way of protecting you, of being with you, of showing you our undying love even when we are long gone.

Beth looked up at Christopher.

'They pretty much come right out and say we're from the future and here's your cheat sheet,' she said.

'And yet they don't,' he said. 'It raises more questions than it answers.'

She browsed randomly through some of the listings.

Invest in real estate in Los Angeles. Buy as much as you can, particularly in downtown, Beverly Hills, Santa Monica, and the San Fernando Valley so you can profit from the city's steady growth well into the next century. There is also great value in the oil underground in Los Angeles and Ventura counties, so be mindful of that. Also invest in Orange County, particularly Anaheim and Newport Beach. Also invest in farmland in Central California and Kern County, and land around Bakersfield. In Northern California, concentrate your investments in Marin County and Contra Costa County.

Invest in Levi Strauss, Heinz Ketchup, Coca-Cola, Eastman Kodak.

Don't smoke cigarettes, cigars, pipes, or any tobacco products – they will kill you. Also, do not chew tobacco, it's not only disgusting, but it will kill you, too. Don't believe anyone who says it has health benefits.

Cash out of any investments or businesses in San Francisco by December 31st, 1905, and under no circumstances should you or any member of your family be in the city in April 1906. All will be lost. This is vitally important.

Do not sail on the Titanic *in 1912 nor invest in the company that built it.*

Do not invest in Europe, or visit there, beginning in 1914. You will understand why by July of that year.

Begin stockpiling food and other resources on our Newberry Springs property and prepare to live there in quarantine with your family from 1918 to 1920. A terrible, fatal flu virus spread by human contact will sweep the world during those two years. If you must interact with people, stand far apart, keep your nose and mouth covered at all times, and wash your hands thoroughly with soap. Your lives will depend on this.

Invest in General Electric, the Ford Motor Company, Bell Telephone, RCA, General Motors, and the National Biscuit Company (NABISCO). Do not invest with Charles Ponzi.

Sell off all your stocks (except Heinz, Levi Strauss, Ford Motor Company, and others we listed before) and withdraw all of your cash from bank accounts before October 1929, when the stock market will crash, and prepare to survive on whatever cash or assets you have until 1933. However, do invest in American Airlines and Kraft Foods when you have the opportunity.

Stay out of Europe in 1939 and withdraw any investments, property, or other assets there by the end of summer. You will understand why within a few months. The situation there will grow worse than you can imagine. Do not, under any circumstances, be in Honolulu, Hawaii in December 1941.

In the 1940s, begin investing in the Walt Disney Company. Also invest in Las Vegas real estate, particularly in areas surrounding the main highway. Don't be swayed by naysayers. It will become a good bet within two decades.

In the 1950s, do not take thalidomide if it's prescribed for any ailment, particularly if you are pregnant. It will cause horrible birth defects. Invest in RCA, Columbia Broadcasting System, International Business Machines (IBM), and McDonald's restaurants and hold on to them.

Beginning in 1979, do not have any unprotected sex – meaning intercourse without a condom – with anyone except your spouse or longtime, monogamous lover, or you risk being infected with a fatal illness. You must trust us on this.

In the 1980s, invest in Apple Computer and stick with it for twenty years, no matter how rocky things get. If you still have stock in Kodak, sell it.

In October 1987, the stock market will crash.

In the 1990s, buy all the Amazon stock you can and hold on to it. It will only keep growing. Don't invest in Enron.

Avoid Los Angeles on April 29, 1992. There will be widespread, deadly rioting.

Do not be in New York City on September 11, 2001, or take any airplane flights that day. This is vitally important.

In 2005, if you still have IBM stock, sell it. Do not invest with Bernie Madoff.

Do not be in Louisiana or Texas in August 2005. Sell any ocean-front property in those states, and any property you have in New Orleans or the surrounding area, before that date. The area will be hit by a devastating storm.

In 2006, if you are in the sub-prime mortgage business, get out, particularly if you invested in Countrywide Mortgage. It will plunge the country into a financial crisis that lasts until 2008.

Do not visit Haiti in 2010.

Do not be on the east coast in October 2012 and sell any ocean-front real estate you have there, particularly in New Jersey, before that date. The area will be hit by a devastating storm.

Avoid West Africa in 2013 & 2014. A nightmarish epidemic will sweep that area.

Do not, under any circumstances, attend an outdoor, country music concert in Las Vegas in October 2017.

Do not, under any circumstances, visit San Bernardino County, particularly the Mojave Valley, on February 2nd, 2019.

Beth looked up at Christopher again.

'Come on. You had to know they were from the future,' Beth said. 'It's the only explanation for such specific predictions.'

'Of course we thought so, but we had no proof.'

'This list is the proof and all the clues they left behind in the open,' she said, handing the documents back to him. 'Like calling himself Ben Cartwright, a character from a TV Western, and opening a restaurant called Denny's.'

'According to history, Ben Cartwright and Denny's in Calico came long before the TV show or the restaurant,' Christopher said, placing the List back in the vault. 'The character and the restaurant could have been inspired by him, by some tourist who visited the Calico tourist trap or read about it.'

'That's true,' she said. 'But there's also the first edition of *The Time Machine*, the names of their mining and construction companies, the inscription on Wendy Cartwright's grave marker.'

'They may have just loved the book. Fans do crazy things, especially when it involved science fiction. How many idiots have learned to speak Klingon?' Christopher pushed the books back into their place on the bookcase, and the shelf slid back over the vault door, hiding it again. 'They are certainly sly hints, but that's not evidence, as I'm sure you know better than anyone. I wanted irrefutable proof and an explanation.'

'So you must have been waiting for February 2nd, 2019, to arrive all of your life. I'm sure you were watching things in the Mojave Valley very closely from afar for weeks, if not months, before that day for any indication of what the solution to the mystery might be,' Beth said. 'You definitely knew about the lightning storm, Owen Slader's disappearance, and everything else that happened, big or small, in the entire county before I showed up at your door.'

'I did, but I didn't have any idea what was relevant and what wasn't,' he said, 'not until our construction crew found the grave and you told me who was in it.'

'That's when you knew Owen Slader was your great-great-great-grandfather and he really was from the future.'

'There's still so much I don't know,' Christopher said.

'Not for much longer,' she said.

Christopher took her back up to the home theater, which was four inclined rows of six plush recliners that faced a wide, curving screen. One seat in the middle of the room served as a command chair, with an array of controls on an arm-rest console that allowed whoever was sitting there to manage the screening. There were also inputs and power outlets for an array of devices, as well as an iPad with a simple interface for controlling everything if the user wanted to move elsewhere. The command chair, he explained to Beth, was also plugged into the home security, communications, and surveillance system.

There was an identical control console in front of the room, off to one side of the screen, so the user wouldn't be blocking the audience's view of the presentation. That was the console Beth chose so she could face everyone. She plugged Owen's MacBook and his iPhone into the system and used the iPad to cue up the videos she wanted to show.

While she was doing that, there was a pinging sound from the command chair in the center of the room. Christopher picked up the iPad and looked at the screen.

'Our guests have arrived,' he said. 'I'll bring them down.'

He left and Beth took a moment to think about how she was going to present her story. There was no way to do it that wouldn't sound ridiculous to everyone except Christopher, so she'd have to confront that issue head-on. It was asking a lot of them, particularly Nicole and Britney. But she hoped the videos would do the convincing for her.

Christopher came down first, followed by Sabine and Nicole, and then Elinor and Britney. Nicole seemed amazed by everything already. The house was like visiting another world, so perhaps, Beth thought, it would prime her to accept the outrageous story she had to tell.

Nicole's long black hair was tied in a ponytail and wore a private school's polo-shirt and skirt uniform. She still had her book bag looped over one shoulder. But the twelve-year-old strode into the room with a confidence and command that seemed beyond her years.

'This experience certainly wasn't on my to-do list for today,' Nicole said.

'You have a to-do list?' Britney said.

'I like to be prepared for things. That way, I am more likely to be at my best,' she said. 'I like to set goals for myself and then exceed them. Don't you?'

'I don't need a list for that,' Britney said.

At least not anymore, Beth thought.

Nicole marched up to Beth and held out her hand. 'I am Nicole Slader. I understand you're a detective with the Sheriff's department.'

'Yes, I am,' Beth said, shaking Nicole's hand. She was impressed and relieved by Nicole's directness. This child would be able to handle what she was about to hear.

'Do you know who killed my father?'

'He wasn't killed,' she said.

'He didn't drop dead and bury himself in the desert.'

'I'll explain everything,' Beth said. 'When I'm done, you'll know exactly what happened to him.'

Nicole frowned, dissatisfied, then looked past her and slowly approached the control console. 'That's Dad's computer and his phone.'

'Yes, it is,' Beth said.

'Where did you find them?'

'In the grave of a woman who died eighty-six years ago,' Beth said, and looked at Christopher and his family. 'Wendy Hale-Cartwright, your great-great-great-grandmother.'

Nicole came back to Beth. 'Why would anyone dig her up and hide my dad's stuff in her coffin?'

'Nobody did,' Beth said. 'They were buried with her in 1933.'

Britney said, 'That's impossible.'

'It was,' she said. 'But now it's not.'

And then she told them why.

It took two hours to tell them almost everything. The only incidents she left out were the bugging of her home and her unpleasant encounter with Bill Knox in the desert. They were too personal and weren't necessary to make her case.

Beth shared almost all of the evidence that she had, including her photos, Owen's wallet, and Wendy's breast implants. She kept her recording of the unboxing, and her discovery of the dog tags to herself, though she wasn't sure why.

But it was Owen's videos and photos that told the story best and were undeniable proof that he'd gone back in time. His Mercedes in the cave, the radioactive isotope test results on the bones, and everything else was just fancy wrapping. When Beth was finished, the only people not shedding tears were Beth and Nicole.

Beth's investigation was over. The evidence had been presented. She'd done her job: she'd discovered the truth behind Owen Slader's disappearance and shared what she'd learned with his loved ones and his descendants. What happened now was beyond the scope of her responsibility, but that didn't mean she was ready to walk away. She couldn't if she'd wanted to. She was a fugitive. Bill Knox had seen to that.

Sabine wiped away her tears and forced a smile, giving Nicole's hand a squeeze. 'Your dad didn't abandon us and he didn't die last week. He lived an entire lifetime before we were born . . . before he was born. He had an incredible adventure, unlike anything anyone has experienced before. It's wondrous.'

'It's heartbreaking,' Elinor said.

Britney looked at her father, who sat between her and Elinor in the middle-row command chair. 'Do you have the List?'

He nodded. 'It's in a vault in the safe room.'

'So it's all true,' Elinor said. 'You've known about this all your life.'

'I only knew about the List,' Christopher said. 'I knew my ancestors could see the future. I didn't know they were from it.'

'But you guessed it and you never told us anything,' she said.

'I couldn't, and as the years went on, there was less and less reason to. The List became insignificant after February 2nd,' Christopher said. 'Besides, would you have believed me if I'd told you, without everything you've just seen?'

'Probably not,' Elinor said.

'Definitely not,' Britney said.

Christopher looked at Beth. 'You did an amazing job, detective. But there is one thing you got wrong.'

'What's that?' she asked.

'The house in Barstow, the one where the truck engine appeared in a man's living room, wasn't dismantled and taken away by the government,' Christopher said. 'It was me. I bought the property and moved the home, and all of its contents, to an old airplane hangar near the Ontario airport.'

The admission took Beth by surprise. 'Why did you do that?'

'Because I wanted to know what happened and I thought the answer could be in that house. I couldn't take the risk that anything might be removed or destroyed. So I took it all so it could be reconstructed, like the wreckage of a crashed airplane, for scientific examination,' he said. 'You can add that to the evidence we have that the military didn't seize.'

'You should have let them have it,' Britney said.

Nicole said, 'Absolutely not. The whole world has to know what happened to my father. He was a hero who made history.'

'And made the future,' Sabine said. 'At least for one family.'

'Nobody can *ever* know that,' Britney said. 'If it comes out, we will be vilified. Everything we have will be taken away from us. We'll be hated by everyone forever.'

'For what?' Christopher asked.

'For cheating,' Britney said, 'though I suppose it's not too late for us to lose it all with stupid decisions. It's not like we got what we have or kept it thanks to any smarts in our family.'

'I wouldn't call it cheating,' Christopher said.

'I would,' Sabine said. 'Your family used knowledge of the future exclusively for your own health, safety, and monetary gain, not to help others. Think of all the lives that could have been saved if you'd warned people about the disasters, plagues, and wars that were coming.'

Elinor said, 'If Christopher, and all the generations in the family that came before him, had shared what they knew about the future, then you and Nicole might not be here. It's possible none of us would be. That's why Owen and Wendy specifically warned against it.'

'That doesn't mean they were right,' Sabine said.

'It means he loved you,' Elinor said, 'and the new family he started. He was in a horrible position. Britney is right. Nobody can know about this. I'm not saying it for selfish reasons, because I am afraid of being hated or losing everything we have. If the government discovers that time travel is possible, they will use it to do much more damage.'

'Perhaps the government already knows or suspects it,' Beth said, 'and they are already thinking about how to replicate the accident.'

'Maybe the damage to time is already done,' Sabine said. 'Who knows what changes Owen and Wendy, as careful as they were, inadvertently caused just by showing up in the 1880s and living in the past for decades before their actual births. All we know is that the timeline of Owen's life in the future didn't significantly change. His life must have played out pretty much as it had before because he went back into the past again and Nicole is still here, safe.'

That's true, Beth thought. The events of his life must have played out at least twice for Nicole to still be here. Or did they? What if the accident was always part of the timeline rather than a break? What if things were happening just the way they were supposed to? Or what if time isn't a loop but an incalculable number of parallel tracks? If so, which one were they in now? Did two tracks merge? Did one diverge? Did it matter?

All of the implications and theories of time travel were difficult for her to grasp and many of them were incompatible with one another. Trying to make sense of it all confused her and gave her a headache. So she stopped trying. It was what it was.

Nicole said, 'Dad wanted what happened to him to be revealed.'

'To you,' Britney said. 'To us. OK, now we know. Job done. Now we have to keep our mouths shut and make sure nobody ever finds out about this.'

'It's too late for that,' Beth said. 'The military will figure it out.'

Everyone turned to her, as if they'd forgotten she was there.

'Not if we destroy the evidence,' Britney said.

'That would be a crime,' Nicole said.

'There's no law that covers this,' Britney said. 'It's never happened before.'

'That doesn't absolve us,' Christopher said.

Elinor stared at him. 'Of what? We haven't done anything wrong.'

'That doesn't matter now,' Beth said. 'The moral and ethical questions about how the Cartwright family used their knowledge can be debated later. We have to deal with the immediate, critical issues.'

'Isn't that what we're doing?' Elinor asked.

'The military doesn't need our evidence to be convinced that they stumbled into time travel. So hiding or destroying what we have won't change anything,' Beth said. 'But if we give it all to them, and it broadens their understanding of what happened, and the consequences, it might prevent other deadly accidents and potentially save lives.'

'Or it might make the world much worse,' Britney said. 'Wasn't that Owen's fear, that a person going back in time, even if he doesn't do anything intentionally to change the future, could still be extremely dangerous?'

'Every scientific advance has the potential to do as much harm as good,' Sabine said.

'There's something else to consider,' Beth said. 'Owen's videos alone are invaluable, not just as evidence of time travel, but for the glimpse they give us into a past that nobody alive, until right now, has ever seen or heard. If Amanda Selby, the coroner, were here, she'd say we have an obligation to science, to history, and to humanity, to share what we've found. It's bigger than all of us.'

'But she's not here,' Britney said.

'But she knows what really happened,' Beth said. 'How many others do? How do we know that Owen Slader, Gwendolyn Hale, and Motor Home Man are the only people who stepped through time?'

She knew they weren't.

'Don't forget the grizzly bear,' Elinor said. 'I'm not saying that as a joke. Other animals may have come through, too, and that could have unforeseen consequences. Maybe it already has.'

Sabine addressed Beth. 'The problem with your argument is that the military aren't known for promoting understanding and improving our way of life. What they *are* good at is killing people. They'll take what they know and use it exclusively as a weapon. They won't share the evidence with anybody. They'll say it's a matter of national security.'

'That's why we can't remove ourselves from the process by hiding what we know and can prove if we release it to the public,' Beth said. 'We need to assert ourselves.'

Christopher asked, 'What do you suggest we do?'

'Use the threat of revealing to the public everything we know about the time-travel accident as leverage to exert some control over how this discovery is used and who is told about it,' Beth said. 'I think, with the help of your lawyers, we can craft an agreement that finds a middle ground, between hiding it all and studying it, that protects everybody in this room and enriches the world at large.'

'You're an optimist,' Britney said.

'I'm a pragmatist,' Beth said.

Nicole turned in her chair to face Britney. 'I agree with Detective McDade. Dad wanted what happened to him, and what he sacrificed, to mean something more than us knowing the truth and you getting to keep your Rolls-Royce.'

'We could lose more than our money and lifestyle,' Britney said. 'The government could lock us up or kill us to keep this quiet.'

Beth said, 'I won't let that happen.'

'You are one person,' Sabine said.

'No, she's not,' Christopher said. 'There is all of us and our resources. I won't let that happen, either.'

Nicole stood up from her seat and faced the room. 'What happens to us doesn't matter. Our responsibility now is to something bigger than we are.'

Elinor stared at her. 'Are you sure you're twelve?'

'I am simply following my dad's example. He sacrificed himself for the future, never leaving that desert, so we could be here,' Nicole said. 'I just think we should be willing to make that same sacrifice or he did it for nothing.'

Christopher's iPad pinged and he looked at the screen. 'This is no longer a hypothetical discussion.' He swiped his screen and what was on it suddenly appeared on the big screen behind Beth. It showed thumbnails of multiple security cameras. Four black Suburbans with impenetrably tinted glass were at the front gate and a helicopter was hovering in front of the house that faced the LA basin. 'The wolves are at the door.'

Beth started unplugging Owen's laptop and the iPhone from the control console. 'Everyone needs to go in the safe room. Now.'

There was another ping, as the driver of the lead Suburban leaned out of the driver's seat and rang the bell at the gate.

'What do we do?' Christopher asked Beth.

'Answer the call.' Beth stuffed everything into her gym bag as Elinor and Britney led Sabine and Nicole out to the lobby.

'He'll be able to hear me but not see me.' Christopher tapped a button on his iPad, which he carried with him as he and Beth hurried to the lobby. 'Yes? Can I help you?'

The man at the wheel held out an ID. 'FBI. Who am I speaking to?'

'Christopher Cartwright.'

'We have a search warrant. Open the gate.'

'What are you looking for?'

'A fugitive with stolen goods,' he said. 'It's a matter of national security.'

The candy counter slid away to reveal the staircase, astonishing Nicole.

'This day just keeps getting better,' she said.

Elinor led the way down the stairs to the vault-like, safe room door.

'That's ridiculous,' Christopher said to the FBI agent. 'You must have the wrong house.'

Elinor opened the door and everyone but Christopher went in. He paused outside the door to hit a switch, which slid the candy counter back over the stairs, concealing the entrance to the safe room again.

'We have the right house,' the FBI agent said on the iPad. 'Open the gate.'

'I'll think about it and let you know,' Christopher said, ending the conversation and closing the vault door behind him.

THIRTY-SEVEN

'I love this place,' Nicole said gleefully, sounding like a twelve-year-old for the first time since Beth had met her. 'Can I explore?'

'Of course,' Elinor said, turning to Britney. 'Give your Aunt Nicole the grand tour.'

'Sure,' Britney said, taking Nicole's hand and leading her out of the living room. 'Wait until you see the game room, Auntie.'

'Actually, I think it's *great*-aunt,' Nicole said. 'Or great-great-great.'

'You just want to be called great all the time.'

'Wouldn't you?' Nicole said.

'What makes you think I'm not?' Britney said.

Once the two girls were gone, Sabine took a seat on a couch and faced Christopher.

'How bad is it?' Sabine asked him.

Christopher tapped a few keys on his iPad. The big flat-screen display of a tropical beach and crashing surf was replaced by multiple security-camera views. One showed the Suburbans parked outside the gate. Another view showed a black unmarked helicopter landing in the front yard and a SWAT team spilling out of it, weapons drawn, ready to engage in a firefight.

'Don't let that worry you,' Christopher said. 'This underground shelter isn't on any plans filed with the city. Even if they find us down here, this structure was designed to withstand nuclear war. It's pretty close to impregnable.'

Sabine said, 'Turn it off anyway, I don't want to frighten Nicole.'

'That girl is stronger than all of us,' Elinor said.

Christopher tapped a key and the restful ocean scene returned.

Beth asked, 'Do you have phone service down here?'

'Landline, cellular, and satellite service are all available,' he said. 'Take your pick.'

'I want you to call your lawyers, tell them to start drafting paperwork that guarantees us immunity from prosecution for any actions arising from the incident on February 2nd, 2019,' Beth said. 'It should also acknowledge our ownership of the digital material we are sharing with the government.'

'When did we decide that?' Britney said.

'We didn't,' she said. 'I just did.'

'What gives you that right?' Sabine asked.

'I found this evidence and I decided to share it with you,' Beth said. 'Now I am deciding to share it with the government, with some strings attached.'

Christopher sighed. 'In that case, the agreement should state that we are only licensing it to them for the limited purpose of research and investigation. We will control how and if it is ever released to the public. They should also be required to brief us regularly on what they learn.'

'Good idea,' Sabine said.

Beth doubted they'd be fully briefed, or that the government would accept any limits on their use of the data, regardless of anything they signed. But there was a way to mitigate that.

'I want something more,' Beth said. 'I want to be part of the continuing investigation into this.'

Christopher nodded. 'Do you have a strategy in mind to pull this off?'

'I do and it starts with me getting all of those commandos off of your nice lawn while you go call your lawyers.'

'I'm on it.' Christopher walked into another room to make his call.

Beth opened her gym bag, took out one of her two unused, throwaway cell phones, and called Bill Knox. He answered on the first ring. She didn't bother introducing herself.

'I want everybody off of the Cartwrights' property five minutes after I finish this call or I will post all the evidence I have on the web.'

'Evidence of what?'

'Teleportation. Time travel. The inept cover-up.'

'You listen to me—' he began angrily, but Beth interrupted him.

'Shut up and listen, Bill. I'm not done. If you have Amanda Selby in custody, you are going to release her with your profound and sincere apologies. If you filed any charges against her, you will drop them, unconditionally. You will also apologize to her employers and make sure she suffers no negative consequences whatsoever for doing her job. I will be calling her at home in an hour and if she is not there with her family, happy and free, I will release everything on the Internet. Every-fucking-thing. Think about it. This is all non-negotiable. I will call you back after I talk to her. The clock starts ticking now.'

Beth hung up. Elinor and Sabine were both looking at her.

'Were you bluffing?' Elinor asked.

'I never bluff,' Beth said. 'Because if you get caught doing it once, nobody ever takes you seriously after that.'

Sabine said, 'You're scaring me, but I like the way you stand up for people.'

'That's my job,' Beth said. 'To protect and serve.'

'I think you've gone above and beyond,' Elinor said. 'You stood up for all of us and Dr Selby, but you forgot to look after yourself.'

'Maybe she did, in her own way,' Sabine said to Elinor, then glanced at Beth. 'I'm not a detective, but there was too much anger behind your words to that guy. It felt personal to me, like there was more going on than just this situation.'

'You're right,' Beth said. 'He made the mistake of mansplaining all of my faults to me and then threatening to destroy me if I didn't drop my investigation.'

'So, this was an opportunity for payback,' Sabine said. 'How did it feel?'

'Wonderful,' Beth said.

Christopher came back into the room. 'The lawyers are ready to strike, though it's going to be hard to bring them into this while also keeping them in the dark about the discovery that's at issue.'

'We'll find a way,' Beth said. 'Can you pull up the security-camera feeds on your iPad?'

Christopher swiped his screen and the feed displayed on the big flat screen. The Suburbans at the gate were backing up, turning around, and leaving. The SWAT team was scrambling back into the chopper, which took off a moment later.

Christopher glanced at Beth, bewildered. 'How did you do that so fast?'

'Charm,' Beth said.

An hour later, Beth went into the library and called Amanda at home. Her call was answered after a few rings and Beth was delighted to hear children wailing playfully in the background when Amanda answered.

'It's me,' Beth said.

'Knox told me you'd be calling,' Amanda said. 'They rushed me out of my cell to a US Air Force chopper and flew me straight home, checking their watches the whole time. They landed on the street, right in front of my house, which my kids absolutely loved. What did you do to scare the Feds into releasing me?'

'I told them I'd post to the web everything I know, and all of the proof we have, about their time-travel accident if they didn't set you free and pardon you for everything since the day you were born.'

'You must have a lot more evidence than you had before.'

'I do and it's extraordinary,' Beth said. 'More than we could ever have imagined. It could change the world.'

'I'd ask you to tell me all about it, but I'm sure Knox and his friends are listening in on this call.'

'Of course they are. How badly were you treated?'

'They took me into custody, interrogated me for hours every day, threatened to throw me in prison for treason, and then asked me how I'd feel about giving birth behind bars and never seeing my child again.'

'They're a bunch of assholes,' Beth said.

'At least they didn't waterboard me. I kept my mouth shut, which just made them more and more angry,' Amanda said. 'Meanwhile, they sent a couple of very nice, clean-cut FBI agents to my house and they reassured my husband that I was safe, but incommunicado, called away on a confidential assignment for the Federal government. They told him they didn't know how long I would be gone.'

'Smart move. They didn't want him making a lot of noise and causing trouble. What did they tell your bosses at the coroner's office?'

'The same thing,' Amanda said. 'The story is so good that I'm sticking with it, too. I'm telling anybody who asks that the Feds swore me to secrecy and leave it at that.'

'How would you feel if that cover story came true?' Beth asked.

'What do you mean?'

'How important to you is it be a part of any continuing investigation into what happened?'

'Enough that I'm willing to forgive and forget being kept in a cell the last few days,' Amanda said. 'Though they did give me a nice fruit basket when I left.'

'You're joking.'

'You really scared the shit out of them,' Amanda said.

'I'll get back to you soon,' Beth said and ended the call, well aware that every word they said was heard and being transcribed and analyzed by the government.

She went back into the living room and sat down with the Cartwrights, Sabine, and Nicole to discuss the compromise with the military that she had in mind. They expressed some concerns, and suggested some tweaks, but basically agreed with her.

So while Christopher copied all of Beth's evidence to his own servers and cloud accounts, Beth placed another call to Bill Knox.

'Here's what's going to happen next, Bill. You're going to hear from the Cartwrights' lawyers, who are going to give you a document for your legal counsel to sign. It basically gives us total immunity from prosecution and equal ownership of the evidence we're going to provide you. Once that is signed, then we want to meet at the Cartwrights' home with whoever is in charge of the investigation into the teleportation mishap. We're done ever dealing with you.'

'We intercepted your packages at FedEx,' Bill said. 'We already have your so-called evidence. There's nothing we can't easily refute as fraudulent or a deep fake. You're one person. I have the full force and resources of the United States government, military, and law enforcement behind me. You have no power here to be dictating terms to anyone.'

'Fine, then there's no sense talking anymore. I'll start uploading it all to ProPublica, CNN, Fox, *New York Times*, the *Washington Post*, CBS News, and all the usual media outlets, or maybe just to YouTube and Facebook,' Beth said. 'We'll save our physical evidence for the Senate hearings. See you in DC.'

She disconnected the call. Everyone stared at her. Beth held up her hand in a halting gesture, urging them to relax. A moment later, her cell phone buzzed. She let it buzz a few more times before answering.

'Make it quick,' Beth said to Bill. 'I'm busy uploading.'

'The penalty for treason is—'

She ended the call, tossed her phone on an easy chair, and smiled at Christopher. 'What do you have to drink down here?'

'I have a Macallan twenty-five-year-old single malt that I haven't opened,' he said. 'Or there's chilled bottles of Coke if you prefer something softer.'

'I'd like a taste of the Macallan,' Beth said.

'Now that you mention it, that makes two of us.' Christopher went into the kitchen, opened a cupboard, and took the bottle out.

Sabine said, 'Make that three.'

'Four,' Elinor said.

'Five,' Britney said.

'Six,' Nicole said.

Sabine turned to her. 'You'll have a Coke.'

'That's hardly the equivalent,' Nicole said.

'It is for your age,' Sabine said. 'How often do I let you drink a glass of sugar?'

Christopher took out five cut-crystal glasses, set them up on the kitchen island, and filled them each with a generous pour of Scotch.

Nicole went to the refrigerator, opened it, and helped herself to a bottle of Coke, twisting off the cap.

Christopher held up his glass. 'To time well spent.'

They all clinked glasses and sipped their drinks. Beth's phone rang again. She let it ring. And ring. And ring.

Sabine glanced at Beth's phone as if it was a live animal. 'Don't you think you should answer it?'

'They can sweat a bit,' Beth said.

'Or they'll play it safe and blast our house off the hillside,' Britney said.

'That would be bad public relations,' Christopher said. 'The last thing they want to do is draw attention to themselves.'

'Yeah, I see your point,' Sabine said, 'I guess that's why they chased Beth through Glendale with sixteen cop cars and a helicopter and dropped a SWAT team on your front lawn. To keep things low-key.'

The phone stopped ringing. Beth held out her glass to Christopher for another pour. He gave her one. She noticed a slight tremble in his hand and smiled at him. 'We have all the cards, Mr Cartwright.'

'I think you can call me Chris,' he said. 'We are way past formalities.'

Nicole said, 'Do you have any candy in this place, Chris?'

Sabine gave her a stern look. 'It's Mr Cartwright to you. You aren't past formalities.'

Chris waved away Sabine's concern. 'We're family. Of course she can call me Chris. But I'm not sure she's my aunt. Perhaps a great-great-great-cousin or a great-great-great-niece?'

'We may be breaking new ground,' Elinor said. 'I don't think there's a precedent to cover this situation.'

'That is a tough one,' Sabine said.

'Where is your dry-erase whiteboard?' Nicole asked Britney.

'Why would we have one?' Britney said.

'For outlining, list-making, calculations, and brainstorming ideas,' Nicole said. 'I have two.'

'Of course you do,' Britney said, downing her Macallan and holding her empty glass out to her father.

Beth's phone rang again. She waited until the second ring to answer.

'This is Admiral Abel Beckett, I want to sincerely apologize for the way you've been treated by some officers under my command. But I think we both can agree that this is an unprecedented situation and there's no playbook for handling it.'

There was a firmness to his voice that reflected his rank and status, but there was also a casual, grandfatherly warmth underlying it, too, that put Beth at ease.

'Yes,' Beth said. 'I suppose we can.'

'That's progress. A terrible accident occurred during a top-secret military experiment that has injured dozens of military personnel, killed one civilian, and irrevocably changed the lives of many others, perhaps even the course of human history. It's a crisis of extraordinary scope and individual pain,' Beckett said. 'In the course of trying to understand what happened and contain the damage, some overzealous officers made serious mistakes. But their intention wasn't to harm anyone.'

'They only threatened it,' Beth said.

'They were doing their jobs under enormous pressure. So were you. Mistakes were made on both sides. It may have seemed that we were all working at cross-purposes, but that's not true. It was two parallel investigations with the same goal – finding out what happened while also considering how to deal with this profound discovery in ways that serve the best interests of science, humanity, and our country.'

'Only your side wanted to cover it up.'

'We both know that going public with this, before any of us truly understands what has occurred or the consequences, would be a grave mistake. You don't want that any more than I do,' Beckett said. 'I'd like us to start afresh, as colleagues and not adversaries.'

'If I step outside this door,' Beth said, 'I'll be arrested.'

'You aren't facing prosecution of any kind, not even for traffic violations. We've already settled with Forest Lawn and the City of Glendale for the minor property damage that was incurred in the chase. We'll even fix your car. You have my word.'

'I'll want more than that,' Beth said.

'I'll gladly sign the immunity agreement you're drawing up,' he said. 'Now, can we please meet and discuss a way forward?'

'Come on over, Admiral,' Beth said. 'We've opened a bottle of twenty-five-year-old Macallan.'

'Why didn't you say so to start with?' he said. 'I'll be there tonight.'

THIRTY-EIGHT

The immediate danger was over, so everyone moved out of the safe room. The Cartwrights, Sabine, and Nicole spent the rest of the day in the home theater, watching Owen's videos and going through his photos. Beth was overcome with exhaustion. She went upstairs and fell asleep on the couch.

She was awakened in the early evening by Christopher and a

blond-haired, blue-eyed young lawyer named Jason Slattery. She could tell from the way his Tom Ford tailored suit hugged his body that he'd made good use of his gym membership. He could have played James Bond.

'What kind of lawyer are you?' Beth asked, sitting up and wishing she looked better than she did after a nap on a couch. Her hair was askew, her clothes were wrinkled and, she suspected, her eyes were puffy.

'An exceptional one,' Slattery said, with a twinkle in his eye. He even had a British accent. 'I've prepared the documents you requested. I obviously don't know what the information or physical material is that you have, or what it's regarding, or what laws you may have broken to acquire it, but this document should give you the control and protections that you want.'

'*Should*?' Beth asked. 'That's not my definition of "exceptional".'

'I'm being modest,' he said.

'He's a Cambridge graduate,' Christopher said. 'The firm says he's their top criminal defense attorney.'

'I'm also a notary,' he said.

'Now I'm impressed,' Beth said. 'You should have led with that.'

She'd be sure to get his number before he left.

'Let's look at those documents,' Christopher said.

Slattery opened his briefcase and handed the copies of the documents to Christopher and Beth and they spent the next half-hour going over them. The language covered everything Beth had demanded and more.

'Is this contract legally binding?' Beth asked.

'Yes, once it's signed and notarized,' Slattery said. 'But I can't imagine any prosecutor or law-enforcement agency agreeing to these terms.'

'You'd be surprised how quickly the unimaginable can become reality,' she said, sharing a smile with Christopher. 'Are you happy with the language?'

'Yes, but still anxious,' Christopher said.

The house rumbled. They looked toward the front yard and saw a helicopter landing on the lawn. A moment later, a man got out of the chopper and strode toward the front door. He was in full dress uniform, his chest covered in medal ribbons, and had a wooden box of some kind under his arm. Admiral Beckett had arrived.

Christopher looked at Beth. 'I think you should answer the door.'

'It's your house,' she said.

'It's your show,' he said.

She got up, went to the door, and opened it. The man on the front step was in his sixties, his warm smile undercutting the formality and authority of his uniform and firm stature.

'I'm Admiral Abel Beckett. You must be Detective McDade.'

'Thank you for coming, sir,' Beth said, stepping aside to let him in.

'Call me Abel,' he said. 'I think we're past formalities.'

'Not judging by how you're dressed.'

'That's because my first obligation is to pay my respects to Slader's family,' he said.

She led the admiral into the living room, where Christopher and Slattery rose to greet him.

'This is Christopher Cartwright and our attorney, Jason Slattery, who has a document we'd like you to sign to protect our interests.'

The admiral shook their outstretched hands. 'There will be time for that later, but I must insist that Mr Slattery be excluded from our discussions.'

'Of course,' Christopher said. 'He's only here to witness and notarize the signing of the agreement.'

'Where can I find the Sladers?' Beckett asked.

'This way,' Christopher said, then gestured to Slattery to stay where he was. Beth and Beckett followed Christopher downstairs to the home theater, where everyone else was still gathered, watching clips from Owen's computer.

Elinor, Britney, Sabine, and Nicole all rose to their feet when the admiral came in.

'Please, don't stand up, that's not necessary. I'm Admiral Abel Beckett. I was in command of the operation that led to the tragic events of February 2nd.' He stepped up to Sabine and Nicole. 'I am deeply sorry for your loss. Owen made an incredible sacrifice for his country.'

'He didn't have a choice,' Sabine said. 'All he wanted to do was get home from Vegas to see his daughter and he ended up in 1882.'

'That's what makes his actions afterwards so impressive and heroic. He took extraordinary steps to make sure we'd understand the significance of what happened to him while, at the same time, he did everything he could to minimize any further harm.' The admiral took the box from under his shoulder. It was V-shaped, like the tightly folded US flag it contained. He handed it to Sabine. 'Owen Slader exemplified the best in all of us in his service to our country.'

'Thank you,' Sabine said.

'But Dad wasn't a soldier,' Nicole said.

Beckett crouched down in front of her. 'No, he wasn't, but what he did, and the sacrifices he made, merit the same respect and gratitude.'

'I think he was more like an astronaut,' Nicole said. 'Except instead of going into space, he went into the past.'

'I agree with you. And if he was here with us today, I'd give him this.' Beckett reached into his pocket and handed her a medal. It was octagonal, and embossed in the brass was an eagle on an anchor, over the word Heroism. 'It is the US Marine Corps Medal, our highest honor for non-combat heroism. But since he's not here, I want you to have it on his behalf and in recognition of your own heroism.'

'I haven't done anything heroic,' she said.

'You're doing it now, by keeping everything you've learned today a secret,' Beckett said. 'I know it will be hard, but it's very, very important. Can I trust you to do that?'

Nicole nodded. 'Will people know some day what he did?'

'I'm sure they will,' Beckett said. 'He will go down in history.'

Britney spoke up: 'He already has. That's the big issue here, isn't it?'

Elinor glared angrily at her, but Beckett smiled, rising to his feet.

'That's true, Britney,' he said. 'And, if you think about it, you wouldn't be here today if not for his sacrifice. You owe him your life.'

'So does this mean you've got no swag for us?' Britney said.

The admiral gestured to the room around them. 'I'd say you've got plenty to mark his achievement.'

Christopher said, 'You can trust us not to say anything, Abel.'

'I know I can,' Beckett said. 'You've certainly done a good job of it for over a hundred years.'

'He even kept it from us,' Elinor said. 'Me and my daughter were kept in the dark about it all until today. I'm still not sure what happened on February 2nd. What were you people doing out there in the desert?'

'It's classified, Elinor,' Beckett said. 'But what I can tell you is that we've been experimenting with teleportation technology for many years and have succeeded in transporting small objects over short distances.'

'Beam me up, Scotty,' Britney said.

'Something like that,' Beckett said. 'We've been gradually increasing the size and complexity of what we teleport. On February 2nd, we attempted to move a vehicle loaded with various materials from our logistics base in Yermo to Fort Irwin. Something went wrong, causing explosions at both bases, and the vehicle apparently disintegrated in transit. We initially thought the debris field was localized to the general area between the two transport points.'

'Maybe geographically,' Beth said. 'But not in time.'

'We didn't discover that until your investigation,' Beckett said. 'We can't even say for sure that the debris was all contained within San Bernardino County.'

'Or in the past?' Sabine asked.

'No, we can't,' Beckett said. 'It's a mystery. We honestly don't know the scope of the catastrophe and what the consequences were, are or might be, given the time-travel element and the potential for changing the course of events.' Suddenly, he looked very tired. He forced a smile and turned to Beth. 'You got me here with an offer of a twenty-five-year-old Macallan. I could sure use that about now.'

Christopher took Beth and Beckett to his study, where he poured them each a glass of Scotch and they took seats in leather-upholstered easy chairs. Slattery was allowed in briefly to give Beckett the document, which the admiral quickly read and signed. Christopher and Beth also signed it. Slattery did his work, gave Beth and Beckett his card, and promptly left with the executed document.

'I can get you a copy of that,' Christopher said to the admiral.

'That won't be necessary,' Beckett said. 'It's for your comfort, not mine.'

'There's still a lot we haven't told you yet,' Christopher said.

'I'm sure there is,' Beckett said. 'This is just the beginning of a lengthy process. We will need to do a thorough and detailed debriefing with you to truly understand the full scope of what we are dealing with.'

'Christopher isn't just referring to his family history,' Beth said. 'We have some physical evidence of time travel you're going to want to see.'

'You mean besides the laptop and iPhone?'

Christopher nodded. 'Your truck's engine landed inside a house in Barstow. I have the house . . . and the engine.'

'We know,' Beckett said. 'We've used satellite imagery to zero in on where you took it.'

'I found Owen's Mercedes,' Beth said. 'It's intact in a cave in Yermo, walking distance from your base.'

'That's amazing and something we certainly didn't know.' Beckett took a sip of the Macallan and shook his head. 'You've accomplished more on your own, Beth, than we have with the full resources of the US Navy at our command.'

'I also have this.' Beth took the dog tags out of her pocket and handed them to Beckett. He studied the name and nodded to himself, as if confirming something in his mind. 'You don't seem surprised.'

'Once we realized about the time-travel aspect of this accident, and you exhumed Wendy Cartwright's grave, we looked into other disappearances on February 2nd now and in the past,' he said. 'Bertrum Gruber went AWOL during a training exercise in 1978. At least now we know where he went.'

'We also know that a miner from 1882 stepped into the present in Yermo and got hit by a motor home.'

'We are aware of that.'

That's because they had his body, Beth thought, which they took from Amanda's morgue. 'What you don't know is that Dr Selby already ran some radioactive isotope tests on his bones and Slader's.'

'How the hell did she do that?' Beckett said. 'She doesn't have that kind of equipment.'

'What matters is that the results are conclusive proof that time travel occurred, in case any doubt remains.'

'Of course it does,' Beckett said. 'We'll need all the evidence we can get to convince the Pentagon, and the President, to give us the considerable resources necessary to fully investigate what happened, and what might still be happening, as a result of the accident.'

Beckett set down his glass and Christopher refilled it. 'Beth, one of your demands in the document I signed was that you and Dr Selby want to be part of the investigation.'

'We do,' she said. 'But we won't work with Bill Knox.'

'He's out,' Beckett said with a wave of his hand. 'Reassigned as our new military liaison in Tasmania. You will report directly to me.' He glanced at Christopher. 'How about you? Do you wish to remain involved?'

'Our family exists entirely because of what happened only a few weeks ago,' Christopher said. 'We're already inextricably involved. Frankly, I don't see how you can investigate this without us.'

'I agree, so I am relieved that you're willing to cooperate. This incident has extreme global, military, political, and scientific implications,' Beckett said. 'Therefore, our work must remain highly classified. It's essential that we maintain a low profile during our investigation. We can't, for example, go into a neighborhood, dismantle a house overnight, and take it away.'

'Understood,' Christopher said.

'That said, I like that you are willing to go to extremes if necessary. It will be very useful at times for us to operate under the cover of a legitimate, private sector business for some of the actions that might be necessary in our investigation. It gives us deniability.' Beckett turned to Beth. 'I'd like you to stay with the Sheriff's department in Barstow and, if possible, do your work for us in the course of your present duties. That will put you in some legal jeopardy, since it will require deceiving your colleagues and probably breaking some laws.'

'I'll take that chance,' Beth said, feeling a tremor of excitement, the anticipation of an adventure about to begin.

'Excellent.' Beckett finished his drink and stood up. 'Let's get to work.'

THIRTY-NINE

B eth spent the next two days at the Cartwrights' home while she and Christopher were thoroughly debriefed by Beckett and one of his subordinates. On the third morning, her perfectly restored Mustang was delivered on a flatbed truck to the house and she headed back to Barstow to begin her new, dual role as a homicide detective and . . . what? Time-travel investigator? X-Files agent? She'd have to huddle with Amanda Selby and come up with a secret title for their secret jobs.

But now, alone with her thoughts, it occurred to her that it had been Owen Slader, his daughter, and the Cartwrights who had been the focus of all her attention, but that she overlooked the interests of a very important person.

Gwendolyn Hale.

Wendy had made as big a sacrifice as Owen, and had shared his dedication to not only keeping their secret, but making sure the truth came out at the right time to give his two families closure and understanding in the future.

And yet she'd been ignored, except as a means to understand what happened to Owen Slader.

Nobody had considered the Hales, the family that Wendy left behind when she stepped into the past, who'd probably spent decades grieving her unexplained disappearance.

That was wrong, and Beth blamed herself.

She decided that Wendy's parents, if they were still alive, deserved to know what happened to their daughter. Their home was going to be her first stop.

She didn't bother clearing the disclosure of the classified information with Beckett first because she didn't care what he or the Pentagon wanted.

If that meant she got fired from her secret job, or thrown in prison for treason, then so be it.

The last known address Beth had for Ed and Myra Hale was the house that they were living in when Wendy disappeared in 1992. And it was only a few blocks away from the rental where Beth lived, so it was actually on her way home.

The Hales' house was a one-story, 1970s-era tract home in a cul-de-sac of nearly identical homes, but theirs had a FOR SALE sign in the lawn.

Beth parked in the Hales' driveway, walked up to the door, and pressed the doorbell. But there was something about the stillness of the house and the air around it that instinctively told her that nobody was there and hadn't been for some time. The drapes were closed, so she couldn't peer in the windows.

There were two cars in the driveway of the neighbor's house, so Beth went next door and rang the bell. A dog started yapping inside and, after a moment, the door was opened by a woman, well into her sixties, wearing a denim pantsuit that hadn't been in style since the house was built. But she still had the figure for the outfit, Beth thought, even if her fake eyelashes, make-up, and big, groovy feathered hair made her look like she'd stepped out of a rip in time herself.

'Can I help you?' the woman asked.

Beth flashed her badge and identified herself as a San Bernardino County Sheriff's detective. 'I'm looking for the Hales. Do you know where I can find them?'

'Is this about their daughter?'

'Why do you ask?' Beth said.

'It was such a tragedy, and it would be so sad if you finally had some news and they weren't here to get it.'

'Have they passed away?'

'Oh no, Ed and Myra are very much alive. They have had some health concerns, haven't we all, but they are doing fine,' she said. 'They even came into some money, though I don't know from where. It could be the Lotto. They bought a lot of those scratchers over the years. But they immediately retired, put their house on the market, and hit the road in their new motor home. They could be anywhere.'

'When did they leave?'

'A couple of weeks ago,' she said. 'I think it was the first of the month.'

Beth felt a chill ride down her spine. 'You wouldn't happen to have a photograph of them?'

'Dozens and dozens. After all, we've been neighbors for over forty years. My son was even Wendy's first high school prom date,' she said. 'But I can tell you that nothing happened that night in the sex department. He's gay, though we didn't know it at the time. I think he wished he was Wendy, the poor girl.'

'Could I please see that photo?'

'Oh yes, sorry, hold on. Be right back.' She closed the door. Beth tapped her foot nervously on the welcome mat. The woman returned a moment later with a fat photo binder and flipped through the laminated pages. 'Here we go. From one of our annual cul-de-sac barbecues.' She turned the book around for Beth to see it.

The photo was a slightly yellowed Polaroid of a teenage Wendy with her parents, standing beside a barbecue grill that they'd wheeled out to their front lawn for the street party. Her father Ed, in a collared shirt and Bermuda shorts, was grilling hamburgers and hot dogs. Her mother Myra held a pitcher of lemonade and wore a floral sun dress that seemed to blend in with her actual flower bed. It was pure 1980s suburban Americana.

Beth used her phone to take a picture of the Polaroid, thanked the woman for her help, and walked away. She didn't start trembling until she sat down in her car and put her hands on the steering wheel.

She'd seen the Hales before, but they were much older at the time.

It was in Yermo, outside of Peggy Sue's diner, not long after they'd run over a man with their motor home.

AUTHOR'S NOTE AND ACKNOWLEDGMENTS

T he mining town of Calico is real. It became a ghost town and was resurrected and re-created *in situ* as a roadside tourist attraction by Walter Knott (of Knotts Berry Farm fame) before becoming a state park, all of which is a pretty incredible story on its own.

But that's where the reality ends.

This is entirely a work of fiction, though I was inspired by actual events that occurred in Calico in the late 1880s. However, I re-envisioned much of the town's history, and invented characters of my own, to suit my storytelling needs.

Capturing what the real Calico was like, but also telling the present-day crime story with some procedural and forensic accuracy, required a huge amount of research, which I did by seeking out the advice of experts and by reading a lot of books and period newspaper articles, including some from the few surviving issues of *The Calico Print*. I also visited and explored Calico, Yermo, and Barstow, filling my iPhone with photos and videos, and taking copious notes.

I am indebted to Kelsey Parsons, Deputy Sheriff, San Bernardino Sheriff's Department; Pamela Sokolik-Putnam, retired Supervising Deputy Coroner Investigator for the San Bernardino County Sheriff-Coroner Department; Alyssa Moser, Deputy Coroner Investigator for the San Bernardino County Sheriff-Coroner Department; Mark Johnson, Deputy Coroner Investigator for the San Bernardino County Sheriff-Coroner Department; Danielle R. Galien, Associate Professor of Criminal Justice at Des Moines Area Community College; and Paul Bishop, Robin Burcell, David Putnam, Mark Forde, Patrick Judge, James Reasoner, Peter Brandvold, and Dr D. P. Lyle for sharing their invaluable experience and knowledge with me. I also want to thank Chris Cooling, of the *Forgotten TV* podcast, for his reporting on the life and career of writer-producer Leslie Stevens, creator of *The Outer Limits*, and the many space-alien conspiracy theories that surround his family history and his work in the television industry.

I read a lot of books for historical reference, but by far the most valuable to me were *Treasure from the Painted Hills: A History of Calico, California, 1882–1907* by Douglas Seeples; *Calico* by Paige M. Peyton; *Calico Memories* by Lucy Bell Lane; *Mining on the Trails of Destiny* by Lawrence and Lucille Coke; *Guide to the Calicos: Ghost Mining Camps and Scenic Areas Vol. 3* by Bill Mann; *Ghosts and Legends of Calico* by Brian Clune with Bob Davis; and *Daggett* by Dix Van Dyke.

Other books that I relied on included *Forensic Odontology and Age Estimation* by Matt Blenkin; *Practical Homicide Investigation, Fifth Edition*, by Vernon J. Geberth; *The Look of the Old West: A Fully Illustrated Guide* by William Foster-Harris; *The Silver Seekers* and *Ghost Towns and Mining Camps of California* by Remi Nadeau; *The National Training Center and Fort Irwin* by Kenneth W. Drylie; *Barstow* by Christine Toppenberg & Donald Atkinson; *Gold Rush Grub* by Ann Chandonnet; *Wagon Wheel Kitchens: Food on the Oregon Trail* by Jacqueline Williams; *The Prevention and Treatment of Epidemic Cholera and Its True Pathological Nature* by George Stewart Hawthorne MD; *Seeking Pleasure in the Old West* by David Dary; *How the West Was Worn* by Chris Enss; *The Cowboy Dictionary* by Ramon F. Adams; and *Desert Country* by Edwin Corle.

All of the errors in history, science, or police procedure that you may have discovered are my fault and were probably done intentionally to simplify things or move my story along. I'm ruthless about discarding facts when they get in the way of telling a good story . . . and not just in my books.

Finally, I'd like to thank my agent Amy Tannenbaum, my editor Rachel Slatter, my publisher Joanne Grant, and everyone at Severn House, without whom you wouldn't be holding this book.